"I'M A .... R, AND I .... CT THAT Y........... NG

Parch went on. "What I need to know from you is who exactly *you* are."

There was no use concealing anything. "Victor Gonser," I responded, my voice sounding odd to my ears.

He nodded. "They got you somewhere on the trail, then. We found several bodies along that way."

"Bodies?" I managed weakly.

"I'm afraid so. They rarely slip up, you know." He took a small spiral notebook from his back pocket and flipped through it. "They usually like to make it look like a heart attack, but they were harried and rushed. They blew your brains out with a pistol, I regret to say."

I seemed to sink deeper into the bed. Somehow, somewhere in the back of my mind, I had harbored the idea that, sometime, I might get back. Now that door was forever closed. Victor Gonser was dead, murdered on the trail in the wilds of Alaska. There was no going back, ever.

"I'M A FEDERAL OFFICER

JACK L. CHALKER
THE
IDENTITY
MATRIX

BAEN
BOOKS

THE IDENTITY MATRIX

This is a work of fiction. All the characters and events portrayed in this book are fictional, and any resemblance to real people or incidents is purely coincidental.

Copyright © 1982 by Jack L. Chalker

All rights reserved, including the right to reproduce this book or portions thereof in any form.

A Baen Book

Baen Enterprises
260 Fifth Avenue
New York, N.Y. 10001

First Baen printing, January 1986

Second Baen printing, December 1989

ISBN: 0-671-69854-0

Cover art by Dawn Wilson

Printed in the United States of America

Distributed by
SIMON & SCHUSTER
MASS MERCHANDISE SALES COMPANY
1230 Avenue of the Americas
New York, N.Y. 10020

This one's for my
technical advisors,
Bill Hixon, Dave Weems,
Ben Yalow, Ron Bounds,
and Mike Lalor, to whom
all nasty cards and
letters should be sent.

This time the horror was an old woman.

She ambled down the little street that was like all slum back alleys in every city in the world: garbage-littered, closed-in, filled with the cries of babies, the yells of aimless adults, and smelling like too many people were cramped into too little space, a fact further attested to by the long lines of frayed washing hung from fire escape to fire escape.

She toddled along, dressed in a faded green and very baggy print dress decorated with faded orange flowers, garb that seemed to accent rather than hide, the effects of age and improper diet. The dress itself was rumpled, as if she slept in it and removed it only for an occasional super-bleached washing.

She halted in the middle of the street as some wisps of wind broke the heat of the day and rolled discarded trash from one side to the other and looked cautiously around.

A lone young black male, barely fifteen, dressed in old, faded shorts that had been cut off from a well-worn pair of blue jeans, and little else, was idly humming an incomprehensible tune as he tossed a little red rubber ball against the wall and caught it.

She stopped to watch him for a moment, her kindly face breaking into a satisfied smile as it squinted to observe the young man.

She liked them young, and he looked in excellent health.

The solitary ball player hadn't even noticed her; he didn't notice as she positioned herself carefully behind him and took one last glance around.

After a few more seconds the kid threw the ball against the cracking brick facade a little too hard and ran into her as he chased the flying red missile that sailed overhead. She fell, then muttered something he couldn't hear under her breath and started to pick herself up.

The kid was extremely apologetic, and she smiled a toothless smile at him.

"That's all right, boy," she told him kindly, "jest hep me back up to my old feet."

She held out her hand, and he took it, pulling her up.

Suddenly, so quickly that he didn't even have time to think, he stiffened, then shook himself and looked down at the old woman again.

She appeared to have fainted and lay collapsed in a heap in the middle of the street. Carefully, he knelt down beside her and groped for something strapped to her leg, a small case, held in place by an elastic band.

Carefully removing the case, he opened it and removed a hypodermic needle. Taking her limp arm, he found a vein, then stuck the needle into it and pushed the plunger slowly, injecting air.

Satisfied, he walked down the street to where it came to another, larger and busier one, and dropped the syringe down the sewer so casually without stopping that no one would have noticed that anything had been discarded.

A little farther down the street a young white woman waited tensely at the wheel of a yellow Volkswagen, motor running.

Without a word, the young black man opened the passenger door, got in, and settled down. Without even a glance, the woman started the car forward, and, within a

minute, was out of sight, lost in a sea of thousands of little
cars heading into and out of the inner city.

He walked into the old morgue with an air of confident authority. A police sergeant greeted him just inside, and after exchanging a few words they made their way down a long, echoey hall lined with ancient marble, their footsteps ghostly intrusions on the quiet.

They entered the main room and both shivered slightly, for it was a good deal colder here than in the rest of the building and in extreme contrast to the heat of the muggy August night.

One wall was filled with what looked like huge airport lockers of a dull gray. The sergeant checked the names and numbers, then nodded and turned the shiny aluminum handle on the third from the bottom.

The compartment slid out on well-greased rollers revealing a body wrapped in a clinical white sheet with the city's seal on it. Methodically, the sergeant pulled back the cover to reveal the body of an elderly woman, Jane Doe #8, wearing a faded green flowered dress.

The man nodded gravely then removed a small fingerprint kit from his suit pocket and took her index finger's indentations carefully.

The sergeant recovered the body and slid it back into the refrigerated compartment, while the man reached into his inside jacket pocket and took a small card from a worn leather billfold.

He put the card next to the one on which the old woman's prints stood out clearly, nodded to himself, and grunted, a sour expression on his face.

"It's her, all right," he said disappointedly. "That old bitch beat me again."

Chapter One

I should have known better than to go to a bar on a Friday night, even in Whitehorse, Yukon territory.

Whitehorse has that aura of backwoods pioneer behind it, but about the only evidence of roughing it left in the now modern, metropolitan city are a few multistory apartments made of logs and the prices you have to pay for everything. Long ago the old frontier gave way not just to traffic lights but traffic jams, parking meters, and modern, plush motels and restaurants. The motel I was in might as well have been in New York, or maybe Cedar Rapids, with its neon, its prefabricated twin double beds and little bands reading "sanitized for your protection" and several channels of cable television—in color, of course.

The bar, too, wasn't much different than anywhere else in North America these days—dark, with a small band (one would think that any act reduced to playing Whitehorse would find a better way to earn a living, but, what the hell, they'd never dream of leaving show business) playing all the latest pop-rock dance tunes

5

pretty badly while lots of the young men and women dressed in suits and designer jeans mingled, talked, and occasionally danced in the small wooden area in front of the stage and barmaids continually looked for potentially thirsty patrons at the tables. About the only rustic touches were the stuffed and mounted moose, elk, and bear trophies over the bar (probably made in Hong Kong) and a few plastic pictures of the Trail of '98 on the walls, all impossible to see clearly in the deliberately dim light.

I sat there, alone, looking over the scene when the barmaid came over and asked if I wanted another drink. I remember looking up at her and wondering what factory made motel barmaids for the world. The same one that made state troopers and cab drivers, probably.

I *did* need a drink and ordered a bourbon and seven, which arrived promptly. I sighed, sipped at it, and nibbled a couple of pretzels, surveying the people in the bar.

There *were* a few differences, of course. Some old people—I mean *really* old people—were incongruously about, looking like retired salesmen from Des Moines and haggard, elderly grandmothers of forty-four kids, which is probably what they were. What they most certainly were were tourists, part of a group that was one of thousands of geriatric groups that came to Alaska and the Yukon every year on the big cruise liners and by fast jet and motor coach combinations. Most of their party would be at one of the "authentic" old frontier bars down the street, of course, all about as authentic as Disneyland; but these were the leftovers, the ones whose arthritis was kicking up or who'd been on one too many tours today and just didn't have any juice left. I reflected that it was a shame that most of those romantic-sounding cruises to exotic Alaska always looked like floating nursing homes, but, I suppose, that age was the only one where you had both the time and the money to do it right. Somebody once said that youth was wasted on the young, who had neither the time nor resources to properly enjoy life, and nowhere was that more graphically illustrated than here. Still, these people had worked hard and lived full, if extremely dull, lives and shouldn't be begrudged for this last fling. They were lucky in a number of ways, at that.

Most people never get the chance to go coast to coast, let alone to someplace far away like Whitehorse, and, of course, their lives had been satisfying to them, anyway.

Lucky . . .

I knew I shouldn't have gone to a bar on a Friday night, not even in Whitehorse. You sat there, drinking a little, watching the beautiful people—and the not-so-beautiful people pretending they were—drift in and out, mix it up, watch couples pair up and others mix and match. You sat there and you watched it and you drank a little more, and the more you watched and the longer you sat the more you drank.

It'd be easier, I often thought, if I were physically scarred or deformed or something like that. At least you could understand it then, maybe come to grips with it then, maybe even find somebody who took pity or had sympathy for you so you'd meet and talk and maybe make a new friend. Harder, far harder on a man's psyche to have the scars, the deformities within, hidden, out of sight but no less crippling or painful.

I finished the bourbon, and, leaving a couple of dollars for the barmaid, left the place. Nobody noticed, not even the barmaids.

It was a little after midnight, yet the July sun shone brightly outside, sort of like six or seven anywhere else. It was hard to get used to that most of all, because your eyes told you it was day while your body said it was really late and you were very tired. One of the tour groups was struggling into the lobby looking haggard, turning the place briefly into a mob scene. I just stood and watched as they bid their goodnights, some laughing or joking, and made their way to the elevators to turn in. None noticed me, or gave me the slightest glance, and I waited there until they'd cleared out before going up myself. No use in fighting that mob, not with only two elevators.

I got a newspaper and glanced idly through it while waiting for the elevators to return. Nothing much, really. Internationally, the Russians were yelling about something the CIA supposedly did in some African country I barely knew, the Americans were yelling about a new Russian airbase in the Middle East, there was some sort of local rebellion in Indonesia, and the Common Market was debating the duties on Albanian tomatoes. An earthquake here, a murder there, the U.S. President was pushing for some new missile system, and the Canadian Prime Minister was in the Maritimes trying to keep Newfoundland from seceding. Big deal. I suspected that this same newspaper could be used, with perhaps a few names and locales changed, for roughly every third day of the past two decades.

The elevator came and I got in, riding it swiftly up to my room, still glancing through the wire-service laden local paper. NORAD scrambled in Alaska when a UFO was sighted south of Fairbanks, but it was gone when they'd gotten there, as usual. Ho hum. UFO stories seemed to run in ten-year cycles, with a particular rash of them right now. I remembered meeting the ambassador to Uranus once in San Francisco, really a balding, gray-haired little man with thick glasses who might never really have been anywhere near Uranus, or even Pittsburgh, but got a lot of attention by saying he had so often he almost certainly believed his fantasy himself by now.

I unlocked the door to my room, went in, and flopped on the bed. All the lonely people ... That was a line from a song once, when I was growing up, and it was certainly true. The world was full of such people—not the nonentities downstairs, both old and young, who live but might as well not have lived, but the lonely ones, the ones who fly to Uranus in their minds or maybe become flashers in Times Square or take a crack at killing a politician. There were degrees and degrees of it, from the horrible to the hilarious, but those nuts had found a release, a way out. For a few there was no release, no way out, except, perhaps, the ultimate way.

Some just got naked in cold, plastic motel rooms and jerked off to some private fantasy they might not ever want to actually experience.

I got up after a while and walked into the bathroom. It was one of those kind with a full-length mirror—you couldn't even shit without watching yourself doing it—and I stopped and stared at myself as I had so many times before.

Behold Victor Gonser, I thought. Age—thirty-five. Height—five eight and a half, something like that. Average. Over-all—average. Caucasian male who'd always been almost scarecrow-thin and still looked that way, only now there was an incongruous double bulge at the tummy that looked totally ridiculous. Most people gained all over, or at least had heavy asses, but, no, mine ballooned around the navel like some hydrogen gas bag.

There wasn't much hair left, and the thin moustache, all I could ever really manage, gave me one of those mild-mannered accountant looks. Truth was, I looked weak in all areas, the face a patsy's face, the kind of face that told you you could walk all over this guy. And even this Caspar Milquetoast was something of a fraud. The uppers were kept in a jar overnight, and I peered at myself from a distance of six inches through glasses that looked like the bottoms of Coke bottles.

There'd be no release tonight, I knew. I was too down, too depressed, too sober despite the double bourbon. It was, I thought, a ridiculous situation for somebody like me, but, damn it, there it was.

Somebody once said that a few of my colleagues envied me, and that had shaken me up for quite a while. The people in question were better looking, more outgoing, seemed to enjoy their lives. Envy? Me? But, of course, there were the things they saw that I'd attained that I'd once also seen as wonderful, only to find they were meaningless once you had them.

Money, for example, was always envied, and I'd had nothing to do with that department. Dad had been a corporate lawyer with a really big-shot firm and he'd made a bundle in his time. Home to me would be a mansion to most people, sitting in the very wealthy Virginia suburbs of Washington, D.C. In a place where a two-bedroom shack was a quarter of a million; we had twenty-two rooms on fourteen wooded acres, complete with pool, riding stable, tennis courts, you name it. It was a lot—particularly when you consider that Mom had to have a hysterectomy for a cancerous condition only a year or so after I was born and that left just the three of us on the place. Two, really, since I guess we saw Dad for about an hour a night and maybe every sixth weekend. That was another of life's little jokes on people, I always thought. Self-made men who worked damned hard and made a couple of million dollars were always so busy they never were home enough, never had time enough, to enjoy any of that money. And, when they started realizing this, as Dad finally did, they'd wind up dropping dead of a heart attack just when they've decided to take it easy and enjoy life.

As Dad did. Dead at forty-six. No geriatric cruises, no graduations, weddings, sailing, none of that for him. That was left to the nonentities, the retired feed grain salesmen from Des Moines with the IRA account.

Life was always full of cruel jokes like that, I thought glumly. And, when I'd stood there, watching him being lowered into the ground surrounded by enough big shots to buy California, I'd felt no loss, no pain, no sense of grief, and I'd felt guilty for that, but damn it all, it's hard to grieve for a man you barely knew.

Mom, now, she was a different case. I had to hand it to my father that he'd remained married to her all that time, although he was no TV sex symbol star himself. She was plain, beyond the best beauty and fashion consultants money could buy, and she'd been poor. They both had been when they'd married just out of college, and she'd gone to work and supported him through law school. There was a bond there, between these two seemingly plain, ordinary people from Moscow, Idaho, one that didn't fall apart as his spectacular law school grades had attracted a large firm well connected to Senator Carlovich and which he'd ridden to Washington and the seats of power. I don't know if it was love—I was never sure of that—but it was more than a strict Catholic upbringing that kept them together. I think, perhaps, that they each had what they wanted out of life, or thought they did. Money, power, prestige.

But Mom wanted more than Washington social life, more than the routine of being married to the powerful and well-connected, more than her political activities and championing of liberal causes. I was the only child she had, and, by damn, I was going to be somebody, too!

A private all-male military style prep school, one of the best, shielded from the world, from the ordinary folk and the roots both she and Dad had risen from, only the best training and prepping for Victor Leigh Gonser, yes, ma'am! Hell, I was eighteen before I even *met* a girl in other than the most rigidly controlled social situations, and by that time it was getting too late. I discovered that I simply didn't know what to do. I hadn't had a childhood, I'd had a mini-business adulthood, so protected from my peers that I could hardly identify with them. It's in the teen years, particularly, that you learn the rules society has set down—how to meet and mix with other people, all the social and sexual signals, the anthropology of your culture. Without them, and out in the world, you find you're as well prepared for socializing as you would be if you were living amongst a New Guinea tribe. You're not a part of it, you don't fit.

And, of course, when you fail out of ignorance to

respond to the rituals of society you get pigeonholed and stereotyped and promptly ignored. In my case the men, and women, at college at first thought I was gay, then decided, finally, that I was sexless, a neuter without the needs they all had. God! How I envied them.

So I threw myself into my studies, for that was all I had, and ignored the social life and activities that the rest of the world enjoyed around me. The work was absurdly easy, even at Harvard—money-hungry universities had gone for the least common denominator in a generation where such basics as reading and math were largely irrelevant, and it had reached even here. Not that there wasn't some intellectual stimulation, but it was the rare professor and the rare course that offered it, and you could tell *those* men and women were not long for the academic life. They did the inexcusable at a modern university—they thought, and, worse, promoted thinking among those with whom they came in contact.

I excelled at university studies, not merely for this reason but because it was the only thing I had to do that I could take some pride in accomplishment. I took massive loads, partly because I was interested in practically everything but also because I had nothing outside the academic life to occupy my time or mind, and the heavier the workload the less time I had to dwell on my lack of humanity. Oddly, the social sciences held the greatest attraction for me, as if, somehow, I could find what was lacking in my own being by studying others in a clinical, professional pattern. I studied human behavior the way the biologist studies the workings of a cell or the life of a paramecium. I wound up graduating *summa cum laude* with double majors in psychology and sociology and a strong minor in political science. For graduate studies I concentrated on psychology simply because I felt that I understood the interaction of human beings in groups as much as anyone did up to then. It was the individual mind, the human psyche, that somehow eluded me. Yet it was political science that I finally got my doctorate in. The truth was, everybody I met in the psychology department was definitely nuts, and a good deal of modern psychology exposed too much of the human being studying it to others—the essence of psychology, of course.

This is not to say that I didn't try analysis. On a one-to-one basis I could be frank, open, and free, but the problem was that I generally seemed to know as much as the psychiatrist and more than many. The foundation of clinical psychology is to get you to admit and recognize the causes of your problems so that you can work them out. My trouble was that I *knew* the causes of my problems, understood myself quite well, but that I could articulate what I needed to join human society only to another similarly afflicted. The rest just couldn't really understand.

Just after my twenty-fifth birthday something truly disheartening happened. I had graduated, received my Ph.D., and I was ready to make my own way in the world from an academic standpoint, but not at all prepared to do so on an emotional level. I was a twenty-five-year-old sexually repressed virgin. There seemed only one thing to do, and I did it, back home in Washington, when outside a restaurant on Connecticut Avenue I was approached by an attractive black woman, nicely dressed and finely featured. I actually approached the proposition clinically, as I did everything, reflecting that I had little to lose with almost no money on me if it were a set-up for a rob-and-roll, and, what the hell . . .

It was legit, and it was fascinating, and it was as coldly businesslike as any academic lab exercise on both sides. It broke my cherry, but it was neither satisfying nor particularly pleasurable in the end. All it showed me was that I was a normal male with the ability to perform; it did nothing to integrate me into the lives of real people.

I was offered an instructor's position in political science from a number of places, but selected Johns Hopkins in Baltimore partly because it was close to home and familiar surroundings and partly because it was the most prestigious institution offering me anything. I did a couple of books that sold moderately well, mostly examinations of political attitudes, and while I found the faculty politics and under-graduate standards at Hopkins to be a mini-Harvard, I managed to find myself a niche. Although my political writings weren't really popular with my colleagues, I was non-threatening, never rocked the boat, and found it easy to say the right thing at the right time to the right person to keep it that way. Not only the psychology, but all those years growing up around Washington hadn't been totally wasted. Still, I tended to associate more with faculty in other, unrelated disciplines than with my own immediate colleagues. It made it easier to keep out of arguments and office politics, and, of course, it helped satiate my never-ending curiosity about practically everything.

And so, I guess, those who could not know what was going on in my head (and no one else could) could envy me—rich, with a solid position at a top school, and with a modest amount of national fame through my books and occasional TV talk show stints. They especially loved me for voter analysis around election time.

Mom died when I was thirty-three. Funny—she'd always been paranoid about cancer since that operation so long ago and it had become a passion with her. So she died of a heart attack on the tennis court at age sixty-one.

I felt real grief for her, even though she was at the heart of most of my problems. She had meant well, and she'd been proud, and, I guess, she'd been the only real human being I could relax with. I considered an offer from American University so I could live in the house, but one look at the place with just me and no social life made that idea ridiculous. I just rented it for a fantastic sum to the Majority Whip of the Senate, who needed it, and took a large old brownstone near Hopkins.

Mom's passing, though, had a serious effect on me. For the first time in my life I was totally, utterly, truly alone. There was no one else now (I suppose Mom went to her grave bewildered that her frenzied matchmaking did no good at all) and every time I looked in a mirror I saw myself growing older, falling apart a little more, losing my last chance at ever joining humanity. I was becoming, had become, not human at all, but a sort of friendly alien, a creature that was nonhuman in all respects and, like Marley's ghost, could only wander the world watching happiness it could not share, existing but somehow apart. I moved through crowds, the only one of my kind.

I often envied women, and even occasionally fantasized myself as one. Not that I was gay, as I said—this was different. It seemed to me that women had an innate social advantage in a society that was male created and, despite years of liberation, still predominantly male dominated. Women, even the most sheltered, were raised to know the rules of the game. Oh, it might be as a warning—if this guy does this, watch out!—but they all knew. They had more options than men, too, in a curious way. I suppose that was why many men feared the women's rights movement. Society—not codified laws, cultural laws—now gave them all the options. Marriage was an option. Children, in or out of marriage, was an option. They could work, with the full backing of the law and the courts, in any field they wanted competing directly with men, or they could opt to be supported by men. Men, on the other hand, had none of these options. The courts still put the burden of divorce and child support on the man while granting custody to the woman, no matter what the relative age or income. Men couldn't have children. Men could not opt to be supported by women if they so chose.

And, in any case, no woman seemed to be in my position in a crowd. Women could walk into a motel bar and be the center of attention, no matter what they looked like, of lonely men on the make. A female colleague of mine once confessed that she'd dropped a bundle in Reno and was left with nothing but a bus ticket home—yet men bought her breakfast, lunch, and dinner with only a little prodding, and she'd made out quite well, thank you. And she was as ugly an old bag as you could imagine.

It wasn't the sexual part of a woman's life I craved, it was the social interaction that was seemingly almost automatic. Academically I knew that there had to be some women, somewhere, who were in my kind of fix, but I couldn't conceive of them in real-life terms.

I wanted a wife, children, parties, dancing, mixing, socializing, feeling, love, tenderness, togetherness with another human being.

And there I stood, looking at reality, in a motel john in Whitehorse and knowing it just wasn't going to happen.

Since Mom died I'd gone away for the whole summer, conscious of the fact that neither of my parents had lived to a very old age and that I could go any time. If I couldn't participate, at least I could visit.

My first year I'd gone on the Grand Tour in Europe. I'd been there before, of course, but this time I poked into everything and anything. I spoke passable German and my French was very good indeed and it helped a lot.

And this time I'd decided on Alaska and the Yukon, mostly because it was already dramatically changed from when I was a boy and I had this strong feeling that, if I didn't see it soon, I'd come back to find it domed over and paved, a chilly California. I'd salmon-fished at Katmai, took a trip into Gates of the Arctic National Park, walked the garbage-strewn streets of Barrow, taken a boat down the Yukon, and now, after a flight from Fairbanks, it had been more than worth it—the place, spoiled or not, still was absolutely the most scenic area in the whole world.

And huge, and wide, and lonely.

I loved the place, but knew that July was not January, and I wasn't so sure I'd like it in the opposite season.

From Whitehorse I intended to take the once-a-day tourist train of the White Pass and Yukon Railway to the trail head at Yukon National Park on the Canadian side, then make my way down the Chillicoot Pass, a reverse Trail of '98, way down to Sitka at the bottom, where I could catch the ferry south. The trail was excellent, thanks to the National Park Service, and while I couldn't have hiked a hundred feet up it the way the pioneers did in the gold strike days, I was wonderful at walking *down* trails. It was a natural capstone to my Alaskan Grand Tour, as it were, and one that I'd have hated myself for passing up. I looked forward to the walk, but not to its ending, for that boat would take me to Seattle and a plane home. I didn't want to go home, really. That bar had brought it all back to me, and, in a sense, represented what home and "real life" was.

I didn't really want real life any more, not that kind, and lying in bed, in the stillness of the early morning, I wondered if I really wanted life at all.

The White Pass and Yukon Railroad owes its existence and continued huge fortune to the gold rush. One look at the Chillicoot Pass showed that only the hardiest could climb it under the best of conditions—yet tens of thousands did, carrying all that they owned on their backs. The lucky ones made it to the top without collapsing or being robbed by Soapy Smith and other professional crooks, but, as with all gold rushes, even the lucky ones who made it to the headwaters of the Yukon River and the boats that men like Jack London piloted downriver to Dawson and the gold fields, rarely struck it rich. Those who did, though, were faced with problems as well, for never had gold been so remotely located and so hard to get not merely out of the ground but out of the area once you did. As the boomtowns grew, their new, swelling populations also needed al-

most all manufactured goods—and it was due to this
that enterprising business pioneers, in a stunning feat of
engineering, built the narrow gage railroad all the way
from the port at Skagway up, over the mountains, to
Whitehorse and the river and road connections. Although
the gold fever was now long gone the railroad prospered, supplying growing population of the Yukon and
dealing now in new, less glamorous but no less needed
resources of the burgeoning north country. So big was
the business that they'd been trying for years to get rid
of the one tourist train a day, as there was still only a
single track and it was needed for more profitable goods,
but, while service was not really what it once was, that
train still ran.

At the beautiful headwaters of the Yukon River, in a
bed of glistening lakes at the river's source, the train
stopped at the old station where once the gold-seekers
had transferred to glittering stern-wheelers, only now it
was to feed the captive tourists a captive lunch and
allow northbound freights to pass. It was here, though,
that I got off with a pack and little else, since, just
around the lake over there, was the top of the Chillicoot.
It was a warm day, around 60 degrees, which meant
almost hot down in Skagway, only a few miles for the
eagle to fly but a long, long way down. The air was crisp
and cleaner than most people have ever known, and,
near the trail head, you could look down through scat-
tered clouds and see the Pacific far beyond gleaming in
the sun.

Although it was a long walk, with all its switchbacks,
it was an easy day trip from this direction—three or
four for the one in great condition coming up the way
the pioneers did—but I had been trapped by the tourist
train's schedule and it was past midday. My ferry wasn't
due in down there until after 7 P.M. the next day, so I
was in no hurry and planned to stop at one of the
convenient Park Service campgrounds about halfway

and say goodbye to the wilderness experience in some grand style.

I met a few people as I descended, mostly young couples or two or three young men, but it was not a busy day for the trail. More would start two days hence, when the ferry came in and disgorged its load, but, for the most part, I had the trail, the views, the clean air and whistling, soft wind to myself the way I wanted it. Finally, leisurely, I reached the camp I'd selected before starting out and was delighted to find no one else using it. It was one of the best according to the parks guide, with a stunning view of Skagway, tiny and glistening below, its harbor, and out past the last point of land, past Haines Junction, to the Pacific and the Inside Passage.

I'd packed light; all cold stuff, prepacks, the sort of thing; for minimum gear and minimum weight, with a small, light folding pup tent I'd already used often on this trip. Still, I had a tiny little gas jet and pot for boiling water, since I couldn't conceive of a day without coffee to get me going, and it not only worked nicely but also provided the added joy of being able to make a cup of bullion.

I sat there for a long time in the late-evening daylight enjoying the view, the solitude, watching a couple of brown eagles circling lazily in the sky, and I thought of what a contrast it was between here and that bar back in Whitehorse. Here, perhaps only here, I was at least partly human, as close to nature and the world as I could get. Here there were no pressures, no social rules, no sign of beautiful people and the kind of normalcy I had never known.

I did very little thinking, really. I just lay there, at peace for the first time in a long, long time, looking out and around and becoming one with nature, riding with the whispering winds, soaring like those eagles, at rest, and free.

I didn't want to go back. I knew that for a certainty.

This sort of peace and freedom was beyond me in any crowded, social setting. Soon it would be back to the cities and the bustling humanity and a world that was very much like that bar, a world in which I was not equipped to live and join and mingle, but only to sit silently at endless dark tables sipping, sipping my drink that might bring forgetfulness while observing the rest of the world in a manner oh, so very clincal and so damnably detached from myself.

I thought again about women, oddly. I'd more than once taken a woman to dinner and had pleasant conversation, or to a show, but after they'd eaten and watched, they'd walk off with somebody they met in the waiting room or at intermission. Oddly, I had no trouble going places with women—they considered me safe, nonthreatening, nonsexist and nonsexual, which, in a way, I was. I didn't even want to go to bed with those women particularly, but it hurt me terribly to watch them going to bed with everybody else in the world except me. More than one grad assistant had put the bite on me for a loan, or propped up my ego so I'd buy them dinner, only to use the money to treat somebody else to a date. I was a soft touch and often used, and I knew I was a sucker, but, damn it, if all hope vanishes what's left?

But I realized, late that night, in the deepening gloom over the mountains above Skagway, that I *had* lost hope. My scars were too deep, too painful, and would never heal, and they had me in agony. I was a human being! Why, then, did everyone around me insist on being treated as a human being but never even think to treat me like one? Hurry! Hurry! See the robotic man! He walks! He talks! He thinks! But he never feels. . . .

But I felt, all right. Every single time was another scar on my soul—no, not a scar, a festering, rotting, infected wound that would never heal, never subside, could only be compounded more and more until the pain grew unbearable. I could feel them now, those wounds, growing worse and worse as I approached a return to civilization and society, already near the threshold of pain. Weeping slightly in my lonely tent, uncaring as to what would happen, I finally, mercifully drifted into sleep.

The sound of horses woke me, and I groaned, turned over, grabbed for my glasses, and glanced at my watch. A bit after seven in the morning, I noted, and rolled over, squinting to see what the noises might be. It was unusual to find horses on a trail like this—it'd take an expert to navigate them on the winding, rough terrain and I didn't even realize that the Park Service allowed them. Still, there they were, coming slowly down, two men and a child, it looked like, on three brownish-red horses breathing hard in the morning chill, nostrils flaring.

I crawled out of the tent and went over to my small pack, where I'd left a pot of water the night before fetched from a small waterfall nearby. I lit the little gas jet, then went over and scooped up some icy cold water from a rivulet on the rocks and splashed my face, trying to wake up and look at least moderately presentable. Only then did I turn to the approaching trio and give them a good looking-at.

Both men looked like hell and neither looked like they should be on a trail in the Alaska panhandle. Both wore suits, although the clothes looked like they'd been slept in for days, and both looked dead tired and somewhat harried. The child, I saw, was an Indian girl, perhaps twelve or thirteen, with long, black hair almost to her waist, but still pre-pubescent, although she was certainly on the verge of turning into a woman. She looked a bit more normal, in a ski jacket, T-shirt and faded, well-worn jeans, with extremely worn cowboy boots that might have been tan at some point in their past.

The lead man had only now spied me, looking somewhat wary and suspiciously in my direction, eyes darting to and fro as if he expected others about. Both men looked to be in their forties, with graying hair and lined faces; the kind of men you'd expect to see in business offices in Juneau or Anchorage but not out here and not looking like that.

"Good morning!" I called out in my friendliest tone. "You look a little tired."

The lead man nodded glumly and stopped near me. The other seemed mostly interested in surveying the terrain not only around the camp but also back along the trail. For a fleeting moment I thought they might be escaping bank robbers with their hostage, and their manner did nothing to reassure me. The Indian girl looked impassive, as if either resigned to her fate or uncaring of it.

"Mornin'," the lead man responded to me. "Yeah, you're right about being tired, I'll tell you."

"Want some coffee?" I offered, trying to stay as friendly as I could. No matter who these people were my best chance was to keep innocently on their good side and let them go.

"Coffee . . ." the lead man repeated, almost dreamily. "God! Could I use some coffee. . . ."

"You sure you wan'ta stop, Dan?" the other man put in, speaking for the first time. "I mean, we don't know. . ."

The man called Dan sighed wearily. "Charlie, after you been here a while you'll see things differently. I'm so damned tired and sore that if I don't get something in me I'm going to fall down to Skagway."

The other shrugged. "O.K. Suit yourself." He sounded nervous and not at all convinced. Both men got off their horses, though, and stretched. I couldn't help but notice as Dan, the nearest to me, got down there was more than a hint of a shoulder holster. I think he realized what I'd seen as well, and I could see him weighing in his mind what to say to me.

"Don't be alarmed," he said at last. "We're not criminals. Not really, anyway. The truth is, we're federal officers."

That stopped me. "Huh?"

He nodded. "What you see here is the culmination of a lot of skullduggery in what might be the most minor diplomatic incident in recent memory." He looked over at the boiling pot. "Coffee ready?"

I nodded idly and went over to the pot. I had only two telescoping plastic cups, so I fixed two cups of instant and decided I'd wait until they were through before having my own. I felt bad about the Indian girl, though, still sitting there atop her horse.

Dan went over to her, sipping hot coffee with a look of extreme ecstasy on his face. She looked down at him quizzically and asked, well, something like, "*U chua krm sbi?*" It was a guttural language pronounced in a manner that would give me a sore throat. In fact, Dan's response would, I'm sure, be beyond me.

"*Gblt zflctri gaggrb,*" it sounded like. "*Srble.*"

Whatever it was, she nodded and dismounted, approaching the pot. Using a little ingenuity, I'd managed to refill it about halfway from the rivulet in which I'd washed my face.

"You know about the Tlingit Indians?" Dan began at last.

I nodded. "A little. The local tribe, I think, along the panhandle."

"That's putting it mildly," he responded. "Fact is, they aren't like any Indians you ever heard about in your history books. They're nuts. More like the Mafia than the Sioux. In the early days they sold protection to the Hudson's Bay Company. The Company'd pay 'em or their trappers just would go into the wild and never come out. Then the Russians moved in, and they decided the Russians were competition for the protection racket, so they went to war and massacred 'em—the Indians massacring the Russians, that is. Real sneaky, real clever. Used the money to buy all sorts of manufactured goods and to throw huge parties. They even started the gold strikes up here just to bring in people so they coule extort more money."

I just nodded, letting him tell his curious story. I couldn't imagine where he was going with it, though.

"Anyway," Dan continued, "today they ride around in huge fishing trawlers. Rich, well-educated, and still as clannish and as trustworthy as the Mafia. The girl, there, is the son of a big shot—chief you might call him. He and his wife had a big falling out and she took a hike with the kid up the Pass to relatives in Whitehorse. The old man threw a fit. Declared war, more or less. Started trying to ram Canadian boats, caused all sorts of trouble, which brought us in. The family's so strong, rich, and powerful we couldn't settle them down without the U.S. Marines and you know what *that* would look like in the papers."

I nodded again, seeing his point exactly. Wouldn't the Russians, for example, have a field day with Marines shooting it out with Indians in this day and time?

"Well, the old lady was stubborn, and the Canadian government wanted no part of it, so we did the only thing our bosses decided we could do. Like common criminals, we snatched the kid and are taking her home to Daddy."

"I gather this wasn't supposed to be your way out," I noted.

"You said a mouthful," he came back. "Hell, all of Momma's relatives are on our trail, not to mention the Mounties, and if we don't beat 'em down to Skagway there's gonna be a *hell* of a stink."

I sighed and shook my head. Your U.S. government tax dollars at work, I thought glumly.

"Dan!" the other man hissed, and got up quickly. "I think I heard horses!"

The other man got up and looked around, also concerned. I strained my ears and, after a moment, thought I *could* hear sounds back up the trail.

"Damn!" the leader swore. "I guess we better get moving."

"Hey, Dan—wait a minute," Charlie said thoughtfully.

"You know, they're looking for the girl most of all. I know there's only one, but we might meet more. It'll mix 'em up, anyway."

The leader paused and considered it. I wasn't following their conversation, but I *did* want them to move. The last thing I wanted was to be in the middle of what might well be a shooting match.

Don turned quickly to the girl, who by this time had also gotten up. *"Grtusi shm du krttha nsi,"* he said to her. Her eyes widened a bit, then she nodded, turned, and looked at me with the oddest expression on her cute little face.

Finally she said, *"Grtusi, mckryss, ka,"* nodded, then walked up to me. I couldn't imagine what was going on and just stood there like an idiot, wondering.

A tiny brown hand reached out, took mine. . . .

My entire body seemed to explode and crackle electrically. There was a searing, all-encompassing pain as if every nerve in my body suddenly cried out, then one massive blow that seemed to explode inside my head. It was as if the entire fibre of my being were being somehow drawn, or sucked from my body, leaving, in an instant, only oblivion.

Chapter Two

I awoke feeling groggy and totally numb, except that my head pounded with a thousand off-key variations of the anvil chorus. I groaned slightly, but couldn't move for a moment.

I opened my eyes and saw only a terrible blur, but, after a moment, my vision seemed to clear and I could see off in the distance. Off—and up. Clearly I had been hit over the head or, perhaps, shot, and my body had been thrown off the side of the cliff. Luckily, I'd landed on a flat patch wedged between rock outcrops, probably the only thing that had saved my life.

Still, I wasn't sure if I were really awake or still dreaming. For one thing, I was *seeing*, and it was perfectly obvious that I was wearing no glasses. The colors, too, seemed slightly wrong, a little darker and different in texture than they should have. Still, my vision was crisp and clear, and, after a moment, I was convinced that in fact I *was* seeing through my eyes. Could the blow and the fall somehow have restored my eyesight?

It didn't seem possible, yet there seemed no other explanation.

Still, I was too numb, too stunned to move, and I was aware that I was in shock.

Voices came to me—men's voices from above, where the camp was. Then, suddenly, I heard the sound of rifle shots, their crisp crackle echoing and re-echoing from the rocks around, and there were men yelling. One of the men in the camp came to the edge of the cliff and I tried to call out to him, to tell him I was here, but all I could manage was a weak gurgling sound. I prayed that he would look down, see me lying here, but he wasn't looking at me. He had a very nasty-looking semiautomatic rifle and he was looking out and down, away from my position.

There was something oddly incongruous about his appearance that made me think it might have been a dream after all. He looked like neither Indian nor Mountie, nor anybody else. He seemed to be dressed in a black suit more out of the 1890s than today, wearing a derby and sporting an outrageously large handlebar moustache. In my shock and delirium I thought perhaps I was seeing the ghost of Soapy Smith—but the rifle he held was very modern indeed.

He didn't look down but turned back to unseen others and yelled something. There was a scramble and a rush, and I heard horses moving out, down, and away from me. Far off in the distance I thought I could hear the sound of a helicopter, and that, at least, gave me some hope. Tlingit kidnapping, indeed. Federal officers indeed. They were what I first suspected, I knew. Fugitives from some crime above, probably in the Yukon. Well, they wouldn't get far, I reassured myself—they were descending into the most totally escape-proof box canyon ever devised by nature, and Skagway had barely 1500 people. Still, if they had copters looking, it meant that I might be able to attract their attention—if I could move, and if I hadn't broken every bone in my body.

A sense of cold came over me, and numbness gradually subsided, to be replaced by aches over much of my body. Still, it was encouraging, and, after a while, I tried once again to move and managed to get somewhat to a sitting position. Almost immediately I felt a sense of wrongness, of something unthinkably different about myself. For a moment I put it down to the after-effects of the blow and fall, but now, as shock wore off and I became more fully aware of myself, I realized at once that several things were terribly wrong.

I had no glasses, yet I saw, sharply, everywhere. I had teeth in the top of my head—not the omnipresent upper plate, but real teeth. And, as I moved my head, I felt weight and something of a drag and I reached up and took hold of a large mass of glossy, coal-black hair.

My reaction to all this was curiously schizophrenic. At once I knew for a certainty that I, now, somehow, was that little Indian girl I'd seen ride in with the two strange men—yet, of course, I knew too that such a thing was unthinkable, impossible. The human mind was an incredibly complex organism—how could you possibly change it for another? I sat there, awestruck and trembling slightly with the certainty that, were I not mad, such an exchange was not only possible but had happened to me. Happened because that girl had wished it to happen—no, had been *ordered* to make it happen.

What kind of a monster was she? What sort of thing, creature, whatever, had the power to trade bodies as casually as it changed a suit of clothes? This went beyond any ESP or similar powers, real or imagined in parapsychology. It smacked, almost, of demonic power, of the supernatural in which I had never really believed. I went back to my memory of her sitting there atop that horse, oblivious to me and to the others.

Relax, keep calm, think it out, I told myself. Consider only the facts first.

Fact: that girl could and did trade bodies with me. My

memory and all that I thought of as me seemed unimpaired in even the slightest detail. If anything, my mind seemed clearer, able to recall more detail about more things than I could ever remember.

Fact: at least one person could trade minds. Maybe more, but at least one.

Fact: somebody else knew it. Those men with her— bodyguards? Allies? Or could they, too, be possessed of that power? But her protectors weren't the only ones who knew. Others knew, and were pursuing them even now, if they hadn't caught them already. So they could be killed—perhaps even captured, although that seemed hard to imagine. Physical touch had been required, that's for sure. The girl had reached out and taken my hand— my *hand!*—and that had done it. That meant no disembodied spirits in the dark. They could swap bodies, but they needed bodies in which to live. They were as mortal as we, and that alone gave me some comfort.

Was she, then, some sort of mutation, some freak of nature or the result of some unknown experiment? She— not the girl, surely. What did the creature look like at birth? Who or what was it? Certainly that was many bodies ago. But such a one would be enormously powerful, almost godlike, I told myself.

And the girl, clearly, hadn't been in charge. Hadn't even spoken any language resembling any one I'd ever heard. The lead man, Dan, *he'd* been the boss. Charlie was the new man. Dan had remarked to him, "When you've been at this as long as I have" or words to that effect. This hadn't been the first time, then.

The UFO report in the paper came back to me— although even if that were related it was hard to see how something that far away could have wound up here. Unless . . . Unless NORAD hadn't lost the object, but almost captured the occupant that it dropped. Come close enough, in fact, to force a wild chase through the bush. If those men's job was to get that alien passenger down to civilization, and if their covers were blown, they might just criss-cross enough, trying to shake pursuit, and so wind up almost anywhere. For the same reason that Skagway was a trap it'd also be the last place most government agents would look for fleeing fugitives.

I considered that angle. Whatever they'd tried hadn't worked. The government—probably both governments, U.S. and Canadian—were on to them, chasing them, closing in. Ordinarily they'd just change bodies and identities and slip into the crowd, but they hadn't—until now. Why? Because too many leftover innocents in wrong bodies would be a trail in itself? Because it would blow their existence wide open, causing panic, suspicion, paranoia. They swapped when they had to, not otherwise. They'd swapped with me because the girl had been a dead giveaway. Now they might split up, two men going one way and one the other, probably losing the horses, playing cat and mouse in the rocks, trying to surprise their pursuers, get one or two off by themselves and swap.

And that left me. First of all, I was no longer who I used to be, possibly forever. My past was gone, everything was gone. Oddly, I felt pangs of regret about that, despite my depression and loneliness, for now, it came home to me, I had lost the one thing I had always had—security. Of course, I could hail the pursuers, those who might understand what had happened to me—but would they? Did they really know or understand the power they were facing? Were they, in fact, a killing party? If so, they'd be looking for an Indian girl and they might shoot first and ask questions later. I couldn't take a chance on it.

Still, what were the alternatives? I stood up, somewhat unsteadily at first, and felt the sore points on my new body. Miraculously, nothing appeared broken, although I knew I was going to feel the bruises even worse as time went on. I checked the pockets of the jacket and jeans but they were empty, except for one stick of chewing gum. Curious, I thought. Or was it just there from the body's original owner?

The fact was that I was now, and possibly forever, suddenly female. That seemed at least interesting. It certainly couldn't be worse than I'd been. I loosened the jeans and felt the area around my crotch. How strange, how different it was. I refastened the pants and felt my chest, where, it seemed, two incipient breasts were just beginning to push out slightly.

I looked at my reddish-brown hand and arm. I was also an Indian, a pureblooded Indian. That didn't really bother me so much, but it *did* mark me socially. In my old circles it would have been a real plus, but up here— the government controlled a lot of Indian life, and there were certainly people who didn't like Indians.

Finally I was twelve, perhaps, certainly no more than thirteen. Just edging into the teen years—but there were drawbacks, too. Mentally and culturally I was a thirty-five-year-old associate professor at Hopkins and graduate Ph.D. from Harvard. Goodbye degrees, unless I somehow got the chance and was willing to do all that work again. If I were picked up, I'd look like an Indian escapee from seventh grade. Going through *that*, at my age, in some Indian orphan asylum—or, worse, being returned to the parents of the original girl—was not something I wanted at all.

I started looking around to see what else they might have tossed down here. I spotted the tent forty or fifty feet below me, which gave me some hope that they'd just tossed everything over in the hopes of disguising the fact that there had been a switch at all. I spotted my pack on another ledge, a little down from me, and, after a pretty precarious climb I managed to reach it. I generally stuck my wallet and other personal things in the pack when sleeping outdoors, both as theft protection and because they were uncomfortable to sleep on. I rummaged around and came up with several things—my spare pair of glasses, for example, which I took out and looked through. My whole head almost was able to fit between the frames, and the world was a horribly blurred, indistinct mess with them. I tossed them away.

Finally I found it—both my wallet and my checkbook! The wallet contained a little over three hundred dollars in U.S. and Canadian cash, and *that* was a godsend. The traveler's checks I regretfully had to conclude were worthless. Even though I could sign them—who'd believe that a little Indian girl was Victor Gonser? Still, it was hard to abandon over five hundred more dollars, and I decided to keep them for a little while. You never knew—one time I might find somebody willing to take them.

The credit cards, too, seemed interesting, but I finally decided against them. They'd just think I stole them. I didn't want to wind up in the clink, an Indian juvenile delinquent, for stealing my own stuff. The checkbook, though, was another matter. If I could make it somehow back to the lower forty-eight I might be able to manage, through my bank in Maryland, a by-mail transaction.

So, keeping only the money, travelers checks, and checkbook, I started to make my way back up to the campground. It was not easy. I hadn't really realized the weight of so much hair, the drag on the neck muscles, and I didn't have the reflexes to automatically compensate that someone born to the body would have had. Too, my arms never *were* very strong, but I found myself positively feeble now. It took me better than an hour and a half to make it back to the top.

Aside from some droppings from several horses there was no sign that anybody had been there, as I expected, and the ground was, overall, too rocky to see much in the way of footprints. Here a crushed cigar, there a couple of cigarette stubs, and that was about all.

I listened for the sounds of people, of gunfire, of, perhaps, the helicopter, and heard nothing. In all the time it'd taken me to get to the pack, then back here, the chase was far beyond now, if not over. I went over and drank some water from the rivulet still flowing nearby as if nothing momentous had happened, then turned and walked back to the ledge up which I'd just climbed. It was a terrible drop down there, with precarious and tiny holds. I realized for the first time what luck I'd had in surviving at all, and noted that what had supported my sixty- or seventy-pound frame on the way up might not have supported my old body. My survival, though, had been a real freak of luck, and I shivered at the thought. No wonder the pursuers hadn't bothered to look down!

I turned away and walked around a little, trying to get used to the balance of my new body, gain some sort of mastery over it. Even the boots had higher heels than I'd ever worn and took some getting used to. Finally, though, I knew I was as ready as I could ever be and started cautiously down the trail. I was determined to hide if at all possible, keep out of sight of any possible pursuers. But, on the long trip down, I met only one person, a park ranger, who simply nodded and continued on up, giving me not a second glance. My biggest problem was a few gusts of wind that occasionally threatened to blow my slight body over, and my constant struggle to keep from falling off my own boots.

The trail became wider now, the slope still sharp but broad, with no sheer cliffs to contend with. You could see almost clear down to Skagway now, and, while anyone else could also see me, there seemed no real way around it. Besides, I had the best vision I could ever remember, and I felt confident that, at least, nobody was going to sneak up on me or lie in hiding.

Approaching Skagway, but still a ways up, you suddenly hit trees and I was thankful for them. Although the chances of ambush were greater, I felt confident in moving off the trail and paralleling it in the brush. Still there seemed no one around, either pursuer or pursued, to threaten. Wherever the battle had gone, it was still ahead of me.

But, then, where would my danger lie? They couldn't put an army in here without alarming the population and making headlines. No, if they were looking for the three fugitives they'd do the obvious things. They'd stake out the train station and probably the rail yards as well to avoid a double-back. They'd stake out the tiny airport, the only place you could fly out of in this small valley surrounded by sheer mountain cliffs two miles high. They'd stake out the ferry terminal, of course, to make sure you didn't get out that way, and the little marina. And they'd start a new team down both the White and Chillicoot Passes from the top just to make sure.

But—would their trap work on such beings as these? Assuming the insane for the moment that these were, indeed, alien beings from some other world, they'd be perfect actors. I saw no signs of a device in the transfer—it was something absolutely natural with them, something they did because they were born with the power to do it. Perhaps they were creatures of pure energy, parasites who invaded bodies—but, no, then why would the process be two-way? Obviously, then, such creatures had to have evolved this power as some sort of natural protection. I wondered, idly, what sort of world it would take for such an ability to evolve? A terribly harsh and competitive one, almost certainly. One with so many enemies that, to survive, it had to learn how to become its enemies.

That was a sobering thought. These would be no pushovers, these alien body-swappers. They'd be tough, accomplished, perfect mimics. About the only problem they had as far as I could see was, in this instance, the newcomer, the one dropped by spaceship, was totally unfamiliar with Earth and its people and customs and hadn't even yet learned the language. The other two, though—they were something else. If "Dan" and "Charlie" were actually creatures like the girl had been and not merely hirelings or agents, they'd become your best friend and you'd spill all your secrets to them.

And they'd kill you without batting an eyelash.

I felt certain that if they'd gotten this far the government or whoever those pursuers were would fail to bottle them in.

But they certainly could bottle *me* in, I realized suddenly, feeling a touch of panic once more. They *knew* what I looked like, certainly—and they'd be watching for me.

I stopped dead and sat down wearily on the grass, cursing softly. Skagway was a trap, all right, but it was a trap for *me*. How the hell was *I* going to get by them?

I wondered what seventh grade in an Indian school would be like—if they let me live that long.

The sheer impossibility of my situation was sinking in on me, and I felt despair rising within. Damn it, I was tired and cold and achy and hungry, and I'd had a lot of water and one stick of gum all day, and I didn't even know how the hell to pee without a toilet without it running all down my legs. . . .

Chapter Three

It occurred to me that, had I been in a large city, not merely a New York or San Francisco but even Anchorage, I'd have had little trouble. I had money, although it wouldn't last long, and I could mix with a crowd, even perhaps enter a shop and buy less conspicuous clothing. Even putting my hair up would be a big help, but I simply didn't know how to do it. The conclusion was obvious and inescapable: to survive to find my own new path in this world, I'd have to get out of the trap that was Skagway.

Air was out, of course. I briefly considered the train—it would be possible to hitch a ride in a boxcar, say, jumping on at one of the slow turns as it went into White Pass—but that would only take me back to Whitehorse, a town as isolated and as staked out as Skagway—and one in which the real little girl's parents and friends might reside. There were no roads out of Skagway. The highway through the pass, long a joke in the region, had been killed forever when most of the area had been made a national park.

Skagway itself was a living museum with its 1898 buildings and boardwalk main street. It might have been possible to do something had there been a horde of tourists, but it was a slow day. I briefly toyed with the idea of waiting for the ferry's crowds to come in, using them as at least a mild shield behind which I could get some sort of disguise, but this was quickly dismissed. They would remain with the area staked out until they accounted for all those they were searching for. The danger was acute here, less the further away I got. That meant that, somehow, I had to go along with my original plan to take the ferry southward in the evening, and that posed its own problems.

Skagway ended a good quarter to half a mile from the water's edge. The area from the end of Main Street, except for some boxcars, was clear and open and absolutely flat. There would be no way to even get close to the boat short of swimming for it—and the water temperature was 50 degrees at best and probably far less than that. Still, I made my way down towards the harbor keeping close to the main line railroad tracks which offered some concealment, trying to see if anything was even remotely possible.

It was late; my stomach fairly growled and writhed in hungry pain and I was somewhat dizzy and exhausted, yet the ferry was now due in only a couple of hours and something had to be done fast. Most of the ferries stopped at the highway connection at Haines Junction; it might be two or three days before the next one put in here.

The railroad yard personnel were busy, it seemed, but it took a moment before I realized what they were doing. A large crane-like device hovered overhead, and, occasionally, it would lower slowly its grasping apparatus over a boxcar. There would be a series of loud metallic *chunks* and then the boxcar was lifted into the air—no! Not the boxcar! Just the top of it. . . .

Containerized cargo. Load the box in a yard, lift it onto a truck flatbed, take it to the Whitehorse rail yard, lift it off the truck and sit it down, securely clamped, on a railroad car frame and wheels, pull it to Skagway, then take it off that rail frame and . . .

And put it back on a truck frame. There was only one truck cab, though, being used to pull the trailer frames away and back new ones into position, and I counted. Six—no, seven large trailers were lined up in a row there, yet there was no freighter in the railroad docks. I felt hope rise within me once again. Why all this work now when there was no freigther in? Why load them onto trailer chassis at all? The only answer had to be that these were being readied to be placed on the ferry. If I could slip into, or somehow get on, one of those trailers, I might be pulled right into the belly of the ship beneath the noses of my watchers!

Slowly and carefully using as much of the railroad's equipment as I could for a shield, I made my way towards those waiting trailers, fearful that at any moment watchers in the yards, or trainmen, would spot me—or that they would begin taking the trailers over to the ferry dock itself. There was a small stretch of open space I had to get to, but it was extremely cloudy and there was a light mist falling by this time, and it seemed worth the risk. Judging my time as best I could, I sprinted for the trailers, adrenaline pumping, and made them, stopping in their shelter to suddenly gasp for breath and get hold of myself.

After a few moments, I looked them over, finding that being four feet tall placed the heavy truck latches out of reach. I might get to one by standing on the ledge and stretching, but it might take more effort than I could muster to move them—if they weren't locked.

My very tininess, though, might serve to some advantage if I could ride in on the undercarriage. I ducked under and checked that possibility out. There were spaces and grooves in the solid steel frame where I might fit, but the handholds would be precarious at best and I would have a long, bumpy pull under the least comfortable of circumstances. I knew, though, that I'd have to chance it. I had no real idea where I was going or what I was going to do once I got there, but I knew for damned sure that any alternative was worse. The only people who would believe my story and accept body-switching were the aliens, who'd tried to kill me, and their hunters, who'd think me one of their enemy and would take no chances, of that I was certain.

Choosing the "shoe" area which helped support the rear axle, I picked one of the lead trailers and wedged myself in as best I could and I tried to relax, waiting for the inevitable.

How long I waited there, so precariously perched, I don't really know—but several times I heard men's voices and heard and saw legs and feet walking between the trailers. Once or twice I heard latches thrown, and loading doors on the trailers thrown back, including the one I was under, but they didn't see or suspect me hiding beneath. Some of the trousers looked too fancy and new to be trainmen, and I was suddenly glad, despite the pain and discomfort, that I hadn't tried to sneak inside one.

I heard the ship come in, a mighty, echoing blast from its air horn signalling arrival at its furthest outpost, but I dared not peek at it. I knew what it looked like, anyway—a great blue ship, more like an ocean liner than a ferry, a representative of the most luxurious, yet necessary, working boats in the world. I waited stuffed inside my precarious perch, hunger and fatigue temporarily recessed as the tension built within and around me. It seemed like hours there, although it must have been far less than that, and I heard the roar of vehicles getting off, the bumps against the concrete and metal ramp, and the myriad voices and shouting that accompanied loading and unloading. Then it was still, for a while, as the ship made ready to load and begin the long journey south once again. At least I knew this one's itinerary—there would be an empty stateroom aboard this time, the one I would have occupied.

Finally, after an eternity, I heard the start-up of engines on the dock and heard the loading begin. There would not be many from Skagway—you couldn't drive anywhere from here—but they would have to be carefully arranged, as Alaska's ferries stopped at all the cities and towns of the panhandle and arranging cars and trucks so they would be able to get off at their proper destinations was a skill in itself.

Finally there was quiet once more, and I became afraid that I had misjudged the situation, that these trailers, after all, were not due to get on. With the fear came a new awareness of the pain in my position was causing, and I shifted slightly.

Suddenly I heard the roar of a diesel cab and was aware that it was backing up to the trailer under which I hid. The rear of the cab slid under as I watched, then stopped with a bump that almost spilled me. A man got quickly out of the cab and walked back, operating the hydraulic couplers, linking the trailer to the cab, then plugging in the air brakes. He looked under to check his work, and I feared he would spot me there, but his mind was on business, and I got lucky. He walked back and got into the cab, then slammed his door and put the truck in gear. The shock of sudden movement spilled me and I grabbed frantically at the metal, trying to pull myself back up before I fell to the ground and was left. I know I cried out in pain and anguish as I did so, but the noise was more than masked by the roar of the diesel. Scraped, with part of my jeans torn, I managed to get back up into the ridiculously small perch and hang on for dear life. Had the truck been in any but the lower gears I know I couldn't have stayed there no matter what I would have tried.

Still, now we roared onto the dock, turned, and moved slowly towards, then into the great ship. Once inside its massive car deck, the truck went through a series of slow maneuvers, backing up and then going forward, then repeating, again and again, until it was in its proper position and lane. Quickly and professionally the driver jumped out, disconnected the air brakes and lowered the hydraulic coupler, then sped out to pick up the next.

There were people all about in the deck area, both passengers and crew, but I wasn't about to wait to be discovered. I got cautiously down, wincing slightly as I discovered that my knee had been badly skinned, then using the trailer as a shield, looked cautiously around. It was obvious that I would have to cross some open deck to get to the stairway up, but I really wasn't concerned. The purser would still be out on the dock—and only he would know or be likely to remember who came aboard. I decided that the best defense was simply to walk over as if I belonged there legally and naturally and hope I made it. After some hesitancy, I took a deep breath and went for the hatch marked "To Passenger Decks" trying to look as if I belonged.

Whether or not I seemed out of the ordinary, nobody gave me a second glance, and the hardest thing I had to do was bear the burning pain as I walked up those interminable stairs, then pushed back the sliding doors at the top, and walked onto the deck of the ferry. The door hadn't been easy—the latch was very high and I'd had to stand on tip-toe to get at it, then push the door back with all my might. I was reminded once again of my new physical situation.

I walked down the corridor, past closed stateroom doors, heading towards the rear of the ship where I could figure out where everything was. I reached the end of the corridor and found a diagram of the ship, a sort of "you are here" thing, and again had to strain, as it was fully eighteen inches higher on the wall than the top of my head.

Nerves suddenly started to get the better of me, and I realized now that this was going to be something new, something I hadn't given any thought to until now. I'd made it—but that fact gave me little comfort. Everything I had done up to this point was borne of necessity and desperation, but now I was reentering society as someone totally different, someone I didn't even know. I was a small, prepubescent Indian girl now to everyone else, and I knew that I would have to *be* that person, act like her, react like her, to be both accepted and inconspicuous.

I'd ridden the ferry on the way up from Seattle to Juneau, but somehow the ship seemed to have doubled in both size and scale, even though this was a smaller ship. Everything, I was discovering, looked larger than life. Nowhere was this brought home more forcefully to me than when I met my first human beings close up. How much we forget of what it's like to be a child in an adult's world! How gigantic the ordinary-sized adults look from four feet or less and perhaps sixty plus pounds.

Aft a bit I saw two illuminated plastic signs that said MEN and MEN'S SHOWERS, and I almost went in until I realized that those signs, which I'd been so conditioned to look for, were now the wrong ones for me. I walked back up, crossed through an intersecting corridor to the other side of the ship, and went into the women's john.

Although hardly a baby, I was so tiny and thin that I almost slipped into the toilet, and my legs barely touched the floor. Still, the relief was the same—or more so, since there seemed even more pressure now.

I had some problem with the latch to the shower—too high again—but managed to get in and close the door. A dressing room and two stalls. I looked around and found a tiny bit of somebody's leftover soap. Not much, but it would have to do. I undressed and, using the dressing room mirror, looked at my new self for the first time. How thin, frail, almost fragile I looked, with ribs you could count and a waist almost impossibly small. My reddish-brown complexion did a lot to hide the many bruises I had, but the aid was only cosmetic—they told

me now constantly that they were there. The scrape
from falling from the truck looked and felt nasty, but I'd
had worse and it'd stopped bleeding.

It took several tries before I got a good hold on the
water handles, but the shower felt good and the soap
helped loosen the grime, wilderness pee, blood and whatever else had accumulated, and I felt my new body
tingle with the warmth and the spray. I had no sham-
poo, but my long hair was already wet because I couldn't
reach up far enough to adjust the shower nozzle and I
rinsed it as best I could.

It wasn't until I was reluctantly through that I realized I had no towel, so I had to stand there in the
dressing room letting myself drip-dry as good as possible, while wringing my hair out again and again. I
hadn't had much hair for a number of years, and never
as much as this, and I hadn't really realized just how
saturated it could get. As I was doing all this I heard the
distant sound of the ship's air horn, felt the slight en-
gine tremble accelerate, and realized that we were under way.

I got back into my clothes, still slightly wet. They
clung, but it wasn't so bad, and all but my hair was dry
in minutes. The hair would be a major problem, I realized now. Before, I hadn't given much thought to wom-
en's long hair, but now I saw that its care and management was a major skill needing tools.

I remained there a moment, thinking of what I should
do next. Get something to eat, certainly, and, if the
ship's store was open, maybe pick up a couple of things
I'd need. Then head for the lounge and try and get some
sleep. I'd need all I could get for the days ahead.

The diagram said there was a cafeteria in the rear
upper deck, so that was the first place to go. I went out
on deck hoping that the wind would help blow-dry my
hair, which currently seemed to resemble a tangled and
sticky wet black mop.

It was raw-cold, suddenly, and extremely windy. The

wetness of the marine climate was all over and went right through you. Away from the shelter of the mountains, the weather was rough even for July. Still, while I was aware that it was cold, made particularly so by the wind, it didn't really affect me as much, while before I'd had to have a sheepskin-lined parka if it dropped to fifty degrees. I recalled seeing pictures once of Eskimos running around in the snow barely clothed, and I recalled that some Oriental skin was colored such because it contained thin layers of insulating fat between the layers of skin. Either my greater tolerance was due to that, or my youth, or a combination of same.

My hair was damp—it would be for hours—but manageable, and I knew that a high priority would be a comb. Despite my near starvation level, I headed amidship for the ship's store, which wasn't going to be open very much longer. Once we stopped and loaded at Haines, it'd pack up for the night.

Amidst the piles of souvenirs were several things I needed, although I had some problems with the large number of people crowding into the very small space and the fact that I was so small myself. Still, a cheap shoulder purse with a ferryboat on it, a comb, box of tissues, toothbrush and toothpaste, and some spray-on salve for the skinned area were easy. They also had some kid's sized T-shirts, a head band that might keep my hair manageable and looked very Indian despite the fact that it was stamped "Singapore" on the back, and I looked at jackets, too. Most were adult sizes at highly adult prices, but there were some kid's thin windbreakers—again with Alaska tourist symbols—and a blue one that fit. I also picked up a small sewing kit, although I hadn't much idea how to use it, in the hopes of patching the tear in my jeans. The place, after all, was a tourist trap, not a clothing store.

I approached the cash register shyly, because I *was* feeling very small and very nervous and insecure, but the gray-haired lady just smiled and took all the stuff and totalled it up.

Fifty-seven fifty. Gad. And the three hundred bucks or so had looked like a lot of money. . . .

Still, I had to pay it, and, without saying a word, I gulped and frankly surprised the woman by peeling out the crumpled bills, which she took, handing me the change. I walked out, away from the people, and, heading again for the trusty john, I sorted out what I had, put the money and other stuff in the purse, then reluctantly removed my original warm, thick ski jacket and left it on a hook, putting on the thinner, cheaper windbreaker. Finally, I laboriously combed my hair, finding it a real and sometimes painful struggle.

While in the john others would enter, and several times I had an involuntary shock at seeing women enter. It would take some getting used to, both their presence and their casualness once inside. I felt like a peeping tom, but forced myself to ignore it as much as possible. I would have to get used to it—I was one of them, now.

Finally I completed what I could and headed back aft to where I longed to go from the start, the cafeteria. My head was barely level with the lowest shelf, but the sight and smell of food almost overwhelmed me. I felt my stomach almost tie itself in knots. What I wound up with was a cheeseburger—at almost three bucks!—and cocoa (mercifully sixty cents) and I found I couldn't really finish the burger. It wasn't my size; my stomach had gone without food for so long it could only barely recognize it any more. The cocoa, however, went down well and tasted fantastic. Now, relaxed for the first time, I felt totally exhausted and slightly dizzy. The clock, which my tired eyes could barely read, said it was almost midnight, which meant that I'd been without sleep, really, for almost forty-eight hours—and who knew how long before that? Still, I couldn't sleep quite yet. I walked forward on this deck, looking over the general passenger lounges, finding hordes of people sprawled out asleep on the floor, on the couches and in the chairs, some just sprawled, others with air mattresses and, in some cases, sleeping bags. There was an area, too, with a lot of gigantic lounge chairs, reclining types like on first-class long distance airlines, and a few were empty. I hadn't seen anyone who looked even vaguely familiar, and no one who looked in the least interested in me except for a few smiles and patronizing glances, and I decided that I was reasonably safe. It was warm here, and quiet. I climbed into one of the lounge chairs, so large it almost engulfed me, and curled up, intending just to rest for a couple of minutes.

The next thing I knew, the sun was shining brightly through the side windows and it was early afternoon of the next day.

I creaked a little from sleeping curled up in a tight little ball in the big chair, and my head was filled with cobwebs. I had the experience of waking out of the deepest sleep humanly possible and, for a while, it felt as if I hadn't slept at all. Some of the bruises were still very much there, but the skinned knee, at least, seemed to have scabbed. I made my way back to the cafeteria once more and found, again, that I felt only slightly hungry. How small *was* my stomach now, I wondered? I got a horribly overpriced bun and some coffee, despite the protestations of a busy-body in line with me that I was too young for the stuff, and went over to a table. The sun had already vanished once again, hidden by clouds and monstrous mountain walls that gave the huge ship very little clearance on either side. The Inside Passage was extremely deep, but very narrow in many parts, and I was startled to see trees on the left side actually tremble as branches brushed against the deck railings.

The bun and coffee positively bloated me, and I discovered that my taste had certainly changed. Sweet stuff seemed to taste much sweeter, and satisfied tremendously, while the coffee, although waking me up, tasted terribly bitter and more acidic than I'd ever remembered. I thought of complaining, then realized that the coffee was probably perfectly all right—it was just that *I* had changed.

And not just taste, either. I'd noticed from the start that color perception was quite different. Oh, red was still red, green was green, and so forth, but they were *different* reds and greens. My big brown eyes definitely saw things a bit differently than my old, weak bluish-gray ones had. Smells, too, seemed sharper, richer, more distinct and in some cases overpowering, yet different, each and every one. A fact that only someone who'd lived in a different body could learn—people's senses were quite different from body to body.

After, I played with my hair, using a couple of purchased rubber bands to make a sort of pony tail and fitting the headband. I was determined to change my appearance as much as I could. It had occurred to me from the start that not only the government agents, or whoever they were, might be aboard but the aliens as well. The only people I feared meeting more than the government men were Dan or Charlie—or, perhaps, myself.

That idea unnerved me a bit. I had hardly been happy with that body, but it *was* me, had been me my whole life. To run into it with somebody else inside, somebody not quite human, would be more than I could have stood, I felt sure.

Still, here I was, heading south, out on my own, with a couple hundred bucks and not much else. Where was I going? What was I going to do?

The coffee was acting like a pep pill on me, the caffeine making me hyperactive, hypersensitive, and a little jittery. I decided to walk the length and breadth of the ship, to see if I could spot any potential threats, and perhaps, work off this nervous energy. I resolved to stick to cocoa after this, anyway.

The ship was crowded now from many stops, crowded

not only by the tourist crowd but also by family groups and lots of young people in rugged clothes who'd been on Alaskan vacations or trips. I stopped by the store again and, despite the prices, blew five bucks on a small red cowgirl's hat with a tie string to keep it on in the wind. It made me look kind of cute, I decided, and it also further changed passing perceptions of me. It was the most I could do to change my looks without help and more resources, and I hoped it would be enough.

I ran into a bunch of kids my physical age and younger playing in the lounge—tag or hide-and-seek or something like that—and while I declined to play several crowded around, asking me if I were a *real* Indian and ooing and ahing when I told them I sure was. I got away from them fairly quickly, but I felt reasonably satisfied. I'd run into a group of my apparent peers and they hadn't noticed anything more unusual about me than my fine, dark Indian features.

Still, it brought me back to the question that lurked about me now, one that I couldn't avoid for very long. What was I going to do now? This ship, in three more days, would put me into Seattle, but then I'd be on my own. Being Indian I could accept. If I made my way back East it'd be an asset instead of the handicap it was west of the Mississippi. Being female, too, I could accept, although it would take a lot more adjusting to. But there was no way around the one central thing that I was that stood in the way of any job, any way to a new life at all. I was at most thirteen years old, for God's sake! Too young for a social security card, driver's license, *any* of the things needed to turn labor into money. Child labor laws stood in the way of any gainful employment, and I wasn't even legally responsible for anything. The world was quite certainly effectively organized to deny any of the basics of life to a thirty-five-year-old pre-teenager.

An hour or so wandering with such gloomy thoughts brought me to an outside stairway on the upper stern deck that I hadn't noticed before. I climbed it, curious, and reached the top deck of the ship, an area which looked flat and barren for a moment, dominated as it was by the giant dark blue smokestacks and mast. But—no, not empty of interest after all, I saw. There *was* an area behind the stacks with people, open on this side but closed on the other three sides and with a roof. The sign said it was the Solarium—which I discovered, was filled with plastic-slatted chaise lounges and camping gear and was heated, sort of, by strong, bare coils attached to its roof.

I ran to it and into it, perhaps a bit too exuberantly, and immediately tripped over somebody's backpack, which in turn sent me sprawling right into someone.

"I—I'm sorry," I mumbled, then looked up.

It was a young woman's face, perhaps eighteen or so, that I saw smiling sweetly at me. She was dressed in a heavy red flannel shirt with red stocking cap, tough-looking jeans and hiking boots, yet she was without a doubt the most beautiful woman I had ever seen in my entire life. Her reddish-blond hair hadn't a hint of dye, her bright, deep blue eyes sparkled with life and inner beauty, and her face, bereft of makeup, was both tremendously sexy and yet somehow angelic. *Angelic*. The word might have been created for her.

"Well, young lady, you were really in a hurry to go nowhere, weren't you?" she said laughingly, her voice soft and musical. "You're not hurt, are you?"

I picked myself up and sat on the cold deck, arms around my knees. "It's kinda wet," was all I could manage, unable to take my eyes off her.

She picked one of the chaises and sat down, looking at me. "You're an Indian, aren't you? What tribe?" She was being friendly with just a hint of patronizing that was inevitable when talking to someone of my age.

I nodded. "I'm a Tlingit," I told her, echoing Dan's lie. For all I knew it could be the truth.

"A Tlingit! Then you come from around here."

I nodded, drawing a little more on Dan's story. "Admiralty Island," I told her.

"Then you'll be getting off soon," she responded, gesturing slightly to her right. "There's Admiralty over there."

"No," I told her. "I'm going all the way to Seattle."

"Seattle!" Her patronizing tone was growing and getting a little hard to take, but I had to grin and bear it. Like it or not, I'd better get used to this sort of thing. "What takes you there?"

I considered my answer carefully. Until this moment I hadn't really considered a cover story, and my creativity was being sorely tested. Still, I had to gamble sometime on somebody else—and she seemed as good as any and less threatening than most.

"They were gonna put me in an orphanage," I told her as sincerely as I could. "Daddy was killed in a boat accident and Mommy's been—gone—for some time. Do you know what kinda orphanages they got for Indians? Horrible, drafty places out in the middle of nowhere run by a bunch of white bureaucrats—no offense—who are just there for the fat paychecks. A *prison's* better than those places."

She looked suitably concerned. Blonde and blue-eyed young women generally felt a lot of social concern at this stage in their lives. I'd taught enough of them to know that it wasn't much of a gamble to play on her inevitable social conscience.

"Oh, come on. I've been to a few orphanages in my time and they aren't that dreadful at all." She pronounced "been" as "bean" and I marked her as a Canadian.

Looking as sadly indignant as I could, I responded, "*White* orphanages. Whites are people. Indians are wards of the state. I'm thirteen now, but as far as the government's concerned all Indians are thirteen forever." Now the *coup de grace*. "Aw, what's the use? You couldn't understand anyway."

It hit home, I could see that. Thanking my entire social science and teaching background fervently, I waited for her move.

Her face was serious now, and she looked at me thoughtfully. "So you're running away," she almost whispered. "How'd you get this far?"

I told her some of the story, altered to make it believable. I said I'd stowed away on a fishing boat north and gotten stuck in Skagway. Realizing I was in a deadend trap, I'd then used the truck trailer gambit to stow away again coming south, this time as far as possible. I told her, too, that the Bureau of Indian Affairs men were looking for me, which is why I had to be careful. I even showed her my torn jeans and skinned knee. The hardest part wasn't the lie, which was less a lie than the truth would have seemed, but keeping to contractions and a slightly more childish vocabulary. I still came out sounding awfully bright for my age, but that was O.K.

The truth was, I really didn't know why I was telling her all this in the first place, nor had I any clear idea of what I could gain by all this. Mostly it was the insecurity, the terrible loneliness of my condition, and my sense of helplessness about it that craved some company, some companionship, some concern. I needed somebody now, even for a little while, more than I had ever needed anybody in my whole life.

"You aren't gonna turn me in, are you?" I asked warily.

She was genuinely touched and concerned, and it showed. "Come," she said. "Sit by me," and I did. She lifted me into her lap and put her arms around me. It felt warm and secure and good. I was so overcome I felt myself starting to cry, and, try though I might, I couldn't really stop it. No gold, no wondrous prize of any kind, could replace that hug. It was a need beyond price.

After a few moments just lying there, weeping slightly, cradled in her arms, I looked up at her, bleary-eyed, and saw that she had tears in her own blue eyes.

"No," she whispered kindly, hugging me tighter, "I won't give you away. But—where will you go? What will you do?"

"I'll go somewhere where they won't send me back," I told her. "Get in a city, maybe do a little begging. I'll get by."

She sighed. "Well, I'll do what I can as far as I can," she told me. She let go and reached down into her bag, coming up with some tissues and a hairbrush. "Let's start by untangling your pretty hair."

She brushed and combed and took out the tangles, and did the sort of things I wanted to do but hadn't known how.

"I'm Dorian Tomlinson," she told me as she brushed and combed. "My friends call me Dory. What's *your* name?"

I hadn't thought of a name yet, but one seemed obvious. Fortunately my male name had a feminine equivalent, as most did. "I'm Vicki," I replied. "Just Vicki—not Victoria or anything like that."

"Vicki what?"

I could hardly use Gonser, and it seemed better for the moment to just cop out. "You'd never pronounce it," I told her. "Let's just keep it on a first-name basis like real friends, O.K.?"

She laughed softly, "O.K., friend." She turned me around, straightening my crumpled clothes. "Well, you don't look so bad now you've been groomed. Now let's go downstairs to the ladies' room and I'll see what I can do about patching your pants."

My little sewing kit in expert hands made short work of the rip, and we adjourned to the cafeteria. She'd spotted the money when I'd reached in for the kit and I'd had to think fast and tell her it was my father's secret savings jar money. As I sipped cocoa and she tea I managed to turn the conversation away from me and towards her.

She was a college student, had just turned twenty,

and she'd accepted an invitation by a classmate—a boyfriend—to go hiking and camping up in Glacier Park. She wasn't too clear on why they had a big fight, but I guessed it was more than just sex since she had to know he'd have some of that on his mind all out there in the wild, but, anyway, they'd fought and she'd stalked out and caught the next plane back to Juneau and caught the first ferry through. As a walk-on she had no chance at a stateroom and the solarium seemed to be the most private place other than a stateroom on the ship. She wanted to be alone, to think things out, she said.

For some reason I felt a consuming jealousy for that nameless young man. I couldn't really explain my emotional reaction, but the longer I was with Dory the more she seemed to loom ever larger before me, like some sort of goddess I was joyful in worshipping. It was much later before I realized that I was develping a mad, passionate crush on her, one caused by her beauty and compassion, my need for a friend, my frustrated (male) previous life, and, probably, the glands of the near-woman I now was.

And I'd eaten a whole hamburger just because she'd asked me to.

As we walked around the ship afterwards, poking into things and looking through the little shop, this feeling grew ever stronger within me. Her merest gesture, word, glance, was heaven to me.

I was totally, madly, completely in love with Dorian Tomlinson.

We walked and talked for most of the afternoon, and generally enjoyed each other's company. I was too busy acting like a lovesick schoolgirl to have to pretend to anything, and later on, when the fatigue wouldn't go away, I went sound asleep in her arms, cradled against her warm, soft breasts.

"We'll be in to Prince Rupert before noon," Dory told me gravely. The comment sobered me, bringing me down

from my secure high of the past day and a half. Dory
was going home to Calgary, a long train trip from Prince
Rupert but definitely out of my way.

"What happens then?" I asked apprehensively.

She sighed. "Well, I can't very well desert you here,
and yet I have a train to catch."

"Let me come with you, then," I pleaded. "I don't eat
much, and I could probably smuggle myself aboard any
old train or something."

She laughed. "I don't think we're that hard up. But,
yes, you're right. The only thing I can do now is take
you. I have a small efficiency apartment just off campus
you could stay at, at least for a while. Think you can
talk your way past customs?"

"Sure," I told her. "Nothing to it. An Indian kid in
Prince Rupert?" I was anxious, even eager for this. It
seemed the way out of all my problems, even if it did
shift the burden onto someone else. In my situation, I
had to be dependent on someone, anyway, at least until
I grew "old" enough to make my own way. And I certainly didn't want to leave Dory—anyplace she was was
where I wanted to be. It looked like things were really
working themselves out, and I wandered forward in the
lounge, feeling content, wondering idly what the small
crowd in front was watching. Curious, both Dory and I
approached, and I suddenly froze solid, gripping Dory's
hand as tightly as I could.

The crowd was watching a man do card tricks. He
was quite good at it, and seemed to be having a good
time. He was a medium-sized, ordinary-built man, but
he'd stand out in any crowd. He was dressed in an
old-fashioned black suit and string tie, wore a bowler
hat, and had a huge, black handlebar moustache.

Although I'd only seen him briefly and at some distance, he was impossible to forget—although the last
time he'd been gripping a semiautomatic rifle and peering off a cliff on a trail above Skagway.

Dory caught my fright and looked down. "What's the matter?"

"That magician," I whispered nervously. "I don't know what's with the funny get-up but he was with the men looking for me."

She frowned and looked at me like I was crazy, but shrugged and turned. "Let's just go back to the lounge and sit for a while, then, O.K.?"

She had no argument from me. We started to walk casually back, away from the strange man's performance. I was beginning to wonder about my original assessment of the pursuers as FBI or somesuch, though. Not only did the man dress outlandishly, but the patter I heard with his card tricks was in an unmistakable Irish accent.

What the hell *was* going on here, anyway?

I wondered when he'd gotten on. I'd pretty well cruised the ship since Skagway time and time again and I'd watched the passengers very carefully. Nobody looking like that had been anywhere around, I was sure of it. If he'd been on from the start, he'd kept himself locked in a stateroom—but, if so, why come out so publicly now? The only possible answers weren't pleasant. I *knew* that he was a pursuer—and that implied that, if he were aboard, so were those he was chasing. He and his people had probably spent some time surveying the passengers even more closely than I had, but hadn't had any luck so far. Although their quarry could be literally anybody, they seemed at least reasonably satisfied that the aliens or whatever they were were still aboard, and they hadn't been able to smoke them out. Moustache, then, would have kept out of sight up to now because he was easy to spot—but now we were only hours from Prince Rupert and through road, rail, and bus connections. Now Moustache would have to make his move, publicly reveal himself, try and get his quarry to panic, make a mistake.

I looked around at all the big people standing around the lounge area with renewed suspicion. Two men in particular caught my attention, one lounging on each side of the doorways going aft, looking relaxed but eyeing everybody who passed with more than idle curiosity. Moustache's pals, I knew instinctively. The ones who wanted to see who turned and ran when they spotted their easily recognizable boss.

There seemed little choice but to try and ignore them and walk right by. After all, they'd probably been on since the start and hadn't picked me up yet. I just held onto Dory's hand and kept going. They'd never catch these aliens like that—but I was damned resolved that they wouldn't catch me, not now, not when I was so close.

Now we were past them and walking down the corridor, and I turned my head slightly and glanced back. One of the men was slowly and casually walking behind us, then stopped, took out a cigarette, and lit it as we continued walking.

There was a stairway ahead, just before the lounge chair section. "Let's go down a deck," I suggested nervously, "and use the ladies' room."

Dory sighed, not having seen what I'd seen and having a sense only that I was paranoid. Oh, Dory, if you only knew the truth!

There were footsteps on the stairs behind us and I turned again, seeing with some relief a middle-aged couple, obviously tourists, instead of Moustache and his boys. We reached the bottom of the stairs and continued on when suddenly I heard a shout and we both turned.

How he'd gotten ahead of us I don't know, but it was Moustache, who'd been flattened against the wall near the stairs. Now he whirled and grabbed at the middle-aged man, who snarled, then yelled, *"Gfrhjty tig smurf!"*

Dory said, "What?" but I dragged her forward. "Come on!" I implored. "For God's sake get into the john!"

I opened the door and practically dragged her in, closing it behind us. The six-stall john was apparently unoccupied.

"Wha—what's going on?" Dory gasped, but before I could answer the door opened again and the middle-aged woman burst in, slamming it behind her. She had a wild look in her eyes and we both just stared at her in mixed apprehension and fear.

The woman reached into her purse and pulled out a shiny-looking .38 pistol. "Just relax," she snapped, gasping for breath. "Oh, that bastard, that devil!" she added, talking now to herself rather than us.

I let go of Dory, who was standing there petrified and speechless. "You may as well just give yourself up," I told the woman with the gun. "Moustache's men will be here any second and you're trapped in here."

The woman grinned evilly. "Not necessarily," she responded, and I knew exactly where her thinking lay.

"We won't do you any good," I pointed out. "They saw us come in here."

It was too much for Dory. "Vicki—who *are* these people?" she asked, amazed and frightened.

The "woman" considered what I said. I could almost see the wheels turning in her stolen brain. Idly I wondered if this were Charlie's or Dan's. She looked at me with a nasty expression on her face. "We should have finished you back there on the trail. Why the hell did you have to follow us?"

"You stole what was rightfully mine," I came back. "What the hell did you expect me to do?"

Dory was confused but she'd overcome her initial fright. She knew that, somehow, Moustache and his men were some sort of cops and that this woman was a fugitive, and that we were now hostages. Initial fear was replaced in her by a sense of indignation, even anger.

"Put that gun away!" she told the woman. "You're not going to shoot us in here. It'd bring everybody running."

"Dory! No!" I almost shouted. "That's just what she wants! Believe me!"

The woman with the pistol grinned, knowing the truth

of what I said. Still, she relaxed rather than tensed and I knew that she was quickly writing the script. "It's the only chance I got," she said, almost apologetically. The pistol came back up, trained on me.

"No!" Dory screamed, and launched herself at the woman, hitting her and knocking her back against the door. I rushed forward, grabbing at Dory to pull her away.

Again there was that terrible explosion in my head and the total numbness of body, the feeling of electrocution, almost combined with something pulling, on me. . .

And I lapsed into shock and unconsciousness.

Chapter Four

I awoke, this time, in a bed. The terrible headache and numbness was there as before, but it seemed less severe this time. Maybe I was just getting used to it, but maybe, too, it became easier the more times you did it. The aliens or whatever they were seemed to have no blackout at all.

I just relaxed, groaned slightly, and let it pass. A soft bed, at least, was a lot easier to take than hard rocks and bruises. Still, my first thought was, *it's happened again. God in Heaven, they got me again!* But who was I? Three of us were involved this time. I could easily have stirred, tried to see, but I found myself unable to do it. It wasn't the shock, I just couldn't make myself do it. It wouldn't matter to the alien, of course. She was counting on the rescuers coming in, finding three unconscious bodies, and making the switch in the confusion. I wondered if the creature had.

It struck me that, for such super-powerful beings, they were awfully ordinary crooks. They got neatly cornered— part of their ego, I suppose, catching up to them—but when they pulled guns they were no Buck Rogers ray guns, just standard old .38s.

The door opened and Moustache looked in. I grew apprehensive suddenly, not knowing where I stood with him—or who or what he was. Even if he were a government man, he'd touched that other alien on the stairs. Who was he now, I wondered, and in whose hands had I fallen? We. Poor Dory, I thought. What a monster I was to get her involved in all this.

Moustache smiled and fully entered the cabin. "Ah, I see that you're awake once more," he said in a friendly tone that retained the Irish accent if not quite so pronounced. He *sounded* like the same man I'd seen doing card tricks in the lounge.

He sat on the edge of the nightstand and looked down at me. "First," he continued, "let me introduce myself. I'm Harold G. Parch, I'm a federal officer, and I know for a fact that you're in the wrong body. That make things easier?"

I nodded hesitantly but said nothing. I'd met "federal officers" before.

"First of all," he went on, "let me assure you that we have all three of them. Two, unfortunately, are quite dead, but we have a third in better condition, strictly controlled and out of this world on some drugs we have found effective with them. What I need to know from you first is who exactly *you* are."

I sighed. There was no use in concealing anything no matter who he really was. "Victor Gonser," I responded, my voice sounding odd to my ears, lower in pitch than I'd gotten used to. I started to have a real bad feeling about all this.

He nodded. "They got you somewhere on the trail, then. Swapped you with the Indian girl. That figures, although we weren't really sure. We found several bodies along the way and, while we knew that one of you had to be the Indian we really didn't know which."

"Bodies?" I managed weakly.

He nodded. "I'm afraid so. They rarely slip up, you know." He took a small spiral notebook from his back pocket and flipped through it. "Yes, I'm afraid so. They usually like to make it look like a heart attack—hypodermic full of air into the bloodstream—but they were harried and rushed. They blew your brains out with the pistol, I regret to say."

I seemed to sink deeper into the bed. Somehow, somewhere in the back of my mind, I harbored the idea that, sometime, I might get back. Now that door was forever closed. Victor Gonser was dead, murdered on the trail in the wilds of Alaska. The final door was shut—there was no going back, ever.

"I'm afraid we played a bit unfairly with you," Parch continued. "We missed you on the trail, but spotted you a couple of times as you came down. At first we thought you were one of them, but you just didn't act like it, and so we simply kept an eye on you. When you passed that park ranger and didn't body-swap we knew we were dealing with a human being, and we got curious. If you could get on the ferry, which we were prepared to let you do, we hoped that you would spook the dybbuks— what we call them—who thought they'd finished you off. And we were right, although it was a close call. I finally had to make an appearance in full regalia to unnerve them a bit."

"You unnerved me, too," I noted.

He nodded. "I had no idea if you knew what I looked like, but it worked out well. You stopped and turned, and they must have felt surrounded. They followed you with the intention of either killing you as they thought they had done or finding out if you were a part of some trap they should know about. We spotted them easy then, since the one was still too new to speak anything except that impossible jabber of theirs."

"I—I saw you leap out and grab the man," I said. "How did you get ahead of us? And why couldn't he change with you?"

Parch smiled. "As to the first, why, 'twas a simple matter. I simply watched you all go, then ran forward, down one flight, with the idea of approaching from the other side. My boys had everybody 'made' by then. As for the second, well, that's why they are so damned scared of me that they have little shit fits at the sight of me. You see, I'm immune. Scares the hell out of 'em—somebody they can't switch with. I suppose I'm the boogeyman in spades to them, the one who hunts them yet can't be disembodied, as it were."

I envied him that distinction, and that immunity. "But why didn't you tell me?" I asked. "At least I wouldn't have gotten Dory sucked in."

He didn't reply immediately, and exhaled audibly. Finally he said, "We would have interceded if you attempted to leave the ship. But you must understand the situation. First, we didn't know who you were—only that you were not one of them. We didn't know who *she* was, either. Remember, these people can be anybody. Whatever, it's twenty-twenty hindsight right now."

I had gotten the courage, finally. I sat up and turned, sitting on the side of the bed. The mirror was directly across from me and it told the story.

"Oh, my god. Does Dory know?"

He shook his head negatively. "She hadn't awakened as yet when I last checked. One of my people is looking in on her and they'll call when she comes around."

I just stared blankly into that mirror for a few moments, and watched Dorian Tomlinson stare back at me. I felt unclean, somehow, and a little sick. Finally I asked, "Who—which is Dory now?"

"The Indian girl," he responded. That made me feel a little better—the thought of Dory trapped in the body of that old lady was more than I could have borne. My conscience was killing me as it was.

"Apparently what the dybbuk did was swap with Dory, then you, then back to the old woman again. They don't go into shock or anything when they switch—it's easier than changing hats to 'em. We were lined up outside and burst in the moment we heard the commotion, only to find all three of you apparently out on the floor. Fortunately I was the one closest to the old lady, and she suddenly got very awake and tried the swap with me. We plugged her on the spot. Messy."

There was a light tap on the door. Parch opened it and I heard a man's voice say, "She's coming around." The agent just nodded and turned back to me.

"I think I'm going to have a very difficult job right now," he told me. "I don't want it, but it has to be done and I'm the boss. I'd like you to come along if you feel up to it."

"Of course," I responded, and followed him. I felt a little dizzy and unbalanced, but that was to be expected.

Of course, Dory would be a much tougher job than me. I, after all, had been there before and knew what was going on. And, I thought glumly, my old body hadn't been a lot to lose when you came down to it. Dory had lost far, far more.

We approached the next cabin door and Parch turned to me and whispered, "I think it'd be best if you stayed just outside here until I prepare the way. Listen in if you want."

I nodded understandingly. She was going to have enough shocks without staring herself in the face the moment she woke up. A man stationed at the door opened it for him and closed it behind, leaving it slightly ajar. I moved nervously to it, slightly irritated at the guard's leering glance in my direction.

Parch greeted her in the same soft, friendly fashion he had me, and introduced himself. I heard a thin, weak voice ask what had happened to her, what all this was about.

Parch cleared his throat. "Something impossible is what happened and what all this is about," he began a little nervously. I didn't envy him this job. "Ms. Tomlinson, we are at war, in a way. A funny war, although not

comical. Our enemies are from a place we don't know
and their weapon is a terrible and formidable, if impossible one. But it is not, alas, impossible. This—enemy—
has the power to change minds with you. Yes, now I
know what you're thinking, and that's what our own
reaction was the first time. We don't know how long it's
been going on, either, since they normally kill those
with whom they swap. A few times they slipped up, and
that's what finally made us aware of their presence. We
still don't know how many people just plain killed themselves or are locked up in crazy wards who may also be
their victims. Your friend was such a victim—and now,
so are you."

I heard her gasp.

"That's right—sit up," he invited soothingly. "Face
the mirror and the truth and the worst will be over."

I heard movement and a sharp little cry, then silence.
Finally I heard her say, in hushed and unbelieving tones,
"It—it's not possible. I'm mad. This can't have hap-
pened, can't be happening!"

And then she broke into tears and it was a long time
before they subsided. I heard Parch pulling tissues and a
nose blow, then silence for a moment. She was a brave
woman, I told myself. She'd launched herself at that—
thing—to save me. She would accept it.

Finally I heard her ask, "My own—body. What's become of it?"

Parch explained the three-way switch and the out-
come, ending with, "So, Vic—Vicki has your body now,
and you have hers."

"Where is she?" Dory pressed. "Can I—see her?"

I sighed, swallowed hard, and stepped slowly into the
room.

"Oh, Dory—I—I'm so *sorry*," I sobbed, fighting back
tears. She just stared at me with those huge brown
Indian eyes for a while, then sighed and shook her head
unbelievingly. Finally she took a couple of deep breaths,

swallowed hard, and said, firmly, "Well, it's done. I can't believe it but I've got to accept it."

"You can see why I couldn't tell you," I tried lamely. "You would have said I was crazy."

Suddenly she got up and ran to me, put her arms around me, and held on tight, sobbing again. I pulled her gently into me and started crying, too. Finally she was all cried out, although I wasn't, and let go, stepping back and grabbing a tissue, wiping her eyes and blowing her nose. "You—you weren't originally that Indian girl, were you?" She said more than asked it.

I shook my head. "No. But I'd accepted having to live my life in that body," I imagined, trying to get hold of myself. "I'm sorry, Dory. I had no idea they were still around. Damn! It was all going to work out, too!"

She tried a wan smile. "Who were you—originally? I think I have the right to know that."

"You have the right to know anything," I told her sincerely. "I was Victor Leigh Gonser, Ph.D., Associate Professor of Political Science at Johns Hopkins University."

I saw Parch chuckle at that last. Dory gasped slightly. "You—were a *man?*"

I nodded. "More or less. A bald and ugly little nebbish, really." This started her laughing hysterically, and we let it run its course.

Finally she calmed down and managed, "I don't believe this. It can't be real." She turned back to me. "I used one of your books—last semester." She sat back down on the bed, still shaking her head. Finally she turned to Parch. "What happens—now? To us, I mean?"

Parch shrugged. "Not my department. I have to get our live friend and his two dead companions out of here, of course. That's pretty tricky because we're in Canadian waters, but we'll manage. You have the run of the ship—enjoy. But don't get off at Prince Rupert. In a couple of hours I'll have my instructions." He softened a bit, realizing how harsh he was sounding. "Look, it'll be all right. We won't abandon you or lock you away or anything. It's just that—well, there are things I can't discuss right now until I get word from my own people. As soon as I know, I'll tell you—O.K.?"

Dory frowned. "I'm not sure I like being the property of the U.S. government," she said with a trace of annoyance. "I'm not even a citizen."

"Right now you are both non-persons," he pointed out. "You, Ms. Tomlinson, can hardly go home and pick up where you left off. You're a thirteen-year-old Indian. And you, Gonser—what'll you do? You can *be* her, body or not, but you can't just go off and be somebody else, either, because the person you appear to be legally exists. Please—just trust me for a few hours. I'm not the enemy."

I looked at Dory and she at me and we gave almost simultaneous sighs and shrugs. Parch was right—we were stuck, at least temporarily.

"All right—we'll play it your way for now," Dory said. "I assume, though, that your government is now picking up the tab?"

He grinned. "Expense account. You're welcome to these two cabins, of course, and if you need any money just ask one of the boys."

There was a knock at the door. He opened it, said a few words, then turned back to us. "We're coming in to Prince Rupert," he told us. "I'm going to be busy for a while. Stay here or walk around all you want. We'll talk when I'm through." And, with that, he was gone. For the first time since the switch we were alone.

Dory got off the bed and stood facing me. She turned up her nose a little and looked around. "Everything's so much higher all of a sudden."

I nodded. "I know what you mean. Oh, hell, Dory, I feel so guilty about all this. I've mucked up your life like they mucked up mine."

She smiled up at me. "Look, that's going to get us nowhere. We're stuck and that's that. I thought about it just now in the way Parch said—it's a war. That old woman was going to shoot you, maybe both of us. In a way we were lucky, I guess. Maybe one day they can put things back again—at least for me. Until then let's accept the fact that we're innocent victims and go on from there." She paused a moment, looking at me with a somewhat critical eye. "In the meantime, maybe I can make a real woman out of you."

I laughed in spite of myself. "What on earth do you mean?"

"The way you're standing. The way you walk. I put a lot of work into building that body and I'm going to see that it's taken care of and treated right while I'm not in it. In the meantime, let's go get something to eat."

I just stared at her, open-mouthed. She was some kind of woman, I decided anew. I envied her confidence and resilience. She opened the door and saw the guard standing there. "Hey! We're going to eat," she told him. "Parch said to tap you for the money."

The man stared a little, a bit put off by this tiny girl giving him orders, but he took out his wallet and gave her a bill. She looked at it, then said, "Uh uh. More. None of that cafeteria crap. We're going to the main dining room."

We talked mostly about inconsequential things through the meal, a very good one in the big, fancy dining room with the very artsy glass seal sculpture in the middle. I was impressed by the quality of the food, compared to the cafeteria, and the fact that prices were actually lower. I was also interested in the fact that I was hungrier than I'd been in some time and ate far more than I had as the little girl. Dory showed that the birdlike appetite I'd experienced was all that that body required.

She was fascinated with the things I had been—the differences in color perception, all the senses, really. As for me, I found Dory's eyes a bit closer to my original ones in color perception—we both had blue eyes, not brown—but I found she was slightly nearsighted, and my sense of smell was a degree different from either my former male self or the Indian girl's. The world was a subtly different place depending on the body you wore, that was for sure.

Dory was making a try on some chocolate ice cream—for some reason, whether weight or complexion or something else, she hadn't had any for a very long time—and I was lingering over a coffee that no longer tasted foul and bitter when Parch joined us. We were already out of Prince Rupert and still headed south. The ship had to get in and out fast, it seemed, because Prince Rupert's single ferry dock was needed for the CN overnighter to Vancouver Island. We sat on the dining room side facing the dock, and had noticed a couple of ambulances pull up and some stretchers being wheeled off, and knew that Parch had done his job efficiently.

He nodded and sat down with us, looking far more relaxed. I took a moment to study his face and decided that there was something very slightly wrong about it, although I couldn't put my finger on it.

"I radioed my field office in Seattle," he began, ordering just coffee. "The IMC wants you, it seems, as I figured. There are very few survivors and we'd like to examine and interrogate you as to the—ah—experience."

"IMC?" I prompted.

He nodded. "You'll find out. We have a pretty big operation going, you must realize. We've been at this over six years and it's not an easy job."

"Six years," Dory put in. "That's a long time to hide something like this."

Parch chuckled. "You have a childish faith in democratic institutions."

"I'll concede that," I agreed, "but it still seems hard to conceal. There's the press, political leaks, you name it."

"I'd have expected more cynicism from a political scientist," the government agent laughed. "Yes, you're right—covering up is a lot of the work. But, you see, this is one area where everybody in the know is in agreement. If this came out, and was believed, the panic and paranoia would be beyond belief. Be frank—knowing what you know, could you *ever* trust a crowd of strangers again? When your best friend might not be? See what I mean? It can give you nightmares—and on a national, even global scale. . . . Well, you see how it is."

"You're pretty free talking about it in a public dining room in normal tones," Dory pointed out.

He shrugged. "Who would believe it in this context? Right now the ship's abuzz with the three kidnappers federal agents nabbed and that's excitement enough for them."

"But who—or what—are they?" I asked him. "And what's their game? They seem awfully lame to be such a huge menace, what with little old ladies and .38s."

"They're a bundle of contradictions, all right," Parch agreed. "And there's no easy answer to any of the questions. We've captured a very few, mostly by sheer luck, over the years, and while they haven't been very helpful we know that one group calls itself the Urulu. We don't know where they're from or what they're like naturally, but they definitely aren't from anyplace any of us have ever visited."

"One group?" I put in, getting a sinking feeling.

He nodded. "There's more than one, that's for sure, and they don't like each other much. Or so the Urulu maintain, but who knows what we can trust? We can knock 'em out, but they don't respond to much of anything in the way of truth serums or any other stock information techniques. Their story is that they're the good guys and they're here to root out the bad guys. You will understand why we take this with a grain of salt."

We both nodded and Dory articulated the thought. "The good guys indiscriminately kill us and pull guns on us. All things considered, how bad can the bad guys be?"

"That's about it," Parch agreed. "And, of course, we have nothing but their word that there's another group. We've certainly not seen any. Either they're more efficient than the Urulu or, more likely, they're part of a convenient cover story and don't really exist."

There seemed little to add to that, so I changed the subject. "You're not an American," I noted. "Not originally."

"Not native born, no," he replied. "Originally I was from Belfast. When I was a wee lad the IRA blew up my parents for the crime of being Presbyterian and leading a peace march. To save me from the orphanage some relatives in Philadelphia offered to take me in and I finished growing up there. But—enough of me. My sort of job may seem very glamorous and dangerous, but it's rather boring, really. A year of plodding routine for one brief moment of action."

"What of us, then?" Dory asked. "I mean—after this exam. What kind of lives can we expect from now on?"

He sighed. "Look, I won't kid you. After the examination, though, which won't last all that long, you can remain and work with us on this problem or we'll set you up somewhere. New identities, complete bios and backgrounds. You can walk out and start new lives on your own that way, or keep within the security of IMC and find a place with us. The choice *will* be yours."

I considered what he said. My thoughts were emotional and confused, but I knew what my decision should be. I had fulfilled a fantasy of sorts, even though it wasn't quite the one I'd imagined. I was young, attractive, definitely the socially accepted type. I'd been oblivious to things when Dory was Dory, but I was already aware of being constantly eyed by men of all ages. I had a free, new start, and it had to be better than my miserable loneliness of so many years. Hell, I'd have been satisfied as the little Indian, really, as long as I didn't have to worry where I was sleeping. So what if I were female? Being male hadn't brought me much; this just *had* to be better. But there was one real hitch in this bright new future.

It was *Dory's* body I wore, and she definitely wanted it back—and I would have to give it back if it were possible. Hell, I was responsible for involving her in this. I couldn't just walk out now, particularly since Dory was such a fantastic person. I still loved her, perhaps more now than before, because of the respect she'd earned by her reaction to all this. The plain truth was that I was less in control of my destiny than I had ever been. The decisions were hers to make, not mine. I was an interloper, a usurper, however involuntary, and my life and future were in her hands.

"Actually," Parch went on, "I hope you'll join us. Both of you have very sharp, open minds that's rare in this day and time. We need people like you."

We spent the rest of the day just relaxing, doing very little and talking less. We were in a waiting phase, really, a holding pattern. Neither of us were yet really free.

We got Dory's things from the solarium and she went through them, taking what was worth saving. Parch had promised us some time in Seattle to shop for what we'd need, so it wasn't much. There were cosmetics, though, and I got something of a short course on their uses and application, and also some criticism on general mannerisms. "No, don't walk like that—more like *this*." Dory had begun her lessons in "making a woman" out of me and I was an eager student. No matter what, I expected to be one for the rest of my life.

A car met us at the dock after we got into Seattle and Parch took us to a a fancy downtown hotel and checked us in. He also gave us, to our surprise, a thousand dollars in blank travelers' checks.

"Go out on the town," he told us. "Buy yourselves new wardrobes, all the essentials."

Dory looked at him playfully. "Aren't you afraid we'll just up and leave?"

He didn't seem disturbed by the idea. "You could, of course. But that money wouldn't last long, and what would it get you? Just take care and be here in the morning—I'll have a wake-up call put in."

He left us then, but both of us knew that he would take no such chances. We might never see them, but we'd never be out of sight of one or more of his operatives.

Dory looked around the luxurious room. "Wow! They sure do it up right when it's the taxpayer's money." She jumped on one of the twin queen-sized beds and seemed almost lost in it. She bounced up and down a few times on it, looking and sounding exactly like a thirteen-year-old kid. She seemed to realize this, and rolled over on her stomach, propping her head on her hands and looking very, very cute.

"Look, if I gotta be thirteen again I may as well enjoy it," she said lightly. "There's some advantages to it. You can act like a kid with nobody looking twice because you *are* a kid."

I chuckled at this and sat down, signing the top line on the travelers' checks. There were a *lot* to sign, and Parch had told me to go ahead and sign them "Dorian Tomlinson," using Dory's driver's license as back-up. I felt a little odd about it, but it was the best way to handle it, I knew.

Finally I was finished, and turned to Dory, who was fooling with the television. "Enough of that," I told her. "Let's go spend this money."

She giggled, turned off the set, and bounded up, ready to go.

Dory was relatively easy to do, since a kid looks like a kid in practically everything that fits, and she opted for the continued informal look of jeans and T-shirts, buying several pairs in different colors, plus some sandals and tennis shoes. She also made one change in her looks, getting her hair cut to a shorter Indian-style with bangs. Having had to manage that ton of black hair I could hardly blame her, although if anything she looked more Indian than ever now.

She spent a lot of time on me, though. I'd never had to shop for women's clothing, let alone wear any, and bowed completely to her advice. It was clear that she still considered this body of mine her own, and she was redesigning it from an unusual vantage point.

By the time I was through I looked like a fashion model. Dorian was, as I'd mentioned, a beautiful woman, and Dory bought, fitted, and matched clothing, cosmetics (about which I had a lot to learn), and the like until I hardly recognized myself. Every time I looked at myself in the mirror it was like looking at somebody else, gorgeous, desirable, stunning. The figure in the glass was everything I'd ever dreamed about in a woman, not only my but many men's fantasy woman come to life. The only trouble was, it wasn't my fantasy I was seeing, it was *me*. *I* was the girl of my dreams, not her lover.

Years ago I'd discovered that people judged you by how you looked, dressed, acted, with no regard for the person inside, the important part of a human being. Women, even beautiful, desirable women, would find the inner me, would come to me with their problems and confidences, make friends with me. But they'd always go to bed with Handsome Harry down the hall, even though his insides were hollow. Everybody does it, even when they condemn it. The cover is everything— what's inside rarely matters at all, and never matters until later.

We wound up still with a couple hundred dollars, and blew that easily on some jewelry for me and a petite watch. Dory insisted on, and got, a Mickey Mouse electric.

We went back, got a meal, then watched a little TV and went to bed. After a short time, Dory said she felt a little lonely in that bed and asked to shift to mine. I agreed readily, and we talked for a little bit, hugged, kissed, and finally drifted off to sleep.

We were up before the wake-up call, and Dory picked

out my wardrobe. Now I looked at myself once again in a mirror and marvelled anew at what I was seeing. My blondish auburn hair had been restyled into a sexy set of curls and bangs, and small crystalline earrings set off my almost perfect Madonna-like face to which cosmetics had been expertly but discreetly applied, and Dory applied a little perfume in the right places.

The clothes were tight-fitting, a black satin pants-suit set off by a gold-colored belt with sunburst pattern, going into long leather boots.

"You're crazy, Dory," I told her. "You've made me into a hell of a sex symbol. I'll have to fight everybody off. Christ! I think I'm madly in love with myself. Is all this really necessary?"

"I told you I was going to make a real woman out of you, Vic Gonser," she responded somewhat playfully. "For as long as it takes you're going to be *me*, the me I never was but always wanted to be. You might as well learn to play the part. And, when I get it back, I'll know what I'm like and you'll know everything about being a woman."

I couldn't really find a response to that. She was obviously neurotic about me, although I couldn't blame her for being a bit odd after what she'd gone through—and what she'd lost, which was what I was seeing in the mirror. I kept wondering why *I* wasn't off myself—or, perhaps I was and just didn't know it. But, damn it, I *owed* her, and she was the boss. I wanted it that way. If she wanted me to be her surrogate self, living her life for her, then I'd do it.

I almost understood it.

Just joining Parch for breakfast gave me a real taste of what being this surrogate was like. Heads turned in my direction when I entered the coffee shop; men cast rather obvious covetous glances at me, women a different sort of look. People scrambled to open the glass doors to the restaurant for me despite the fact that I was not only capable of it myself but had to step carefully to keep from tripping over them, and waiters seemed to vie with one another to offer me a chair in their territory. I was the center of attention, no doubt about it. And, I found, I kind of liked it, too.

Everything I'd done in my whole life was an attempt to escape the psychological barriers to humanity that my sequestered youth had built up. I had never broken free on my own, not with my learning, my books, my position of respect. Suddenly it had been done to me, and for me, without me having to even lift a finger. It was, in a way, the confirmation of my whole dismal view of human behavior. Not one of those people scrambling for the door or chairs or eyeing me either lustfully or enviously knew who I was, what I did or didn't do for a living, whether I was rotten or nice, brutal or gentle, any of these things. It was irrelevant what I was; only what I looked like really counted.

Parch had been surprised and a little taken aback at my appearance. Still, he remained rock-solid, as distant as always, barriers up. I wondered about him—his strange background, his odd vocation, his outlandish moustache and manner of dress. Somewhere in that head was a very strange mind, I knew, and a tremendously private one hidden behind granite layers as mine had been. I couldn't help wondering if it was as fragile as mine, or, perhaps, hid something far darker. No matter what, all we could see of him was a carefully crafted and totally masked *persona*.

"Where to from here?" I asked him over eggs and coffee.

He put down his knife and took a long drink of brewed tea. "South, eventually to IMC, if only for your own protection. No telling if there might be more around, tracking us, trying to find out where their comrade has been taken. I can tell you no more now—you will be thoroughly briefed after you arrive and settle in."

"What's this IMC you keep mentioning?" Dory wanted to know.

Parch just smiled. "You'll find out soon enough." He glanced at his watch. "After ten. We'd best be going, I think. I'll ring for a car to pick us up and we'll be off."

This was quickly done, and a nondescript blue Ford soon pulled up and two serious-looking men got out and helped us load our new baggage and Parch's one small case into the car. Dory insisted on sitting up front and I found myself in the middle of the back seat sort of squashed between Parch and one of the security men. The stranger bothered me a bit, mostly because he kept making subtle moves directed at me. His arm somehow kept finding its way around me, and he seemed to press in on me a bit more than was necessary. I found it more than irritating but couldn't think of anything to do; Parch seemed oblivious and gazed idly out the window. I could only pretend I didn't notice, try to squirm out when possible, and make the best of it. Dory, I noticed, looked back at me from time to time, saw the problem, and seemed somewhat amused by it.

It wasn't a long ride. As we neared the Seattle-Tacoma Airport we turned off on a side road, then went up through the freight terminals and over to a small building that bore the insignia of an Air National Guard unit. I sighed in relief as we got out, then noticed Parch take out a small walkie-talkie and speak into it. He looked up, and we followed his gaze, seeing a small helicopter in that direction now turn and go swiftly away from us.

Parch turned back to us and put the walkie-talkie away. "No obvious tails," he told us with a little bit of disappointment in his tone. "I think we're safe."

We walked through the small building with all of us getting curious looks from the uniformed servicemen there and me getting some different kinds of looks, then quickly out onto the tarmac. Waiting for us was not the military plane I'd envisioned but a sleek Lear Jet.

The interior was wonderfully appointed; it looked like it had been decorated by Gucci for a millionaire. Parch told us it was a VIP plane used for ferrying congressmen, senators, Pentagon bigwigs and the like. It had a bar, music system, and wide and comfortable seats, which, fortunately, were individual and of the swivel-type, so I didn't have to put up with any amorous security men there.

Once airborne, Parch served some coffee and cookies and seemed to relax quite a bit. "No more problems for now," he almost sighed, and for the first time I got an idea of the tension he'd been under.

"All right, then—what is the IMC and where is it?" I wanted to know.

"Nevada," he responded unhesitatingly, telling me that we were heading now straight for the place. "It's near where they used to test atom bombs years ago. We still have what is referred to as a 'Nuclear Research Facility' there—that's IMC as it appears in the federal budget, Pentagon budget, official ledgers and such. Initial funding was a bloody bitch—we took a little from just about every DoD program—but, since then, our maintenance budget hasn't really been out of line with what we're supposed to be. That's one way we get away with it. Most senators and congressmen are simply too busy and too rushed to check out every single project, particularly established routine expenditures, and we can get pretty convincing should one ever decide to inspect the place."

"I still can't believe you can keep such a thing secret," I told him. "You said DoD—that's defense. *Somebody* has to know."

He chuckled. "You'll see that we can be most effective there. But, you see, it has to be that way. There's perhaps half a dozen senators and two dozen congressmen who can keep a secret. The rest would cause more stupid, ignorant panic than anything else. Our work depends on secrecy, not really from our own people although that is necessary, but from the aliens. We can, after all, be penetrated. We don't know who's who—let's face it. That's why it's essentially a sealed facility, like a good

top secret research project working on anything dangerous. Once in, you're in until we feel we can let you out."

I wasn't sure I liked the implications of that. I wondered just how free our choice was going to be, but I
said nothing.

"IMC," he continued, "stands for Identity Matrix Center. When we discovered that we had been penetrated,
invaded, whatever you like, by aliens who could body-
switch it was the logical choice. Heretofore body-
switching had been considered a total impossibility, a
fantasy thing and nothing more. The very concept was
unthinkable, for it meant that no one anywhere could be
trusted and literally nothing could be safe for long. We
were then forced, by a couple of blunders like the one
that left you alive, to confront the reality of the thing—
and there seemed only one logical response. In the forties this country decided upon an atom bomb, found the
money, got the best experts on atomic physics together
with as unlimited a budget as was possible, and told
them to design and build one. They did. In the sixties,
we decided to put a man on the moon and created
NASA. It was more public, of course, but the approach
was the same—get the money you need and the top
experts in the field together in the best research facilities you have and tell 'em to do it. They did and there's
American flags all over the moon now. The same approach was tried with the Alternate Energies Task Force,
although that's been underfunded. The same thing is
applied to IMC. Body-switching exists. It's possible. Therefore, we need a defense against it as priority number
one. A secondary priority is to learn how to do it ourselves if we can—for obvious reasons."

I nodded, only beginning to see the scope of this thing.
"And have you made any progress?"

He shrugged. "We know *what* happens when they do
it, but not *how* they can do it. I am living proof that
they have made a lot of progress—I was not *born* immune to the aliens. The trouble is that it still requires

enormous technological backup to do even that to one person. Mass protection is still practically impossible although theoretically we could do it. What we lack the most is concrete informatin on our enemy—how many they are, where they come from, just what they're doing here. Without those we're still somewhat defenseless, since we assume their technology to be far in advance of ours. Were we to just go to a big program, let the cat out of the bag as it were, they might well easily invent a counter and then we're worse off than we were. See what I mean?"

"You're military, then?"

He chuckled. "Oh, no. Most of the boys you've met are FBI, of course, and the Defense Intelligence Agency actually manages the security of IMC, but I'm the top watchdog. I'm the Chief Security Officer of the General Services Administration."

Chapter Five

Imc didn't look like much from the air—miles and miles of miles and miles, composed of yellow, red, and orange sand, mostly flat, with a few high sharp mountains far in the distance. We passed Yucca Flat, where long ago the first atomic weapons were tested—you could still see the ghostly remains of old mock villages and protective concrete bunkers as we circled for a landing.

Twenty or thirty miles from all this an airstrip loomed ahead on the barren desert. There was no question it was in use—a squadron of sleek fighter-bombers was berthed in two concrete parking areas and a couple of huge transports were parked near the tiny terminal, nearly dwarfing it. The base itself was small—a few dozen squads at best of what looked to be regulation Air Force barracks, all looking like long veterans of continuous occupation. All badly needed paint at the very least. I felt something of a let-down and said so.

"That's only the top of it," Parch laughed. "The main base is underground, going down more than half a mile. They built them deep for the atomic stuff, and we made it even deeper. Our computer banks alone run for miles under the desert, a couple thousand feet down and very isolated from any outside influences."

I frowned. "A computer that large? I thought that went out with the integrated circuit."

"Ordinarily that'd be true," he admitted, "but even when you consider that a hand-held computer with a phone plug can do almost anything, it's limited by the amount of information that can be stored in it. Consider the human brain, then, with every single thing in it reduced to computer bytes. That's what that computer—computers, really—down there is for. We need mechanical equivalents of human brains plus. There's never been a computer complex like IMC."

We rolled up to the little terminal building, almost under the wing of one of the giant transports. Again a car, this time from the government interagency motor pool, picked us up and drove us from the plane to one of the barrack-like buildings. Entering, we discovered it was a complex of small offices. Nasty-looking Air Force guards with menacing automatic rifles, checked us out and quizzed us every fifteen or twenty feet. I had the distinct feeling that, if Parch didn't give the correct response each time—and each was different—we would all have been shot down where we stood.

A huge and incongruous freight elevator was in the middle of the first floor, with two more Air Force guards on either side of the door. Again the routine, then both guards plugged in keys on opposite sides—too far, I noted, for any one person to do it—and turned together, opening the elevator door. We stepped aboard and the door rumbled closed once more. Parch then punched a numerical combination in the elevator wall, there was a click, and he extracted from a small compartment yet another key and placed it in a slot, turning it not like a key but more like a combination lock. I began to feel very, very trapped.

We descended, and, passing the next floor, then the

next, and still another, I knew we were sinking into the Nevada desert. Level five was ours, but I had the impression that the shaft continued on a lot further, and walked out into a long, lighted tiled corridor with an antiseptic smell. The ceiling was lit with indirect fluorescent lighting, and except for the lack of windows it looked like any modern office building. Uniformed Marine guards seemed to be everywhere.

Parch led us down a side corridor, then through a series of double doors. I saw that we were in some kind of dispensary, although that wasn't quite right.

Men and women in medical whites looked up at us and one woman walked over and had a conversation with Parch. Finally he came back to us.

"Processing first," he told us. "Just believe it's all necessary. It won't take long, anyway."

He waited while the efficient team photographed us, took our fingerprints, retinal patterns, EKG and EEG, blood sample—the whole thing. The end result was going over to a small window and receiving two small cards, one for each of us, that looked like credit cards. On the front was our photographs, fingerprints, and a lot of zebra-stripe coding, the back was entirely coated with a magnetic surface.

"Guard those cards," Parch told us. "To get into and out of your room, or anywhere here, you'll need them. They contain everything about you that we know now, all linked to a cross-checking computer. You'll need them even to eat. There's some paperwork to fill out, which I have here, but I'll take you to your quarters and get you settled in first. You can fill it out there and give it to me later."

We followed him down another corridor and the decor changed a bit. The floor was even carpeted and the doors were evenly spaced. "I feel like I'm in a motel," I noted.

"You are," he replied. "The IMC Hilton, we call it." He went up to a door about halfway down with the

number 574 on it. "No keys, though. Go ahead, Gonser—
try your card in the little slot there."

I hesitated, then put the little plastic card in the
small, narrow slit next to the door. The card went in
about halfway, then something seemed to grab it, pull it
all the way in, and there was a click. I didn't immediately try the door, expecting the card to come back.

Parch realized the problem. "Just go on in. It keeps
the card until you leave the room and close the door.
When the computer control senses the room's empty
it'll offer the card back to you in the slot. Take it and it
automatically locks. Neat, huh?"

I shrugged, turned the knob, and opened the door.

The quarters were quite nice, like a luxury hotel suite.
There was a single queen-sized bed, dresser with mirror,
nightstands, a table and couch, a couple of comfortable-
looking chairs, lots of lights and lots more closet space,
and, in the other room, a large bath with shower. The
main room even had a color TV and there were remote
controls for it and all lights beside the bed. Parch showed
us everything like an experienced bellman, even trying
the TV to make sure it worked.

In back of the parlor area was a small portabar which
was mildly stocked and a miniature refrigerator for ice,
also containing some fresh fruit, milk and juice, and the
like. A cabinet held glasses.

I was impressed. It was far more than I'd expected
from the U.S. government. Parch just shrugged it off.
"Look, we have some of the top brains in biophysics,
biochemistry, computer sciences, you name it—and, in
some cases, their families as well. We can hardly take
such people and lock them away in some fallen-down
barracks, can we? All your things have been brought
here and unpacked, by the way, along with a number of
extras in your size; lab whites, that sort of thing. You'll
notice the phone has no dial—it's not a line to the
outside. But there's a directory there, so you can call

anybody in IMC, even arrange wake-up calls. There's daily maid service and the bar and fridge are kept stocked. If you need more, or pharmacy items, anything like that, the numbers to call are there."

Dory looked around the room with a mild look of disapproval. "The bed's for both of us? Don't you have a king size?"

"This is Ms. Gonser's room, not yours. You have an almost identical one next door in 576."

"Why can't we stay together?" we both asked, almost together.

"Rules," Parch told us. "Get used to them—there are a lot of them, I'm afraid." He hesitated a moment, looking a little apologetic. "Look, you'll be next door and can visit all you want. The only thing is, well, you're still on probation, so to speak. Please go along with us for now and trust me that there are good reasons born of past experiences behind those rules. O.K.?"

There seemed little choice but to accept it—for now.

"Come, Ms. Tomlinson, I'll show you your room," he said, turning to Dory. "And I'll leave the papers here. Take a little time, stretch out, relax, fill the things out, and after I check in and tend to my own business we'll get together again. Take advantage of this time—you're going to be very busy soon."

They went out and the door closed behind them. I went over to it and saw that there was one difference between it and a motel that made me vaguely uncomfortable—no inside lock. I finally just sighed, turned, and went over to the bed. Hell, if you can't trust a setup as guarded as this a puny little lock wasn't going to help, I told myself.

Finally I explored the room. In addition to the other features I found a clock, a radio, some recent magazines, and the day's Las Vegas newspaper.

I checked the clothes, all neatly unpacked and put where they should be. I got undressed, then stood there, looking at my nude body in the dresser mirror.

Damn it all, I told myself, I still turn myself on.

Suddenly, on impulse, I got up, lugged one of the chairs over to the door and propped it against the knob. It made me feel better, even if it made no sense. I wanted no sudden surprises, and the guards in the local area I'd seen were all male.

I took a brief shower, which felt good, then just plopped on the bed, looking at that supine reflection in the mirror.

It was no good, I thought moodily. I've joined the human race, all right, but I've joined the wrong half. Oh, it might be fun to act like a woman—all the way, with my choice of men, just to see what it was like, but, somehow, I didn't think so. It wasn't my body—it was *hers*.

As much as I enjoyed the attention now being paid to me, the courtesies, the fact that I was the automatic center of attention, the ogled rather than the withdrawn and hopeless ogler, I couldn't pretend that my inner self had really changed. Mentally, I was still male. All those handsome young men I'd met that morning hadn't done anything for or to me. I still looked sideways at some of the cute and attractive women we'd passed in Seattle, and the only time I'd felt any sort of sexual stirring was in the women's room of the coffee shop back at the hotel. I still was attracted to women. I would rather be in bed *with* this reflection than *be* this reflection.

I reached over and flipped on the TV. It was the news, something I usually immersed myself in. The usual was going on. Two dead in hotel fire ... Secretary of State hopes for new arms treaty with the Russians.... President of the Central African Republic shot in coup attempt.... And so it went. Somehow, it just didn't seem important anymore.

I flipped off the TV and lay back face up on the bed, closing my eyes for a moment. What the hell kind of future did I have? I was a gorgeous sex symbol who was the opposite of what I appeared to be. In a sense, nothing had really changed. I was still the alien, the outsider, the non-participator in society because my inner and outer selves were so damnably different.

Idly, I became aware that parts of my body were reacting to my inner thoughts, a pleasurable tension building, and I was only half aware that my hands were touching, stroking those parts. My nipples felt like tiny, miniature erections, and responded to rubbing with a tremendous feeling of eroticism. I kept rubbing one, almost unable to stop, and reached down between my legs, doing to myself what I *wanted* to do to myself. I could imagine me—the old me—here, in bed, next to this beautiful sex goddess, doing this to bring her to a fever pitch, then penetrating, thrusting. . . . I grew tremendously wet, my finger feeling so good, my thumb massaging the clitoris, until, finally, I experienced an orgasmic explosion that shook my entire body. It felt so good I kept at it, accomplishing it several more times. It felt *so* good and I think I just about screamed with ecstasy at the repeated orgasms. Finally I stopped, a sudden fear that my outcry had been overheard bringing me down a bit, and I just went limp, breathing hard on the bed, savoring the afterglow. Male and female orgasms were certainly related experiences, but very different in the way the sexual sensation was transmitted. It was a wonderful feeling, but it did little to snap my depression.

For it was still me inside this sensuous body, me, Victor Gonser, male, all by myself, alone in the quiet of the room.

After a while I managed to get up and went over to the desk to look at the forms to be filled out. There were a *lot* of them, and they were very detailed about my past life, work, interests. I filled them out almost haphazardly, not really caring very much.

The phone rang and I picked it up. It was Parch, asking me to come down to his office. "The guard will show you the way," he told me. "We'll have a light dinner, then I want to go and wake up our prisoner."

"He's *here?*"

"Oh, yes—and still sleeping like a baby. We've prepared a special room for him and it's about time we tried to find out what we can."

"Is Dory coming?"

"No, just me and you, then a couple of specialists. Don't worry—she's fine. You can visit her later on tonight if you like."

I hung up, got up, and looked through the clothing. I had never appreciated before how much trouble women go through to look the way they do. It all felt funny, cumbersome, and slightly uncomfortable. The bra was the most uncomfortable of the lot, but with my ample chest I thought I needed it.

I went through the clothing Dory had bought for me and cursed her for it. All the stuff was clingy and sexy and that was not what I wanted, definitely. I looked over at the added stuff and decided on it for the moment, choosing a pair of white pants, a plain white T-shirt, and sandals. It looked just as sexy as all the elaborate stuff, but, what the hell, it was comfortable and practical. With my shape I hardly needed a belt, didn't see one that worked, and decided against one. Finally I brushed my hair, which I hadn't washed, nodded to myself in the mirror, then walked over and pulled the chair from the door. I opened it and spotted the Marine guard at the end of the corridor. I stepped out, letting the door shut behind me. There was a click and a whirring sound and my card reappeared in the little slot. I'd almost forgotten it, but I removed it now and stuck it in my hip pocket.

The guard gave me the kind of look that betrayed every thought in his licentious mind, but he was *very* disciplined and directed me down the corridor to another, small elevator. The guard on that one had been expecting me and inserted and turned his single key. I stepped in, was told to punch the next level up—four— and the door closed. It was more like a normal elevator than the other, but, I noted, the buttons went only from levels three to sixteen. No way out on this one.

I punched four, noted the implications of level sixteen, and was quickly taken up. The guard on four directed me to Parch's office, which proved to be a large affair, with two secretaries in the outer office, teletypewriters chattering away, computer terminals like mad, and lots of different colored telephones. It looked more like the city desk on a newspaper than the office of a man like Harry Parch.

He was carefully putting his costume back on as I entered. I noticed more comfortable military khakis draped over a chair, and a makeup and dressing table resembling an actor's off to one side.

When he turned around he was the Parch we'd seen from the start—but now knew. I wouldn't recognize the real Parch from Adam in any group of men. No wonder I hadn't seen him on the ferry earlier than that showdown day—he probably was all over the place, but as someone entirely different. The blue eyes were special contact lenses; I saw a pair of glasses on the table. The moustache was one of several different types he kept in a small case, and there were more wigs and a wardrobe of differently styled clothing in a rear closet.

Everything, I realized, about Harry Parch was phoney.

He brightened and smiled. "Well! You certainly have adjusted well. Most folks in your—er—situation go a bit off the deep end, you know. Some worse than others."

I nodded. "I think Dory's a bit off. Nothing serious—but she's not quite herself, I'd say."

He shrugged. "Could be worse. We have an entire psychiatric unit here just to treat problems like that. They're good, but nobody can work miracles. I suspect we'll let them take a good long look at your friend when you take the routine tests tomorrow. Maybe they can help her adjust. She's going to be no good to anyone, even herself, unless she does."

It was clear as we walked down the hall who was the

boss here. Sentries snapped to when he approached, nobody once questioned him about anything at all, and he walked to a small executive dining room like he owned the place. In a sense, he did. The dining room with its own chef and fancy meals, was obviously for the select few at the top.

"Why the costume?" I couldn't help asking him as the salad came.

He smiled softly. "Symbols are important to anyone. I head the people who track the dybbuks down, and I'm immune to their biggest trick. I'm not Superman, though—a bullet does the same thing to me that it does to you. They both hate and fear me—and so I let them hate and fear *this*. It affords a physical magnet for them that also serves as a terror symbol—the man with the stake out after the vampire, so to speak. And it protects me as well, of course. If they knew my real identity and appearance I could never venture anywhere without an armed guard."

"The accent—is that phoney, too?"

"Oh, my, yes, ducks!" he came back in thick Cockney. "Any bluddy toime y'want, luv." He chuckled, then switched to Brooklynese. "Dem bums ain't gonna know wud I'm like." He switched back to the familiar soft Irish he normally used. "You see? I've studied accents for years. Makeup, too. In my younger days I was going to be a great actor. Maybe I am. I like to think so."

"That Belfast story—it was a phoney, then?"

He thought for a moment, and I wondered if he were deciding whether to elaborate a lie, invent another, or tell me the truth. Would I ever know? This strange man exuded something vaguely sinister, something I couldn't really pin down intellectually but felt, deep down. Perhaps it was his total lack of anything real—or was that cold and analytical tone the real man coming out? In his own way, Harry Parch was as chameleon-like as the alien dybbuks he chased.

"Yes, I'm a naturalized citizen," he said hesitantly.

"The early part is genuine. I'll be quite frank, Ms. Gonser—that experience shaped my entire life. You have no idea what it's like to grow up with the army on every street corner, neighbor against neighbor depending on what church your folks went to, not knowing whether the next parked car contained a bomb or the next ordinary man or woman you passed wasn't going to turn and blow your kneecaps off." His tone grew very serious. "You have no idea what it is like to see your parents blown to bits before your twelve-year-old eyes."

There was nothing I could say to that, but I couldn't help thinking that he was either being honest or was one hell of an actor.

"Those early nerves—Belfast reflexes, I call 'em—stand me in good stead now. Coming down that trail up north, not knowing who was who . . . And I'm well-suited for this battle, I think. I *always* doubt strangers, but only a Belfast boy doubts his old friends."

I more or less believed him, but it didn't make me feel any better about him. I had the strong feeling that Harry Parch loved no one, trusted no one, lived in a violent world where all could be enemies. If his story were true he was undoubtedly so paranoid as to be in many ways insane; if it were not true, then he was even worse—a man who loved the game, to whom patriotism, ideology, and human beings were all just words to him, labels on chess pieces to be moved and sacrificed at will. I wondered which he was. A little of both, probably. Pragmatically, governments need people like Harry Parch, I reflected, but always as agents of someone else, never as the boss.

We continued talking as dessert came, but it was all small talk. That was all I was going to get from Harry Parch, on himself or on anything else. I was just another pawn to him in his grand game and I would get only what he decided I should get.

We left the dining room and he led me back to the elevator which we took three more levels down. The new area looked like a clinic—which, in a sense, it was. Three people met us—two women and a man—all dressed in sharp medical whites. He talked with them for a minute, then introduced me to them, and finally said, "Well, I have to go in there with him. I'm supposedly immune but you never know—so what about a password?"

I thought a minute. "How about—Machiavelli?"

He laughed sharply, although I could see he was somewhat nervous. "Machiavelli it is, then. You all hear that?" The others nodded and I was a little surprised to see that it was the two women who drew nasty-looking pistols from their pockets. One I recognized as a vet's dart pistol, the kind used for putting zoo animals to sleep, but the other was a vicious-looking magnum.

We walked down another corridor and entered what looked like a recording studio. No, I thought again, maybe like the place where police hold line-ups of suspects for witnesses. There were several comfortable seats in front of a thick pane of safety glass, with microphones in front of each chair. The two women took positions on either side of me, putting their weapons in swivel vises, then opening small doors in the glass window through which the pistols could protrude. I saw that there was a wire mesh on the other side of those tiny openings, preventing anyone from touching the weapons. For a moment I was uneasy about this, since I wondered if these aliens might not be some sophisticated collection of microbes, an alien symbiote or parasite—but I quickly dismissed the idea. Not only would they have known that, at least, by now but the odds of any alien organism being able to affect humans was slight to none.

Behind the glass lay the man, on a hospital bed, a bottle of some clear fluid hanging on the side, dripping a little bit of itself into the unconscious figure through a small needle inserted in a vein in his wrist. The body was strapped securely to the table.

Parch and the male technician in white slid a number of bolts and locks from the door to one side of the glass—I could hear each lock give—and Parch stepped inside. The door closed behind him and I could hear every lock going back into place. Only when that was done did the inner door open electrically, allowing Parch to step into the chamber.

"Now, everyone, I'm going to slowly bring him around," Parch's voice came from the speakers, sounding oddly distant. "I'm simply going to prompt him with some elementary stuff, perhaps sprinkled with some little white lies, so we can get the measure of him a little better." He took a deep breath. "Let's do it."

I had to admire Parch's coolness, even though he was clearly a little nervous. Carefully he removed the needle from the dybbuk's wrist and hung it to one side, then quickly left. I noticed that the medical technician who remained outside gazed anxiously at an electronic console. Obviously the alien's body was monitored—and perhaps Parch as well.

"Now, no shooting unless my life is in danger," Parch ordered, and I realized that it was his fellow humans, not aliens, that worried him. "Also, please no one say anything until and unless I ask you to. He can not see you; the glass is one-way."

We sat there, waiting expectantly, intently watching the figure on the hospital bed. It took about five tense minutes before the man seemed to stir, groan, then, finally, groggily open his eyes.

Abruptly, his eyes focused, found Parch, and widened in what I could only think was fear. He struggled to get out of his bonds but got nowhere.

"You'll not break those shackles very easily," Parch warned him. "You should have chosen a weightlifter or someone else more muscular. However, that still would do you little good. You're covered by both a sleep gun and a magnum, and both would be used as unhesitatingly on me or on you."

The man—a rather good-looking man of thirty or so, with sandy hair and a ruddy, outdoorsy complexion—looked around the chamber and stopped struggling. "Where am I?" he asked in clear and accentless American English.

"You're at IMC, and at IMC you'll stay," Parch told him. "It's where your folks have been trying to get to all this time anyway. Well, you made it. Now, let's be civil about this—introductions?" He looked around with annoyance. "I should remember to bring a chair in here." He sighed. "Well, I'm Harry Parch, Security Officer for IMC—but I expect you know that."

The man just stared at him.

"What do we call you?" Parch asked, shuffling a bit from foot to foot.

"My name would mean nothing to you—literally," the man on the table responded. "For general purposes, I use the name Dan Pauley."

I started slightly. So this was Dan, the leader on the trail.

Parch nodded to him. "All right, then, Mr. Dan Pauley it is. You know, this is the first time I've ever had the chance to talk civilly to one of your kind. This *is* quite an occasion. Sorry I forgot the champagne."

"You've killed a lot of us, though," Pauley almost spat.

Parch assumed a mock-hurt look. "Oh, come now! *I'm* not the one who picks innocent people and shoots air bubbles into their veins after stealing the bodies they were born in."

"I never liked the killing," Pauley responded in a sincere tone. "At first, I admit, none of us gave it a second thought—to them you seemed barely higher than the apes, if you'll pardon the expression. But I've lived here a long time, got to know this place, and it became more and more unpleasant. We simply had no choice if we were to stay undetected."

"Oh, my! Pardon me!" Parch responded, his tone if

anything more cynical than before. "Isn't it fortunate that the first of you that we capture in one piece is a moralist, an idealist, and even has a guilty conscience! My, my!" His tone suddenly changed to chilling hatred. "And I'm so glad that all your murders were necessary! How much comfort that is to your victims, their spouses, children, friends. How *very* comforting."

Pauley sighed. "All right, all right. But don't make such a moral crusade out of it yourself. The human race hasn't been very kind to any of its own who happened to be in the way if they were more primitive than the civilization moving in on them. To a race that practices genocide on parts of itself that differ only in color, or religion, or some other trivial thing I think we're pretty civilized about it. We killed only when necessary, and we killed only to safeguard our own mission."

Parch had started pacing a bit, but suddenly he stopped, turned, and looked directly at the man strapped on the table. "Ah, the mission. If the killing and body-stealing is an abhorrent necessity, then you must have quite a good reason for doing so, at least in your own mind. What? Anthropology? Conquest? What?"

The man thought for a while, obviously wrestling with his inner self. If he told too much he'd betray his people to his worst enemy. If he told nothing he would be unable to escape the moral corner into which he'd painted himself. I felt a little sorry for him. He couldn't know that he was not the first Harry Parch had caught nor, I suspected would he.

"Look," he said at last, "my people—we call ourselves Urulu, which just means people, really—are in trouble. In many ways we're quite different from you, maybe more so than you can imagine, but in some ways we're the same. We evolved on a life-sustaining world, became dominant, and built a civilization. Finally, we reached the stars, as you may someday do, and began looking for other civilizations. We found a lot, but none capable of interstellar flight, and things went along pretty well for a while. Like most expanding cultures, we stole from the civilizations we discovered, but not anything you might guess. We stole ideas—art, new ways of looking at things, scientific breakthroughs in areas we never considered, things like that. They're the true treasures of a civilization, and we could steal them to our profit without injuring any other cultures. They never really guessed we were there."

"Like Earth."

"Well, not really. Frankly, Earth is just a bit too primitive and too alien to have much to offer us. But, finally, we bumped into another civilization, a far different one, also spreading out to the stars. We frankly don't know much about them, although they're technologically our equals. In many ways they seemed like us, even to the body-switching capabilities, but when they'd reached our level they had made different choices about how to use their powers. They weren't a civilization you could even talk to, identify with, or really understand. They were—well, missionaries, I guess, interested only in converts. When we met they tried it on us, we resisted, and war resulted. A gigantic war, really, on a no-win scale. They won't surrender—they *can't* surrender, it wouldn't be something they'd comprehend—but we're so strong militarily that they can't win, either. This state of perpetual stalemate has existed now for thousands of years. And we can't win, either—they're too many and we too few."

Parch's expression was both grim and thoughtful and I saw him nod once or twice to himself. I had the feeling that Pauley was confirming what Parch had been told by others, and I thought I could see how his mind was going. Either the Urulu had one hell of a convincing and consistent cover story or they were telling the truth— and they seemed too egocentric to bother concocting anything this elaborate. It would be hard for them to imagine being caught like this. And if this war were true—where was the other side?

"How does all this involve the Earth?" Parch wanted to know. "Are we now the front? Or might we be?"

"I—I really don't know. There's no front in the normal sense. We have a military stalemate, remember—and destroying a planet doesn't get you anything but one more dead planet. The war now is a battle for the minds, the souls, if you will, of various planets. There's some evidence that they are active on Earth, but it wouldn't be a high priority item for them. You're very rare in the galaxy, you know. Most—maybe 95 percent—aren't like you at all. Most races couldn't exist here in their natural forms, we included. But there are enough planets with what you might call humanoid life to make it worth their while—and ours. We have few allies, and those we have are much closer to our form of life than yours, and we occasionally need, well, warm bodies to work those planets.You're out here on a spiral arm, pretty far away from the action, but you're the closest, most convenient source of warm-blooded mammalian oxygen-breathers we have."

I was appalled, and even Parch looked disturbed, at all this.

"We're your spare parts depot, then, for humanoid worlds," Parch said more than asked.

Pauley nodded slowly, a sheepish look on his face. "Look, this world's massively overpopulated anyway, and I think you'd admit that most of those people are vegetative—subsistence farmers, primitives of all kinds. They die young, of curable diseases and terrible customs, sometimes of starvation, and it makes absolutely no difference whatsoever to your race, your history, if such people live or die. We try to concentrate on people like that—we really do. Most of the bodies we take are from people who matter not a bit to Earth but they matter a great deal to us. In a sense, we give them purpose."

"At the cost of their lives," Parch responded darkly.

"This is a war! You'd react the same way and do the same things if you were in our shoes! You *know* it!"

Parch didn't reply to that because he knew as well as I did that the whole of human history supported the alien's point of view. We really weren't that different after all.

"So those people on the trail and in Skagway and on that ship—they were all expendable?"

Pauley sighed. "Look, I was a—station chief, I guess you'd call it. I've been here a very long time, and I was due to go home as soon as I could break in my relief. That's who I picked up in Alaska—but something went wrong. You know more about that than I do. We got chased halfway across Alaska and the Yukon by you, no matter what tricks we tried. I wish I knew how you did it, I really do. All those we left—well, it was them or us. You'll understand that a body-switching race doesn't face death easily because there's a good chance it won't happen."

Parch nodded at that, and I considered it. A race of body switchers *would* be potentially immortal, subject only to accidents and acts of violence. Particularly a spacefaring race with access to all the bodies of many worlds. It was a staggering concept.

"Now what happens?" Pauley asked. "You can kill me, of course—and I admit the thought terrifies me. But I'm a soldier and a volunteer—I'll die if I have to. You can keep me prisoner, but that won't gain you much, either. I don't mind telling you the general things but there's much, the important parts, no amount of coercion can get from me. You can try torture, but I can shut down the pain centers—I have far more control over this body than you have of yours. You can't use drugs—although I'm sure you'll try. All you'll get is a Urulu mind and unless you know Urulu, a language with few common references to yours, it'll get you nothing but a lot of bad sounds."

"Or I could let you go," Parch said softly.

To my surprise that caused the alien to laugh. "Come

on, Parch! You and I both know I couldn't do anything now if I wanted to. You have me in your sights. You have some way of tracking me—how I can't imagine. I'm not about to betray my people."

"We have your matrix, you know," Parch said in that same soft tone.

The man stiffened. "My ma—" He seemed to collapse, to deflate as if a balloon newly pricked by a needle. "So you've come that far," he managed weakly.

"You started it, you know," the IMC agent pointed out. I wished I knew what they were talking about.

Pauley seemed to regain a little of his composure. "I suppose we did, although it's hard to believe you're advanced enough to manage it. I wish my people knew. It might change everything. Make us allies instead of adversaries." He hesitated a moment, thinking. "Maybe that's what *they* are doing here. We thought it was just to try and cut off our body bank, but if *they* even guessed ..." Again a pause, then, "You may be in far more danger than you realize."

"If they know—and we have only your word that they even exist—we're already doomed," Parch noted. "I rather suspect they do not know, Mr. Pauley, if you didn't."

"Which brings us back to question one," the Urulu said. "What do we do for now?"

"Well, I can't trust you, of course, for I have only your word on these matters, and you can't trust me, since you can hardly place your faith in my hands childishly. What I think we shall do for the moment is leave things as they are while we get to know each other better. For now, I'm going to release you from this bed, and we have rigged up a small apartment in back, through that door there. It is, of course, totally bugged and monitored and is not the world's most comfortable accommodations, but it should do. Food will be passed in to you. Automatic and human-controlled weapons will be trained upon you at all times, of course, so please keep that in mind. Just consider yourself, well, a prisoner of war."

The man nodded. "I understand." Parch undid the straps holding the alien down and Pauley got up unsteadily, rubbing the places where the tight restraints had cut into him. Finally he got unsteadily to his feet and went over to Parch. "Truce?" he asked, and put out his hand.

We all tensed, knowing what Pauley was trying to pull. Parch did not hesitate, taking Pauley's hand and shaking it vigorously, a wide smile on his face.

"Now that we have that established, yes, a truce," Parch told him.

Pauley looked more than a little astonished and somewhat worried. "The only people I ever knew that were immune are other Urulu, who can consent or not, and our enemy," he said suspiciously. "Which are you, Parch?"

For the first time I understood just why Harry Parch was such a terror figure to them. They knew all their own people on our little world, so Parch, who had the power to block a switch, had to be their enemy in human guise. It seemed to me that Parch, too, must have thought of that, perhaps long ago. For a second I wondered if it might not just be true, but I quickly dismissed the idea. That way lay madness, and you could be paranoid enough just knowing what I knew.

"I'm no alien," Parch assured him. "I was born in this body on this planet, I promise you. I am—a prototype, you might say. A few of us have been rendered immune to you, although at great cost."

Pauley just stared at him and I did likewise. "Cost?" The alien repeated.

He nodded. "I am totally immune. I am myself—forever. Forever, Pauley. You yourself mentioned the promise of immortality from the process. You can see, then, why so few working on this project have been willing to take the cure."

Pauley's mouth dropped slightly, and, for the first time, I understood IMC's problem, why the defense wasn't "perfected" as Parch had said. If we really *could* learn how to switch bodies then immortality, at least for some, would be attainable. Attainable, yes, like the Urulu— but not for Parch. Never for Harry Parch . . .

"I must leave you now," the agent told the alien. "However, I'm assigning someone directly to you, to talk to you, discuss ways out of this mess, give us some common ground. I think you two will get along famously—considering you are responsible for her being in the body she's in. Your partner, anyway. Does the prospect interest you, Ms. Gonser?"

I almost jumped at the sound of my name. Finally I leaned over and keyed the microphone. "There's nothing I'd like better," I told them both.

Chapter Six

I was escorted by Marine guard back to my room, and I decided to drop in on Dory and fill her in. I went to her door and knocked, finally hearing a muffled question. I called out who I was and heard the sound of something being pulled back from the door. The motion made me chuckle a bit, and feel a little better, too. I wasn't alone in my privacy demands, it seemed.

Finally the door opened a crack and Dory said, "Come on in. I'm not really fit for those gorillas at either ends of the hall."

I pushed the door open and walked through, shutting it behind me. She was nude and had a towel wrapped around her hair. The TV was on, and I saw a mirror, scissors, and make-up kit on the bed.

It was already getting hard to remember myself in that slight, dark body, and I reflected how odd it was that I'd adjusted so easily to all this. Humans were adaptable animals, all right.

She was extremely thin and quite cute in an exotic sort of way. Although not quite there as yet, you could tell she was going to be an attractive, if small, young woman.

"What've you been doing?" I asked her.

She went over and snapped off the television. "Sitting around, mostly. Watching TV. They got a couple of movie channels here I never saw before—one's all porn. Interesting. I been sitting here doing my hair and taking notes for when I can use it properly."

I smiled and took a seat on the couch. "Did you get anything to eat?"

"Oh, yeah, hours ago. One of the Marines came by and we went up to the dining hall. The food's not bad, although I have a thing against cafeterias. They got some setup here, though. Bar with dance floor, movie theater with first-run stuff, game rooms—you name it. Like a luxury hotel. Swimming pool, jaccuzi, saunas, you name it. Even tennis courts. They live pretty good here, I'd say."

"I'll have to see it," I told her, then proceeded to fill her in on my evening. She followed my story with rapt attention, occasionally breaking in with questions. When I was through she considered it all for a while.

"You know, you sound like you really *liked* that alien thing," she noted.

I shrugged. "I don't know what I think. I *can* say that I found him reasonable, at least. I don't like the idea of my planet being a body bank for some alien species, but I can understand his point of view without approving. I think, inside, we're more alike—his people and us—than either of our groups wants to admit."

"Or he just understands humans better than we understand his kind," she responded a bit cynically, then changed the subject. "Any idea what happens next to us?"

I shook my head. "Parch said we'd spend most of the day tomorrow taking a battery of tests."

"Tests?"

"Psychological tests, mostly, I think. They want to

find out if there's anything wrong with our minds after the switching, how we look at ourselves, the world, that kind of thing."

She nodded. "I guess I understand. The truth is, I've been looking a little at myself lately. I'm not really sure I know myself anymore, if I ever did. I mean, it's kind of funny, but the more I think about all this the less I *mind* it. Isn't that weird?"

I frowned. "I don't understand what you're saying, frankly."

"It's—well, it's hard to explain. I think maybe you'll find out for yourself. But, well, things weren't going right for me. I was pretty screwed up inside, and I didn't really know where I was going, only that I couldn't really go back to my old life, my old friends, be the kind of girl they wanted. It's—well, hard to explain. But life was getting to be such a pisser this wasn't so bad—once you get over the shock. For a day or two I really went off the deep end, particularly with my old self standing there in front of me. It's passed, though. I keep thinking that this was the best thing that could have happened to me—becoming somebody else, that is." She hesitated, realizing she wasn't getting through. I had the impression that there was more to this than she was telling me, some missing piece of the complex puzzle that was Dorian Tomlinson. For my part, I couldn't imagine a nineteen-year-old stunner of a woman with money, brains, and looks having any problems I could recognize as problems.

"What about you, Vicki? How are you holding up? I mean, you had a lot more of a change than *I* did. All I did was lose some height, about six years, and gain reddish-brown skin."

My own sense of loneliness and isolation, of being out of place, returned to me with a vengeance. The interlude with Parch and the alien had allowed me to temporarily push it to the back of my mind, but it never really left, and now here it was back full once again. In a way,

I thought, I was worse off than I was before, for the only way I got any release was by pretending I was doing it to somebody else. I felt a need, almost a hunger, to share this feeling with somebody and Dory was, now, closer to me than anyone else in the world. I began cautiously, but eventually it just poured out, my whole life story, my frustrations, the whole thing. "I feel as alien as that Urulu or whatever it is in that cage," I told her. "Just like I always have. God, Dory! I have such a need to *belong*, somewhere, just once."

She came over to me and kissed me softly on the forehead. "Poor Vicki," she sympathized, "you really have the worst of it, I think." She curled up into a cute little ball on the couch opposite me, looking at me thoughtfully.

"You know," she said, "it's really crazy. I never knew you as a man and I have a tough time thinking of you in those terms. You're *mannish*, yes, in your movements and gestures, but not *male*, if that makes any sense. Part of that's my own conditioning, I guess. I knew a lot of women who dreamed of being men, but you're the first man I know who admitted fantasizing being a woman. It's the old image thing, I guess. Women say they want men to be more emotional, tender, all that—but you got me to thinking that maybe that's all wrong. Maybe men *are* all those things women are, but it's all locked inside somehow. Maybe we contribute to it—I know many of my friends say they want a warm, tender man but they only go to bed with macho types."

I nodded. "That's my bitter experience. Men who really *are* what our liberated women say they want are often friends, confidants, of those women—but never sexual partners. That was my experience. I always wondered if the male stereotypes everybody decries—the macho types, that sort of thing—aren't reinforced by women's behavior towards them. A man with normal sexual drives who tries to be a warm, friendly human being to women only to see them march off with what they say they abhor might *become* more of that macho type himself. In the process he loses his humanity, and maybe his pride, which makes him inwardly bitter, but he does it because he's forced to. And then there were those like me who *couldn't* lower themselves that way, and so became the permanent outsiders. You have no idea the hurt it causes—and the cynicism it breeds against women in general, fair or not."

She considered that. "So you envied women. The pretty ones got all the attention, while the more open economy gave them all equal competition with men in the marketplace and other options. You know, I wonder if we haven't hit on one of the basics of human behavior. Still, you know, it's a man's world in most respects. Men still run the country, most of the businesses, make most of the decisions, make more money and seem generally freer to us women. Male culture dominates so much that the successful businesswomen really get there and stay there by imitating the men, being as aggressive, as macho, maybe, as they are."

"We begin as little babies, but there it departs. Everything in a boy's life is competition—winning. Sports. Fighting to establish pecking orders in gangs. Showing off. But, you see, the necessary basic training is there because men can't do anything else. Women now have the same career choices as men, but they can opt not to work, to have and raise babies, their choices clear early in life. Men have only that sense of purpose in the job. Even if they marry, the law gives the man the obligation to support the wife and kids, and in a divorce gives the kids almost invariably to the mother while making Dad pay for it, even if Mom's a cultist murderer with a fifty-thousand-dollar-a-year job while Dad's a kind, devoted, loving ten-thousand-dollar-a-year janitor. He has no rights, only responsibilities, and no real options. No wonder men die so much earlier than women."

"It's no picnic as a woman, either," Dory responded. "We get the dolls, the toy stoves, the frilly little dresses.

We rarely get the attention our brothers do, the preparation for something big. Then along comes puberty and you get periods that make you feel yucky, and suddenly you can't go to the store alone. If your parents aren't scared for you then you soon get scared yourself. Rape becomes a threat you live with. You envy your brother going downtown alone to pick up something at the store or take in a movie. The boys see you as a thing, not a person, and usually have only one thing in mind. I was seventeen before my parents would trust me out on a date after dark! And most girls have to decide in the college years—career or family. The pressure's big, you get hurt fast and often, and if, like me, you're good looking you're even more limited. It's understood you'll work for a while until you get married and settle down, but aside from modeling or show business or something like that you can *get* any job—if you want to pay the price for keeping it, and if you don't expect to go anywhere.

"Pretty women aren't supposed to be smart, and they don't have to be. You quickly learn what you're expected to do to get what you want—and you either do it, or don't and go nowhere, or get married and settle down. You get a dozen passes just going to lunch. You wind up a prisoner in your own skin without options at all. You know, I really envied men. I had two older brothers and I really wanted to be one of them. Come and go when you please, free to pick and choose careers, free to be left alone in a crowded party if you wanted to be or go on the make if you felt like it. No period, no danger of getting pregnant, none of that."

I shook my head sadly from side to side. "The grass is always greener. You wonder how anybody winds up happy in this life, or satisfied, or content.

"Luck, mostly," Dory decided. "Enough people, enough combinations. But not either of us, it seems." She chuckled dryly. "How did two such miserable outsiders wind up together in this fix?"

I looked at her without comprehending. "Surely you were better off comparatively than me. You had a lot more of your life ahead of you, were still far along from making those choices. You had the *potential* to find happiness, a potential I really ended."

"No, Vicki," she responded gently. "It wasn't that way at all." She sighed and was silent for a moment, as if making a decision. Finally she shook her head slightly and mumbled to herself, "O.K. True confessions time, I guess." She looked back up at me. "What I'm going to tell you I've never told a living soul. I just really got to telling myself a few days ago, for real."

"You don't have to tell me anything you don't want to."

She shook her head. "No, I *want* to tell you. Particularly now." She sighed once more and looked a little thoughtful. "Look, I knew what growing up was supposed to mean, supposed to feel like. I had a lot of girl friends in the neighborhood, and they all had crushes on big pop stars or TV actors, things like that. Even on some local boys. I never did, but I figured I was just more picky, smarter, or something. I just stuck mostly with my girl friends, never really feeling too comfortable around boys. I was a virgin until I was seventeen—that's weird in this day and time, but I never really thought it was until I hit college. I was sure horny all the time—the tension inside me was unbelievable. I tried a couple of boys in college—after all, I had my pick— but it just didn't do much for me. I never got off and hardly even got wet. I got to wondering if maybe most of this stuff I'd heard was bullshit, that women just faked it but didn't really get out of sex what men seemed to. But I could get *myself* off, and it felt great— but I felt like a freak."

She paused here but I said nothing, having a feeling as to the direction she was going. It was most difficult to remember that she'd been in college only a year—and so all this was only fourteen or fifteen months at most, still very fresh to her. Despite the tiny thirteen-year-old body and childish voice she seemed so very much older than nineteen.

"After school ended last May, we had a big party off-campus to celebrate," she continued. "Lots of stuff around. Booze, pot, pills, coke, even opium, would you believe? I never really was much into that whole thing, but it was that kind of party, you know, and I drank a hell of a lot more than I should and did a little hash with the group and the next thing you know I'm rolling around on the floor making out passionately . . ." She sighed. ". . . With Mary Forester."

I nodded, although it felt very strange to hear it. She looked up at me and there was genuine anguish in her face.

"You see? Well, when I woke up on the floor much later there, I got out fast and went back to my little off-campus apartment. I was sick at myself as well as being hung over. I kept telling myself that it was the booze and drugs, and I had myself halfway believing it, but I didn't want to see any of those people again. I was embarrassed, afraid, I guess. I just wanted to run, get away—not home, either, although that's where I went. My folks were glad to see me, of course, and Mom was trying to fix me up with dates while Dad was talking about my future and all that and all I wanted to do was crawl into a hole and die."

"And after a month of hiding out, with your family pressing you to get out, you decided to pack off to Alaska."

She nodded. "Tommy Coyne wasn't at the party—he'd already gone home to Vancouver. I decided to call him, he invited me along on his trip to Glacier, and we managed to con my parents—not hard to do—into believing it was a summer trip for college credit. There really *was* a course like that so I had all the brochures. Tommy was a nice guy who had the hots for me but we'd never made it. I figured this trip would not only let me sort myself out but maybe reassure me."

"It didn't, though," I guessed.

She nodded grimly. "It was worse. Even worse because he *is* such a nice guy. I knew it even before. That roll with Mary Forester had unlocked something in me and I found myself looking at women in a whole new way every time I passed them, talked to them, whatever. Look, I didn't *want* it. God! Here I was a sexy young woman in college with a bright future someplace and then *this*. Of course, once I came face to face with it I could see that it'd been that way all along. I just hadn't considered it, hadn't wanted to think about it. And now my whole world was crumbling around me. Choices closed, options closed. I walked out on Tommy without explaining—I just couldn't think of what to say, how to tell him—and caught the next boat through. I could've flown, but I wanted the trip, the time to think things through and sort things out. All I could think of was that I couldn't tell my parents—they wouldn't understand, couldn't understand. They're conservative, solid, all that. The scandal alone would have killed Mom, at least. But I couldn't just turn my back on it, either. I wasn't cut out to be celibate. I was still trying to make my decisions, find a way out for myself short of suicide, when you showed up and gave me somebody else to think about. You know the rest."

I nodded. "And what about now? Has anything changed for the better?"

She smiled thoughtfully. "At first, as I said, I was real upset. I wasn't *me* any more. I wasn't really free. But where had I been going, anyway? The more I've thought about this, the better it seems, the more like a godsend. I'm somebody else and somewhere else. Cut off from the past completely. No matter what I do now, it's not my old problems. In a way this has solved my problems. I don't know if I'm going to still feel the same sexually or not—I rather think so—but I don't care any more. I can live that life if it's divorced, now and forever, from my family, friends, classmates." She sounded genuinely relieved, sincerely satisfied, although it was as if she herself were seeing all this for the first time. "Dorian Tomlinson is dead," she breathed. "I'm free."

I looked at her and tried to smile a little. Dorian Tomlinson was dead and she was free, yes, perhaps. But Dorian Tomlinson was also looking at her and sitting very near her this very moment, imprisoning a very different sort of person with a different problem not at all resolved.

Chapter Seven

Most of the next day was taken with the testing we'd been told to expect. It was quite involved and elaborate, with all sorts of written exams—some forcing pretty bizarre choices—plus interviews, extensive questions on personal background and attitudes, everything. There were even a couple of very involved I.Q. tests, and those results they were willing to tell us. Mine was 162, down a couple of points from my old tests but well within the margin of error. Dory's was 144, lower than mine but still well above any norms, confirming my opinion of her. She was a little disappointed. "Not quite a genius," she grumped. "The story of my life."

We hadn't had much time to talk to each other, but after it was all over, a little after 5 in the afternoon, and we were in the cafeteria getting a bite to eat, she brought it up briefly.

"You know our talk last night?"

"Uh huh."

"I was pretty free with the same information today. I tell you, Vicki, it's like a gigantic weight has been lifted from my shoulders. I didn't even flinch at the word. I really do think, maybe for the first time in my life, that I like myself, that I'm at peace with myself."

I squeezed her hand. "I'm glad for you," I told her, and I really was.

She smiled back. "I know. The funny thing was, they didn't seem at all bothered by it. Lesbian. Such a weird word. They even told me there might be nothing really wrong at all. One of 'em said it was partly physiological— a function of brain development. I want to find out more about that angle. If I could know that for a fact it would kind of, well, knock out the last guilty stab wound."

I admitted I didn't kow much about it, but I pointed out that IMC was probably the greatest assemblage of experts on the brain and human behavior ever assembled in one place—certainly assembled with such facilities and such a budget. She'd get her answers here.

We had the evening free, and Dory delighted in showing me around the luxurious facilities. She was almost a different person, half girl-child, half wise adult, but I knew that she'd probably slept solidly and without real worries or guilt for the first time in a couple of months the past night.

I found, too, that she was right about this body I wore. I don't know how many passes men made—I'm sure I missed some of them—but it was not only annoying, I really did begin to feel like some kind of object, a pretty piece of art or sculpture. A part of me wanted to take one of them up on it, to really *be* a woman, but I wasn't one, not really.

We'd gotten up early and were, therefore, tired early. I had a message from Parch that we were cleared now and that we had tomorrow for the grand tour and then to work. Dory would be placed in a training program for technicians—she'd have her choice of several types—while I'd begin the process of making friends with, and trying to draw out, the mysterious Dan Pauley. I was looking forward to that.

In one way, at least, Dory's own revelations, her own emotional outpouring and honesty about herself to others, had done me some good. She no longer dreamed of getting this body back, and I was no longer a caretaker. That made things a little easier on me—I could begin to think of this as a permanent condition and make my plans accordingly. Still, I didn't want to think much beyond IMC, at least not right now. In a sense, I was where I would have wanted to be had I known of the place in my old existence. An encounter with aliens from another world was the most momentous act in the history of modern man, one that would forever change the way human beings saw themselves and their place in the universe. I was *still* a social scientist, and still wanted to be one, and, for that field as well as the others here, this was the place to be.

Parch met us after breakfast and took us down to Level 10, lower than we'd ever been allowed before. We were ushered into a large, spacious office even grander than Parch's, and the sign on the glass door read, "S. Eisenstadt, Ph.D.—IMC Project Director." I was a little shocked at that name—hell, I *knew* Stu Eisenstadt! He'd been on the faculty at Hopkins until mysteriously leaving for "government work" four years ago. Now I knew what that work was and where he'd gone.

He came out to meet us and I couldn't help thinking how little he'd changed. He always reminded me of a fat Albert Einstein, even to a thin, reedy, and slightly accented voice. He'd been in the United States most of his life but he still couldn't tell the difference between a V and a W.

He stopped when he saw us, gave a look of slight distaste, I thought, to Parch, then eyed us, eyes lighting up and a large smile growing under his bushy white moustache. "Vell, vell, vell! You bring me two beautiful ladies!"

He was the kind of person who was charismatic in an

odd way, exuding a grandfatherly warmth you could feel. He had always been among the most highly regarded men I could remember by those who knew him, always doing favors, always willing to listen, sympathize, give advice. His father, a Lutheran minister, had died in a concentration camp during World War II and he remained a deeply, if inwardly, religious man, seeing no conflict between his science and his faith. He never pushed it on you; he just lived it and that was far more impressive.

I went up to him and offered my hand. To my surprise he didn't shake it but took it gently and kissed it. "Dear lady," he said softly, and suddenly I was yanked back to the present and my own new form. This wasn't Hopkins, and he was seeing a far different person he'd never known.

"Stuart, it may be hard to believe, but inside this body is Vic Gonser, an old colleague of yours."

He grinned broadly, and there was added twinkle in his eyes. "My! *Victor!* How you have *changed!*" He turned to Dory. "And you must be Miss Dorian Tomlinson." He bent down slightly and repeated the hand-kissing routine.

I cursed myself for underestimating the wily old bastard and not remembering that "Project Director" title on his door. His often comic personality masked a brilliant mind fully as devious as anyone's. Of *course*, he'd known all about us, who we were, how and why we were here, all the facts well ahead of time.

He gestured to chairs and we all took seats except Parch, who excused himself and left with a few whispered words to the professor we couldn't hear. I couldn't help noticing that the others in and around the office kept glancing nervously at Parch, while the security chief was anything but deferential to Stuart. When Harry Parch left, he seemed to take a black cloud with him.

Eisenstadt sighed. "Vell, Victor! So—it is a great improvement, this change in you. I find you positively radiant to look at." He turned to Dory and said with mock seriousness, "He was a bald little schmoo of a man ven he vas a he." She giggled, and I could see she was falling under his spell.

"Stuart, I may look different and you the same, but I have to say I'm surprised to see you here—surprised and pleased," I told him. "Project Director, huh?"

He nodded. "This is vere it's all done. Parch, he chases the aliens and keeps us a secret, but *here* ve find out how they do it, what they do, and open up the frontiers of knowledge. I tell you, Vict—Vicki—that here ve have already taken quantum leaps—quantum leaps!—in man's knowledge of himself, the most important frontier you can imagine."

I was interested. "You've made real progress, then?"

"Wery much so. I'll be glad to explain it to you, but first ve begin at the beginning, yes? Some old college biology. Ve have not vun brain in our head, you know, but three. Vun, the medulla oblongata, is the first, the basic, the *primal* brain from our reptilian ancestors. It controls much of our automatic functions. Then there's the cerebellum, our mammalian brain. Body temperature, blood pressure, voluntary muscles, that sort of thing. If you have both these you are perfectly equipped to be an ape, yes? A primitive ape, anyway. Memory data, too, is mostly stored here. But to use it for anything but the most basic stuff you need the cerebrum, yes? In computer terms, the cerebrum is the programmer, the cerebellum is data storage, and the medulla is the electric company, you see?"

I had to laugh at the analogy, which was simple but apt. I would like to admit that such basic stuff was unnecessary, and it was to me, but I could see that Dory was getting her memory jogged.

"Now, that's a simplified model—extremely so." Stuart continued, "but it's vat ve need for our purposes. Ve will keep to the computer analogy for all this, but it is important you not think of the brain as an integrated whole but a series of assembled components. All right?"

We both nodded.

"All right, then. Ve have known for a long time that the memory process is basically holographic—you see complete, integrated ideas or images in your cerebrum, not individual data bits. Ve had some success back at Johns Hopkins with feeding additional information into the brain in such a manner, but it vas child's stuff. But this holographic idea vas a wrong direction, even though it was right. No, don't look at me like that. I mean it. It meant ve didn't ask the right question next."

"And that was?" I prompted.

"How that information is *stored* rather than how it is *processed*," he replied. "Look, basically we vould have claimed that what we can now do vas, if not totally impossible, then unlikely in our lifetime. What shocked us all was the self-evident fact that complete memory and personalities could be changed with no apparent physical harm. Incredible! Impossible! But a fact. The process itself is so complex that it defies rational explanation among my colleagues. The fact is, like gravity and magnetism, ve're not quite sure *how* it works but ve know it does."

"You *can* do it, then?"

He shrugged. "Not vat these aliens do, no. They do in moments vat it takes this entire complex of the most sophisticated computers to do. No machines, no vorry, just touch and *pfft!* It is something inside them, something to do with the nature of what they really are. I think they are some sort of energy creatures, bound together in a complex pattern, that needs a body to vork. They are born in bodies, yes, same as ve, but they are not that body. They are symbiotic organisms inside animal bodies, although they can not exist outside bodies at all. So, vat they do naturally ve are not physically equipped to do. But if they can do it to us, there is a vay, vith technology, for *us* to do it to *us*."

"I'm sitting here listening to all this," I said, "in a

body so different from my own it's incredible, yet it's still hard to believe."

He nodded. "I know, I know. I don't believe it myself sometime. But, let's make a try at it, yes? Let's start by saying that the brain is everything. The most incredible, complex, and vonderful computer ever designed. It is made up of cells called neurons that are so densely packed that there are one hundred thousand of them in a square inch! And interconnected by ten thousand miles or more of nerves. The whole brain contains over ten trillion neurons—a staggering number, bigger than ve can really conceive. So much ve don't live long enough to fill it all up.

"But the brain is a prisoner, you see, an isolated thing with no sensations, not even pain. It is totally input-dependent for its information, and this input comes from everyvere else in our bodies—eyes, ears, nose, throat, and the nerve cells that cover our bodies inside and out. It can be fooled—that is the basis of hypnosis. If it can be convinced by its receptors, its input, that something false is true, it accepts it. It has no independent vay of checking out that information."

I glanced over at Dory and saw her rapt attention. Stuart was a good teacher, and he was obviously relishing the role once more.

"Now, input—sensory data, whether it be light, shape, color, anything—is sent to the brain and routed to the proper place for it," he continued. "It indexes by area. There's really no difference in the neurons, but our genes set up a pattern, a matrix if you will, that the brain follows as its own unique coding and indexing system. Evolution, in other vords, produced an incredibly efficient indexing system. Each individual matrix is unique, like fingerprints, and so our first problem is how to discover how the brain indexes for each personality— their identity matrix, you might call it. Ve do this by a sophisticated probe—actually millions of tiny energy probes—that finally find the right place and are able to plug in, as it were, to the individual's brain. The process is new—invented here—and quite complex."

"You don't have to shave the head and drill, then?" Dory put in.

He chuckled. "Oh, no. At the start, yes, but no more. It is necessary only to establish a direct, electrical connection to the brain. The Urulu, they do it at almost any set of nerve ends in the body, but ve believe there is actual entry by the Urulu organism along the nervous system and into the brain. Ve based our own work on that hypothesis and it vorked. Our computer system and probes is the mechanical replacement for the organic, as it were, Urulu."

"But you said each matrix was unique," I pointed out. "So how can you replace one pattern for another?"

"Vell, ve start by shooting tremendous amounts of stimuli into the cerebrum directly. You say 'name' and your name is brought forth into the cerebrum. The computer seizes on that and follows it back, and so on. But after a vile it can ask questions far faster than ve, and it asks millions of them per second. Ultimately it learns the code, the matrix, for the information center and can track down miscellaneous material until it has complete access to memory storage. It generally needs an external stimuli—like us asking questions—to start, then it takes over, and, at computer speed, it still takes twenty or more minutes, sometimes longer, to completely map a matrix. At the end it is just recognizing the existence of data, of course, not caring vat that data is."

I was starting to feel a little uneasy about what he was saying. The idea of mapping the memory, the very core of being, of an individual like Rand McNally did roads was unsettling.

"Now, let's go back to the brain itself," Eisenstadt went on. "Although retrieval is holographic, storage is not really so. The hologram is constructed in the cerebrum from retrieved data. How is that data stored? Vell, all the input, all the information from your senses, goes to the cerebrum—but not as you perceive them. All external stimuli are instantly converted into brain language—and that brain language is chemical in nature. But there are two languages. One, the holographic one, is transmitted to the brain. There it is broken down into bytes of information and recoded. Each byte becomes a synapse, a chemical messenger that is hustled along and routed by a tiny electrical impulse. Each little messenger gets to the brain where neurons route it, according to the matrix, to its proper place. When it gets to that proper place the individual neuron in charge, as it vere, make a tiny copy in its *own* individual language. All this at incredible speed, you understand. Like trillions of tiny chemical tape recorders, infinitely specialized, who record the message ven the chemical messenger runs past its little recording head.

"Ven you remember something, or use something, or need to retrieve something, then the command is sent out from the real 'you'—your cerebral cortex, or command center—and, instantly, the little bits of information that apply rush back with copies of the information needed—copies, note, the original stays there—where the cerebrum reintegrates this information into a holographic picture. An idea. A memory. You name it. Naturally, the information that is most frequently used is easiest to get at. The less it is used the more difficult it is to get at that information—you 'try to remember' but can't, quite, because you have had no need for it for so long the track is overgrown with veeds. It has to be this way. Most information you get from cradle to grave simply isn't needed or relevant, no matter how big it vas at the time, and it is stored avay in the cranial closet, so to speak, to make room in the more efficient areas for more pressing stuff. Once out of the main matrix and off in that closet, it becomes hard to find, like any attic overfilled with unused and unvanted stuff, becoming even harder as you grow older as those closets fill with all the junk. That's why much of the brain appears to be doing nothing and ve don't even miss some of that stuff if it has to be removed, say, in an operation."

"Does the brain ever—erase?" Dory asked hesitantly. I got the impression she was a bit unsettled by all this, too.

"Oh, yes," he replied. "Sometimes it's accidental. Sometimes it's the result of an injury—repairs inside the brain may require it. Self-repairs, I mean. In fact, some of it is automatically erased very qvickly. Vy should it bother to keep instructions it gave to the gastrointestinal tract for digesting a specific meal when you vere three? So, after a decent interval, it erases and generally keeps this sort of expendable information in one area for constant re-use. So, to sum, the neurons store the information, the synapses feed the input to the brain, copy and transmit stored input, and erase. They also do much more, of course—they create enzymes that do different things in and to the brain and the like in response to stimuli."

"That explains the brain in layman's terms," I agreed, "but not how the Urulu swap minds."

"Ah, the Urulu. Vell, vat they do seems to go something like this. By simple touch they are able to plug into anyone's nervous system the same as our computer. Automatically, in no more than a few seconds, they are able to do vat ve vith our huge computer take half an hour or so to do—get a complete picture of your matrix, and, as such, know exactly vere and how your information is stored and processed. And they know instinctively what to ignore—the automatic functions, for example. Then they are able to order the neurons to disgorge this information and it flows in an electrochemical rush to the point of contact and from there to the Urulu brain. The same thing happens to the other matrix, which flows, simultaneously, in the opposite direction. The amazing thing is not only is the exchange complete in both directions, without disrupting the body functions, but it is accompanied by a 'carrier' signal, as it were, which is the exact opposite of the information being extracted. In other words, the neurons receive a signal that is absolutely complimentary to the chemical code they already are storing—in effect canceling it out. The effect is that each brain rearranges itself into an exact chemical copy of the other. *Not* a hundred percent, mind you—memories, personality, yes, but not vat is necessary to keep the body going, to manage the unique physical body into which it is now placed. Vether this is an actual transfer of information or vether this is simply a rearrangement is something ve don't really understand yet, although ve tend to think it is a rearrangement rather than an actual exchange considering the speed at vich it is done. If memory, personality, whatever is chemically stored, then prior information is duplicated by the other brain and then totally erased in the original by giving such commands to the cerebral cortexes of each brain and a channel through which the information needed may be exchanged."

"Then—I'm not really Victor Gonser at all," I said, feeling a little hollow and distant. "Dory's mind just thinks it's me. And that Indian girl, whoever she was, just thinks she's Dory."

Stuart shrugged. "If all that vas you, your id, ego, super-ego, all the memories and bits of information that went into forming them, your identity matrix, in other words, is duplicated exactly—vat is the difference? I think of it as an exchange of souls in a marvellously mathematical way."

"These chemical messages—you already said false ones could be sent and that total erasure was possible," Dory put in, thankfully changing the subject. "You also said that the computer can figure out our entire filing system. Does that mean what I think it means?"

"If you are thinking vat I think you're thinking, then, yes. An unforseen side product, but a revolutionary discovery. In its own vay the equivalent of atomic energy—with the same potential both vays."

I suddenly felt very stupid. "What are you two talking about?"

"Selective memory," Dory responded. "If that computer tells you you're Joan of Arc you'll set the fire yourself."

"It is a fact," Stuart admitted. "Ve can read out the mind and record it, even store it like Beethoven symphonies are recorded. Feed it into any mind. It's still very primitive right now, and there are too many risks to try it on humans, but it is coming, it is coming!"

I felt sick. "And anything that can be digitally recorded can be selectively doctored."

Stuart nodded, apparently not bothered by that. "Oh, yes. Ve have high hopes that ve can bypass brain disorders, cure cerebral palsy, for example, epilepsy, and other such things. Do away vith dyslexia. Perhaps, eventually, be able to order cancer cells to self-destruct. The potential for ending much human misery and suffering is unlimited!"

I grew increasingly uneasy, and I could see Dory was the same way. "You could also turn an entire population into loyal, loving, obedient slaves."

The scientist shrugged. "Like all discoveries, the potential for abuse is awesome. It is our responsibility, our trust, to see that it does not happen. Fortunately, ve have much time—the technology involved in such a thing is not yet here, and, for now, ve alone have it. But ve cannot unlearn vat ve have learned, cannot undo vat ve have done any more than the atomic genie could be pushed back into the bottle once released. It is a grave responsibility, but it is no more grave than other great discoveries of mankind. Ve have the responsibility vether ve vant it or not, and, as always, ve puny little fallible humans have to deal with it. Considering how far ve have come to now, I think ve vill."

An assistant brought Stuart and Dory tea and me coffee. I couldn't help thinking about the potential, and wondering about the possibilities of abuse. I looked around at the people at IMC and thought about the others I'd met. Except for Parch they seemed very ordinary people, middle-level bureaucrats in administration, technicians and scientists and their families as well. Not evil threatening people. Not headed by Stuart, particularly, one of the finest men I'd ever known. Still, they would worry me, particularly Parch. In the hands of such a man as he, the pontential was horrible.

It was Dory who shifted subject again, possibly partly in self-defense against thinking too hard on what was bothering me.

"What about genetics?" she asked Stuart. "I mean, you can't change the genetic code when you change this information in the brain."

"I'll admit that is a puzzle," Eisenstadt admitted. "There are so many things about a person that are determined by his physiology and science is no closer to solving the heredity-versus-environment debate now than twenty years ago. Perhaps people like *you* vill eventually solve the puzzle, although there is debate even on that. After all, your personalities were shaped by your original genetic and other makeup and might by this time be too fixed to be measurably changed. Maybe not. If you find out vill you tell us?"

We both laughed, and Dory kept to this point for a reason I slowly started understanding.

"What sort of things are you certain are genetically caused?" she asked him.

He shrugged. "Studies vith tvins have shown a little but it is more puzzling than before. They make a great thing about identical twins separated at birth using the same shaving lotion—but might that not be because their taste and smell are the same so the same stuff vould be pleasurable? Ve don't know."

"What about—sex?" she pressed, becoming obvious.

"Sex is obviously genetic in the most basic sense," Stuart replied, at first missing the real question. "The degree of sex and of sexual response is partly a matter of enzyme and hormone production, stuff like that. You *can* be oversexed or undersexed, for example, even in the drive, as determined by your genetic make-up. Beyond that, though, so many cultural factors go into it that it is hard to say. Victor, here, vas Victor for thirty-five years and is now Vicki, but not in the usual sex-change vay. Fully functioning, vith all the body's genetic drives, hormones, that sort of thing. I vould suspect the head to respond to vomen and the body to men, vich vill give you the life of a real svinger for a vile—but you vill settle down into vichever pattern body and mind compromise on, feel best vith, over the long run."

"That was *my* body," Dory pointed out.

"I'm avare of that."

"Doc—I was a lesbian."

That stopped him, but only for a moment. He thought over the possiblities, then said, "Vell, that puts a little more of a strain on Vicki, here. There is a tiny area in the cerebellum discovered in 1980, a small group of neurons that is normally sexually consistent—it looks vun vay in men, the other in vomen. It came out of studies to see if the male and female brain differed in any significant vay. Now, this is not the cause of all homosexual tendencies—much of it is psychological and environmental. But it has been found that some vomen have the male configuration—not many, but some—and some men have the female. Who knows vy? A mistake in genetic coding? A mutation? Something the mama drank? Extreme sexual mirror-imaging vas found in hermaphrodites, but a small but important percentage have the thing tilted a bit towards the wrong sex, if you'll pardon me. It might cause extra—complications—for Victor if that body's sexual identity center is more male than female. Only time vill tell—or, of course, ve could do a computer scan and find out."

"You mean hook me up to your computer? Uh uh, Stuart. Not now, anyway. I've had enough fooling around with my mind for the time being."

He chuckled softly. "Come. I vill show you the heart of IMC and maybe you vill not feel so bad."

We got up and left the office, going down a hall to a set of large double doors with all sorts of security warnings on them. He ignored them and held the doors for us to pass inside.

The room was huge, looking more like the control center for some space system than anything related to biology. An orange wall-to-wall carpet went around the floor in a semi-circle, but it was almost obscured by the computer terminals, control centers and chairs, that made it seem like Mission Control. They all faced a raised semicircular platform carpeted in light green, on which sat two large chairs looking like nothing so much as dental chairs with large beauty-parlor hair dryers attached. Enormous masses of cable ran from the chair assemblies into the floor.

"The soul of IMC," Stuart told us with obvious pride.

We walked onto the orange-carpeted area and Stuart went over to a large and forbidding looking console. He opened the top and reached down, removing from it a ruby-colored translucent cube perhaps a foot square. He handed it to me and I looked at it curiously. It weighed no more than two or three pounds at best. I handed it back and asked, "What is it?"

"A digital recording module," he replied. "Inside it can be stored over ten trillion bytes of information. In a sense, a couple of these can hold the sum total of a human brain's knowledge and experience. It is a revolutionary vay of storing information and the key to our progress here. The equivalent of tventy thousand kilometers of magnetic tape fifty centimeters wide. Two or three of these, in the computer system, and ve can record and play back a human mind."

I shivered. "Then you can actually remove information from the brain, like they can?"

He nodded. "Yes, yes, ve can do that. It is simply a matter of applying the correct electrical signal at the correct point in the cerebral cortex. Ve can now get a readout."

I looked down at Dory and thought that her expression must be matched by my own face. "So can you—switch minds?"

"Ve are not *that* far along yet, although ve are very close. So far ve have managed first to copy someone's identity matrix and store it on the cubes. Then it was but a short step to learning how to erase as ve recorded. Ve can take it out and erase now, and put it back in the same head from which it vas took, vith no apparent loss. In fact, ven ve do that the person always remembers much more of their life, seems to think a bit more clearly. Remember—ve are cleaning out not only the active memory and personality but also that attic full of forgotten junk, opening new pathways to it and for it. It becomes accessible again. But only for a vile. Since it vas stored there in the first place because it vas no longer needed, it fades with disuse, in a veek or two at the most."

I nodded to myself. "Yes, I remember the first time I got switched. I seemed to remember things back to babyhood and everything seemed so crisp and clear, like my I.Q. had been doubled. But it faded."

"Can you—put people back into other bodies?" Dory asked hesitantly.

He saw her concern and smiled reassuringly. "No. Not yet. Not really, anyvay. Tolerances are too critical. Ve just don't know enough. There is anyvere from a ten to fifty percent insertion loss, or the information is there but can't be gotten at. The roadblock seems to be the brain vaves, the voltage inside the head. It, too, is different for different people and the old values won't do since that would interfere with the autonomic functions of the body ve don't touch. The values of the new body aren't matched to vat the old matrix system is used to. It appears there is an almost no-tolerance compromise between vat the input needs and the new body requires that is unique with each individual. But the Urulu find it—find it and automatically match it in moments. Vun day, perhaps soon, ve vill find it, too."

And, somehow, I knew he would. I shuddered at the idea of an "insertion loss" of ten to fifty percent. An I.Q. 150 might become a below-normal I.Q. 75.

Stuart had to go about his business after that, and we left him in the command center of IMC. We headed for the cafeteria, although neither of us felt like eating. I, for one, felt the need to sit down and get control of myself for a few moments.

"It scares the hell out of me," I told Dory. "Right now he can read us out and store us in little cubes. You know it won't be long before they'll know how to switch. Considering how far they've come in such a short time now, it could be today, or tomorrow. Certainly it's a matter of months, not years. And all that will be put in the hands of men like Harry Parch. Worse. Can you imagine them with a bunch of bodies, clearing them out, then feeding Parch's recording into all of them? An army of Harry Parches. He wouldn't need his makeup kit any more."

"It's worse than that, if you remember our earlier conversation with Eisenstadt," Dory replied. "Look, I own—used to own—a good digital tape recorder. Puts the signal on tape as a binary code, millions of tiny dots, each representing a single element of the music. Mine won't edit much—it's a cheap model—but at the store where I got it they had this real fancy kind, the kind professional recording companies and TV companies use. They had a string quartet—four instruments playing together—on tape. They used to show what you could do with an editor by removing one instrument—the violin, say—and replacing it with a piccolo playing the same part. Sounded stupid and weird, but that computer tape recorder-editor of theirs could figure out which little dots applied *only* to violins—even reverb, echo, you name it—then separate it from all the other sounds and replace it."

For a moment I didn't see it, but suddenly it hit me. Holographic memory ... That meant that the brain didn't store your name, for example, in a billion places. Inefficient. It stored that in one place and went to it when forming its thoughts. If they learned which little digital dots, which bytes of information, were which, and could locate your name as easily as the musical engineer located Dory's violin, they could replace that information when reading it back into you. Edit your memories.

"You see what I mean," she said gravely. "They could redo everybody. We'd be happy little robots. And Dr. Eisenstadt seemed so *nice*."

"He is," I assured her. "I'm sure he and his colleagues are thinking along the lines he said. Curing disease, treating hopeless mental illness, that sort of thing."

"These people—the ones we've met—they seem like decent sorts, I guess. They have husbands and wives and kids and many live on the surface, in normal homes, having normal family lives. They join the PTA, play tennis, laugh at comedies, bowl. Am I wrong to be so afraid?"

I reached over and squeezed her hand. "No, you're not. History is on the side of your nightmares, I'm afraid. Oh, I doubt if anybody here, even Parch, is acting from selfish, power-seeking motives. Whatever they do with this power they will do for the best of reasons, from the purest of motives. Their psychiatric screening is damned good, as good as for the guys who fire the nuclear missiles in case of atomic war—and we've never had one fired incorrectly yet. But good motives don't make actions good. These people aren't monsters or crazy dictator types, they're worse—middle-level government bureaucrats and naive scientists. But consider—I'll just bet there is, or soon will be, a Genetic Research Center that's the equivalent of IMC somewhere. So that IMC and GRC combined can produce the sanest, healthiest, most perfect human specimens government bureaucrats can devise. Perfect people made to order—a glorious ideal. Without hatred, without prejudice, all equal. And all somebody else's idea—and ideal—of perfection."

She shivered. "What a horrible idea. Surely there must be *something* we can do about it."

I shook my head slowly from side to side. "There isn't much. The only thing that might undo it would be the full glare of publicity. And, no matter what Parch said, we're prisoners here, really, Dory. They aren't going to let us out of here until they can be assured of our silence. And as long as they are in a wartime type situation, with everybody concerned with meeting an alien menace from the stars, they'll have a Harry Parch around to make sure nothing gets out." I sighed. "We're in the position of knowing the danger, but we have to sit back and hope somebody else blows the whistle. It's out of our hands, damn it."

"At least they aren't there yet," she said, trying to convince herself that there was some light at the end of the tunnel.

That very afternoon they put me to work. By this time Dan Pauley had been transferred to a more automated and more secure glass cage, and I was able to work without a lot of gunslingers around. Remote monitoring would stop Pauley before he could do just about anything; a rat caught in a very frustrating trap.

This left me with Jeff Overmeyer as the one man always there for my sessions with the alien. Overmeyer was a nice young technician who oversaw the technical aspects of my talks, made certain the recordings were clear and that all systems in the alien's security were working properly. Although officially Parch's man, a security man, he was neither as sinister nor as secretive as his boss and generally tended to be a really nice guy. It wasn't an act, either, and more than once I suspected that the usual government games were being played and that he might be Eisenstadt's man in Parch's organization the same as Parch undoubtedly had people with Eisenstadt's technician crew. Both men were co-equals who often got in each other's way, and both would be always trying to circumvent the other.

As for Pauley, he seemed to enjoy talking, particularly with me, although never about things he didn't want to discuss. Overmeyer assured me that they had already tried the drugs and other tricks short of physical torture on Pauley and found him not only impervious, as he'd said, but infuriatingly amused by their attempts. It was up to me.

Some things I learned explained a little. The Urulu didn't like airplanes, for example. I found it amusing that a race that flew across countless light-years of space was terrified of airplanes, so much so that they'd gone from car to train to horseback to ferry in Alaska rather than easily circumvent Parch by switching bodies secretly and taking a plane south. It was an odd bit of alien psychology that helped remind me that this normal, pleasant young man was neither normal nor a man. The best explanation I got was that the normal Urulu form was so different from ours that their normal environment posed its greatest threat in changes in pressure. Although unaffected physically by small changes while in human form, their inborn alien fear of such a thing was so great they couldn't bring themselves to do it. It was a handy fact, anyway, as Overmeyer pointed out. It meant they didn't have to check airplanes and airports as much, and that a really good test of whether a body was taken over or not might be to take them for a plane ride.

They'd played pressurization games on Pauley here, but it hadn't worked. The terror was so complete that the knee-jerk reaction he had was to pass out cold. Nobody won again.

As to how the Urulu switched bodies, he was no help

at all. Not that he withheld much information—he just didn't know. It was like raising your right arm, or blinking, or anything else normal—you just *did* it, that's all.

About the Urulu he was no other real help, although he was willing to discuss his enemies, a group that translated out as The Association. The master races of that alliance had apparently developed the technique mechanically, much as IMC was trying to do, and had hit upon our wildest nightmares.

It was odd, in fact, how much Dan's description of the Association matched Dory's and my own fears about IMC. Theirs was a race—the original one—that had used the process to create "perfect" people according to an idealized standard. It was a dull, soulless, mechanical society but everybody was happy because they couldn't be anything else, and nobody had any doubts, fears, jealousies, nor love, hate, or any of the emotions we would recognize. Their sole drive, their sole aim, was to bring that driving "perfection" to all sentient races in the universe. They would find a race on a world, study it in cool, computer-like terms, analyze the "imperfections" of the society and the race—and the world—and then slowly, surreptitiously, they would worm their way in, gain converts, create a force of native devotees, and eventually they would gain the seat of power in each and every nation, tribe, you name it. The world, then, could be easily remade.

"That's why the very existence of IMC worries us," Pauley told me. "We don't think they've found it yet, or infiltrated it yet, but it's tailor-made for them to take over. If, of course, it doesn't become a homemade and homegrown version of The Association without their help."

That last, I think, disturbed me more than any external threat. I asked him what his people would do if they discovered IMC.

"Destroy it, certainly," he responded instantly. "But not the minds who created it. Just the physical plant.

With that done, they would then try to enlist the Earth as an ally against The Association. Space and potential immortality in exchange for fighting a war Earth had a stake in winning."

"That didn't seem your direction as of Alaska," I pointed out coolly.

He shrugged. "Alaska was another era. If my people now knew just of IMC and how much progress it had made they might well destroy the entire planet, writing it off as lost to The Association."

That was a chilling thought. "So we have the cooperation of the dead? Some alliance!"

"No, no! You must understand Earth, as I said, is very peculiar. Evolution went a wildly different way here. That's why we needed the bodies and had to come all this way to get them. Maybe ten, fifteen planets out of tens of thousands, went your way. There is some, well, prejudice there, of course. The belief that such a world and such a race can't develop the kind of human qualities we see as valuable. You see, the mother race of The Association was more like yours than ours. My people would have to be convinced that Earth wouldn't inevitably take The Association's path. Soulless, we call such races. But I've been here. I know you're capable of the kind of qualities we value so highly—individuality, love, warmth, feeling, caring for one another. They looked and saw only the bad points—the terrible hatred and prejudices on such petty grounds, the dehumanizing philosophies, the cruelty and hatred and suspicion. If my people could be convinced that you are not on one side of the ledger but poised on the line, able to go both ways, they'd fall over backwards to make sure this planet developed its true potential for greatness."

"And who will convince them?" I asked skeptically. "You? If we let you go will you usher in this great new era? Even if you could, why should we believe you? Why trust you to do that?"

He just shook his head sadly. "No, I *don't* know if I

could convince them. I'm not sure how to do it in the limited amount of time we'd have to make a decision. Even if I'd get listened to by somebody who could make such a decision." He hesitated, then concluded, his tone one of total defeat, "And I have no way at all to show that I'm not a dirty villain lying through my teeth. That's what's so frustrating, Vicki—knowing what has to be done, and knowing that you can't do a damned thing about it, not even knowing if you could if you had the chance."

I nodded sadly. I knew exactly what he was feeling. It was close enough to home I felt more comfortable changing the subject.

"Dan—why do your people need live bodies at all? Why wouldn't cloning do as well?"

"It won't work," he told me. "Don't ask me why but it won't. An experienced, complex mind just doesn't mesh right with a cloned body that has no history of its own. If you raise the clone as a total individual, yes it'll work—but not an unused mind grown for that purpose." He looked apologetic. "When you think of Earth people the way most Urulu do, as little more than complex animals, it's easier just to nab bodies as you need them."

Every day I was continually fighting off men's advances. I began to realize what Dory meant by beauty being a curse. All men seemed to think they were God's gift to women, none seemed to think I could do anything for myself, and, since very few knew that I was not born in this body, all assumed I was "making it" regularly with somebody or other. Trouble was, this damned body looked good in a potato sack.

I found what relief I could in masturbation but couldn't bring myself to anything more overt, although I hardly lacked for opportunity even with a few of the women around, lesbians themselves. They were more tolerant of such things at IMC, where the brain was the object and the subject. Ultimately, though, I knew I would have to face up to the problem, since my body was more and more insistent and had far greater needs than my old one had, and, of course, I badly needed some sort of companionship in this cold, underground city. Dory was around, of course, but not much after a while, as her training program took her to far distant levels and required a lot of practice and studying. Besides, I told myself, she'd *found* her new life, her new start. I still felt that I owed her, but she didn't necessarily feel the same towards me, and I couldn't blame her.

I was also, now, experiencing menstruation, and it still shocked me every time my "period" came. It was messy, smelly, uncomfortable, you name it, and every month on the first day of it I got the most horrible, debilitating cramps I'd ever experienced. The IMC medical staff prescribed some stuff which helped enormously, but I was still experiencing the underside of what it was like to be a woman, and the physical discomfort and mental shifts were far greater than I'd ever realized from the viewpoint of being a man.

I was pretty well reconciled to being in this body the rest of my life, though. That, at least, grew easier every day. I no longer awoke with a feeling of surprise at who and what I was, and I'd long ago gotten used to the bras, the odd feeling of women's undergarments, not to mention all the cosmetic stuff, hair care, and the rest. Real high heels were still a bit beyond me, but I was practicing, in the private places, and I was also consciously studying and imitating women's mannerisms, ways of walking, that sort of thing. I was a long way from being completely natural, but it was coming. I wanted to fit.

And that, finally, brought me to the decision point. I *had* to know about myself, and that meant taking the plunge.

There was no question as to who would be the first experiment. Jeff Overmeyer had been the closest thing I had to a confidant and friend since Dory'd gotten so busy, and he was young, experienced with women, knew my background but didn't mind, and had never once pushed himself on me or treated me as other than an equal. I liked him a lot, even if I didn't fully trust him, and although I hesitated for weeks I was the one who finally made the first move.

After, coming back to my quarters, I saw that Dory was still up and went in to tell her.

"Well, you don't look any worse for wear," she noted. "What did you think?"

"I don't know what I think," I told her honestly. "It was—well, strange. On the one hand, I'm now convinced that women get a little more out of it than men. A man's only got one place to feel it, while we've got four."

"We," she noted. "You *are* adjusting."

I shrugged. "On the one hand, it felt really good. On the other, well, it felt *wrong*. I kept wanting to be the aggressor, for one thing. And while the preliminaries were fine, during intercourse I kept wanting to stick it in, to feel that total sensation, and instead I had a whole different set of feelings. Not unpleasant, in any way, but not what I knew *he* was feeling. Put it down to mixed reviews, I guess. I haven't gone sour on the deal, although the idea of a blow job is pretty repulsive."

"Did he come?"

"Yes."

"Did you get off?"

I hesitated, then replied, "No."

She just nodded for a moment, then asked, "Did he use a condom? Or have you started on the pill?"

I felt a slight shock go through me. "No on all counts," I said uneasily.

"Jesus! How far along are you? How long since your last period?"

"I thought a moment. "Two weeks. I'm about mid-way."

"Holy shit! You took a chance there! Or do you plan to have his baby?"

I just sat there, stunned, for a bit. It simply hadn't occurred to me.

Dory whistled. "You're really in the club now. You got two weeks or more of heavy sweating to do. As much as you hate your period, you're gonna be praying for it to come. And if it doesn't, and the feds don't do abortions here, you're gonna go through more than I ever did. *Now* you're *really* gonna find out what it's like to be a woman."

Chapter Eight

The next three weeks were among the most miserable of my life. I grew increasingly nervous and irritable, and even throwing myself into the reports and mounds of paperwork on Pauley and the Urulu didn't help. I screwed up form after form, couldn't type worth a damn, and every little thing made me furious where in other circumstances I'd have laughed them off. I was a holy terror to be around and I knew it, but I just couldn't help it.

I certainly didn't blame Jeff Overmeyer. In fact, I didn't even tell him, although he didn't quite escape blame in my mind. I was irritated with myself, of course, for not thinking things through, and the primary blame was mine, but there seemed something unfair about the fact that he had assumed that I had taken precautions rather than think along those lines himself. Score another one culturally for men, I thought sourly, realizing that, as a man myself, in my very infrequent sexual acts not once had I considered any kind of male birth control.

Dory tried to cheer me up by noting how much against

the odds any intercourse leading to pregnancy was, but I was sure that the venerated Murphy's basic law would apply. When I was a week late, I got one of those home pregnancy test kits from the pharmacy and tried it, only to get some chemical confirmation of my worst fears.

I was pregnant.

The very news, knowing for sure that the worst had happened, calmed me a bit, since, at least, it outlined a series of actions. I knew from the start that I wasn't ready for this sort of thing, not yet, anyway, and that left abortion as the only option. The trouble was, the medical facilities at IMC were entirely governed by government regulations, and while they see-sawed on the abortion question and had for many years they currently didn't allow it in government facilities except to save the life of the mother. I was furious at this—*they* didn't have to carry the kid, let alone bear it under these circumstances—but they wouldn't let me take the only obvious way out. There seemed a particular irony to my problem, since we were of undetermined status (although officially on the government payroll) at IMC and it had been many months since either Dory or I had seen the sun. I wasn't about to take this, though, and finally confessed the problem to Jeff.

He arranged an appointment with Harry Parch.

I'd seen almost nothing of the man since the first few days at IMC, and I'd had the impression that he'd been away more than here which suited everybody just fine, but walking into his office once again I found him the same cool fish, only more cruel and infuriating than ever.

"So you got knocked up and you're stuck," he said with a trace of amusement. I grew furious at his tone and felt myself becoming flush with anger, yet I held it in. No matter what kind of slimy eel the man was, he was the only one who could help.

So instead of yelling at him, I just replied, "I'm in trouble, I have a problem, and my status here keeps me from resolving it. I'm asking—pleading—for your help. It's only a problem because of your goddamned government restrictions."

He nodded. "I'll agree that the situation is complicated beyond normal bounds. Just what do you want me to do about it? I can't order the clinic to ignore those policies—the folks that slap them on pay our bills and our salaries. Frankly, my influence just doesn't extend into the medical field."

"I know that. They already explained that to me. But we're in Nevada, a state with liberal laws on almost everything. I've talked to several women here, and they tell me there are abortion clinics in Las Vegas."

"I thought it was something like that." He sighed. "I don't mind telling you that you present me with a real problem, since you certainly know too much at this point for true security's sake." He paused, hands together, thinking it over. Finally he said, "However, I can sympathize with your situation. If it were strictly up to me, there'd be no problem. I doubt if you could do much harm anyway, unless you ran into some Urulu. You're too trusting, too much of an idealist. Tell you what, though—I'll pass this on to the full Directorate of IMC, which includes myself and Dr. Eisenstadt, and recommend we allow it. It could be a little while, though, so you'll have to just grin and bear it until then. Everyone's not here right now and I have to leave again shortly for Washington."

I had a sinking feeling. "How long?"

He shrugged. "As soon as possible. That's all I can promise."

"It'll have to do," I agreed, resignedly.

I had, naturally, talked all this over with Dory, and she seemed interested in the idea of me getting out, however briefly.

"Look, I've been in lots of places you haven't," she told me. "I told you about some of the things I've seen."

She had been giving me regular reports, since my own

areas of IMC were now routinely familiar but off the beaten track. It was clear that IMC was experimenting on human beings, starting with some terminally ill volunteers from various government hospitals. Close to death and without hope, these people had allowed themselves to be placed in the two sinister chairs downstairs. Early results, rumor said, had been very encouraging. Finally some volunteers who were themselves on the project had been tested—with horribly mixed results. Bright young men and women who now had pieces of themselves missing, muddled, or scrambled, now kept around in whatever menial tasks they could do until the bugs were worked out. Eisenstadt, it had been said, opposed the experiments at this point but was overruled by the Pentagon bosses in Washington who were desperate for results. Now he was working eighteen-hour days and seven-day weeks to break the puzzle, because, of course, those damaged people had had their "identity matrices" recorded prior to the experiment. He was determined to restore them.

It rang true to me, first because it sounded like Stuart, and also because the pressures *would* be mounting. From my security contacts, mostly through Jeff, I had learned of some independent confirmation that a second alien group might well be operating and that the Urulu story might not be just a common bluff. If the Urulu scared them, The Association practically terrified them, not just because of its philosophy (since we had no real way of knowing if the Urulu were any better) but because it represented Earth as a potential battleground between two superior alien forces and technologies, helpless to do anything about it. The pressure to crack the last bits of the identity matrix puzzle would be enormous.

That they would do it neither Dory nor I doubted. But when they did—what would they do with it, these faceless, nameless Pentagon bosses? It made some sort of public disclosure even more imperative.

Time passed, though, with my own problems taking

on more urgency than the larger, global picture. If they went too long without a decision, I might have to have a far more dangerous and drastic type of abortion and that scared me most of all. I began to think that, in spite of everything, I might have to bear the child.

Six weeks after that fateful intercourse I finally got a summons to Parch's office once again. He looked tired and haggard and not at all in the mood for trivialities like me. Still, he said, "All right. They approved it. We've made an appointment for you at one of these places for one tomorrow afternoon, and will, of course, deduct the considerable cost from your account here. Overmeyer will drive you there and stick with you. It's almost a three-hour drive, and who knows how long there, so we've approved your staying at a motel in town for the night, then driving back in the morning. I picked Overmeyer because he's at least partially responsible for this, but it'll be his head if anything, and I mean *anything*, goes wrong. His and yours, too. Understand?"

"I understand," I nodded glumly.

"Oh—the motel's on you, too. We'll pay for the gas."

"Thanks a lot," I muttered sourly, and left him.

I met Dory for lunch—she was now working in one of the computer centers as an operator, seemingly enjoying it, although she had some problems with everyone taking a thirteen-year-old kid seriously as a co-worker— and told her the news.

She brightened at the news I was getting out. "Look," she whispered, her tone becoming somewhat conspiratorial, "while you're there you can get word out."

I was startled. "To who? And how? I'm not going to be alone—except for, well, you know. . . ."

"You've gotta know somebody's home phone number. Send a telegram by phone and charge it to that number."

I considered it. It actually sounded plausible. My own old number would, of course, have been long disconnected, but there *were* a number of people whose numbers I knew and who wouldn't even notice such a charge on their bill. "But who?"

She thought a moment. "How about Harl Calvert?"

I thought about it and the more I thought the more sense it made. Calvert was the biggest syndicated muckraking columnist in Washington. He'd sell his soul for a story like this if he hadn't already sold it long ago—but once he had it he wouldn't let go. And he was listed, so they could phone in the telegram without my having to give specific addresses.

Still, I was extremely nervous about the abortion and this only doubled my anxiety. Yet, the abortion might disguise my actions, and it was worth a try. That was all I could promise. I'd try.

I won't dwell on the ride into Vegas in the scorching sun, nor the abortion experience, except to say that Jeff seemed as worried and depressed as I was, so there was little conversation, and the clinic was the most dehumanizing cattle barn I'd ever been in, with loads of miserable looking women, mostly teens it seemed, sitting around waiting to be called. The experience itself was administered by doctors who had the same regard for you as they did for a piece of meat and it was painful and horrible to undergo, and more of a shock to my nervous system than I'd expected.

It was also, in a more personal way, very depressing. No matter what my liberal feelings on abortion, they'd sprung from the viewpoint of being a man, one who would never have even the threat of undergoing one himself and not the slightest idea of what it was like. And, somewhere deep inside me, I realized I'd always bear the cross of the action, always feel like I'd killed, if not someone else, then at least a little part of me.

Jeff was solicitous and left me alone when I wanted to be. We were registered in as "Mr. and Mrs. Jeffrey Overmeyer" which, I supposed, was only fitting. It was odd, somehow, that the most abnormal combination of

circumstances imaginable gave such an air of total social normalcy.

Still, he left me alone in the room to sleep a little—I
was pretty shaky still and hadn't slept at all the night
before—and, there I was, alone in the motel room with a
motel phone.

I admit I lay there on that bed staring at that phone,
knowing what I had to do but also knowing that if I
waited much longer, Jeff would return and my chance
would be gone.

Finally I got up the nerve to do it.

I charged the telegram to my father's law firm. Although he was long dead the firm continued and even
prospered and it'd never much changed its number. I
took a chance in identifying myself as George Lloyd's
secretary, since it'd been long enough she might not still
work there, but they took the message and didn't seem
to have any problems.

I sent, "Top secret government mind control project
well underway in Nevada desert near Yucca Flat. People
held virtual prisoners to security there." I didn't sign it,
of course.

But it was done—and now it was up to Harl Calvert.

I had barely finished when the key rattled in the door
and I almost jumped back into bed as Jeff opened it.
The initial scare was followed by some relief—if he were
this close he couldn't have been overhearing me at the
switchboard, and if he were lurking just outside he would
have come in earlier.

He brought the local papers and seemed totally free of
suspicion. "How are you feeling?"

"Much better," I told him, and I was, although a bit
weak. "I feel starved, though. What time is it?"

He looked at his watch. "About seven thirty."

I got up, and found myself slightly dizzy. "Umph. Still
a little weak. They said it was all in the mind, though,
so I guess my mind decides what's important. What's
for dinner?"

He laughed, looking relieved. "Glad to see you more like yourself again. Look, there's no room service in this dump, and none of my instructions covered barring the doors. Parch is pretty convinced you could shout to the rooftops 'the aliens are coming!' and only get thrown in the asylum anyway. What say we make the most of tonight? Go down to a good restaurant, hit a casino, then get a good night's sleep."

I smiled. "That's the first bright spot I've had in weeks," I told him with total sincerity. "Just let me get dressed."

I dressed quickly, not only because I genuinely *was* anxious to get out but also because I feared that something would go wrong, that they'd call back and inquire about a telegram or something.

And it *was* a good night, although I was still feeling slightly weak and it didn't last very late. It was the first time since Seattle, so very long ago, that I'd been out in public, and I was a different person now even if in the same body. It was fun to be out *with* someone, to walk arm-in-arm down a casino-lit strip, to let go a little and hug him when he hit on the crap table. Being with him I felt very normal and very secure. I was still aware of the heads turning, the admiring glances, but it didn't bother me that night.

And, later, in the motel room, he held me when I wanted to be held and we kissed goodnight and I thought that he was probably the only man who had any understanding of me.

I wasn't falling in love with Jeff, and still felt no real sexual passion for him, but I liked him a lot, not just for being a nice person but for understanding. I didn't really know myself yet, or what I wanted or even could be, but I *did* know that Jeff had brought me, in the worst of circumstances, the closest I'd ever felt to belonging, to fitting in, to being a part of the human race, and I owed him for that.

It almost made me feel guilty that I had betrayed his kindness and trust in me with the telegram. Almost, but not quite. For looming behind Jeff was IMC, and Harry Parch, and I certainly felt the same about them.

I had taken the risk and done what I could, and I could do no more. It was out of my hands now. But I had some satisfaction in the wording of the message. Parch had been right—had I even mentioned "alien invaders" or "body switching" in my telegram it would have been tossed right in the circular file with the other nut cases. But I hadn't. I had lived in and around Washington too long to make that kind of mistake. I had offered instead the irresistible.

We had been taken to IMC in July; it was now February of the next year and things were still running according to routine. I'd long since finished with Dan Pauley; I had no idea where he was or even if he still was anyplace. I was now working with the computer techs on assembling a basic history and psychological profile of the Urulu and it was proving fascinating to me, although it would probably have driven most people nuts to go through all that minutiae for some little scrap here and there. Much of what I found confirmed the essentials of Pauley's own statements, although, I had to note, they had all been the most casual, friendly talkers any interrogator would want and yet they'd told precious little anybody wanted to know.

I also turned twenty in February, according to Dory— February 16. Dory remained in the technicians ranks, mostly by choice. She had never had much interest in some grandiose career or the joys of college learning; she was far more practical-minded than I was and found a hands-on job far more satisfying. She'd grown a little, and near the end of the year had begun the final stages of passage into puberty, the change into womanhood bringing out an innate beauty in her.

My telegram had been sent in late October, apparently to no avail. I'd lived in some fear of discovery for weeks after, but now my greater fear was that it had either not reached its intended party or had been disregarded by Calvert's column. All I could tell Dory and myself was that I had tried, done what I could, and it just hadn't been enough.

It was, therefore, a major surprise late in February when the whole of IMC was abuzz with the news: a big-shot congressman, Chairman of the House Intelligence Committee, Phillip Kelleam, was paying us a visit—and, word was, there would be at least one reporter with him.

The rumors were soon confirmed as we were commanded to attend little after-hours seminars by Parch's people on what to say and what not to say, who we could talk to and who we couldn't.

I had continued to see Jeff Overmeyer, although not romantically, on a social basis and got more details.

"Somehow, Calvert—that Washington columnist with spies in every department—got wind of IMC," he told me. "We don't know how, but, then again, it's a miracle something this big has managed to escape the public this long. He dug up enough supporting stuff to make a real stink and threatened to go public with it unless he got the whole story and could be convinced not to run it. That got Kelleam involved, since it's his ass as much as anybody's, and so they're orchestrating this little tour. All Parch wants is for nobody except hand-picked people to say more than polite nothings to them and leave them to him."

"He'll get that much," I noted. "After all, who wants to be the one that broke the rules who's still here with Parch after they leave? But I think you're blown now, Jeff. Even if Kelleam's in on this Calvert won't sit still no matter what bullshit he's fed. If he finds out the truth he'll splash it over the whole world; if he doesn't, he'll mount a massive attack on us as a wasteful extravagance."

Overmeyer just sighed. "No, I don't think so. You just don't *know*, Vicki, what we can now do."

He wouldn't go any further, but it worried me.

Kelleam turned out to look like everybody's favorite uncle; he was a twenty-four-year veteran of the House and one of its masters, in line, some said, for the Speaker's chair. I stared at him, going around, shaking hands like anybody here could vote for him, and being so much the saccharine politician that I knew he was anything but what he appeared. He was a damned smart and shrewd political manipulator, a power-lover with guts, and one of the few men who'd know all about IMC. As different as the two men appeared on the surface, if Harry Parch had a friend and soul-mate in this world it was almost certainly Phil Kelleam.

He brought an entourage, of course, mostly bright-looking young men and women, his aides and yes-men whose very souls he owned but who had dreams one day of being at the center of power themselves. How much *they* knew of IMC's true job was unknown, but, courts or no courts, I bet myself that every one of their phones were tapped, their every waking moment spied upon or monitored by somebody.

Calvert was by himself, nobody else allowed from his side. He looked much older than the little picture they always put with his column and not at all well, but his brown eyes darted everywhere and his expession showed that he was not here for any pleasure trip.

When Parch, Eisenstadt, and another man in a business suit whom I'd not come across before but who was, obviously, IMC's own chief of administration, Joe Parks, shook hands around with the party, it was Calvert who spoke up.

"I want to know the truth about this place," he snapped to Parch in a somewhat threatening tone. "You have a lot to account for, you know. The budget for a whole nonexistent nuclear aircraft carrier is here and the public has a right to know how you can float a ship in Nevada."

Parch didn't seem at all disturbed. "We'll show you

everything," he assured the columnist. "Answer any questions, anything you want. Even give you demonstrations. At the end, if you still think this place should see print at this time, we'll do nothing to stop you."

Calvert just nodded dubiously and walked to catch up with the Congressman. From my office I just watched the group fade down the long hall until they were gone.

Something definitely stunk to high heaven, though. The level of cover-up necessary to fool somebody like Calvert just hadn't been done at IMC, and Harry Parch had sounded a little *too* confident of himself. I began to worry a bit. Would they dare kill Calvert? I hoped not, not only because I'd feel like a murderer but also because it would mean a sense of power here beyond any in the country. But, no, I told myself, they wouldn't do it anyway. All you'd need to blow this place irrevocably would be to have Calvert die in the course of its investigation, even by the most accidental of causes.

I didn't see them again, but Dory did, twice, and what she saw made us both even more nervous.

"I saw Calvert twice," she told me. "Once on the same day you did, then again two days later when they were leaving. It was incredible, the change in him, Vicki. I swear to you that I heard him talking to Kelleam and Parch like old buddies and assuring him that he'd do everything in his power to keep the lid on! Calvert!"

I felt defeated. "You think this is all an act of his, then? That he's really with them."

"He wasn't with them, wasn't acting, when he came here," she responded ominously. "Oh, Vicki, I'm *really* scared now. I think they've done it—broken the roadblock wide open! I think they did what they told him they'd do—show him around, answer every question, and give him a demonstration. I think they demonstrated all right—on him!"

I was wrapping up my work in early March. They seemed quite pleased with it, despite my own estimation that it was full of holes in all the important places. We were winding down now, though, and I expected to find out in another few days what my next assignment would be.

I, therefore, wasn't all that surprised late one afternoon to get a summons to Parch's office. Technically I worked in his area, although far removed from his nastier jobs, and it would be from him or one of his administrative assistants that I would get my new assignment.

I was, however, surprised to find Dory there, and I got a very uneasy feeling. As I walked into that familiar office I noticed an immediate change. The secretaries and technicians were nowhere about, but present were several well-dressed men who could only be some of Parch's agents.

Parch himself looked grimly at us and gestured for me to take a seat. Still, his opening remark was very routine. "You've finished the master report?"

I nodded nervously. "It just needs to be correlated and printed out."

"That's good, that's fine," he responded. I glanced anxiously at Dory but she had the same nervous look I was feeling and her eyes and expression told me that she had no idea what this was about.

Parch leaned back in his office chair and sighed. "Ms. Gonser, Ms. Tomlinson. The time has come to discuss both your futures, I'm afraid. You've been most helpful to us in a number of ways, and I'd like to just pay you off, give you new identities, and be rid of you. Unfortunately, I cannot. You have also been a wee bit harmful, I'm afraid, and even if we could overlook or fix that part, neither of you are very trustworthy when it comes to making my job easier. I am charged with keeping this installation secure. I do not believe that this is possible were I to let you go, even if we could, somehow, erase the location of it from your minds."

"I don't know what you're talking about, Parch," I managed, my mouth feeling suddenly very dry.

He shook his head sadly. "Look, I'll not play games with you, nor can I spare the time in needless cat-and-mouse talks. We know you sent the telegram to Calvert. It was quite a good try, really. We had no idea at the time, but once his people got to poking and probing we managed to get into his files and discover the text of it, then compare it with Western Union. Although it was charged to a Washington law firm—your father's old one, I believe—the official file copy contained the number from which it was placed. That proved to be where, from its date, we already suspected—the Mirage Motel in Las Vegas, Nevada. It was not nice, Ms. Gonser, to abuse our hospitality like that."

He had me cold. There was really nothing to say. He turned to Dory. "As for you," he continued, "while we have few places totally monitored on a routine basis, since this place is so large, we did, because of your psychological profile, take extra precautions with you. During your initial medical exam here we placed a tiny micro-miniature transmitter under your skin. It ran down a week or so ago, finally, but we have a nice tape recording of your conversations with Ms. Gonser, particularly one just before she went for her abortion."

"You bastard," she muttered.

He shrugged off the insult. "Now, even with all that, I wouldn't normally be worried. But, as I said, we can't really remove IMC from your minds, not all the people, physical layout, you name it, unless we induced amnesia from the point of the final switch on the ferry. That I could do, but it wouldn't mean much to your futures and your life. It simply wouldn't be fair."

"Since when has something like fair play ever been a part of your behavior?" Dory snapped, and a little part of me cheered.

He sighed. "Look, I'm not the evil mastermind you think me, I assure you—for all the good it does. I do not make the final decisions, although discretion is left to me on how those decisions will be carried out. If it were strictly up to me, I would just let you continue until the time, here, when we know enough to go public and face down our threats. But it's come down to a matter of security. The Urulu were telling the truth, in one regard, at least. They are at war with another alien power and that war is reaching us more and more. Because we lack the defenses we cannot yet meet the threat. The security of IMC is important now first and foremost because either of those alien sides would destroy it in an instant and the warfare would become open and blatant. Millions of lives are at stake, I firmly believe—and in that condition, what can a few individuals count for? Not only the two of you, but me, anyone here, no matter how high and mighty."

"The land of the free and the home of the brave," Dory sneered.

Again he was surprisingly defensive. "Yes, it *is* ironic that we claim to be defending freedom and yet must resort to unfree methods. Still, free has a whole new meaning now. We're talking about the potential for the most absolute form of slavery—tyranny of the mind of every human being on earth by an alien power." He grew quite intense, and I began to think that, perhaps, he really *didn't* like all this. "I believe that what we are doing here will determine forever whether or not the human race can be free. I cannot, will not, allow personal feelings or considerations to jeopardize that sacred trust."

There was silence for a moment. Finally, feeling wooden and empty, I said, "So you're going to kill us, then."

"No, I'm not," he replied, sounding a little hurt. "First of all, both of you are already dead. The Indian girl is forever just plain missing, of course, but any records traceable to her original identity were removed totally. Fingerprints, footprints, you name it. They appear on no official record anywhere. You, Gonser, are dead and buried as you know. And as for the Tomlinsons, a bit of scouring morgues throughout the northwest turned up a decent candidate. You, Ms. Tomlinson, missed your train at Prince Rupert, decided to hitchhike, were in an accident and burned almost beyond recognition. You were identified by your personal effects, and are buried in Parklawn Cemetery, Winnipeg."

Dory started, and I was almost as surprised.

"Again, records were gotten to, but, this time, other data was substituted. Ours is a society of records, of bureaucracy. Both of you, as you currently are, are anomalies in the world today—people on whom not a single solitary record exists."

I felt sick, like I was going to throw up.

"However, this is the United States of America, not Soviet Russia or China or some two-bit dictatorship. We simply don't shoot and dump people, at least anywhere I'm in charge."

"Then you're going to imprison us here? Maybe for years?" Dory gasped, and, odd as it sounds, there was a note of hope within her. If we remained alive, there was always a future.

"We have no budget for such a thing, and no authority," Parch told us. "Besides, it would be controversial here and it would be such a waste. No, there is another way, a way that will make things as right as they can be, allowing you to live normal lives while keeping us secure and you removed as any possible threat. We have come a long way technically here, as you certainly have guessed by now. It was the only reason we could deal with your Mr. Calvert. Unfortunately, the remedy for him, as I said, is not possible with you. You're still not at peace with yourself anyway, Gonser, and you, Ms. Tomlinson, shouldn't be cooped up here, perhaps for years, unable to live any sort of life."

"You're going to make us into robots, slaves," Dory gasped, horrified.

"No, nothing like that. Consider it from my viewpoint. We can not continue as before. It's bad for you, and it presents a continual risk to us. We can't morally justify killing you. It would be almost as criminal to have you both wake up strangers with a nine-month gap in your memories, not to mention embarrassing things that are possible if you *did* decide to return home and convince people you're who you really are. To imprison you would be illegal and unconscionable. To process you like we did Mr. Calvert and a couple of Kelleam's aides would be impossible if we were to release you because we can't be that selective, and anything like that would open up one of the possible cans of worms I already mentioned. We can't simply turn you around to our point of view, either, since you have been here nine months, gotten to know a very large number of people, and such a personality change would be noticed, they'd put two and two together, and we'd get a holy stink from Eisenstadt's crowd."

"What, then?" I wanted to know, just wishing it was all over with.

"Dr. Eisenstadt and his top people are all in Washington for a conference," Parch replied. "We arranged it that way. The rest of his people who are not also *my* people are, interestingly, not working this evening. In the course of research, our people took the matrices of a huge number of people. Thousands, I'd say. They didn't know what was being done, of course, and the process isn't important. We were looking to see the differences, of course. To compare them. When it became clear that we would reach this point, my people started working on looking at those matrices, taking parts from various ones, literally creating *new* identity matrices, complete people who never lived."

"Violins," Dory mumbled.

Parch ignored her. "Each of you received quite detailed individual attention. We needed real people—that is, ones that *might* be—and we needed ways of life for each of you that would allow you to live normal, if obscure, lives, out of the mainstream as it were, where you wouldn't be likely to even be discovered by accident."

"A retired salesman from Akron and his homemaking wife," I sighed, resigned to almost anything now.

"Huh?"

"Like the people in bars and dance saloons, on vacation. The kind that go to Vegas on a four-day, three-night package holiday. The normal folks who live and die and nobody cares."

He looked at me a bit puzzled. Finally he said, "This is the best way, believe me. Best for you, too. No more sexual or identity hangups. No more learning how to walk in high heels. No more lusting after other women, either. I'm aware of its partial physiological basis, but it can be overridden. The brain can be fooled into almost anything."

"I'll bet," I said sourly. I was shaking slightly and I couldn't stop.

"You'll be real people," he went on. "You'll remember your pasts, you'll fit in where you're put comfortably, and you'll live your lives with not even a thought of us, a hint, a lingering memory."

"When are you going to do this to us?" I asked him.

The men in the back of the office stepped forward. "In a few minutes," he said. I felt a prick on my arm and turned with a jerk to see a man already holding a spent syringe. Dory had received the same treatment.

"Wha—" I managed.

"You'll be fully conscious," Parch assured us. "We need that. But we find this drug will make you much less inclined to argue and much more eager to cooperate. Just relax and let it take hold."

Already I could feel it working. A strange numbness came over me, as if my whole body were going to sleep. My eyelids grew heavy and finally closed, my mouth became dry, my tongue felt thick and limp, and I struggled unsuccessfully as my thoughts seemed, also, to go to sleep. And yet, as Parch said, I was somehow fully conscious, a lump of clay.

"Open your eyes," Parch said gently, and I stirred

slightly and did so. "I'm your friend," he told me. "I'm the only really good friend you have."

Yes, I knew him now. He was my friend. My very *best* friend.

"You trust me," he continued in that same soothing tone. "You know I won't do anything to hurt you. I want to help you. I want only good things for you. You'd trust me with your life, wouldn't you?"

I nodded, both awake and not awake. He was my very best friend and I trusted him with my life.

"You'll do anything I tell you to do, won't you?" he prodded. "Just *anything.*"

I nodded eagerly. I'd sure do anything at all he asked me to do. He was my very best friend and I trusted him.

"Now, get up from the chair and go with these nice men. They are your friends, too, and mine. Go with them to where they take you and do what they ask. You *want* to go, don't you?"

I smiled, nodded, and got up. Such nice men. Friends of my very best friend. I trusted him so I trusted them, too. I'd go with them anyplace they wanted and do just what they said.

One of them took my hand. "Let's go," he said, and we walked out of the office. Behind me I could hear Harry Parch speaking to Dory, but it just didn't concern me and registered not a bit.

They seated us in the large chairs on the raised, green-carpeted area of the lab center. A tiny part of me seemed to know what was going on and tried to fight against the drug, but it was hopeless.

Seated where I was, I could see part of the lower level. The consoles were all on, with thousands of multicolored switches thrown, some blinking, some changing colors, while CRT screens showed everything from odd patterns to rows upon rows of print. Technicians sat at the different consoles, many with headsets, fiddling with dials, controls, and keyboards.

A white-clad technician came up to me, fixing straps around my arms, legs, and below my breasts, securing me in one position in the chair. Then she reached behind me, there was a clicking sound, and the large helmet-like device came down over my head. The technician guided it with one hand while fixing my hair in a certain way for ease of the probes, I suppose.

Parch came into the room and looked around, then nodded. He went over to one of the technicians.

"Gonser first," he told the man at the screen. "You set up?"

"All systems normal," the man responded, then, into his headset, "Loud cubes. Memory insertion modules six through eight. On my mark. Now."

The screen flickered. Idly I thought, *he isn't even looking at me. He has his back to me.* It was an independent thought and I tried to grab onto it, cling to it, but I failed. I steeled myself for what might come next, marshalling as much will as I could. It wasn't going to work. Somehow, they were going to blow it. Somehow, I was still going to be me, that little part of myself not drugged cried out.

"Initial I.M. sequence, probes out, Chair One," the chief technician said, and suddenly I was aware of a tremendous vibration from the middle of my forehead up and all around me. The humming sound was quite uncomfortable.

"Matrix probes go, report on probe lock."

My whole head started to feel funny, like millions of tiny needles were being stuck in it. Actually there was nothing physical at all; there would not be until one of the little light probes found what it was looking for.

The humming subsided, to my relief, and so did the odd, ticklish sensation of the probes.

"Probe lock on," a voice from one of the other consoles said crisply.

"Probe lock, aye," the chief responded. "Prepare primary sequencing."

"Prepared. Locked on."

"Stage one. Begin manual stimulus."

The woman who had strapped me in and lowered and adjusted the helmet now spoke to me.

"What is your name?" she asked. "You needn't respond to these. Just relax. Do not answer the questions."

I struggled against the drug, against everything, but it was no use. Everytime she asked a question the answer would always come to mind, the same way it was impossible not to think of the word "hippopotamus" once you'd been told not to think of it.

"Where were you born? Sex? Mother and father?"

The questions went on and on, like a job questionnaire you didn't have to fill out, only read. The questions, however, covered a wide range of my personal life and experiences, my attitudes, quite a bit more than the basics with which they'd started. It was frustrating to realize what they were doing—locating holographic keys, master bits of cross-referenced material which the computer itself could trace from there. There was no sensation.

"We've got sequencing!" Somebody shouted, and the woman stopped asking me questions and stepped back. I recalled Stuart's explanation and knew what they were doing now. The computer had located enough key pieces of information that it was now asking the questions itself, asking them directly of my brain at a speed so fast my consciousness wasn't even aware of it. I have no idea how it works, but I have no doubts about it.

It seemed to go on forever. Finally a buzzer sounded somewhere and the chief technician, still huddled over his console, nodded.

"Initial sequencing completed. Begin recording on one, two, and three," he ordered. "Read out on my mark . . . now!"

Again there was no sensation, but there wouldn't be. The brain had no senses of its own, and this was a read-out, a copy of what was there, not anything actually being done to it.

For the slowness of the first stage, this one seemed to be over before I knew it. Again the buzzer sounded.

"Recording complete. Analysis. Run two-six-five."

"Running."

"Analysis completed."

"Run comparator with new I.M. on 4-5-6."

"Running . . . Completed. Comparator confirmed. Some slight adjustment in levels required. Got it. Matched. Go."

"Very good," the chief technician said. "Prepare for manual check."

"Manual check ready, aye. All systems stable and normal."

"Begin manual check."

Again the woman technician next to me spoke. "What is your name?" she asked.

"Victor Leigh Gonser," I responded aloud, and with it I felt some triumph. The drug was wearing off! I felt sure of it! If I could just hold on I could break this control!

"What is your name?" she asked again.

"Misty Ann Carpenter," I replied, feeling more confident now. It wasn't working!

"How old are you?"

"Thirty-six," I responded.

"How old again?"

"Twenty—just."

"What sex were you born, Misty?"

"Male."

"What sex?"

"Female." Dumb questions. I was beginning to relax. They couldn't do anything to me! Maybe it was the double switch, but I was sure now I was immune.

"And where were you born?"

"Alexandria, Virginia."

"Where?"

"Cedar Point, Oregon." I was feeling relaxed now, the tension easing out of me. It wasn't going to work. Sooner or later they'd realize that. I didn't know what Parch would do then but at least I would still be me.

"We've got it," a technician called. "No problem. Run program."

"Running."

Yes, I was still me. I was still Misty Ann Carpenter, twenty, female, from Cedar Point, Oregon, and I damned well was gonna stay that way.

Chapter Nine

I woke up slowly, as if from a very deep sleep. For a minute I didn't know who or where I was, but it all came back to me as I opened my eyes and looked out the large window of the Greyhound bus.

Ain't it funny how things go, I thought, and, for a moment, I just lay there, leaned back in the seat, and remembered.

Cedar Point was a small logging town. Just that. Daddy was a logger, and his Daddy'd been one, too. There weren't nothin' else to do. Mama was right pretty, but she didn't have much schoolin' and they got hitched when she was just sixteen. Three of us kids, me the only girl, later they closed the logging. Made a park outta it. Daddy, he didn't have nothin' and no place to go, so he started drinkin' hard. When he was drunk he was mean, and when he was mean he beat us, Momma hardest of all, and he was drunk more and more of the time. I remember him, all big and fierce and mean, with the blaze of drink in his eyes.

Mama, she was so pretty even after that, but she cried

a lot and tried to bring us up proper, sendin' us t'church Sundays and doin' what she could on the welfare and the food stamps. 'Cept Daddy kept gettin' 'em and tradin' for booze. One day he didn't come home at all, and they come and tole us he was in jail for killin' a man in a drunk fight. Things was better after that, but Mama she just couldn't get ahold of us.

Me 'specially. I kinda felt bad about it now, but what's done is done, as Mama us'ta say. In my teens I skipped school mor'n I was in it. It was dull and I never was too good at that readin' and writin' stuff, anyway. The boys, now, that's what I was good at. I finally just quit school, said the hell with it. Why go? I was just gonna finally find the right boy, get married, and have my own mess of babies. Didn't need school for that.

That's how I'd finally got in with Jeremy Stukes. He was a big hunk of muscle, real strong, and the biggest prick I ever did see. I fell for him like a ton of bricks, and, afore I knew it, I was listenin' to his big dreams about goin' to the big city and makin' a pile. I was seventeen then and the most I'd been from Cedar Point was Klamath Falls, once, with Mama when she had trouble with the food stamps.

Jeremy, he and me made plans, and one night we got the big escape. I snuck out with a bag, and he picked me up in this real big, fancy car. I was so took I never even asked whose it was. Turned out it was stole, damn him. A cop picked us up goin' south and we beat him out, all right, but by then I was both scared and mad as hell at him. I started tellin' him what I thought of him and, 'fore I knowed it, he'd throwed me outta that car and drove off, leavin' me there in the middle of nowhere with a bag and a couple of bucks.

Well, I was plenty scared, sure, but I wasn't gonna go home, either. For all I knew they might 'a thought *I* stole the car, and, besides, wasn't anything to go back to anyways. So I just started hitchin'—found it was real easy. Hell, I always knew I was pretty and stuck out in all the right places, so I didn't have much problem.

One ride was this nice salesman, and I needed a shower and he was *real* friendly, so we stayed overnight in a motel together. I knew what he had in mind, but I kinda needed it myself, and the only real surprise was that he give me twenty dollars when he let me off. I hadn't really thought of it before, but suddenly I saw there was lots of lonely men out there and somebody like me, well, she could maybe help 'em out and make some bucks at the same time.

I finally made Sacramento, but I got busted kinda quick there and it scared me. They couldn't tell how old I was, though, and they weren't real tough, just told me I hadta get outa town right fast. This one vice cop was real friendly, and him and me made it together, and he told me I should go to Nevada, where what I was best at wasn't a crime.

So I worked the roads up to Reno, only to find that it was legal everyplace *but* Reno and Vegas. Still, I had no place to go and nothin' else to do, and the money was good enough that I managed to pay the fines. Got to be a regular down at vice. Funny, though, cops in vice ain't like real cops. I kinda think they don't like some of the laws they carry out. Anyways, this one cop introduces me to this other guy he knows and, last week, I get an offer from this place called Cougar Lodge. This guy tells me I can get four hundred a week free and clear plus room, board, clothes, you name it, by turnin' one trick a day, minimum, more if I wanted. All nice an' legal.

After almost two years on the streets, makin' it for peanuts as a free-lance, I knew I'd either hav'ta hook up with one of the pimps in town or I'd finally get tossed in the joint for real, not just do a few thirty-day stretches in County Jail like usual. My cop friend told me this Cougar Lodge was a high-class house, run right and with state exams and stuff like that. I'd already had to use the free clinic a few times, for one abortion and lots of times for VD checks, and while I was clean still I knew it wouldn't last. Not with the kinda Johns I was gettin'. So I tole the guy O.K., I'd try it, and he took me to his own Doc—a fancy one—and I came out clean. And then I got this bus ticket, and here I was, goin' south to who knew what? Who cared, either?

"Stateline, Nevada casinos," the driver called out, and pulled in. I looked around. So this was Tahoe, I thought. Looked like the Reno Strip in the Oregon mountains.

I got off and found it was real cold. I didn't expect that, although I had my heavy jacket on. Reno was cold, but we'd been goin' *south*, for Christ's sake!

The same guy I'd met in Reno was there to meet me, all bundled up, and he got my bag, real gentleman-like, and we walked to his car. It was somethin' else, I'll say. A big, fancy Mercedes all shiny and new. Maybe, Misty old girl, you got hooked up right. Maybe you finally got the breaks.

His name was Al Jordan, a little, fat guy about fifty or so puffin' a big fat cigar. He was the manager, he told me, and went over the terms once more. I reminded myself that I was twenty-one, at least to him, since at twenty I was still too young for the legal stuff, but I'd been lyin' about my age for a while now.

The place was real beautiful, up in the mountains and all. Kind of a winter resort, with snow and everything. I didn't mind, since Cedar Point was sure colder'n this sometimes and Reno wasn't exactly Miami Beach in February.

The place looked like a big old hotel, which I guess it was once. It was real pretty inside, too, with a big hall, blazin' fireplace, bear rug, all that. But I really knew I was in the big time when I saw that they took all the big credit cards. That was a giggle. Wonder what they put on the little slips?

I got introduced to the staff by Al, then we went into his big, fancy office and he gave me a bunch of forms. I looked at 'em but had a little trouble readin' 'em, and he helped me. They was the damndest things. Tax withholding forms, social security, shit like that. I really started feelin' like I'd found a home.

"You'll work a six day week, with Mondays off," Al told me. "But you'll get six days around your period off, and you can go anywhere you want, stay here, go into Tahoe, whatever. You're paid once a month, at the beginning of your break, into a bank account in your name—that's one of the forms there, the yellow one. You can take as much out as you want any time at the desk, or let it stay. It'll be in the bank, making money for you, until you want to use it."

That sounded fine to me.

I had my own big room, with bathroom, and big, round bed. Al let me decorate it the way I wanted, on the Lodge, and I had a lot of fun doin' that. We also went on a shoppin' trip to Tahoe, with me pickin' up a buncha really sexy clothes and all.

The other girls were real pretty, too. Some were real smart, some came from the streets like me, but all looked *gorgeous*. I never got along much with other girls—men was my style—but they was nice enough as a bunch and we each had our own room and place.

Al brought this one guy to me who was a beauty expert, they said, and I really got the works. After he was through I almost didn't know myself, and when I got into my workin' outfit I decided I was at least as sexy as the other girls.

The workin' outfit was real high heels, panty hose with black mesh, and a kinda bikini, plus nice, long earrings, a sexy hairdo done for us by a guy who came through a lot, cosmetics, and the like. We was told to let our hair grow long, keep our fingernails long and them and toenails painted, and all that.

When a customer—we was told never to say trick or John—came in, we kinda paraded in the lobby struttin' our stuff and he picked whichever of us he wanted.

There was some bad feelin' among some of the other girls against the ones that got picked most often, but as I got picked a lot I didn't mind. Let 'em eat their hearts out.

The guys weren't real kinky types, either. Oh, a couple, but mostly those types were weeded out. We serviced the best in the West, Al always said—salesmen, big shots, show-biz people (sometimes even makin' house calls down to town for them types). Some were into bondage and S&M, which was cool, as long as they didn't hurt *me*. Al knew which way we all bent and he tried to steer the customers to the right girls when he thought he should. He seldom made mistakes.

I never liked the S&M types, and so I never got 'em. Oh, once, a goof, but I put that straight. Bondage, though, I didn't mind, and all the other kinky stuff, the role-playing and other games, that sort of thing. Some of the guys got off just from the mirrors I had all around, includin' on the ceiling.

I told myself every day when I woke up, around two or so, that I had found paradise, maybe for a lot of years. Carole, for example, was thirty-seven, looked younger, and still goin' strong. I could do it forever. I made a lot of lonely guys happy, gave high-class sex to guys who hardly knew how to fuck, and I couldn't get enough. I really liked the ones on power-trips, though. I was so submissive bondage was just an extra turn-on, and I loved it. I couldn't get enough.

The rest of the time I just stayed home, mostly, watchin' TV and shit like that, including the porn movie channel to get ideas. Every once in a while I'd go down to Tahoe, 'specially after the weather got warm and the ski bums cleared out, to swim a little in the pools of the big hotels, gamble some, and, once in a while, get picked up and treated for a night, sometimes for a freebie but mostly not. I spent some dough, though, not so much on that—I found I never really had to buy a meal—but on pretty clothes, jewelry, that sort of thing.

Hell, I had nothin' else to spend it on, and I could die young or somethin' and what good would it do me? At the end of a year I got a big raise, too, so it kept buildin' up. I bought mink and jewels and fancy, sexy clothes and still had money in the bank, even after the government took out its cut.

Over that first year, though, a real funny thing happened. It was so graduallike I didn't even think about it 'cept when buyin' clothes, but here I was, a growed woman, and I outgrew my bra!! Got thinner at the waist, too. Changed a bit. My 35-24-35, which wasn't bad, became a 42-23-36, which was real weird at my age. I was always sexy, but I started bein' almost always horny, even always dreamin' of sex. I thought maybe Al was puttin' somethin' in the the food, but even he and the other girls noticed it and said somethin' after a while. I never really tried to figure it out, but while it was better than ever for business the big boobs sometimes made my back hurt and I started findin' myself rubbing my workin' parts just sittin' around. It was like I was becomin' an *animal* or somethin', and it worried me a little. I told Al, but he just said this life was what God had made me for and now that I'd found it I'd just turned completely on. "All your juices are flowing full-tilt," he said.

But it *was* a change. My voice was a little lower and all-the-time super-sexy without me even havin' to shift gears, and I knew my moves were all super-sexy, animallike. But as time went on I worried less and less about it. I got lots of customers every day, and a lot of repeat business, and a couple of the big show-biz stars started wantin' me only. Pretty soon I stopped worryin' about things, or even thinkin' much about anything except fucking and pleasing men and getting as many as I could.

Finally, after I'd been at the Lodge a long while, one of Al's friends, Joe Samuels, who ran a fancy strip club in town, asked me if I'd ever thought about doin' that. I told him I had—I'd watched them fancy strippers and really liked the idea of takin' it all off while all them men watched.

It turned out that Al owned part of the Copa Club and didn't mind. He was such a sweet guy. I got up a little early and went to school again, but this was a different kind of school. A stripper's school—only they said "exotic dancer" or some such shit. There was a lot more to learn than I figured. Not just the dances, the moves, but the timing. When to turn, when to drop this or that, all that.

So I started stripping for the Copa Club part of the time and as I got to be more of a draw I got less and less of the walk-ins at the Cougar, stayin' only with my old regulars and the really big shots.

I loved stripping almost as much as fucking, and there was no reason not to do both. I was goin' up in the world I loved, and I was havin' a ball at it.

I got recognized on the street, not just for bein' sexy but for bein' a big shot, a *celebrity.* I got a rush just lookin' at the Copa Club's big sign now, with a picture of me on it and just one word, "MISTY." All capitals like that. I didn't like to read and never read much of anything but that one sign I read over and over.

I got a driver's license—I don't think the testing guy was payin' any mind at all to how I was doin'—and credit cards and a little sports car in a fancy pink shade.

Pretty soon Joe was gonna open a new, bigger Copa Club in Vegas, and he and Al wanted me to go down there. I liked it in Tahoe, but Vegas was big time, and I couldn't say no. Besides, it was warm, even in the winter.

I didn't want to leave Al, and it was kinda a tearful goodbye, but I knew I hadta go. I went down a couple weeks early to get settled in and look around my new home town.

It was Reno and Tahoe all rolled into one. I had no troubles there, even if I wasn't really known yet—I knew I'd own this town, at least the part of it I wanted, real quick. I stayed at the Sahara while lookin' for my own place and I had a lot of fun cruisin' the strip, tryin' to have a good time each night without liftin' a finger or payin' a dime.

My third night in town, I met this nice-looking young guy, said his name was Jeff something-or-other, and we went out on the town and had a real good time, even if we did lose at the tables. After, we went up to my room at the Sahara and, well, one thing led to another, and I was gettin' all set, when I turned my back on him for something or other and felt a sharp sting right in my ass. I let out a sharp "Ow!" and started to turn around, but the whole world just blacked out.

Chapter Ten

"Run program!"

Again there was no sensation, no idea that anything was going on, but funny things, lots of big words and memories and all sorts of stuff, rushed back into my head.

An elderly man who looked like Einstein, only fatter and older, stepped up to me. "How do you feel?" he asked gently in a soft accent that was central European, I guessed. I seemed to know him from somewhere, and I struggled to recall.

"Stuart," I managed.

He smiled. "Excellent! You know me. Now—who are you?"

I tried to think. Who? It was all so mixed up. "Mis-ty Vic-tor Gon-ser Carpen-ter," I managed.

"Which is it?" he prodded. "Which one are you?"

I tried to think for a minute, sort things out in my head, and they wouldn't quite come together. It upset me, not knowing, not being able to put it all together.

I tried to think. I remembered Misty Ann Carpenter

and her life perfectly. I *was* Misty Carpenter and it *was* my life. On the other hand, I was also Victor Leigh Gonser, male, mid-thirties, somehow in the body of Dory Tomlinson. I tried to look at my body, feel my body. It was Dory's body, yes, but it was also *my* body. Misty's body, Vicki's body. It felt both natural and odd.

"I—I'm both," I said in wonder.

Eisenstadt nodded again. "Good. Very good to come so far so fast. I think that as you go on the two parts of you vill more and more come together. You vill be a new person, not Victor, not Vicki, not Misty, but a blend of all three. I think that is all ve can hope for, and I think it might just be for the best."

He signalled and the apparatus was lifted from me. He offered his arm and I got up from that chair, that damnable chair, and unsteadily followed him back into his office. He gestured for me to sit down, then poured a little brandy for me which I gulped greedily.

"Do you know how long it's been?" he asked gently.

I shook my head, still trying to get a grip on myself. "Long, I think. The only attention I've paid to time recently was when to take the yellow pills and when to take the green ones."

He chuckled, then grew suddenly serious. "It's been more than three years."

That stunned me. Three *years!* I was twenty-three now, then, and Dory would be almost seventeen. . . . That brought up a thought. "Dory?"

He turned and gestured behind me, and I recognized an older Jeff Overmeyer enter with a strange, dark young woman. She was a tiny woman, not just in height but she seemed so small and fragile, with dark reddish-brown skin, wide, flashing eyes that looked almost coal black, and long, almost blue-black hair. But she was extremely attractive, narrow-waisted, small-boned yet somehow with the toughness of leather about her. Her face was a classical Amerind beauty's, with high cheek-bones and the look of the exotic, almost mystical, about her. She wore tight, faded jeans and an old T-shirt with some Indian design, showing small but firm breasts beneath. A faded pair of cowboy boots seemed perfectly in place on her.

"Dory?" I gasped.

She just stood there a moment, staring at me, wide-eyed. "Vicki?" she responded, unbelievingly. "Is that *really* you?"

I got up, she ran to me, and we hugged and held each other close. I found that I was crying, and, looking at her, I saw that she was, too.

I was conscious of how different I now appeared to her, and felt a little odd about it. We finally let go, and Eisenstadt offered her another chair. She just sat there for a moment, staring at me.

The scientist looked past us. "Jeff! You might as well come on in, too." The agent came over and took another seat, facing us. He looked older, I thought, but still the same. Only Stuart never changes, it seemed.

"I can't believe it!" Dory said in an amazed tone. "What did they *do* to you? You shouldn't look all that different after three years."

"I can explain that," Overmeyer said. "Parch arranged with a man named Al Jordan, who runs a high-class sex palace up in Tahoe, to take on a new recruit. Jordan has some ties to organized crime, and was nailed a number of years back, but never spent any time in jail. Instead, he does favors for the U.S. on occasion, from sexual blackmail to taking on people like Vicki here—or should I still call you Vicki? It doesn't seem the same any more."

My mind was reeling from all this. Al a Parch man? It didn't seem possible! I felt somehow betrayed and used. Still, Jeff's question deserved an answer. Which one was I?

"Make it Misty," I told him. "I've been her for a long time now, and it's the only real identity I have. It seems—*right*. I dunno."

"O.K., Misty. Anyway, knowing where you were going, they fiddled with some areas of your brain. Doc? You know more than me about that."

He nodded. "Yes, they changed the orders to parts of your body. Increased hormone production, that sort of thing. It's wery complicated to explain, but easy to do. Basically, they adapted your physical body perfectly to your, er, occupation, in the same way they might increase steroid production in a bricklayer to develop bigger muscles. They overrode the genetic instructions—but while it is permanent it is not inheritable."

I was shocked, but also oddly relieved to find the changes in me explained. Still, I said, "A tailor-made *nymphomaniac?*"

He shrugged apologetically. "That is the potential of this process, I fear. Tailor-made anything. That is vy ve had to find you both and get you back now. They are to the point vere they are starting to process the staff here, actually *inwiting* big shot politicians to come in, that sort of thing. They are out of control. Acting now vas a big risk, but acting later may have been impossible."

Overmeyer nodded. "I'm due next week. Oh, not for processing, not officially. Just having my matrix taken, they say. But I know better. I've seen the people they've been processing lately and it's scary."

"Wait a minute! Let me get my breath and bearings!" I protested. "We—we *do* have some time, don't we?"

"A little," Stuart replied. "I took a leaf from Herr Parch's own book. Only their routine duty staff is on right now—and I have some of my people at key stations. Ve are not being monitored here, and the big vuns in Security, like Parch, are all back East until tomorrow."

I relaxed a little. I had to trust these two men, since I knew so little myself about this labyrinthine place.

Labyrinthine, I thought idly. Misty wouldn't even be able to *think* of the word, let alone pronounce it.

I looked at Dory. "What—where did they send you?" I wanted to know. "Speaking of changes—you're some little sexy bomb yourself. If I'd known I was gonna grow up to be that I wouldn't have changed bodies."

She laughed a little. "It is hard on me, too," she replied. "But, for the last few years, I've been growing up on an Indian reservation in northeast Arizona. A school for Indian orphans. Oh, they knew I wasn't Navaho, but they finally sort of accepted me. While you were having all that fun, I was going through high school again—or a poor excuse for one. It's terrible what's been done to the Indian, and they're such good people. I wasn't much of a student anyway. All I knew was I'd finally get married to some buck and we'd live in some hovel out in the wilds and have babies and try and manage."

I nodded, seeing the pattern of Parch's "placement" concept. "You sound different, you know," I told her. "Sort of an accent there."

She nodded. "They programmed me with Navaho—a real bitch of a language, by the way—and Corho, which is a northwest language so it'd seem right, but not much English. I was supposed to be a half-breed by their standards—half Navaho, half Corho. A good part of me, maybe proportionately more of me than you considering our ages, is Delores Eagle Feather, and everything I say is sort of filtered through Navaho. I find I think in Navaho, mostly, where there are word equivalents, but my whole English and French vocabulary is there for the asking."

"So are you Dory—or Delores?" I asked.

She screwed up her face a little. "I never liked Delores much, although, like you, it's the only legal identity I've got. I'm going to go back to Dory, I think. It's gonna be harder getting used to you as the old Vicki, though. You sure don't look like I remember."

"I'm not the old Vicki," I told her. "But I don't know who I am yet, either."

"Both of you have some adjusting to do," Stuart said, "and it vill take some time. It vill come gradual, not in one *woosh*. I had the option of restoring you vere you left off or just feeding your old matrix back in on top the new, and I decided it vas best to do the latter. You should know your whole life, and, particularly in your case, Vic—Misty, the new parts of you are better equipped to handle that body of yours. I could erase the new encoding for the genetic instruction override, but it vouldn't be a service. Your body vould be out of balance. It vould cause fat, and your enlarged boobs they vouldn't shrink, just kind of deflate and sag. Better ve keep both of you in at this stage."

Dory nodded. "I prefer it that way anyway. I'm not the same person I was when I left here, but I think I'm the better for it in some ways. I feel more Indian now, and that's good, not only because of what I now am but also because, for all the terrible life most Indians have, they still are a great people. I learned a lot from them, and I'll always be a part of them."

I looked at Stuart. "You must have had more of a reason than this to bring us back now. Where do we go from here?"

He looked at us seriously. "Listen, the both of you. A lot has happened in the past three years. For vun thing, obviously, ve can do anything they can do and at least as vell. Parch, and the people over Parch, are mad vith power. If they aren't stopped, I don't know vere it vill lead. I fear that I, too, might be put under my little babies out there after a vile. Eventually—vell, the whole country? The vorld?"

"But there's an equal threat," Overmeyer put in. "This Association, or whatever, is on the march. It's winning. You can't really see 'em, just smell 'em, in a nasty way. Last month the four largest religious cult organizations, different as night and day, all merged into one huge body. Their followers can't be deprogrammed by anybody short of IMC. Their combined assets are in the *billions*, their followers fanatical and growing, and they're everywhere, not just the U.S."

I frowned. "But most of the world is communist. That wouldn't work there—unless you're suggesting a war."

He shook his head. "Not a war between us and the communists, no. But they're working there, too. A whole new Chinese philosophical group has arisen, cultlike, and has gathered powerful friends in Peking. It appeals to the ideals of communism and argues their present attainability. The Soviets will probably be the hardest nut to crack, but even there we see similar forces at work. They're patient, this Association. I think they'd be willing to simply grow up into powerful positions in the party until they *were* the leadership. Once in charge of even a single Soviet Republic, their work efficiency, dedication, and production would propel their leaders to the top in Moscow—and in that kind of society people can be ordered to be processed."

I shook my head, a feeling of hopelessness coming into me. How much nicer, more comfortable, to be Misty Carpenter, to not worry about things like this or even be able to conceive of them in her little world.

"What can we do?" I asked.

"Ve can do the only thing possible," Stuart responded. "Ve can take the biggest gamble in all of human history. Listen, you remember long, long ago, interviewing the alien Pauley?"

I nodded.

"Vell, remember vat he said? That the Urulu vould save us if they could be convinced ve vere vorth saving?"

I strained to remember. It seemed a long time and another life ago. Still, I nodded. "Go on."

"Vic—Misty, look, ve have talked about it and ve think now that it may be our only hope. Ve must contact the Urulu, somehow conwince them that ve are vorth redemption, and get them to come in. To destroy IMC and face down this Association before it is too late."

My old conversation came back to me now, and I was

dubious. "But he said there was a chance they'd just decide we were infested and destroy the entire planet."

"Misty, the planet's already *being* destroyed," Overmeyer put in. "Weren't you listening? Ten years, twenty, and you might neither recognize nor want to *be* human on this planet, if that word has any long-term meaning. IMC is making the enemy's task easier here, although you can't convince them of it. The world isn't going to collapse tonight, or tomorrow, or next year, but it's rapidly reaching the point of no return, when they'll be in such control that this sort of plan will be impossible. The Urulu have to see us humans the way we are, not the way we'll be remade. Dr. Eisenstadt and the rest of us who are sick at the way things are going are convinced that we must make our move now."

"Which brings us back to what we have to do with this," Dory responded. "Why us?"

"I vould like to say it's because I love the both of you, vich I do, but it goes deeper than that. This fellow Pauley, he was the most reasonable of the vuns they caught. The most *human*, you might say. He'd lived vith us a long time and understood us a bit better. Also, according to your own reports, he seemed to feel some sort of guilty conscience, particularly around you. Ve think he is our only hope. Ve intend to free him—and, vunce ve do, you may be the only hold on him ve have."

Dory looked dubious. "I don't like it. I can still remember the absolute *contempt* that woman, that alien, on the ferryboat had for us. I can't imagine that they'd be any better than the enemy."

Overmeyer looked at her. "They are because they *have* to be—don't you see that, Dory? If they're no better, then we're already lost. It's a gamble, sure. Lots of things could go wrong. They might be as bad as the others—they can't be any worse. They might not listen. Pauley might just say to hell with us and leave. They might blow us all up. But *what is the alternative?*"

She didn't like the idea despite the arguments, that

was clear, but she could only shrug. "I'm just along for the ride."

"Not qvite," Stuart told her. "There vere several reasons for taking the added risk of bringing you back, all carefully vorked out and thought out. For vun thing, if Pauley *does* feel real guilt about—Misty—then you are a double dose, and a reminder to him. She will also need somevun to help and support her. It is a big burden to carry alone. And, of course, you are more practical than she—sorry, my lady, but it's true. *You* came up vit the plan for the newspaperman, yes? *You* had better sources of information within IMC than did Vicki, who vas in a much higher place. You complement each other. You are a better team than either alone. You see?"

I was a little put out by Stuart's assessment of me, but the more I thought of it the more I had to agree, particularly now. I was being raised from the dead, as it were, and entrusted with the fate of the whole human race, the heroine of a bad thriller that just happened to be so damnably *true*, and I needed somebody badly.

"How do we begin?" I asked them.

"First we talk with Pauley," Overmeyer said.

"He's *here*?"

He nodded. "Always has been, on a special security level with the few others we have. It's computer-monitored and watched, but we have the computer here, and if we can feed false data into brains it's no trick at all to feed false data into security pictures, sound monitors, and the like. Once we spring him, we arrange the computer so you walk right out of here. It's the wonderful thing about relying on computerized security systems—they only work if the programmer's honest. We've had time to prepare this, Misty." He reached in his pocket, pulled out several cards and handed them to us. I recognized them at once—the same credit card-like security keys as before. "Your voice codes we'll give you in a few minutes, and we'll arrange for instructions to reach the elevator guards ahead of time. Isn't bureaucracy wonderful? As much as it obscures and slows, it also makes things painfully simple—if you understand it, and if you get the paperwork right. You will be able to leave—but once you're in that parking lot upstairs you're on your own."

"You're not gonna be able to keep this from Parch for long," Dory pointed out. "Even if we get out, he'll know when he gets back."

Stuart nodded. "Yes, but ve vill give him a little something to puzzle over first. It is time ve vill buy, no matter how little. An hour, a day, can make the difference."

I looked down at myself. "Some getaway," I commented. "Super low-cut slit, sparkling green evening dress, high heels . . . I'm really going to be inconspicuous."

"You couldn't be inconspicuous anywhere," Jeff noted. I smiled sweetly at him. How different it would be for the two of us now, I thought wistfully.

I looked over at Dory. "Well? What do you think now?"

She smiled and shook her head in wonder. "God! You're so *sexy!* I can't believe it!" Then she turned back to the two men.

"Let's do it," she said.

Chapter Eleven

Stuart and Jeff left us to prepare our going away party. I felt uneasy about it all, but, as Jeff had said, there really wasn't any choice in the matter. The alternative was that Parch or this Association or both would take over, remaking us into happy little robots. I only hoped that the two of them were up to matching Parch trick for trick; otherwise, I'd still open Joe's new joint in Vegas and Dory would be opening a beads and trinkets stand on U.S. 89.

The trouble was, a part of me wanted nothing to do with it all. I had what I really wanted now, popularity, adulation, fun. . . . It didn't seem fair, somehow, to wrench me back and load the world on my shoulders.

"Three years," I said to Dory. "It doesn't seem possible. All that time, such a different life."

She nodded. "Out of curiosity, why the long peroxide curls? I always thought my fluffy auburn hair was real pretty."

"It was and is," I told her. "But it's—professional.

The big body, big boob look seems to require a blond. Look at all your past sex symbols."

She sighed. "I suppose so. I'll tell you, though, that I would not have recognized you. I still can't really believe it. You've changed so much. . . . Inside as well as out. That sultry voice, those moves. I can hardly wait to see you eat a banana. They said you were a high class prostitute. Was that true?"

I nodded. "It's not nearly as bad as it sounds. Lately I'd moved up into stripping. I was going to headline a new club in Vegas. Dory, this may sound funny, but I *like* my new self. If—*when* we get out of this, I'll go back to it. Still, speaking of changes—you're a small package of dynamite yourself. You really grew up with the right stuff—again. But you seem a little more thoughtful, more reflective, more comfortable with yourself."

"Maybe some of this did us a favor. The blend of new and old made us new people, but whole ones."

Whole people. I liked that idea. Victor Gonser had never been a whole person; he was all act, introspection, aloof from the humanity he craved to join, but could not. Vicki Gonser, too, had been trapped in a nasty transsexual web, out of place and time. Misty Carpenter, the original, had been shallow, dumb, totally self-centered and egotistical, a hollow person, somehow. Parch's idea of what women should be—beautiful, sexy, seductive, submissive, and without a brain in their heads.

Dory, too, had been trapped in her old body, cut off from the society she wanted to be a part of even more cruelly than Victor had been; sexy, attractive, bright, and lesbian, not confident of herself, her future, her place in society, facing a new kind of life she didn't really want but couldn't avoid. I looked at her now with a great deal of affection, and felt a few unbidden tears rise inside me. Whole people.

I suddenly reached out, grabbed her, hugged and kissed her once more, and cried softly.

Victor wouldn't have done that, and the old Misty wouldn't have understood why.

"I'm so very glad to see you," I whispered softly.

She hugged me and kissed me again, and I could see that there were tears in her eyes, too. "Me, too, Vicki Misty Gonser Carpenter."

I laughed and we hugged and kissed and touched and, in that moment, I think, we both did become truly whole.

The battle was for the minds, Pauley had once told me, not the shells.

Stuart came back in. "Ve have located him and talked to him," he told us, and I had no doubt who "him" was. "Ve brought him up to date. He seems quite agreeable, and particularly anxious to see the two of you. Ve told him vat happened to you both."

Jeff Overmeyer stepped into the room and I looked at him. "How will you get him out?" I asked.

"He already *is* out," Jeff replied, and I froze. There was something terribly wrong about him, something I couldn't quite put my finger on.

"Oh, *no!*" I almost sobbed.

"Yes, it's true," he sighed. "I'm not Jeff. We switched. But it was voluntary, I promise. He knew what he was doing."

Both Dory and I were on our feet now, staring at him. "But—why?" I looked at Stuart.

"Ve discussed it early on. Somebody had to do it. Jeff has been on the outs with Parch for some time. He couldn't get avay and he knew it, but if he stayed he vould go under the computer. This way his mind, at least, is safe—for a vile—and no Urulu are missing. That extra time is bought a bit more, but it is bought dear, yes?"

I nodded glumly. "Dear indeed."

"Oh, come on," Pauley said, sounding relaxed and sure of himself. "My old body wasn't much older than Jeff's and is in good shape." His tone grew grimmer.

"He was a dead duck and he knew it. Better this way than no way at all." He walked over to us and looked us over. "Let me take a look at you."

Involuntarily, we both stepped back, away from his grasp. "Don't you touch me!" Dory snapped.

"Wait a minute! I'm not going to switch with you—I promise." He saw we were still hesitant. "Look, if we're going to do anything at all together we have to trust each other. If you don't trust me now then we're lost before we start."

I shivered slightly, but stood still. "All right," I said nervously.

He took my hand, then placed his other hand, fingers spread, on my forehead. I could feel nothing. Finally he nodded to himself and let go, turning to Eisenstadt. "Interesting. You have it all now, although some of the approaches are unique. Dory? May I?"

She took another step back nervously, but steeled herself finally and let him repeat the process. Finally he said, "All right. I sense the conflict within each of you, the problem of integrating two lives. Being holographic, your brain still has trouble handling both and is frantically re-sorting, re-filing, and trying new and different pathways. But it'll work itself out. You may find your mind playing little tricks on you but it won't matter in the long run. I think they're capable, Doctor. Shall we get out of here?"

"Wait a minute!" Dory exclaimed. "If Jeff's so hot how do you expect to get out of here as him? And if you switch, it'll leave a real loose end."

"That is true," Stuart admitted, "but, you understand, if it vas only Jeff and myself this would never have been possible even to now. Misty, Dory, these are *good* people on the whole. Normal, decent people. Even Parch, in his own odd way, is no monster. But there *are* monsters in the chain of command—ordinary, normal fellows vith vives and kids who vorship power. It is, in some vays, like Hitler vithout Hitler—the monster cannot be pinned down, but he is there. Now ve, of IMC, have vun chance to show that ve are not just good Germans, following orders no matter vere they go. Everyvun looks for the Hitler, but it is the banality of evil that makes it so insidious." He stepped to his door and gestured. Two technicians came on the run.

Stuart nodded to them. "These brave fellows are John Castellano and Villy Stroyer. Johnny, here, is my chief administrative aide. Both are too young to know the horrors of vich I speak first hand, yet they are vith us. They know the horror that is *here*."

Castellano, a small, dark, hawk-nosed man with long black hair, spoke. "We're volunteers, Miss. And we have clearance to leave if we want." He turned to Pauley. "Which do you want?"

Pauley looked both surprised and impressed, both by their commitment and their casual acceptance of him. "Either of you married?" he asked.

"No sir," the other man, a bit older but still a decent-looking man with a fine-lined Nordic face and a slight paunch. "I was—once."

Pauley considered it, then turned to Eisenstadt. "Why not you, too, Doctor? John—you've worked with him. Think you could *be* him? Until we come back, anyway, and can get you into a younger body."

Castellano looked nervous—they both did—but he sighed and said, "I think ve can pull it off, yes."

The voice was all wrong, but he had the tone, accent, and inflection down pat.

Eisenstadt stared at them and I thought I saw the tiniest glimmer of a tear in his eye. "You vould do this?"

Castellano nodded. "Doctor, I don't want to see you under that thing with Parch at the controls. I was ready to do it as Jeff Overmeyer, I'm willing to do it now."

Pauley became all business. "Lie down on the floor, then—all three of you. Good. Now, grip each other's hands tight. Just relax—it won't hurt."

We watched, fascinated. For the first time I was going to see the Urulu exchange bodies without being a party to it.

It was very odd to watch. Pauley alone was not knocked out by the process, but Pauley kept changing from body to body, so three would be out cold and the fourth would move, then drop and another would move, and so forth. I realized he was trying to put the right people in the correct, although wrong, bodies. Suddenly it was over, and Stroyer got up fairly confidently. "We'll have to wait for them to come around," said Dan Pauley. "Partly to see if I got it right, and partly so we can see how convincing it all is."

It took seven or eight minutes for the first to come around, the Jeff Overmeyer body which was now occupied by the original Stroyer. He rubbed himself, groaned, sat up, shook his head, and tried to get a grip on his new self. I could sympathize.

Castellano's body was next, with the same trouble, but with a slight difference in manner and tone.

"Whew!" gasped Stuart Eisenstadt. "Ven ve do it it's slower but not such a jolt to the central nerwous system!"

His own body was last to revive and had the most trouble adjusting. "The biggest problem, though, will be remembering that accent," Pauley warned him. He looked pleased.

"Well, now we have left them a Dan Pauley, a Jeff Overmeyer, and a Stuart Eisenstadt, all of whom would be missed. And two technicians will leave at the end of their shift as normal, not to be missed at least until they fail to show up tomorrow morning."

Stuart nodded. "Yes. I have the codes in my head, so ve are safe there. But—see, you vomen—give me your cards."

We were a bit puzzled, but handed over the little plastic keys he'd given us not long before.

"Let us make it look *very* right," he said conspiratorially, and went to his inner office where there was a computer terminal. He switched it on, began typing, then stopped and inserted one of the cards in the slot on the side. There was a rat-tat-tat noise, and the card popped out again. Now he inserted the other card and repeated the process.

Finally he handed the cards back to us, took his own—that is, Castellano's—card and punched in, then Stroyer /Pauley's. I looked at mine but could see no differences.

"Ve are now married," he said with some amusement. "Me to you, Misty, and Dory to, ah, Stroyer. Isn't bureaucracy amazing? There is now even a statement on file in the computer files of Las Vegas County to that effect."

I shook my head. "But—why?"

He grinned. "It vill register now on the computer record that ve vere met by our vives, who vere cleared to this point, and left with them a couple of hours later. When they do a cross-check by computer, they vill find ve *are* married and things vill look normal. Every little step ve cover is important." Besides, he added, giving a mock leer, "I feel so much younger and better and now the feeling it is legal."

For such an absolute security prison it was remarkably easy to just walk out as we'd walked in so long ago. The right words were spoken, the right combinations turned in the elevators, and all went smoothly. Stuart was right, I realized. The most burglar-proof safe in the world is no better than paper if someone wanting to break into it knows the combination.

"Ve'll take Castellano's car," Stuart suggested. "It is the largest." He stopped a moment. "*If* you have the keys, Pauley, in his pocket."

Pauley looked surprised, fumbled, came up with a small key ring, and we all sighed.

Although large by today's standards it was still a small car, and while Pauley took the driver's seat and

Dory the front bucket Stuart and I squeezed in the back.
There was little room.

"Where to?" the Urulu asked.

"Avay. Out of here," Stuart replied. "Vunce on the
vay ve vill make better plans."

He started the car, backed out, and switched on the
air conditioner. I was already starting to bake, and the
hatchback in the rear gave the little compressor a real
workout. We drove out of the parking lot and down the
base road.

"Gate coming up," Dory warned.

The sentry came out as we stopped at the gate, gave
us an odd look as he saw the assemblage in the car, but
after looking at all four of our cards he waved us on. In
twenty more minutes we were on U.S. Route 95, headed
south.

We'd done it!

Take that, Harry Parch! I thought smugly.

"Where are we headed for?" I asked.

"Sign back there said Las Vegas 250, which I assume
means kilometers," Pauley replied. Not much in between, either. We could use a road map."

Stuart was a little worried. "I don't like the idea of
going to Las Vegas," he told us. "Too much Harry Parch
there."

"Well, I could turn around and head north," Pauley
suggested, "but I remember there's even less there. We're
on the wrong side of the mountains and they could cut
us off fast on any of those roads. I'd say Las Vegas is our
best bet—we have lots of options from there."

"Most of my stuff's in storage there," I noted, "but
I've got a room at the Sahara with a change of clothes.
I'm not gonna get anywhere dressed like this."

Stuart frowned. "I don't like it. If anything goes wrong
it'll be the first place they look."

"That's true," I agreed, "but, remember, I'm *supposed*

to be there. Poor Joe—how will he take his opening big act skipping out on him?"

Stuart thought about it. "Yes, there is something in that. Tell you vat, Dan. Let's go into Vegas, then try to change cars if at all possible vile Misty tends to her affairs. I think you could cover her from the street and help in case things go wrong. Misty—how much money do you have?"

I laughed. "I don't have much need for it," I told him. "But I've got a bunch of credit cards."

He shook his head vigorously. "No. No credit cards except maybe to check out. They can trace you easy from those cards. I mean *cash*."

I thought a minute. "Misty—the old Misty—never paid much attention," I told him. "Most of it's in savings, just a little in checking."

"Hmmm . . . The banks vill be closed by the time ve get there. But ve need money. *Any* idea how much you got?"

I shook my head. "Only roughly. Ten or fifteen thousand at least."

Everybody seemed to react in shock at once. Dory whirled and said, "*That* much? In three years? You *must* be something!"

I shrugged. "I started at four hundred a week, but top-draw strippers make a lot more."

Stuart sighed. "Vell, I don't like it, but it looks like ve have to stay in or near Las Vegas until the banks open tomorrow morning. Ve need that money. Dan?"

"I have to agree," he told us. "We'll need travel money at least. And if I can't contact a station tonight, which is unlikely—we used to change 'em every month or two anyway—it might be a long trip finding which is active."

I looked at Stuart. "You didn't say I had to finance this whole thing. Couldn't you at least have thought of the cash angle?"

He looked defensive. "I said the plan was *good*, not that ve had thought of everything."

We drove along, and I had to look at my companions and marvel a bit. What an unlikely team out to save the world, I thought: A well-meaning, idealistic scientist who could change the world from a computer terminal but forgot things like money, an alien cut off from his species and an unknown quantity beneath his slick veneer, a Navaho girl of uncertain personality and little background for any such intrigue, and a former male political science professor now happy as a voluptuous blond bombshell of a stripper. What an insane team.

And me—just who was I, anyway? I knew the answer almost instinctively, from every cell and nerve in my body. I was Misty Ann Carpenter, queen of the strippers and sometimes lady of the evening, that's who. And I felt comfortable and right that way.

What had happened to Victor Gonser, I mused, as the miles of desert and mountain roared past. Where had he gone? I was Misty Carpenter—but she didn't exist. She'd been created in that same computer by Harry Parch and his technical crew. Was I real—or some embodiment of a male sexual fantasy? Certainly I wasn't what the average woman wanted to be or admired. I was a toy, a pampered pet, a plaything for other people, a mistress, a lover, too good to be true for the common male libido. And I *liked* it. If anything I alone was setting women's liberation back twenty years or more. And I didn't *care*,

So, in a sense, Parch had won a victory over me even with my old memories restored. And because it worked, it didn't really matter.

But where was the old Victor Gonser? I looked for him, but found only traces here and there. Oh, I remembered my past all right, but it seemed distant, remote, as if it'd happened to somebody else, like in a very long, boring movie or something.

Data. Computers again. I had the data of Victor's life. The data but not the—matrix? Soul? I couldn't be sure. I tried to think back to when I was he—how long? Four years? I was that person for thirty-five years, my present self for four, so why was he so less real to me than Misty Carpenter?

I thought back, tried to get inside him, and found I could not. Even the little things—being much taller, stronger. It just didn't relate. All the episodes of his life were there, but I could only see myself behind those eyes that witnessed it. I tried to remember the sex and even there I couldn't get it right. I'd remember the woman, remember the room, everything, but when it came to doing it I was always being penetrated, not the other way around. I couldn't even remember what it had been like to even *have* a penis. Why couldn't I?

Memory is holographic. The phrase echoed in my mind, but now I began to understand what Stuart and Dan had been talking about. Your data wasn't stored redundantly, over and over. The brain would quickly fill despite its huge capacity. But if reference A were stored only once, and all the bits and pieces were stored only once, the cerebrum would simply pull from those spots to create a picture, a complete thought, in the mind.

Or a self-image.

And that was what was happening to me. The Gonser data bits were there, of course, complete and ready for use, but the core of me, my self-image, could either fragment into two totally split personalities, in which case I would be schizoid, or one would attain dominance, would establish itself in the primacy seat of the identity matrix.

Did anything of Victor Gonser remain? Well, Misty Carpenter was a stripper and prostitute who could discuss Von Clauswitz, A.J.P. Taylor, and the fine points of Jungian psychology before going to bed with you.

"We're coming into Vegas," Dory announced, bringing me out of my thoughts. I opened my eyes and looked out, seeing the bright lights in the distance although it was still twilight. Vegas was beautiful by night, I thought, but ugly as hell in the daytime.

"Two motels, fairly near but outside the Strip," Stuart suggested.

"Why two?" I asked.

"If they are avare of us they vill be looking for four," he explained. "And off the beaten track the rates are cheaper and the traffic thinner. Better ve stay extra cautious and get avay."

There was no argument for that, although I, at least, felt a little more secure. I had walked the Strip for almost a week and checked it out, and I was a legitimate visitor.

We dropped Dory and Dan off at one little motel, a nothing sort of place, really, a few blocks off Las Vegas Boulevard, and they registered without problems. I was glad to see Dory accepting it so well considering her ill-concealed distrust of Pauley. She had guts, I had to admit that.

Stuart and I took a room in another place just down the street. It looked O.K., and after we were all settled in we met again at a Sambo's for a bite to eat and some discussion.

"I think I should go directly to the Sahara and get my things," I told them. "The longer we wait the more the risk."

"Agreed," Pauley replied. "Look—no use in all of us going. Doctor, you and Dory stay here—I'll drive Misty down close to the Strip and let her off. She can walk down to the Sahara and get what she has to." He paused, looking at me seriously. "This and the bank tomorrow will be the riskiest part of this stage of the trip. Be extra careful."

"I will," I assured them all.

Dan let me off quickly and sped away, but I knew he was just going to stash the car in the Sahara's back lot. I walked slowly but confidently towards the hotel-casino, acting like I had every right to be there—which I did. I took it slow and easy, though, to allow Dan enough time to park and make his way around to the lobby area.

Walking into the casino was like coming home, the sights and sounds and bright lights, the clunk of slots turning and stopping and the bells going off signalling jackpots, seemed like lost friends welcoming me back. Three guys tried to pick me up on the way to the elevators, a little above average, but nobody looked particularly suspicious. That didn't mean much, of course, since Parch's agents were visible only when they wanted to be. It would be up to Pauley to protect my rear.

There *did* seem an abnormal number of people just lounging about, though, and it gave me pause. For the first time since hitting Vegas I started getting nervous, looking sideways at people. Was that clerk the same one as yesterday? Was that guy with the racing form lounging against that post over there ogling me surreptitiously for the right reasons? I suddenly didn't feel so sure.

I reached the elevators and punched the button, conscious of eyes on me that, perhaps, weren't friendly or lustful eyes. It seemed to take forever for the damned car to come, but finally it did. I stepped in, and as the door started to close two men ran for it. I stepped back involuntarily, fear shooting through me as the lead man caught the door, hit the rubber safety stop, and, as the doors went back, got on with me. The other man followed.

I had already pressed 6, my floor, and now I cursed myself for it. Who were these men, these strangers so insistent on riding with me?

One man pushed 8, the other 11. Higher floors than mine. Could they be planning to walk back down from 8 and surprise me at my door?

The elevator stopped at 6 and I got off, not very relieved that the two men stayed on. I fumbled for my key in my small purse and almost ran to my room. I put the key to the lock, then hesitated once more. Were they waiting for me inside? Would Harry Parch's chilling voice greet me when I opened it?

I had no choice, but still I hesitated. I wished Dory were here, or Dan, or somebody. I was suddenly feeling very alone and frightened. Finally I took a deep breath, put the key in the lock, turned it, and pushed the door in.

It was dark in the room, and I quickly and apprehensively turned on the lights. Nobody there. It didn't reassure me. Closets, bathroom, they could be anywhere.

Scared to death now and cursing myself for insisting on this little side trip, I cautiously explored the entire room. Nothing. I sighed, knowing it might only be a brief reprieve. Quickly I hauled out my smaller suitcase and looked at my wardrobe. Finally I hauled out the big one, too, and started sorting. Undergarments, panty hose, toiletries, cosmetics, all went in the small one, along with some different shoes and some miscellaneous outfits. For now I decided that the simple, casual look was appropriate. Some blue jeans, sandals, and a thin sweater over just a bra.

The rest of the stuff I threw into the large suitcase. I hesitated on the short mink jacket. It was too warm and I wasn't dressed for wearing it, but it seemed like it might come in handy when we left the desert. Somehow I managed to cram it into the small suitcase and get it shut.

I tried picking them up but while the small one was barely manageable with two hands, the big one was impossible. I would need help.

Feeling that the world was closing in on me, I thought frantically for a moment, then realized that I would have to have a bellman. I sighed, picked up the phone, and called the bell captain.

A young man was up very quickly with a small cart—too quickly, I thought with suspicion. He quickly loaded the bags and took them down to the lobby. I began to think the worst, that, perhaps, they *were* on to me, all around me, but wouldn't pounce. They were waiting for me to lead them back to the others.

I checked out, and at least the cashier was a familiar face and a woman. I found that I could leave the large case in hotel storage, at a few bucks a day, until I sent word of where to send it, and that relieved my mind a bit. I had them put two weeks worth on the credit card and signed it, hoping I'd remember to keep up payments. I really didn't want to lose all that good stuff.

I looked for Dan in the lobby and finally spotted him, but tried not to look directly at him. He was down a bit towards the casino, playing the slot machine nearest the lobby.

I managed the small suitcase as best I could, and it was only a moment before a middle-aged man came over and offered to help. In any other circumstances I would have been delighted, but I found myself wondering if this was legit or not. But I couldn't move that thing very far—my back was killing me anyway—and I accepted his help to move the bag to the main entrance, where cabs normally lined up.

I thanked the man and he responded, "Any time at all, Babe," which sounded sincere and natural enough and then he went back into the casino.

Cabs weren't prevalent, but one pulled up in five minutes or so which I told to take me to the bus station. At the station, I walked in, waited until that cab had picked up another fare, then came back out again, thanking God that it wasn't too far to lug the case. I got in another cab and took *it* to the Sambo's where we'd eaten. He thought it was an odd destination, but didn't argue. I waited there a long twenty minutes or so, and finally a small car, a red one, pulled up and Pauley stuck his head out. "Misty! Get in!"

I frowned at this car change, but lugged the case to the curb and managed to lift it in to Dan. I got in and he took off.

"What happened? Where'd you get this car?"

"It's not good," he told me. "I think we got away with this but by a whisker. I was just heading back to the car when several cop and plainclothes cars pulled up front and back of the Sahara. One local boy, probably proud of himself, was already standing at the car and some of them ran to him. I checked the front and saw others rushing inside. I knew you were away, so I just walked away, slowly and naturally. Finally I found this one, parked and unlocked on a side street, and I stole it. Somebody'd gone into a laundromat and left the keys in. So it's hot, and I'll have to ditch it. Look, I'm taking you back to the room. Brief Stuart, then have him get Dory and come to your room, or you do it. I want to find out what's what in this city, and I have to dump this far away. O.K.?"

"All right," I replied, sounding worried. "Look—take care of yourself. Without you this is all for nothing."

He pulled up in front of the motel room and surprised me by leaning over and kissing me. I was startled. Then he winked, took my suitcase out with one hand, and said, "You just sit tight. Nobody catches me twice. Just get Dory with you and don't move from that room until I get back no matter what—hear?"

I nodded, and he roared off. Off in the distance I could hear the wail of sirens, off in the direction of The Strip.

I knocked on the door and Stuart opened it cautiously, saw me, then came out and helped both me and my suitcase inside. I quickly filled him in on the developments.

"Probably poor Castellano," he sighed. "He probably forgot the accent and let New Jersey come through."

"We have to get Dory," I told him, but he held up his hand. "No, let's do it the smart vay." He pointed to the telephone. "No sense in all of us getting exposed."

I was so rattled I could hardly think straight, not to mention dead tired and achy. I was damned glad to have Stuart around to do the thinking for me.

I called Dory. She answered almost immediately and

took the news pretty well, but she said, "Look, I'm just about to get in the shower. Give me twenty minutes or so. I'll be over then. I'll knock twice. O.K.?"

"O.K.," I responded, hung up, and told Stuart the news. Then I sat down on the bed and found myself suddenly trembling, unable to stop.

Stuart came and sat beside me and put his arm around me. "Poor Misty," he said as gently as possible, "you are not equivipped for this sort of thing. Vell, neither am I. But ve do vat ve must, yes?"

I nodded and squeezed his hand very hard. He held me tightly, and I needed to be held, and made me feel at least a tiny bit secure.

Dory was almost on schedule, still dressed as before but with a large motel towel wrapped turban-like around her hair. "They didn't have much time to grab anything of mine when they snatched me," she explained. "No loss, though."

Something in my manner seemed to betray my recent attack of nerves, and she came over and squeezed my hand, then looked at me face to face. "Huh. I'm almost as tall as you when you're in sandals." She grinned. "I don't think I'm ever gonna make five feet, though, so you got me by three inches."

It broke the tension a bit and I relaxed a little more, laughing at her. I began to have even more respect for her now, knowing she realized how tightly wound I was and diverting me with trivialities.

Finally she sighed and looked at the two of us. "Look, I don't know about you but I'm really dead tired. I haven't been to sleep in almost two days and that shower was the last straw. Would you mind?"

"Of course not," I said. "Pick a bed."

She stripped without hesitancy, noting that her clothes had to last her a while yet, and climbed into bed. Stuart idly started looking through the Las Vegas promotional literature, and I finally relaxed enough to get undressed myself. I flexed my back muscles, which were really starting to ache, and Stuart, seeing this, came over and started giving me what felt like the most orgasmic backrub I could imagine.

"It is the breasts," he explained, although I'd already figured that out. "A lot of veight pulling you forward, a bit more than your genes designed your back muscles for. Unless you get reduction surgery it's something you'll have to live vith."

I nodded. "I know. Maybe someday I'll be settled down, not need 'em so much any more, or the back will finally get to me and I'll do something." I lifted them up with my hands and looked down at them. "Good Lord, Stuart—was there ever a woman born naturally who grew a pair like these? Sometimes I feel like a cow."

He chuckled. "Thousands, probably. But few in such delightful combination." He sighed. "Ah, if I were only thirty years younger!"

I looked over at Dory in the other bed. She was out like a light, mouth open slightly, totally oblivious to the world.

"But, Stuart," I whispered, "you *are* thirty years younger."

He started a moment, then looked thoughtful. "So I am," he said, wondering, then undressed himself.

God! I needed him!

I was tired, and he was tired, but we lay there in the darkness after, neither of us really able to sleep, thinking about things that the past few minutes, at least, had helped us forget.

I stirred a bit. "Why do I always get the wet spot on my side?" I whispered.

"It's a male plot. Ve're trained to work it out that vay," he responded lightly, and we both chuckled softly and were silent for a moment.

"Still vorried?" he asked.

"A little," I admitted. "About a lot of things. Not just tonight, although that's bad enough, Lord knows."

"Vant to tell your doctor about it?"

I smiled in the darkness. "It's me, Stuart. Since I—came back—today, I've been struggling with myself, with who I am."

"Ve varned you about that."

"No, no, it's more than that. In the car this afternoon—I *knew* that I had undergone a profound change. Victor Gonser is dead. Gone. And not just physically. There is only me, and I'm Misty Carpenter."

He thought for a moment. "No, I think you have the right solution but the problem it is backvards."

"Huh? What do you mean?"

"The solution, the *only* solution for you, is to be Misty Carpenter, now and forever. It is not only a person you like but one you *must* be, for you will be Misty Carpenter to the vorld no matter vat. The problem you have is that this Victor fellow, he is not as dead as he should be. You are looking at yourself through his mind, his morality, and you think, vell, it is wrong that I like being a voman, like being Misty Carpenter, like the heads turning, doors opening, the sex, the exhibitionism. Because he is not dead, this Victor, he makes you feel guilty, doubt yourself. Look—this Victor fellow ve both knew. Did you like him?"

I considered the question. "No. Well, not exactly. I didn't mind *him* so much as the way he was forced to live."

"He vas an egomaniac and an insufferable bore," Stuart responded. "A man who lived in his own private little hell, vich he built himself, and preferred self-pity, vallowed in it, even kind of enjoyed it. So—you start! Vy should you care? You are not he, you are Misty Carpenter!"

I tried to respond to that, but I was all confused inside now. It had seemed so *simple*.

"You see? Now *vy* vas he such a bore, a stick-in-the-mud? He never could join. He was dark, not very good-looking, bald, and had a pot belly. No girls paid him any mind. He had built such a mountain of defenses against a lonely childhood and a possessive Mama that he could not break them."

Tears came unbidden into my eyes as his comments brought back a lifetime of anguish and bitter loneliness.

"So now he is gone, *pfft!* And in his place is Misty Carpenter. She, too, has her problems, but they are not Victor's problems. Heads turn ven she valks into the room. Men fall over themselves to gain her favor. Misty can never be lonely. A dancer? Look at those big, beautiful eyes! Everyvun vants her. Everyvun loves her. Money? Vatever she vants she gets. Inhibitions? No. She loves the crowd and they love her—she valks naked in their midst if she vants. Is she used? Exploited? No, not really, for she loves vat she does and does it by choice, yes?"

"You make it sound so trite," I said bitterly.

He hugged me. "And so it is! But that is *all* it is. You have a golden opportunity here. Vat have you done so far? You have taught. You have done brilliant research, written many books that have caused young people to think—a very rare thing these days. That alone is more than most human beings *ever* accomplish. Far more. Now, you are born again, yes? You experience anew, are able to give anew, learn and grow in new and impossible vays, vithout losing any that you have already accomplished. This is not bad—it is vunderful. The only hard part to understand is vy you feel guilty about it. You should be *proud*, not ashamed! Trite? Perhaps, perhaps not. But if they are trite they are the trivial things as vell, yes? They are not the main things in life. But joy is important, *love* is important, *caring* is important. Yes—become Misty Carpenter, body and soul. You must. For only then can you live and love and give and get."

I sat there quietly for a while, digesting what he said, and he left me alone to do it. He was right, of course. I was Misty Carpenter because I wanted desperately to be Misty, who was always adored and never alone.

Stuart was right, though. Victor was not dead. Victor was transformed, raised up. A part of me would always be Victor and should always remember him, understand him in order to know and help all the Victors of this world. But I was not Victor. I was *me*.

I kissed him with feeling, then turned and my hand touched the little plastic alarm clock on the nightstand. I took it, suddenly, and looked at it. "Stuart—it's almost one-thirty."

"So?"

"Dan's not back yet."

"That has been on my mind, but I haven't let it get to me. He vas tough enough to trap on your boat, yes? He vould be almost impregnable in a big city. I think he is spying for us."

"But—suppose he doesn't come back? Suppose he just takes off?"

"If he'd vanted to he could have done it any time, yes? If he has, then ve have lost, of course. But I think not. He vill come back."

"I almost hope he doesn't," I said. "Then we would be out of this."

"For a vile, yes; for a very short vile. But then the campaign begins. And ve—you, me, Dory, all of us—vill be its wictims. No—he *must* return. He *vill!* And you must hope so, too, deep down. No matter who or vat you are you have a responsibility."

"I didn't ask for it."

"No, but few of us *do* ask such things. Fools, perhaps. You studied history. It is not extraordinary men doing great things. It is, mostly, ordinary men propelled by events, by circumstance, into extraordinary positions."

I could almost hate Stuart then. He was too insufferably *right* all the time.

Finally I said, "Stuart—when he does come back, what then? If the alarm's out and they know I've been to the

Sahara, have the car, then the bank is out. I have less than twenty dollars left in cash. Dory has almost nothing. And you've got—what?''

"Tvelve dollars and sixteen cents," he admitted.

I nodded. "And we have no car now. They'll be looking for us anyway. We need money and a way out. I don't know about the way out, but I *can* get us some money. More than we got, anyway."

He knew what I meant. It didn't really bother me, of course, but I couldn't help thinking of Dory.

Stuart understood. "Look, you forget—you who should of all people not forget—that she is a twenty-three-year-old voman, yes? A modern voman. You are not—you are vat you vant to be, a concept of a voman, but not of her background. She is not naive, nor stupid. She was raised on the tradition that vomen can do anything, be anything. You are in some vays the old model, she the new. You have decided vat is the right sort of vomen you vant to be—you can not change that, nor can you act on vat is right for her. That is her choice."

"But—I—we—damn! It's kind of weird, but, Stuart, I'm in love with her! I have been in love with her ever since I first met her. I don't want to hurt her!"

"So? Vat is so veird? She loves you, you love her. You two of all people are the best sort of lovers. You know it's vat's *inside* that counts, not the body you vear."

"But I like—men."

"So again? Sex is love, maybe? Since ven? Sex can be vith love or vithout it. You should know. But vun is not necessarily the other." He sighed. "Still, if you must do it for us, you must, even if she vould have some hurt—vich I'm not too sure about. Our responsibility is to those people who can not know vat is going on. They have no choice, and so neither do ve, if they are not to become victims, yes? First ve do vat ve must. Then ve decide our own lives. So vat is the alternative? Ve all shack up vile you get a dance job and the rest of us sveep floors, yes? Or?"

"What would I have done without you, Stuart?"

"The same thing—only more slowly, and vith more pain."

I hoped that he was right, not so much for his sake but for mine.

The night wore on towards morning, and, in spite of ourselves, we finally fell asleep.

A gentle knock on the door awakened me. I glanced at the clock—a little after five. Not even light yet. I began to think I'd dreamed it when the knock came again, a little more insistently. I got up as quietly as I could and went to the door, checking to see that the chain was on.

I opened it a crack and whispered, "Who is it?"

"Dan," came a hissed reply. "Let me in—quick."

I undid the chain and he slipped in, then I closed it and chained it again. I stared at the shape in the dark, which looked smaller, different, somehow. "Dan—is that really you?"

"Yes," he responded. "I—had to switch, Misty. It was a close call. Turn on the light and get ready for a shock. We better wake the others, too."

I reached over and flipped the lights on and gasped. The figure in the room was a tiny one, wearing a brown monklike robe with hood and sandals.

Dory and Stuart stirred with the light, woke up, and looked blearily in our direction. Both saw the new Pauley and gasped.

"Relax—it's Dan," I told them, and I really hoped it was.

He reached up and pulled back his hood. The head was totally shaved, even the eyebrows, and the face, which once might have held some human attraction, looked bony and emaciated.

"Are you—male or female?" Dory asked, staring in wonder.

"Female," he responded, "although sexless is more naturally true." Speaking aloud his voice did have a feminine tone to it, but the inflection, the manner, was all Pauley's.

"Who or what was *that?*" I wanted to know.

Pauley sighed and collapsed tiredly into a chair. "Look, I'll tell you the whole thing from the beginning. I ditched the car on the north side, in a motel parking lot, then started walking back towards downtown. Thank God they have busses all night here, and one came along and I grabbed it, heading back for the Sahara area. I *had* to know what they were doing. I tried to be as inconspicuous as possible, but I no sooner entered the casino when I spotted a very familiar figure across the way talking to a couple of security men. It was Harry Parch."

"Parch!" Dory gasped, then turned to Stuart. "I thought you said he wouldn't be back until late today."

"Something must have tipped earlier than planned," the scientist responded. "They got him back here on the next plane."

"Well, anyway, there I was in a known body, target number one, fifty feet from my worst enemy. I turned to walk out the door and as soon as I hit the street this girl in this long robe, here, comes up to me and starts a pitch to sell me flowers. I tried to put her off, but a glance back showed Parch and the security men heading my way, so I eased her down towards the parking lot. I couldn't help noticing how nice, how *trusting* she was, smile always on her face. Well, there was this dark area, and I got ready, figuring at least I wouldn't have to kill anybody. No use hiding with Parch around. So, I reach out to her, and, by God, she reached out and grabbed me first! Not just her hand—I mean with her mind!"

"She was Urulu?" I gasped.

That strange face was grim. "No, not Urulu. But *I felt the push*—it's hard to describe. Let's just say she let her mind flow out, flooding mine. I had an instant reaction, first an instinctive block, then I rushed in and made the switch on my terms. Her ego—her matrix—was so simple, so uncomplicated, that I damned near crushed it, and I left my old body sitting in the phone booth with a stupid smile on his face."

"But she could make the svitch, like you, yes?" Stuart prodded. "But this ve have not yet developed. I vould know it if ve had."

Pauley shook his head. "It wasn't IMC, either. It's a new wrinkle, but an old pattern. I wouldn't have guessed it, not yet—but it is The Association."

I thought back to the tapes, and the conversations we'd had, and shivered.

"So ve *are* under attack after all!" Stuart murmured.

Pauley nodded slowly. "The war is here. How long it's been here I can't tell—we've all been out of circulation for three years. That's why I can't just contact Urulu here. I tried a couple of the numbers but they were disconnected." He turned to Stuart. "Tell me about the Redeemers."

The scientist shrugged. "Ve have had such cults around this country for years. They are mostly young, mostly made up from runaways, former addicts, teens vith unhappy homes."

"I remember the Children of God, the Moonies, lots of others, from when I was growing up," I added. "I suppose Hari Khrishna is still around."

"Most have merged," Stuart told us. "This new church svept them up, a big movement. You cannot escape them, and, thanks to the courts and the First Amendment, you can't interfere with them. Many of the older ones have come together vith them. They own huge tracts of land, are rich and pervasive."

"I know how rich they must be," Pauley responded. "I left the mongol sitting there and went over to this cart that read 'Flower Power for Love and Godhead.' I saw two others similar to myself working further down the airport, and I checked in my pocket. There was almost $230 there.

"That much was good. You ought to have seen those

APs when I tried to sell them flowers! I even pressed Harry Parch himself!"

"You didn't!" Dory gasped. "And did he buy one?"

"He looked at me kind of funny for a minute, and I thought I'd gone too far, that he knew who I was despite all. But, I'll be damned if he didn't gentle up and buy a nice carnation! I even chivvied him out of his change for a 'contribution.'"

"Dan!" I scolded. "You shouldn't have! How did you ever—"

That strange, shaven head came up, and I'd swear there was a definite change in the form. It seemed to be eerily transformed, to shrink, change, become someone else.

It rose, an incredibly sincere pleading in its eyes.

"Buy some flowers?" this plaintive voice asked, so genuine and convincing that we all seemed to pull back a little. "Would you convert some money to beauty?" it pleaded, so genuinely that it scared the hell out of me.

Suddenly the effect was gone, replaced by Pauley's confident manner and smile that shone through that odd body. He chuckled.

"My God! That's *incredible!*" I managed.

His face turned serious. "You see," he said, "my people developed the IM transfer without mechanical aid, as an evolutionary device. We were weak, our brains our only defense in a world unremittingly hostile. Our brains gave us IM if we needed it, and gave us a certain illusory power as well. There would be this terrible creature, ready to eat us, and we'd activate this protective circuit. Suddenly we weren't Urulu food any more, we were a plant, another carnivore, something like that. We can still do it—the power of the Urulu is all in the mind. We've been fighting all our existence, and we still have it."

It was unsettling to all of us. Frankly, Dan Pauley had been a real person, even in different forms. He was not a friend on the trail or on the ferry, but he'd become a nice sort of guy in imprisonment and escape.

But he wasn't a nice sort of guy at all, I thought.

He was an alien creature whose very thought patterns were different from us. He was simply imitating us, giving us what we wanted him to be. That's why everybody liked Pauley, everybody felt comfortable with him.

Stuart, ever practical, broke the mood. "Did you keep the money?" he asked.

Pauley smiled. "Sure. Two hundred and thirty flower power bucks plus five from Mr. Harry Parch."

"But what good does it do us?" I protested. "We're still known, and now Parch knows we're in town. He can smoke us out—it isn't that big a place. And now The Association will know that a Urulu is here, too."

Pauley shook his head. "No, not much threat from The Association at this stage. These are drones. Their minds have been drained, the useful information, if any, filed, and they have been given identical, empty *personas*. They're robots, that's all. That's why the girl's mind cracked when I resisted. It simply wasn't equipped for it. The other two won't even recognize that one of their own is missing. They'll go on until relieved, then go back to their living quarters. Nobody will notice or care. The biggies will only show up to make sure everything's going right and collect the money. They won't even count. Individuals don't exist in The Association."

I started to press for more information on the enemy but Stuart was ever practical. "The fact remains that Harry Parch is here and he knows *ve* are here. He can lock up this town tighter than a drum but very qvietly, vith full government authority. Ve have to get out of here. As the crow flies, ve are less than eighty miles from IMC."

"Well, we've gotten this far—we can't give up now," Dory put in. "I won't give that son of a bitch another crack at me!" She started thinking. Finally she said, "Look, I'm the least known and most unobtrusive person here. Parch hasn't seen me since I was a kid and my odds of meeting him head on are pretty slim anyway."

There was no arguing with that.

"O.K., then," she went on, fire in her tone, "so we've got $235, plus whatever we have left over. That's a lot. Now, when the stores open, I'm gonna take that money and buy us a way outta here."

Check-out was noon, but, despite some nervousness, we needed a little more time and I managed to sweet-talk the manager, a kindly old guy. I was a little apprehensive about letting Dory out alone, but Dan and I were both conspicuous, for different reasons, and even if Stuart's current face wasn't familiar to them, which it was, he would have been lost on such a shopping expedition.

She came back in a taxi with a pile of stuff we had to help unload. I looked over it, somewhat approvingly, the only one who, at least, didn't need a wardrobe.

"I kept it simple," she told us. "Things we needed, things for a good disguise, all from the discount stores except the wigs, which I had to pick up at Sears."

We sorted the stuff out and I was amazed at the variety. She handed me a package. "Mix it," she told me. "It's hair dye. Sensual Auburn, it says. Seems stupid to dye it its natural color, but I couldn't stand black on you, red always looks phoney, and it looked the best."

I took her advice, although with a bit of regret, and filled the sink.

A bit later she took over the bathtub and started pouring in small packets that turned the water into what looked like really thin mud. "What," I asked her, "is *that?*"

"Skin tint," she replied. "You mean you never saw it? It was just getting to be the in thing a few years ago. It's out now, I guess, but it's still around. It's a dye, it won't wash off, and this particular batch is called 'Bronze

Goddess.' You can get 'em in any color—even blues and pinks and stuff like that."

I looked at it dubiously. "How *do* you get it off, then?"

"You can use an alcohol sponge, but most folks just let it wear off. It fades out in a couple of days. Now, strip and get in—we got to cover every part of your nice, white skin with it."

The stuff actually didn't look bad *on* the skin, or in it, or whatever it was. Like a really deep suntan, a real golden bronze. She spent a lot of time making sure I had a complete coat, using a sponge applicator. When she was finished my skin and hair just about matched, although my blue eyes were a little incongruous. Dory was even prepared for that. "I knew you might have sunglasses," she said, "but not with a light frame." She handed me a pair and they looked pretty good. A golden nail polish and light lipstick completed the job, and I had to admit, looking at myself in the mirror, I looked like an entirely different person. With my hair now up and back, my ears showing, I looked exotic, all right, but not like Misty Carpenter. I decided to stick to the jeans, sweater, and sandals. It was simple, and comfortable.

She had gotten Pauley a short brown wig that looked pretty good, some false eyebrows that gave the Urulu a more human look, and a simple jeans and T-shirt outfit. "You'll have to wear the cult sandals, though," she apologized. "I couldn't guess your shoe size."

For herself she put her hair up and fitted a black Afro wig over it, applied some judicious cosmetics, and got some new jeans and a souvenir T-shirt but she added a matching denim vest. "Had to go to the children's department," she grumped. She stuck to her boots, on the theory that she still was the least recognizable, and pulled out a denim cowgirl-type hat with fancy stitching.

Stuart was the hardest, since we couldn't change him much. A complete change of clothes made him look touristy, a light jacket, more sunglasses and a brown cowboy hat completed the picture. He had a two-day growth of stubble, and we suggested he not shave for a while. We did, however, give him a dye job, changing his black hair to a browner shade, with just a touch of gray on the sides. It made him look different enough that he seemed satisfied.

Pauley was amazed. "How did you even know the sizes?"

She grinned. "When you've been a woman all your life you get to guessing other women's sizes pretty well."

We stood back and looked critically at one another. "What do you think?" Pauley asked.

"They'll do," Dory replied. "Look, it was the best I could do for a hundred and fifteen dollars. You never had problems, I am least likely to be known, Stuart— well, if he came face to face with somebody who'd known the original owner he'd be in trouble, but not casually, or from an I.D. photo. No, Misty's the only one with problems."

"What do you mean? I think I look terrific!"

"Yeah, you do—as usual, which is the problem. Honey, you have a forty-two-inch bust on a twenty-four-inch waist. There's no disguising that. Your every move is an advertisement. One sex goddess attracts as much attention as another—and attention is what we don't want to attract."

"What can I do?" I wailed. "This is *me*." I felt that it was a ridiculous position. Who'd ever thought that not being noticed, being nondescript, fading into the background, being very common and ordinary, would be such an asset?

Where are you, Victor Gonser, when I really need you?

"Let's get something to eat," Pauley suggested. "The usual place, I think. It's a good test, since our old selves have been in there before—*your* old selves, anyway."

I nodded, then had a sudden thought. "What about my suitcase? It's got all my stuff in it!"

He sighed and looked at it. "You can't even lift it," he

pointed out. "I'd say take what little you can in your purse and forget it."

"Forget it hell! That's my *life* in there!"

"Or it might be your life if you keep it," he shot back.

I sighed and almost cried when I thought of the stuff I would be losing. But one thing I wouldn't abandon. I opened the thing and took out the mink jacket. It was a nice brown and would go with my dyed self.

"Wow!" Dory whistled. "Is that *real?*"

I nodded. I also took the jewelry case, opened it, and dumped it into my shoulder bag, along with the contents of the smaller purse I'd been going to use. The rest was really nice, and had some fond memories attached, but it could be more easily replaced. I looked at it sadly and shook my head, then sighed. "O.K. Let's go before I start bawling my head off."

Stuart and I went first, dropping the key off and then going off arm-in-arm. It served to draw some attention away from me to him for having me on his arm, which was good psychology.

Dory and Dan followed a few minutes behind, and we met in a corner booth at the restaurant. At the end, after figuring the bill, we figured we still had about $120 and some change. That was only $30 apiece. Not very much at all. Not even enough for bus tickets.

"We'll have to split up and get out of town," Pauley told us. "I don't like it, but they'll be looking for groups. Ordinarily, I'd say Misty and Stuart were the ideal couple, but not here. Putting our most recognizable people together would be a mistake. Better he and I—much less visibility that way, since they won't know me at all—and you and Dory."

I nodded. "Sounds O.K. to me."

"I'd still not travel around too close together while in Vegas," Pauley went on. "You've got to face it, Misty—even in a city full of beautiful showgirls you get noticed, and that could cause them to put you and a smaller Indian woman together."

"We'll take it easy," I promised him. "Look—you two take care of yourselves and don't worry about us. I think we can handle ourselves in the city."

"O.K., then. I'll leave it to you how to get out. Train, plane, and bus stations are bound to be watched closely, as will all rental car agencies."

"They can plug right into the computers," Stuart put in. "Get a readout—and you'd have to use your right name and driver's license and credit cards."

"I didn't say it would be easy—for any of us. I'd say bus is the best bet—it's the one thing we can probably get for the money we've got, although maybe not all the way. Take separate busses. Let's see . . . This is a Thursday. We'll meet in Los Angeles, at the Farmer's Market, at noon."

"Tomorrow?" I asked.

"Every day until we all link up," he replied. "But don't give it too long. Anybody not there by, say, Monday, you have to write off. If I can get out of here and get a little money I'll check a safe house we have between here and there. Maybe I can make contact."

"And if not?" Dory asked him.

He sighed. "Then we've got real big problems. Not insurmountable ones, but a lot harder. Look, I'd rather not go into that now. Better you don't know until you have to."

I saw what he meant.

The hot, bright, cheery look of Las Vegas was, somehow, suddenly more sinister. I began to feel the fear again, gnawing inside me. *They're out there,* I thought. *Out there looking for me.*

Suddenly it wasn't quite so much fun being Misty Carpenter.

Chapter Twelve

Dory and I paid our bills and left them there, then walked out onto the street. We didn't even look back to see where they went. It was better that way.

And lonelier.

I took Dory's hand and squeezed it tight. She looked up at me and gave a confident smile, and I felt better.

I wasn't alone. It was the two of us against the world, at least, and while that wasn't much it was far better than just one.

She looked down the bleak highway. "It's a ways down to the Strip and the bus station," she noted. "May as well start walking."

Nobody walked in Las Vegas, not from this far away from the casinos. There wasn't even much provision for sidewalks, and the gleaming towers of the Strip looked ugly in the distance, set against the bright sun and dirty sand and hills. It should never be day here, I thought.

"We can't do it this way," I told her. The Strip was there, but it was a good mile away. A couple of hotels

and casinos were closer, but they weren't where we had
to be.

"Yeah," Dory agreed sourly. "My feet won't take this,
and I'm sweating like a stuck pig."

"C'mon!" I urged. "I've got an idea!"

We ran across the street when traffic allowed, and
stood there.

"If I'm going to be a sex goddess," I told her, "I
should be able to get us a ride."

And I did. As a matter of fact, the guy almost lost
control of the car. I had a hot thumb.

He leaned over and opened the front door, and we
both squeezed in. It wasn't a big car, but it was air
conditioned and felt good. I was in the middle, so I put
my arms behind the two.

"Where you girls heading?" the guy asked pleasantly.
He didn't look like a gambler or tourist. More like a
salesman, I thought.

It took no effort at all to turn on Misty Carpenter's full
charms.

"Down to the Strip," I said in my best voice. "Going
to look around for a while."

"I have to go over to the residential section," he replied, regret evident in his voice. "I'll run you down to
the Frontier, though. That ought to put you in the center
of things."

The trip by car was too short for many questions, and
I made sure he didn't think of any. It was so *easy*, I
thought. It amazed me, this power I had. Not just that it
worked, but that it didn't have to be worked. It was
there when needed.

We got out, and I made his day by kissing him.

Las Vegas at 2 P.M. isn't the world's most thrilling
town. This place ran by night, came alive by night,
although it was always open.

I shifted my shoulder-purse, which seemed to weigh a
ton—and no wonder. Even after giving a little of my

best jewels to Dan to pawn when he cleared town, I had a lot in it. Mink was also warm at eighty-one degrees.

"Well, we can't stand out and fry," I said with a lightness I didn't feel. "Let's go in where it's cool."

Once inside, with the clank of slot machines and the ringing bells and flashing lights, I felt nervous again. Everybody seemed to be looking at me, but instead of the admiring glances they probably were I saw each as a Harry Parch spy.

I noticed Dory was staring at me. "What's the matter?" I said, suddenly concerned.

"I'm trying to figure out just what you do, how you do it," she replied.

"Do what?" I asked.

"That's what I mean," she said sulkily. "The moves, the stance, the walk, everything."

"Oh," was all I could manage at first, relief sweeping over me. Then I added, "Besides, you're too young for that."

"Like hell," she retorted.

I remembered Stuart's words and frowned. We needed more money, certainly, and I could get it. It was here, available. Vicki Lee shouldn't need money at all.

I looked at Dory, and she read my thoughts.

"If you do it, I will, too," she said, teeth clenched.

And that upset me for some reason I couldn't understand. "No," I said in the same tone.

"You go ahead," she urged. "I'll watch. Then—well, I'll meet you in the L.A. bus depot, that's all. Don't worry. Remember, I'm twenty-five and this body's *ready*." She paused. "I go *both* ways now, you know."

I started to protest, to argue, then turned and walked away from her, towards the bar.

She was small, but she was a well-developed seventeen-year-old. They wouldn't have any problems believing her old enough, particularly with that manner and speech, and an experienced woman.

Which, of course, she was.

Even this early in the afternoon, I didn't even have to sit down before I had to choose which John looked most promising.

His name was John K. Jessup, he was about forty-five, paunchy and slightly gray, dressed in a brown tweed suit and matching tie. He was there for a convention, he was lonely, and he had the bread.

He reminded me a lot of Victor Gonser. I wondered if the old Misty would have targeted him, or whether this was *because* of the resemblance.

It was right out of the books and old movies. He was a machine tool salesman, of all things, from Iowa City, of all places, and he bought me some drinks until we both felt good, and he talked of his business and his life while I just gushed all over him.

It was simple. I just stopped thinking and it worked on impulse.

Then we gambled a little, caught a nice little lounge act, danced a bit after—he really wasn't a bad dancer—and he had the time of his life. Everyone was looking at him, envious of him, wondering why they couldn't have such luck.

For that was my protection—in context, I was a cypher, a symbol, a thing, a precious object that was coveted.

But not a wanted human being, sought by certain people.

Then a nice dinner, a few more drinks, and up to John K. Jessup's room, where he fulfilled his fantasies.

It was a life I liked, would have gladly stuck with.

But I was wanted in this town, I had a responsibility, and I had an appointment in L.A.

He didn't want me to go, begged me to stay at least to breakfast, but I couldn't.

I never once asked for money, I never once asked for anything.

He slipped me some money; insisted I take it, and seemed slightly embarrassed by the action.

I was in the elevator before I looked.

It was two hundred bucks.

That easy.

For having fun.

For giving somebody else a good time, too.

I walked to the bus station, the hot night air feeling just great, me feeling just great.

There was a cop car parked around the corner from the bus station, and a suspicious-looking guy in sports shirt and slacks leaning on the wall near the door.

Suddenly I didn't feel so good anymore.

I was alone, all alone.

And Misty Carpenter feared that most of all.

I backed away from the streetlights, back into the shadows and waited, barely daring to breathe. I was trembling slightly, and I turned and walked back down the street, back into the Strip, which somehow seemed now to be threatening; the garish lights and weird sounds loomed and swooped and pressed in at me.

I realized suddenly that I'd started to run, and slowed to a nervous pace.

People passed me on the street, the heads turning as always to look at me, only this time I didn't want them to look, didn't want them to notice. I felt like I was lit up, an advertising billboard, which, in a way, I was.

I needed a drink and a place to sit down for a few minutes, and I turned into a small bar and slot machine parlor on the fringe of the Strip. It was crowded, and heads turned when I entered, men staring, gesturing.

"Hey Babe! Lonely?" somebody yelled out, and I turned, pushing back out onto the street, that suddenly cold, lonely street.

Misty was, in herself, a trap.

I reached an intersection turning off to a small, dark street. As I turned the corner, not thinking of where I could go, not thinking of anything but getting away from the lights, a figure suddenly loomed before me, strange and horrible.

"A pretty flower for a pretty flower, both to glorify God?" piped a voice. It was one of the Redeemed, and I almost screamed, and pushed the poor creature out of the way.

There are no really bad sections of Las Vegas, but there are some not so well lit, not so garish, not so public, and I was in one of these now.

I was cloaked in the darkness, and for a moment, it felt good.

Suddenly a man came out of the shadows, a bottle in his hand.

"Hey! Honey! Wanna drink?" he called out in a filthy, ugly voice as he reached for me. I almost screamed, but evaded him. He followed me, and I started running again.

Finally I came to a corner and rounded it. There was a house and some small trees watered by a sprinkler, and I quickly crouched down in their protective, dark shelter, and held my breath.

He came around the corner seconds later, and stood there for what seemed like forever, breathing hard and looking around.

So this is what it's like, I thought. Is this what every woman feels and fears if she ventures out alone? Is every walk in a strange place a potential threat, a promise that, perhaps, horror is lurking there?

Victor Gonser wouldn't have hesitated in walking into that bar, down this street. Victor wouldn't be crouching, trembling in fear as some bastard stalked him. Men couldn't comprehend this terror, as I waited breathless, certain I would cough, or fall and give myself away to this man of the dark.

He drained the bottle, and threw it into the yard. It hit the tree, and landed just a few inches from me.

I heard him mumbling something to himself, then he turned and walked slowly down the street toward the Strip.

I remained there for some time, shaking terribly, realizing that while Victor Gonser hated being alone, I, Misty, could not *survive* alone.

I heard a clock somewhere strike three. Three in the morning, and I was crouching in the darkness of somebody's front yard.

Just as I could not turn Misty off physically, I could not shed her mentally, either. She was not cut out for this and she was terrified, out of her element completely, overcome with that emotionalism that now worked against me.

I shuddered, and forced myself to stop crying, to calm down. I took deep breaths, and tried to regain control.

Think, dammit, think! I told myself over and over.

Cautiously, I made my way back to the walk, and could see nothing, nobody but a few cars going to and fro.

Now the Strip was closed to me as well. *He* had gone that way, and I must go the other.

I walked, forcing myself to be slow and deliberate, afraid as I walked under every streetlight, more afraid of the darkness between.

I was suddenly out of sidewalk and streetlights again, and walking on the sandy shoulder of what the sign said was State Route 6. How long or how fast I'd walked I didn't know. Over to the right of me I saw the start of an Interstate highway, and beyond it a cluster of lights in the darkness.

Route 6 and the Interstate seemed to get further apart, so I cut overland, crossing the dark gulf between; desert grass and brush stung my feet, and I felt in total despair.

Then, suddenly, I was at the big highway, which was carrying a moderate amount of traffic. I looked over and saw that the lights I'd seen were not merely lights but a truck stop of some sort.

It was difficult crossing the highway, and there was a slope down the other side which caused me to fall more than once, but I was over, and walking toward the bright lights.

Frankly, I was in a state of shock yet, had been since the man had almost caught up to me. I could just think of the lights, of people, lots of people, with no dark places.

The place smelled of diesel fuel and a young attendant rushed around checking green pumps, using extenders to wash the windshields of the big rigs.

Even so, it was fairly new, and one of those complete types—a restaurant, complete with slot machine banks, and a trucker's store of sorts. I walked in and headed first for the women's bathroom, which was fairly difficult to find. This was still mostly a man's world.

Once inside, the shock seemed to wear off a bit, and I almost collapsed, bracing myself against a sink. Slowly my head came up and I looked at myself in the mirror.

My God! I thought. I looked like hell, and even looking like hell I looked sexy.

I straightened myself up and went into a stall. I sat there for several minutes on the toilet, trying to get ahold of myself.

Now what? I asked myself, fearing that the answer was that I was doomed to wander forever like this, cut off and alone.

Something within me seemed to snap. *No!* I told myself suddenly, and dried my flowing tears of hopelessness.

I was back in control, tired but thinking once more. The terror wasn't gone, but it had been superceded by desperation. If the terror came, then it would come. I had to accept that. But, if that was all I could look forward to, I might as well slit my throat right here, now.

That's where Victor Gonser had been, back up on the trail, I realized. Thinking about jumping off a cliff, wasn't he?

I fumbled in the big, cheap purse. Some makeup there, yes, a small towel, and about $230.00. All my worldly goods.

I straightened myself up and went out over to the trucker's store. It was mostly men's stuff, but I found a cute straw cowboy hat that looked really nice, some hankies, deodorant, and other toiletries. Even a spare couple of shirts. They stuffed the bag to bulging, but it was much better.

I went back into the john and used what I'd bought, carefully brushed my hair, cleaned up, got looking and smelling nice.

Terror there might be, but I had a mind inside this body, and I had this body, too.

I walked into the restaurant. It was mostly empty except for a few truckers talking in a special area reserved for them, sipping coffee or eating hamburgers.

The waitress came over, and I asked for coffee and some eggs, all I thought I could manage.

But I radiated, and I knew it. Nature abhors a vacuum, and I had a vacuum on both sides of me, while nature was staring from the trucker's lounge.

One of them, a tired-looking man in his mid-forties dressed somewhat cowboy-style, a day or so's growth of beard giving him something of the rugged look, called over.

"Hay!" he said loudly, in an accent that was strictly hillbilly. "Hay Sweet Thang! You lonesome? C'mon' over!"

I drank my coffee and pretended to ignore him. Finally he got up, mostly, I think, at the whispered taunting of two other drivers, and came over.

"What's the matter, gal? Troubles?" he asked pleasantly. "You look too sad sittin' here like that with that expression on yore face."

I turned to him. "I'm stuck, if you want to know the truth. I used to dance at the Mauritania Lounge here, but the boss decided he wanted to use me in another end of his business, and I quit. I've just been drifting around all night, trying to think about what to do next."

He seemed genuinely sympathetic. "I know what you mean, I think. Where y'all headin' now?"

I sighed. "I was thinking of getting a waitress's job or something," I told him. I had seen a sign near the front door. "Now, I don't know. I have a lot of friends, but they're all back in L.A., and I have no way to get there."

He rubbed his chin, and looked about as sincere as I was.

"Well, now," he thought. "No money?"

"Some," I replied, then told him about the encounter with the would-be rapist. I told it straight, sparing nothing except the fact that I was not about to go back into town for entirely different reasons than the fear of meeting him again.

He nodded sympathetically, and there seemed real concern in his voice.

"Look," he suggested, "I've just dropped a load at the air base here, and I'm deadheadin' back to Barstow. You're welcome as far as there. After that, well, I don't think we got a problem gettin' no ride into L.A. for a beaver pretty as you, ma'am."

And it was as simple as that.

He was a perfect gentleman all the way, and I slept the not so long ride to Barstow.

Once he got in C.B. range of the I-15, I-40 junction, he got on the radio and described me in incredible, somewhat colorful language, and explained my need.

The others didn't believe him, and so I got on myself and asked for help.

I hope I didn't cause a smash-up somewhere, but finally the man with the strongest radio got through the jam and we linked up. I kissed my savior good-bye, and changed trucks.

The new man was not as nice or as gentlemanly, but he seemed satisfied to pet and snuggle as best he could with fourteen gears to control, and damned if he didn't wind up driving miles out of his way to drop me at the Farmer's Market!

I had made it with two hours to spare, not costing me a thing, and I was dead tired but little else.

Meeting in the Farmer's Market, I found, was more difficult than anyone would think. It's a huge place, full of stalls selling just about everything, and crowds of people all about. I finally decided that I was too tired to hunt; if I was going to be a magnet, I might as well be one and let them find me.

I got a small bun from a Greek-style bakery stall, and some strong coffee and sat down at one of the picnic tables that were spread all over the inside of the place.

People were all around, and I got the usual looks, but nobody bothered me. *This* kind of crowd, the tourists and the locals, was the kind I liked best right now.

About 11:15, wandering around just looking at things, I heard a familiar voice shout "Misty!" and before I could move Dory was all over me, kissing and hugging. I finally calmed her down and we found a place that, while not exactly quiet, was at least out of the mainstream, and sat down.

"Well," I said to her. "You don't look exactly worn down and away. Tell me what happened after we split up."

"Well," she echoed me, "after you went off with Mr. Middle America I stood around for a while, then walked into the bar—and immediately got challenged for my I.D.! I didn't believe it, but I had to leave, and they escorted me completely out of the casino.

"So, there I was, out on the streets with no place to go. I saw some of the Redeemed selling their flowers, and I wanted to get away from there."

"I know," I responded with a slight shudder. "I saw some on the way here. It's a wonder they aren't all over here."

"They wouldn't allow it," Dory said flatly. "They're selling, so they'd have to have a stall." She twisted in her seat a bit, getting more comfortable. "So, anyway, I didn't want to be around those creeps, and so I headed for the bus station. I saw all the stakeouts, but I figured that if this getup wouldn't get me past them then I was gone anyway, and they gave me barely a glance!"

I took a deep breath, thinking of my own fears and what that had led to, and said nothing.

"Well, there I was, so I bought the ticket and started to come here. They were pretty thorough—had somebody at the ticket counter and bus gate, too. Well, anyway, I passed, and got a seat, and a few minutes later this young black guy, a real cool sort, took the seat next to me. He tried to look disinterested, but I've been around. We got to talking, and he was very nice.

"So we got in about a little after one in the morning, and we took a cab to his apartment—"

"Dory! You didn't!" I exclaimed.

She smiled. "C'mon, I *said* he was a nice guy. I spent the night there, he had a real nice place. A computer programmer, I think he said. He played some records— Man! Are they ever weird now!—and blew some smoke and had a real great night. He was gone to work when I got up, so I fixed myself some breakfast and came on over. You know, I heard they didn't have any busses in L.A., but they do—occasionally. I got here, and that's all there is to it. What about you?"

I hesitated, feeling a little funny. I didn't know exactly what I felt, or why I felt it, but it was a crazy sort of combination. Joy that she was here, and safe, and without any problems, some resentment that she'd done it all so easily after what I'd gone through, and, for some reason, a touch of possessive jealousy, strange from someone like me.

I tried to push it back and considered how much to tell her. In the end, I felt a little mad at myself and thought, hell, this is *Dory*, dammit. I told her everything, sparing nothing, and she listened in quiet concentration. When I was through, she sighed.

"You've had it rough, even though most of it was of your own making. After all, you had over two hundred bucks. Hell, you coulda taken a *cab* to L.A., at least to Barstow, anyway."

I was thunderstruck. It simply hadn't occurred to me. Now that she'd said it, I saw a dozen easy ways that a girl with money could have gone.

Blind, dumb fear had done it to me.

I started to cry, and this upset her. "Now, don't do that, or I'll feel bad and we'll both be bawling," she said sharply. "Look, you just went through something that every woman grows up with, has to face. It's the real world. Men can sympathize, but they can never *feel* it, so they can't ever understand how limiting it is to be a woman."

There was nothing I could say. Once I'd written of my hatred and contempt for all restraints, for anything that limited choices.

But there were some decisions you couldn't escape from.

Unless you went Harry Parch's route, or The Association's, and gave up *all* choices.

I glanced over at a clock nearby, and gasped. "It's after twelve," I said suddenly.

We moved out into the mainstream again, got some drinks, and started staring at the increasing crowds of people milling about, eating, and going back and forth.

Over two hours later we were still waiting.

I couldn't conceal my mounting agitation, and neither could Dory. Neither of us, though, would say it for some time more.

When it got to be three o'clock, she finally uttered the unspeakable.

"I don't think they're coming," she said softly.

I sighed. "So what do we do now?"

"I think we take a bus and go shopping for some clothes with that money of yours, then find a place for the night," she responded.

I nodded glumly. "Then?"

She shrugged. "We come back here tomorrow, same time. And the next day, and the next. If they don't show by then, I think we both go out and get jobs."

Chapter Thirteen

A hundred bucks doesn't go far these days when you're shopping for clothes, but Dory was ever the practical one and it's surprising what you can get at big discount and drug stores.

For another forty we found a room at a cheap hotel, not the kind of place I really liked but the most we could afford in these days of $150 rooms. That left about $70 for food, transportation, and emergencies. It wouldn't last long, but it only had to last until Monday, when, I hoped, I could find a pawn shop.

By early evening I was dead on my feet and just about passed out. I think I slept ten or eleven solid hours, but, despite a headache, I felt better than I had since I'd last been in Stuart's little chair at IMC.

It was a little after ten on Saturday. Dory came into the room from the outside, newspapers in hand. "Well! Sleeping Beauty awaketh!"

I managed a smile, and shook the sleep from me. I took a cool shower to get fully awake, then got dressed, sticking to the casual outfit. It was warmer in L.A. than I'd expected.

Trying to manage with the city's less-than-great mass transit system was a pain, but we couldn't afford cabs at today's prices, not now. We got to Farmer's Market just before noon, and I managed to get coffee, a danish, and some aspirin. We idly read the papers, thin for a Saturday, which contained little of interest to us, and waited.

Suddenly, thumbing through the inside back section, Dory let out a little gasp.

"What is it?"

"Listen. 'Man, Woman Die in Flaming Crash. Victorville, October 2. An unidentified man and woman were killed tonight when their car swerved to avoid a pedestrian and rolled over, bursting into flame. The car had been reported stolen in Las Vegas hours earlier. Highway Patrol officers are investigating.' " She looked up at me, a pained expression on her face.

"You don't suppose ..." I managed, supposing exactly that.

She nodded slowly. "Sure. It fits. Although it's almost certainly not the way it really happened."

I thought sadly of poor, gentle Stuart, and of the strange alien who called himself Dan Pauley. I couldn't bring myself to believe it, although, deep down, I knew it was true. Stuart, in particular ... The thought of a world without him was almost unbearable.

They were gone.

I fought back tears, not very successfully. "So it's over. The great expedition to save the world is over. Well, if anybody saves it, it won't be us, now."

Dory nodded glumly. "No use hanging around here any more."

"What do you want to do?"

"Get drunk, or stoned, or both. Then wait for the Sunday papers and see what's available."

"Like hell I will," I snapped, getting mad now. "Damn it, I'm through running. Where's a phone booth?"

She looked at me strangely. "What . . . ?"

I stalked over to the booth, picked the receiver up, fed it a quarter, dialed O and got the quarter back. "Operator? Give me Al Jordan, Stateline, Nevada. I don't know the area code but I know the number." I gave it to her. "Collect," I told her. "Tell him it's Misty Carpenter."

I listened for all the relays and operator-connected conversations. I was using Al's private number, though. If he were there—and he almost certainly was about this time, I'd get him.

"Hello! Misty! Good to hear from ya," he enthused.

"Listen, Al, don't give me that bullshit," I shot him. "You're a no-good son of a bitch in the pocket of Harry Parch and I know it."

"Hey! Wait a *minute*, Baby!"

"Just shut up and listen, Al. I know you can call Parch. He's in Vegas, most likely. You call him and tell him to call off his dogs. We surrender. We want to have normal lives. I want to open that club, Al! I want to pick up where I left off! And I don't want any Harry Parch or his type whiskin' me off anywhere in the dead of night. You tell him Dory and me'll keep quiet, we'll be good girls and he can check on us all he wants, but we've had it, we're through, all we want is to be left alone, as we are—*as we are*, Al—to live normal, decent lives. Y'hear me?"

He was silent for a moment. Finally he said, "Jesus, you can get mad! O.K., O.K., I won't bullshit you. I can get ahold of Parch. But I dunno if he'll buy it—or if you can trust him if he says he'll buy it, Babe."

"He's a skunk and a rat but I think he *will* buy it, Al. How long do you figure it'll take to get hold of him?"

He thought a moment. "Give me 'til eight tonight, at least. Call me back then or give me a number."

"Uh uh. I'll call. Talk to you later, then. And, Al . . ."

"Yeah, Babe?"

"I can't do anything about Harry Parch or to him. But I wrote down a whole list of names and dates of some pretty big customers at Cougar over the years and I got it so it'll hit the papers if I disappear. You got that?"

"Take it easy, Babe. I'll do what I can!"

I hung up on him, feeling a lot better.

Dory, I found, was standing next to me, and she was staring at me, open-mouthed. "Wow. I didn't think you had it in you."

"Neither did I, but, damn it, I'm tired of being pushed, shoved, brain processed, chased, and all. We done what we could and that's that."

"Your grammar slipped, you know," she noted. "You sounded like a whole different person, accent and all."

I nodded. "Meet the real Misty Carpenter."

"Think Parch'll buy it?"

"I think so," I told her honestly. "If we're in Vegas we're under his thumb, so to speak, and he has nothing to gain now. In his own way he's a reasonable man. We just don't matter any more, Dory."

"I hope you're right," she said sincerely.

I wasn't about to call Al from the hotel, but we went back there to settle down and wait for the magic hour.

We didn't say much about the future, or the risks involved, nor did I, at least, dwell on them. I think I'd just been tensioned and pressured out. I was just too sick and tired of this to be scared any more. I'd had plenty of sleep, yet I felt completely worn out, inside and out.

There wasn't much on TV and we finally went through the papers, and, for a while, we just sat around listlessly, letting it all wear off. Finally I said, "I think I'm going to take a shower and just wind down."

Dory looked over and smiled. "Want company? We can save water and do each other's backs."

I laughed and said "sure" and we did. In the process, the tension seemed to lift, and we got to playing around with each other, scrubbing the sensitive spots, and when we got out and dried off we both flopped nude on the bed.

"Misty?"

"Yes?"

"What happens if Parch buys the deal? What happens then?"

"I use the credit cards for a plane to Vegas, we rent a car—mine's still up in Tahoe—and pick up all the left luggage. Then we check into the best hotel suite we can find and get the best dinner in Vegas."

"No, not immediately. After. In the long term."

"I make a pretty good living, and I have a lot of contacts from my old clientele," I told her. "I got a solid four-week contract with the Imperial Lounge, which is Joe's place, which I can parlay into a lot more, either with Joe or some of the others there, if I'm a hit."

"You'll be a hit. With those moves you're the best in the business, I bet."

I smiled. "And, if I get long-term work, we find a condo or something there and settle in. Buy furniture, clothes, you name it."

"And where do I come in? I mean—what's *my* future? Yours is pretty secure."

"As long as the looks last," I admitted, turning on my side to look at her. "But I don't see what you're concerned about. You can do anything you want to do."

"I'm not sure just what I *do* want to do. Since—coming back—I really haven't allowed myself to think about the next day. Now I have to—and I have no place to go, no money, no job, not even a real cover identity so I can get a driver's license or social security card or anything like that. No high school diploma, nothing—and I at least deserve that, having gone through it twice."

I looked at her strangely. "Dory, you have a place. Wherever I am you have a place, money, whatever you need. I can't hack this world alone, not any more. Maybe the original Misty could, but *I* can't. I need you very badly."

"Sure, for now. But when you get the big time and all those big-shots are around with their flashy everything, it might be different."

I sat up, turned, and stared at her. "Dory, you little idiot! I'm in *love* with you! Don't you understand that? I've been in love with you since the first day we met on the boat. I need you terribly, with me, always. Without you, all the rest doesn't mean a thing."

Her face broke into a broad smile and she got up and hugged me. "Oh, Misty! That's all I wanted to hear!"

And we made love there, for the first time, an act stronger than sex but which made sex all the better. It was as Stuart said. It wasn't who you were on the outside but who you really were, on the inside, that mattered most, that was the only thing that was really important.

And the lovemaking lasted and lasted and lasted. . . .

I would not give up men—and possibly she wouldn't, either. A part of me, at least, required the physical act. But I knew then that I could love only this one, and make love only to this one person, this individual, this wonderful human being.

And after we just lay there, caressing each other tenderly, saying very little for a while. Finally Dory sighed and said, "Misty? You know, after all this, I *finally* found it."

"Found what, honey?"

"My place. Normalcy. A real life. For the first time I *like* myself, see a real future. I'm whole, Misty! I'm not a freak any more! I'm a real person and I'm very, very happy."

I smiled, recalling my own conflicts. Whole people. Neither of us would ever have been whole or happy as our former selves, doomed to go through life slightly askew. The Urulu, although it wasn't their motive, had accomplished a lot, and, oddly, so had IMC, even Harry

Parch. Not deliberately, of course, but it was there all the same. I didn't know, had never known, two people as much in love and so filled with caring for each other as Dory and I were now, yet, even there, those external forces had twisted and turned us for the better. I rid myself of my male-ness, so to speak, and became a real woman, while Dory faced down and made peace with her inner demon. And, knowing that body-switching was not only possible but was practiced by all sorts of creatures, including the U.S. Government, removed any last stigma that might linger in the mind about love between two women. When men could be women, or women, men, at the flick of a switch or the touch of an alien hand, what difference did your body really make? Tall, short, fat, thin, old, young, male, female, black, white, red, yellow . . . all irrelevant.

Was this, perhaps, the Urulu promise? A civilization that never looked to the outside, only *inside?* Who saw and reacted only to the real person within, regardless of physical form? It was an exciting possibility, one made all the more likely by the Urulu's own nature. Would *any* race that evolved with this ability pay any attention to looks or superficialities at all? Not among their own people, certainly.

I wondered again what they were really like. Not at all like us, certainly. And not totally free themselves of prejudices and hang-ups, since they had so little regard for us warm-blooded mammals.

And there was the rub. The authoritarian empire they had encountered had been led by a race like ours, a race that had itself discovered, rather than evolved, the mystery of the identity matrix. Had evolved with our concept of physical, superficial differences being important. Their prejudices, like those of Harry Parch and those who pulled his strings, shaped their use of the identity matrix, and had distorted and perverted its potential. No wonder the Urulu couldn't grasp us as a race worth saving! They couldn't see how we could evolve except into a new mini-Association.

And they might well be right, I told myself. Certainly we had failed, but, damn it, we had done our best. Done everything that was asked of us, to the best of our ability. We could only hope now that there were others to take up the fight and that one of them would succeed. A pity, though, I thought. We—Dory and I—were, I felt, closer to the Urulu, or at least its ideal, than any other human beings on Earth. Stuart, though, poor Stuart, had at least seen this potential.

Suddenly I had a thought and sat up, grabbing for the clock.

"What's the matter?"

"It's after nine! I didn't call Al back!"

Dory got up and shook her head. "We were at it for *hours*. Wow."

I kissed her and jumped out of bed. "And it was wonderful, too. But I have to make that call."

I was still only half-dressed when the telephone rang in the hotel room. I jumped at the sound, then turned and stared at it for a moment. It was one of those internal things, without even a dial. Who would be calling *this* room?

Hesitantly, I picked up the receiver. "Yes?"

"Miss, ah, Carpenter, when you failed to call at eight I decided to wait a bit, but finally decided to call you, instead," said Harry Parch.

I almost dropped the phone. Dory saw my horrified expression and I mouthed Parch to her. That made her sit up fast.

"Go on," I told him, trying to sound brave.

"I took this step as a demonstration of good faith," he continued. "As you can see, we know where you are, and could have picked you up at any time if we'd wanted. Actually, I must congratulate you. We did not pick *you* up at all, and I have no idea how you got where you are. However, we had excellent photos of your friend from the Indian school, and we spotted her when she boarded the bus. From that point we just followed her directly to you."

I nodded glumly to myself. It *had* seemed all too easy. "So why didn't you pick us up yesterday?" I asked him.

"Basically, we wanted to see what you'd do. We have not been kind to the two of you, who are the most innocent people in this mess, and we would prefer not to do any more. You *didn't* go to the papers, you *didn't* run around hysterically, you just accepted things, and that is what we wanted to know. Miss Carpenter, when I received your message today I can not tell you how happy it made us. You have chosen the best course for you, for us, for everyone. I believe we can finally end all this, or, at least, your part in it, and you and your friend can go about the rest of your lives."

I felt excitement and relief rising in me. I covered the mouthpiece and whispered to Dory, "He's going to buy it!"

"Then we're free to leave? To go back and pick up our lives?"

"Yes, indeed. You understand, of course, that we will keep a watch on both of you, and that if you cause trouble in the future this arrangement may have to be modified. But, as long as you don't rock the boat, neither will we."

"That sounds fair enough," I told him. "But there's one minor point you could help with."

"Oh?"

"Legal identities. I'm sort of real, but Dory's got real problems. She needs proof of citizenship."

He sounded surprised. "Why, she's got it—and so have you. We don't do things halfway. There really *was* a Misty Ann Carpenter, but she died at the age of three months and is buried in Cedar Point Cemetery in a pauper's gravesite. Delores Eagle Feather had a similar fate in Yakima, Washington, but her birth certificate's on file there. Use those. No one will ask or question you about them. It's done all the time."

I nodded to myself. Finally, I said, "Parch—one more last thing on this matter."

"Yes?"

"Pauley. He said the Redeemed were the enemy and that they could switch."

He sighed. "I know. They use the First Amendment as a weapon. But we're working on it, that's all I can say. It's not your battle now. Go find a home. There are others more qualified to carry the burden. Goodbye, Miss Carpenter."

"Goodbye, Mr. Parch."

And that was that.

It was, in fact, as easy as Parch claimed. We blew the last of the cash on a quick flight back, called the Sands for a minibus, and were settled in in less than four hours. I was relieved to find that not only was my big wardrobe still in storage, but the nice old geezer at the motel still had the bag I'd left.

The city lost its ugliness and was alit with neon splendor at two in the morning, open and doing business all around. There are no clocks in casinos, and they work on a timeless schedule which many of the restaurants and other places also follow.

On Monday we went to the bank and then on something of a shopping spree. It was far different than before. Las Vegas was its former glamorous, unthreatening self once again, and we had each other and were no longer alone.

A black, heavy weight had been lifted from both of us and we were like kids. Both of us had ourselves practically done over, the only complaint from Dory that I needed my hair blond and curly again, and Dory seemed almost born anew. She had her hair styled into a pageboy, bought some really nice clinging fashions, and, in a slinky, satiny silk dress, heels, and some jewelry transformed herself into a stunningly beautiful woman.

We wrote for our birth certificates and got them, applying for passports, the ultimate stamp of legitimacy although we didn't feel like going anywhere, got her a driver's license, and had her name added to my charge accounts and bank accounts, and found a small but comfortable apartment away from the Strip in a nice, safe neighborhood.

Joe was delighted to see me and launched the club with a big publicity blitz. It was a real class show in a real class setting, and a damned good location—no gambling, of course, but sandwiched between two busy casinos. We did really great business, and Joe was so happy he offered me thirty weeks for thirty thousand. I took it, of course, but not before Dory looked over all the contracts, deals, and exclusions. It was clear I was the star and centerpiece of the show, she said, and if I could establish my dominance during that run the place would be so identified with me that they'd wind up eventually giving me a piece of the club.

She got around the high school problem by taking the G.E.D., a real snap according to her, then enrolled in night courses in business administration. She became my manager, more or less, making most of the decisions, controlling the money and spending, even getting me on some local TV and, through that, an agent with powerful connections.

Nobody raised an eyelash at our obvious intimate relationship, not in Vegas, although some of the guys I knew couldn't figure out how I could go to bed with an attractive guy and obviously enjoy it and then go home to my "wife." Dory seemed to understand and not to mind my promiscuity as long as I always came home to her. For her own part, she didn't seem interested in anybody but me—although I hardly could have stood in her way—and she seemed happy and content. I might have been the star, but she was the boss in the household, no question about it, and I liked it that way.

If anything, our relationship deepened even beyond what I would have thought possible. At times we almost seemed two different sides of the same person, knowing what each other was thinking and feeling, understanding each other and trusting each other totally.

On her official eighteenth birthday she came of legal age for most things and applied for a legal change of name, from Delores Eagle Feather to just Dory Carpenter. I was flattered, but she did it because she wanted to and I didn't object. She had a lot of fun changing names on accounts and her driver's license and even passport when it came through. She had taken the last step, that of becoming her own person and not somebody else, and she was radiant.

The publicity campaign paid off. I got written up by one columnist as "The Queen of Las Vegas" and I loved it. I did talk shows and supermarket openings and loved to shock the hell out of people by proving myself an intellectual, conversant with a lot of topics, although never in the act. That wasn't the image the public was buying.

Again the old hang-up, of course. What I was outside was what was important to the masses.

Dory had been right, too, about the club's dependence on me. When I made a move to leave, they jumped, had long discussions with my agent, and, since they really couldn't offer me more money—without a casino, which a strip club couldn't have under the weird laws there, their top gross was limited—but they did wind up offering me a slightly lower salary and a profit percentage, which we took, along with the biggest piece of ego I could imagine—a name change to "Misty's Harbor," complete with large, sexy portrait of me framed in Vegas neon.

The only dark spot was the numbers of the Redeemed that seemed to be growing everywhere. You couldn't go anywhere without running into them with their flowers, candy, shaved bodies and raped and gutted minds. They had bought large buildings, huge tracts of land, and were gaining political influence, the kind that comes with massive amounts of tax-free money and power. They swelled in membership and never seemed to lose converts, a fact that actually attracted more young people and lost souls to the movement. As usual, the press was mixed, the conservatives upset at losing their kids, the liberals shocked at the gutting of a generation's spirit, but with Constitutional guarantees there was nothing, it seemed, that could be done to slow them.

They were spreading worldwide, in the Latin countries, in Africa, in Europe and parts of Asia, tailoring their public beliefs to fit local concerns. It was hard to tell what they were doing in the Iron Curtain countries, but I had no doubt they were there and working successfully.

The cult alone soon had a worldwide following estimated at more than twenty *million*. Dory and I watched the TV and headlines and understood anew what Dan Pauley had meant. The Association planted, and grew, and moved out to conquer all.

I couldn't believe that Parch and IMC would take this lying down, and I wondered if, somehow, they'd just discovered an enemy they could not fight without making themselves into the enemy. It must be frustrating, I thought more than once, to *know* and have the power and be so impotent.

We'd been living our own life of peaceful glamour for more than two years now, and it showed no signs of slacking off. Some tentative investments Dory had made in local real estate had already paid off, and we were very comfortable and secure. To celebrate our second "anniversary" I'd taken some time off and we'd gone to Hawaii and Tahiti, a sort of belated honeymoon, just the two of us doing what all lovers do—or would like to do, if they had the time and money.

Coming home from the club late one night, about four or so, I was feeling a little off and just wanted to get in, eat, and relax. On such days Dory would have a light supper waiting, and I could just relax and unwind.

I walked in and saw nothing cooking and Dory in the living room avidly watching TV. For a moment I just thought she'd got engrossed in a movie or something, but then I realized it was a newscast and that she was very intent on it. I frowned. A newscast? At this hour?

She looked up as I entered, looking worried and haggard, and I grew concerned. "What's up?" I asked. "What's happening?"

She got up and came over, giving me a hug and a kiss. "You haven't *heard?* You don't *know?*"

I shook my head. News didn't travel much in my circles, at least not while it was happening.

"They shot the President!"

"What?"

She nodded. "He was comin' out of a hotel in Chicago where he was campaigning and they zapped him!"

"What? *Who?*"

"The Redeemed! About an hour ago. Opened up on all sides with automatic weapons! Mowed down a *huge* crowd."

My God! I thought, and sank back into the sofa. What insulated lives we've led. I wasn't a fan of the President's, but I still felt a deep sense of outrage at the deed.

"Why would they do it?" I asked aloud. "It doesn't make sense for The Association to do something like this."

We both went over and turned back to the TV. They were showing an instant replay of the thing—it seemed to have been in front of the network cameras. It was a stunning, horrible, grotesque sight. "They're all *smiling,*" I breathed, unable to tear myself away from it. "Oh, my God!"

They switched back to the studio, where a tired-looking anchorman, not one of the regulars, continued the story.

"Vice President Arnold was awakened and told the news at 3:45 Pacific Time. Arnold immediately cut short his campaign swing through California and is expected to fly to Washington later on this evening. His motorcade is already getting ready to go to the airport and he is expected to leave for there as soon as possible.

"Repeating our earlier story. President Long is dead, shot to death by gunmen waiting for him with submachine guns outside the Trevor House Hotel in Chicago where he had been in an early morning political strategy session with Illinois Republican bigwigs. He emerged from the hotel at about six fifteen Chicago time and was immediately cut down, along with at least twenty-six others, by a squad of at least six gunmen with automatic weapons who were allegedly members of the Church of the Redeemed. All six were killed. A complete list of the dead will follow shortly.

"President Long had to fit the session into a crowded schedule, and scheduled it only as a last-minute bid to end party bickering in the crucial midwestern state. The unusually early time was caused by his schedule. He was due to fly to Kansas City at eight Central Time."

I did a mental calculation. If he was shot at 6:15 Central, it was 4:15 here—only twenty minutes or so before I got home.

The announcer was going on and on about the whole thing. The list of dead included the Secret Service agents, some well-known press people, his top campaign aide and two Congressmen from Illinois.

"FBI and Secret Service agents immediately went to the local and national headquarters of the International Brotherhood Church of the Redeemed, but spokespersons for that organization deny any responsibility for the slaying and state categorically that they are as shocked as the rest of us."

"I'll bet," Dory grumbled.

I thought a moment. "No. Wait a minute. Maybe they are."

"Huh? You know those idiots don't do anything without orders!"

I sat back, feeling stunned. "Dory—suppose it *isn't* The Association. Suppose it *isn't* the Redeemed."

She looked at me quizzically. "What do you mean? You saw 'em. You remember how Dan looked: Who else could it be?"

I thought furiously. "Dory—who's the Speaker of the House?"

"Huh? I dunno. Why? I guess I can look it up in the almanac." She got up, rooted around, found it, struggled with the contents, then found the right page. "Well I'll be damned," she said. "Phillip J. Kelleam."

"Arnold's a dead man," I told her. "If not today, then as soon as possible."

"I don't get you."

"Dory—if the President *and* Vice-President are killed before a successor be named, the Speaker of the House becomes President."

"Oh, Jesus!" she breathed. "It's Harry Parch!"

I nodded.

"We gotta do something. Warn the Secret Service or something!"

I shook my head sadly. "We can't. He's probably got our phone tapped and us monitored very closely right now. Besides—who'd believe us? And why would they?" I got up, went over to the small bar, and poured myself a stiff one.

Dory came over and looked at it. "Pour me one, too. A good stiff one. I think we both need it."

In the background, a remote announcer was saying, "The Vice-President is emerging now, absolutely covered by Secret Service agents. He's in the car—they're roaring off. They want to take no chances tonight."

But, as night passed and the dawn rose over the desert, my prediction was already true. More of the so-called "Redeemed" had planted a huge series of bombs on a key overpass any limo would have to take to get to the airport. It exploded as Arnold's limo went over it, then dozens of the Redeemed, all smiling, closed in and machine-gunned everything that moved. Some of the cops who survived finally got them—it was a suicidal attack with none of them even trying to find cover—but they had done their job.

And so had Harry Parch.

In a way, it was a master stroke. Kill the two top men. Put your own man in power, probably backed up by a huge contingent of people either on the inside at IMC or those who had been invited out to scenic Nevada for a demonstration. . . . Kidnap some of the Redeemed and reprogram them. Make sure it was on national television, the nightmare of young, hollow faces in robes and hoods smiling as they shot those people down in cold blood. Knocking off both the top spots absolutely demonstrates the conspiracy in the public mind, allowing Kelleam to take control and move decisively, as a result of massive public outrage and pressure, to close down the Redeemed. Was it any coincidence that the bomb-planters had waited to be cut down at that bridge when they could have easily slipped away?

So all we could do was sit there and get very drunk so we wouldn't have to decide whether or not Phil Kelleam and Harry Parch were really any improvement over The Association.

We awoke hung over when the phone rang the next afternoon. I reached blearily over Dory and answered it. It was Joe, of course, telling me that the club would be closed for a few days, through the funerals, anyway. I just told him I expected it, hung up, and rolled back on the bed again.

I felt really lousy, but Dory was even worse, so I struggled up, finally, sticking some coffee on, then flipped on the TV. The usual stuff, mostly, what you would expect under these conditions.

Kelleam had wasted no time while we slept, declaring

four days of public mourning, scheduling the unprece-
dented double funerals, and, almost before he was sworn
in, authorizing the FBI and Secret Service to move in on
the Redeemed all over the country with National Guard
and regular military supporting them. He had almost
unlimited power for the moment to deal with the obvious menace, and he was making good use of it—to the
applause of Congress and the people. He moved so efficiently that you'd almost swear he'd been expecting
something like this and had the plans already drawn up.

Most everything was closed, even in Vegas, except the
casinos, of course.

Dory struggled into the kitchen, groaning, and looked
like I felt. She reached into a drawer, took out a plastic
bag, and rolled a joint. It didn't make the hangovers go
away, but we didn't care so much about them anymore.

The TV showed the military moving on Association
buildings, temples, and holdings with exceptional speed
and thoroughness. Tens of thousands were being rounded
up, and large camps were being established in different
parts of the country to hold them all. A quick session of
Congress had authorized exceptional emergency measures, thereby reinforcing what Kelleam was already
doing by executive order. Many other countries were
moving, too, either frightened by the Redeemed or using
the events in the U.S. as an excuse to move. All over the
world the cult, which had enjoyed such fantastic success, was being rapidly and systematically crushed. Rumors were already circulating that really strange things
were being discovered in examinations of church papers
and property; implications were being made that this
was far more than the simple religion it appeared.

About five that afternoon we'd both come down suffi-
ciently to eat something and function in a more or less
normal manner, but we both felt down, depressed, and
helpless. It seemed obvious to us that the country was
being softened up in order to be faced with the threat of

alien invasion, an invasion by mind control which needed defense.

It would take a while, of course, to build the pressure up and do it right, but it wouldn't be a very long time. They would want to capitalize on the emotional shocks and the resultant national mood. They would introduce the devices all over the country, the processors that would make you safe from the aliens. They were probably quite rapid and efficient now, and maybe even portable. People would beat down the doors of government demanding protection, and they would get it. Yes, they'd get it—and what else? A few ideas, a few attitudes, perhaps, that they didn't have before? Neither of us could fully shake the feeling that it wasn't the beginning of the end.

"Don't worry," Dory said, trying to put as cheery a front on things as she could, "you're proof positive they'll have exotic dancing and sexy women in their brave new world."

But I still wasn't sure if I wanted to live in a world run by men who would cruelly cut down their own leaders and program the rest. Still, *our* life would continue, somehow, and there was nothing we could do about it, anyway.

"Let's take a little trip," I suggested. "Just the two of us."

"Where?"

"Away. Someplace without a lot of people and newscasts. It's the middle of the summer." I glanced at the calendar. "In two days it'll be six years since we first met on the ferry."

"Think you can get away?"

"Sure," I told her. "I don't have anything big scheduled, nothing I can't cancel. And it's a hundred and eight out there, for Christ's sake! Things aren't going to be normal for some time."

"Where are you thinkin' of?"

I went over some possibilities in my head. "Why don't

we just get in the car and drive? I'd like to go to the ocean, I think. Maybe the Sonoma Coast of California. Nice and deserted, and I haven't been there in a long, long time."

"Well, it beats sitting around here gettin' stoned," she agreed, and it was settled.

I had some trouble getting hold of Joe, but no real trouble in getting three weeks. With the club closed for the next four days, he had plenty of time to line up some good alternates and put in a little last-minute plugging.

I still had my little Fiat sports car in shocking metallic pink, a car I'd been attracted to in the first place because it was one of only two or three convertibles you could still buy. We packed and got a road atlas and got started the next day.

It felt funny driving north, since we drove along the boundaries of Nellis Air Force Base and Test Range, beyond which, buried under thousands of feet, was IMC. When we passed the small, nondescript road leading off into the dry hills to the east leading to it I felt a slight shudder, but nothing more.

We stopped for the night in Stateline, mostly for old time's sake, although I didn't go up to the lodge. I was afraid that if I ran into Al up there I'd ring his pudgy neck.

The next day we hit San Francisco, officially in mourning but still functioning, and I showed Dory some of the sights. We had a good seafood dinner near Fisherman's Wharf and rode a cable car hanging to the outside like only tourists do, but it was still too filled with people and news and reminders of the world situation, not the least of which was a San Francisco in which not a single member of a cult was on the street corner trying to peddle you something. In *that* town their *absence* was bizarre.

The next day we took California 1 up the coast. It's never been a good road, being two-lane, winding and twisty, but it is, I'm convinced, the most scenic road in

America, perhaps anywhere. Built originally by the Spanish starting back in the 1600s, it follows the winding coastline at the edge of the Pacific providing unlimited scenery as well as a real test of driving skills. It had changed since my youth, becoming more developed with fancy houses on many of the scenic bluffs, but it was still really pretty most of the way.

It was warm but not hot, a really refreshing change from what we'd been used to, and the salt-smell, sea birds, and sound of crashing breakers on the cliff walls far below the road acted as something of a tonic.

Out here, it seemed, bad things couldn't happen. Out here was only the sun and sea and the creatures of nature, true peace and quiet. Traffic, too, was abnormally low because of the mourning period, and the only reminder of the larger world were the flags we occasionally passed, all at half-staff.

We stopped often at the frequent turnouts—it's a little better driving south than north, as you're on the ocean side of the road—and once we climbed down to the rocky beach below, played a little, and played tag with the waves at the water's edge. For a moment, at least, it was good to be alive.

Finally, late in the day, we reached the coastal town of Fort Bragg, a resort and logging town despite its military name dating from Civil War days, and took a motel room for the night, agreeing that we would neither buy a newspaper or watch TV, and we didn't. We had ourselves, and we occupied ourselves with each other, and we had a good time. Finally, we fell to sleep.

The ringing phone awakened me, and, for a moment, I thought I was back home and started to reach over Dory for it, only to suddenly realize where I was, groan, get up and walk over to the phone on the dresser. I didn't know what time it was, but it was still dark.

Cursing whoever it was for getting a wrong number, I

picked it up, ready to give the caller a piece of my mind. "Yeah?" I snapped.

"Misty?" responded a low, pleasant man's voice. "This is Dan Pauley."

I dropped the phone.

Chapter Fourteen

"What is it?" Dory called sleepily.

"There's a man on the other end who says he's Dan Pauley!" I told her, picking up the phone and getting a little mad. "Listen, you," I told him, "I don't know what the game is but we quit, remember? Harry Parch said to leave us alone!"

"I'm not from Parch," the voice replied. "I really *am* Dan, Misty. I'm not dead—and neither is Stuart Eisenstadt. Look, I'll explain everything but not on the phone. You're still being shadowed, particularly now, and I don't know how much I can do like this. Look, the Surf Motel, about a half-mile up the road from you, has an all-night pancake house. Meet me there in half an hour and I'll explain everything."

I started to say something, but the line was dead. He'd hung up on me.

I detailed the conversation to Dory, and she was even more dubious about this mystery man than I was. "You have to learn not to answer phones in hotel rooms where nobody's supposed to know you," she grumped. "Still, I guess we better get dressed."

I picked up my watch. "It's four in the morning!"

"Yeah," she responded sourly, "but we gotta go anyway. If it's some kind of Parch trick we're better off in a place like that than here. And if it's not, well, we'll always wonder."

I nodded, knowing she was right. "You're the boss," I told her, then turned on the lights, pulled on some jeans, a sweater, and sandals, gave my hair a quick brush, and was ready.

Dory looked at me critically. "You let it all hang out like that and you'll drive the truck drivers wild."

"I don't plan to be too long," I shot back.

"Yeah, well, just don't jog anyplace, huh?"

We left, got in the car, and drove up Route 1. It was dark and deserted, with almost nobody on the road. It was fairly easy to spot the place, though, on the right hand side, and we pulled into the parking lot and looked around. After a minute or so, I turned to Dory and said, "Well, we haven't been arrested or anything yet. Might as well go in and get some coffee."

She nodded, and we walked nervously into the place, picking a booth and looking around. It was nearly deserted, only a few people sitting at various tables.

A young man entered looking like something out of a bad old movie. Long, black hair, frizzy beard, leather jacket, motorcycle helmet under one arm, studded black boots and even, so help me, a tattoo on the back of his right hand. A cigarette dangled from his lips, and he looked around the place, his eyes finally settling on me.

"Oh, boy," Dory breathed disgustedly. "For this we get up in the middle of the night, right?"

He finally sauntered on over to us, as I knew he would, and looked down, almost dripping invisible slime. "Hi, mind if I join you ladies?"

Frost was too mild for my tone. "Buzz off, buddy. We're waiting for somebody."

"You're waiting for me," he mumbled, then straightened a little, his tone becoming clearer, more normal. "I'm Dan Pauley."

"*That'll* take some doing," Dory snapped nastily.

"Yeah, I know what you must be thinking, but it's not. Look—mind if I sit down? There's a cop coming in and he may give me a pain."

Seeing that Dory wasn't going to give ground, I shifted over a bit and he sat. "It's good to see you both again. I—owe you a lot of explanation."

"Yeah, at least," Dory responded. "How do we know you're who you say you are, anyway? Or, if you *are* Dan, if you haven't been turned around by Parch and his buddies?"

He sighed. "You can't. You'll have to trust me. What motive could I have, anyway? You got off pretty free by facing up to them and adjusting. You've done pretty well, I know, both of you. You've got no real kick coming." He turned to me. "Look at you. The Queen of Las Vegas." He turned back to Dory. "And you, the Indian paramour and real estate genius. But, you're right. I *do* owe you an explanation."

"At least," I agreed, adjusting to the fact that his tone and manner did sort of remind me of Pauley, what I'd seen of him, anyway.

"Why weren't you at the Farmer's Market?" Dory asked.

He nodded. "O.K. From the top. After you left the restaurant, the Doctor and I wandered down to the Strip. I decided he should go to the bus station first, while I could cover—they didn't know me at all, remember, in that body and that disguise. He bought his ticket O.K., but in the line to get on the bus two of Parch's men just slid up on either side of him and walked him off. I couldn't do a damned thing without jeopardizing myself, and maybe you. I made a good fifteen agents in that station, including some working the counter. All I'd get would be another dart or maybe a shot in the head. It was damned frustrating, but there wasn't anything I could do. The only thing I could think of was to wait for you and see what happened then. About half an hour later Dory came in, bought her ticket, and made it onto the bus. I was pretty sure they'd made you, but they let you go. I had to ask myself why."

She nodded grimly. "They made me, all right. All the way."

"Well, I waited as long as I could for Misty, but you never showed, and I couldn't live in that station without somebody getting suspicious, so I got my ticket and rode out. Nobody made me, since they weren't sure who they were looking for. I had to figure Misty'd been picked up, too, and that Dory and I were going to be on our own. I headed straight for the Farmer's Market when I got in, then staked out the area. Imagine my surprise when Misty walked up to a counter in the inner courtyard."

I nodded. "I remember."

"Well, I waited, and finally Dory came, too, but I spotted her tails. I suddenly realized why they'd let you slip through, Dory. You were bait. Bait for me. You were the only way they could get to me, since I could be anybody, even if Stuart blabbed. Of course they couldn't afford to let *him* run loose, but you, well, you weren't really important to them. I tailed you all day, kept watch on Parch's tails, and when I saw just how well covered you were I knew that I would have no chance if I contacted you. He even had somebody on the hotel switchboard ten minutes after you checked in."

I nodded, and even Dory seemed to be warming a bit to him. The waitress brought our coffee and we sipped at it while Dan continued his story.

"Well, I'm sorry for how it sounds, but I was just forced to write off getting to you. I hocked those diamonds you gave me, Misty, and that gave me a little money to work with. I was still in trouble—I had no idea how to contact my people and almost no money, so I did what I had to do. I cased a small suburban bank, picked a victim, studied her for a couple of days, then intercepted her on her way to work, switched with her, tied her up, and, using her master keys, managed to steal several thousand dollars. I left, switched her back, and left her there. Poor woman. Either she's in a mental ward, or maybe in jail, but it was the only way."

"You could've gotten a *job*," Dory snapped.

He sighed. "Look, we've been down that moral road before. Maybe Parch got wind of it and cleared her. I hope so. Anyway, I knew about the planted news item where we were apparently killed, and I figured you'd take it at face value. Parch obviously wanted to see if you had a contingency place to run to that would lead him to me or other Urulu, and he got fooled. I think at least half the reason he let you go back to your life was that he still hoped that, sometime, I'd contact you. It cost him very little."

I was starting to get paranoid again. "Are we still being tailed?"

He nodded. "Oh, I don't think he's paid much attention to you for the last year or so, but when you took off on a trip at this critical time he had a man on you. *A* man." He grinned. "I'm him."

I gasped. "And what is he—now?"

He smiled. "A member of the Redeemed. I got the drop on him, switched, tied him up, then called the cops. He's been hauled to the local slammer by now."

"Where'd you find one of the Redeemed?" I asked. "I thought they were *all* locked up by now."

"Mostly," he admtted. "But I never changed bodies. There wasn't any need to, so I didn't. It was the same one I'd nabbed back in Vegas. You know, the eyebrows grew in but the hair never did. They must have used a chemical or something. That's gonna make it even easier for Parch to round 'em up." He paused a moment. "You know, they didn't come up with a bad plan. This'll set The Association back years here. They'll have to devise a whole new strategy, start over—unless they take the military option. IMC's gambling they won't, and I kind of agree. A major force moving this way would alert the Urulu, and it really isn't worth that kind of a fight. It can be won other ways. If it weren't for the fact that the same scheme to discredit the Church also was cleverly disguised to put their people totally in power and soften up the population for IMC's debut in their hands, I wouldn't even be here now."

We let that go for a moment. "Where did you go after you robbed the bank?" I asked.

"Well, we had a safe house and station in the desert near Death Valley. An old abandoned government installation. Missiles or something, but overgrown with weeds and overrun with sidewinders after the years. I figured that was my best bet, so I took the tourist bus out to Furnace Creek, then hitched down to where I had to be. I walked over that hot desert for several hours and finally reached the place. It was gone. Destroyed totally."

"Parch?" I asked.

He shook his head no. "Not self-destruct, either. The place was melted, fused together. A high energy weapon from the air beyond what you have and very different from what we would use. The Association had hit it quick and hard."

"So you were still stuck," Dory noted.

He nodded. "Stuck was right. I almost died in that damned desert just getting back to the road. I thought a car would *never* come along. I was sick for two days. But I recovered, and eventually worked my way around to two other isolated safe houses, one in Utah and one in northeastern California. Fused too, into nothing. Oh, I could have gone on around the continent and maybe overseas, but I got the message. They'd made us, somehow, and attacked all locations simultaneously and so thoroughly that there was little use. That left me only one way out, and I didn't want to take it."

"Which was?" I prompted.

"There's an emergency ship out there, in orbit," he

told us. "It's pretty well disguised and its screens would keep anybody from The Association to NORAD from getting curious. The type of attack they launched, the signs that it'd been at least a year earlier, maybe more, and the fact that there had been no Urulu reprisals told me that nobody, probably, got away. Maybe there's a few loose like me, but, if so, they're laying so low they wouldn't make a move. Besides, even if they took the emergency craft they'd arrange for another. No use stranding some of your own people for nothing."

"Won't your own people start wondering and check up on you?" I asked him.

He shook his head. "Not unless they get a real distress signal. This is off the beaten path, considered not worth bothering about. The only way they'll come is if somebody gave them a call and asked them in, like from the emergency ship."

"Dan—why haven't you just gone to that ship?" Dory wanted to know. "Why wait so long? And why come back and see us—now?"

He sighed. "Look, if I'd taken that ship out and filed my report on what I knew, they might just write Earth off, or, instead, they might come over and wipe out every man, woman, and child on the planet in the same way as a doctor would kill disease germs. I've been here too long. I like the people, and I see the potential here for it to go either way. Look—long ago, I was in a similar situation far away from here. Different world, different kinds of people, night and day, but it was still comparable. I took the easy way then, and that world got destroyed. I simply can not bear the responsibility of that twice, at least not without trying to do something about it. But once I report, I have about as much influence in the final decision as an army sergeant in the field has with his commanding general. You see my problem?"

We nodded, and, still, Dory pressed the questions that were on both our minds. "So why now? And why *us*?"

He hesitated a moment, then replied, "O.K., I'll put it right on the line. IMC's moves have pitted them directly against The Association. They've written us off and joined battle directly. I think the nationalism, petty jealousies, prejudices, and rivalries of this world favor The Association hands down, but, in the long run, it makes little difference to humans who might win. It forces my hand. I know neither of you liked being in the position of having to decide the fate of the planet—the responsibility is too terrible. But *I've* had that choice dumped on me, and I can't avoid it any more. I think Dr. Eisenstadt was right in the beginning, but we were a lot more naive then and the timing was wrong. It may still be, but I think we've reached the deadline, and I feel I've got to call that ship and report. I want you two to come with me. I want them to see you, talk to you, examine you. I think you two are the only hope left for saving this planet."

I shook my head unbelievingly. *"Us?"*

He nodded. "You know the process. Neither of you are what we call 'body-native' so you'll be more acceptable. And, frankly, I think, as Dr. Eisenstadt did, that you two, particularly now, have grown so much inside that you best represent the qualities my people will be looking for."

"I find that hard to believe," I told him sincerely. "We're not in the least representative of humanity."

"Exactly," he agreed. "That's why. With so much at stake we have to rig the game a bit, but you'll admit I know my people better than you. I know what I'm asking. Risk again. Putting yourself on the line, maybe your lives. At the mercy of an alien race so different from you that they aren't superficially human, like me. I can't force you. You have to make your own decision."

I didn't know what to think or how I felt, and I could only look over at Dory. Her face was inscrutable, but her big brown eyes met my gaze for a moment, and I knew, then, what we would do.

"You're going anyway, aren't you?" she asked me.

He nodded.

She sighed. "Then I guess we really have no choice."

And she was right, of course, although it seemed like nothing had really been our choice for the past six years. It just didn't seem *fair*, somehow, to risk all that we now had, to ask us to do it, because of some duty, some responsibility, to the future of the human race. The human race had never felt much duty or responsibility for us. They had felt no responsibility for poor Victor's plight, certainly, when and if they recognized it at all—it just wasn't any of their business. They were forcing Dorian Tomlinson into extreme personal agony, to live a life in some sort of gray ghetto cut off from family and friends or, perhaps, commit suicide somewhere in what would have been a terrible waste of a wonderful individual. Even Misty Carpenter was really a cypher, a cartoon in the public's mind, an object of lust because of what was really a physical deformity of the sexual parts of her body. Would those lusting people still be around when I grew old and saggy? Did one of them even think of the physical pain, the back strain and other side effects, I lived with because of that?

Stuart's old, original face seemed to come to my mind. *He* cared. And Pauley, too, telling Harry Parch that most people's lives were so empty, so devoid of meaning, that they might as well have never lived at all. Make your life matter, Stuart had said. I thought of history, of the faces and personalities that marched forever in our minds for good or ill. History was the account of people who *mattered*.

Dory was right. We *had* to go.

"What next?" I asked him. "I mean, that agent will be missed no matter what."

He nodded. "But we have a long journey to complete. There's only one place for me to call the ship. We have to return to Alaska."

Full circle, I thought. *For better or worse, it will end where it began.*

Chapter Fifteen

There seemed to be very little point in subterfuge. If Parch really wanted us, he could have us, although it seemed we'd have to either keep some distance from Pauley as long as possible while headed in the same direction. We agreed that the best way to handle it was to go back and go to bed—as if I were capable of anything else at that point—and proceed normally up the coast. Since we weren't supposed to know about our tail, we just had to act as if we didn't have one. Had the tail vanished and we with him there might be a big outcry—but if we continued openly and normally up the coast and made no effort to hide, they could never be sure that their man's disappearance was directly connected to us or not.

Pauley checked our car, found a small electronic tracer, and decided to leave it there. The more open we were, the better. We agreed on an itinerary for each night up the coast, and Pauley warned us that he would certainly have to switch bodies again but would pace us all the way.

Dory was a bit upset at this. "You're gonna do to somebody else what you did to *us*," she protested.

He nodded. "Or worse. But it *has* to be done, Dory."

"You mean—*kill?*"

"If I have to," he replied. "I want no trails. There's too much at stake. Dory, all I can promise is that I'll try my best to cause as little harm and pain as I can."

She was irreconcilable, but he left us shortly after that and there was nothing either of us could do or say.

The next day we continued on up the coast, not going too far because of our lack of sleep, then continued on U.S. 101 now, still along the coast for a while. We continued to hit the sights although our mood was far different from the previous few days at the start. Finally, though, we relaxed and had a really good time, perhaps being even more carefree and uninhibited than normal as it went on. Deep down, neither of us knew if we'd ever be able to do this again.

We finally cut over in Washington State and reached Seattle, a pretty city that had changed little in six years. We were back in civilization again, for a little bit, anyway, but things were already starting to return to normal with the funerals now over. Only the still half-staffed flags reminded us of the momentous change that had taken place.

A ferry was due to leave for Alaska in two days, but, in July, a stateroom was just out of the question and taking the car even less possible. The fact was, the tourists and their agents had the best all sewn up every year, and, unless you were very lucky the only thing you could get was a general ticket, which entitled you to go on board but little else. Although we were told that a cabin could be squeezed in between Ketchikan and Juneau we decided, what the hell, we'd rough it. I arranged with a long-term parking agency to keep the car and we went on a shopping spree far different than the one we'd gone on in Seattle so very long ago, haunting the best camping supply dealers for sleeping bags, air mattresses, and a small portapump of light plastic. We were delighted to find one that slept two, and took it. With Dory's slight build and my disproportionate one we decided against backpacking, but the whole thing was put in a large, thin casing with handles that, although it weighed a ton, was manageable. We also bought some heavier-duty clothing for the trip and seemed set, finally heading down to the huge blue ship at the dock in the late afternoon.

Because we were getting on in Seattle we had among the first choices of location, and chose an inside place in the forward lounge, just putting our suitcases and bedroll there so that others wouldn't usurp it. Flying was never considered as an option in our talks with Dan; he still wouldn't fly unless his life depended on it, and maybe not even then, and that gave us the excuse to be nostalgic.

We'd been bothered with men most of the trip, and I was used to cooling them down anyway, but I think we were so openly and blatantly affectionate on shipboard that it scared a lot of them off. Oh, the occasional "You never had a *real* man" slob, sure, but nothing we couldn't handle. Still, it always irritated me that men had more relative freedom than women. I doubt if either Dory or I had gone anywhere without a little can of mace and a portable scream alarm in our purses, and you were never sure whether the next guy you met was a nice fellow, a jerk, or a would-be rapist. It was infuriating to be walking to my car back at the club and then have to drive home even if it was a nice night, but I always was conscious of how damned lucky I'd been, and I'd known a few women who hadn't.

That, I guess, was why it was nice to be alone with Dory on a trip like this. The undercurrent of fear was still there, but it didn't seem intrusive when you were with someone.

There had been no sign of Dan Pauley during the whole trip, but we suspected he was never far away. We also suspected that Parch's men—two, probably now, at least—were also somewhere about. We didn't let it worry us.

The ferry was a different one than the one on which we'd met, larger, fancier, but it was similar enough in design to make us a little nostalgic and bring back the old memories. The topside solarium, the gift shop, cafeteria, you name it—and the young campers, backpackers, and hordes of tourists.

It took three and a half days to reach Haines Junction, end of the line in this case, and I couldn't suppress a look to the east, where, out of sight beyond high mountains, Skagway and the Chillicoot Pass lay.

It was another day's bumpy bus ride from Haines to Fairbanks, but it was new territory now for the both of us and we enjoyed it while we could. Still, there was tension underlying the journey now, building with each passing kilometer marker on the highway, as we knew that we were approaching the moment of truth.

It occurred to me that Parch might well know, or at least suspect, where we were heading, and that worried me. He could be there, waiting, as he had been when the shuttle had landed six years before to disgorge another occupant for an Indian girl's body.

We stayed the night in Fairbanks, still very much on schedule, and in the morning rented a car and drove south along Route 3 past Mt. McKinley National Park—the mountain was socked in and we could see nothing—to Cantwell, then turned east on Route 8, a good dirt road with occasional paved spots, for several miles.

Traffic had been heavy on 3 but aside from an occasional pickup truck we neither passed nor were passed by much on the dirt road.

We proceeded until we hit Milepost 12, then stopped, turned around, and proceeded back a mile. If all was well, Pauley should be waiting with a signal by the side of the road, a sign reading, "Need a lift to McKinley," which would be fairly natural except that this wasn't exactly the world's best-travelled road, and a code-phrase to double-check.

At almost the 11 Milepost we saw somebody. He was a tall, thin, black man in his forties dressd casually, and he was holding a sign.

"Need a lift to McKinley."

"I'll be damned," I muttered, and came to a stop. He ran up to the car, looked in at us, nodded, and said, "Screw Harry Parch."

"Get in," I told him, and Dory popped up the back door lock for him. He got in and said, "Just go a few hundred yards further up—there's a tree with a white mark on it. Stop there."

I saw it as he said it and pulled over once more. He got out, removed some very substantial-looking brush, revealing a rough and overgrown dirt track. I drove up it, and he quickly replaced the brush, which seemed wired together, and rejoined us. "Just follow the track to the end and park under some trees," he ordered.

I did as instructed. The road curved and twisted and hadn't been used in what looked like years, and it took all my reflexes to keep us on track. Finally, though, it ended at a small stream under a clump of small trees. This was not really tree country, but it offered some concealment.

He got out again and beckoned for us to follow, which we did. There was a small trail, hardly noticeable now, once you crossed the stream, leading a half a mile or so farther along to an open meadow strewn with large and small rocks. He studied the area for a moment, then went over to a particularly large rock and strained to lift it.

"He'll never lift *that* boulder," I said, and, as I said it, the whole thing seemed to flip up. We went over to it curiously and saw that the rock was something artificial. Revealed now was a faceplate with several sets of ringlike markings on it. His fingers tapped on the rings in what looked like random order but had to be some prearranged code, and suddenly one of the rings glowed a dull red. He nodded again to himself, looked satisfied, and closed the "rock," then exhaled deeply.

"Well, that's that. You don't know how I had nightmares that I'd find this place booby-trapped or melted or the power gone."

I looked up at the sky. "How long before it gets here?"

He thought a moment. "An hour, maybe more. It'll have to sneak itself out of wherever it's hiding and figure the best emergency approach in and out. We don't want to attract missiles or any other attention until it's too late."

"You don't *know* where it is?" Dory asked.

He shook his head. "Nope. It's a pretty smart little mechanical bugger. It thinks for itself pretty much. I just hope it comes before we have company."

I looked around nervously. "You think we will?"

"Oh, sure—sooner or later. Later, I hope. The only tail you had as far as I could see was the one pickup truck and you passed it. I expect they're discovering you're gone right about now, but until our baby lands they won't find us unless they spot the car from a helicopter. It's a risk we had to take."

I shivered. This was going to be a *nervous* hour.

"Who did you kill for that hunk?" Dory wanted to know.

He shrugged. "No appeasing you, is there? If you *must* know he was a pimp and a drug pusher in Eureka I happened on. Believe me—he's no loss to this world. I picked him for that, and also because he was a black male, which gives us physically three major races and both sexes."

"Is that important?" I asked him.

He nodded. "Trust me. I'm trying to load the dice as much as possible, like I told you."

We sat and waited because there was nothing else to do. The temperature was comfortably in the seventies, and the only sound and annoyance around seemed to be the buzzing of some particularly large mosquitoes. Swatting at one brought another thought to mind.

"Dan—your people. The Urulu. What are they like? Physically, I mean."

He thought a moment. Finally he said, "Do you have any prejudices against jellyfish?"

I shivered slightly. The fact was, I *did* have a little against them. Every summer in Chesapeake Bay the stinging sea nettles would make water fun impossible without a protective net. "You're a jellyfish?"

He chuckled. "No, not really. Nothing like one, actually. But the Urulu might remind you, superficially, of jellyfish."

"Whew! That's a relief," Dory responded sincerely. "I had visions of scaly horrors with big eyes and nasty teeth."

We both just looked at her strangely.

"I always liked monster movies," she said defensively.

"Dan—shouldn't you brief us?" I asked him. "I mean, we're going into this pretty cold turkey."

"It's got to be that way, Misty. If you're coached they'll know it and we'll blow it. Don't worry—I'll be there to lend support. Just be yourselves. I don't think either of you really realizes what really superior human beings you are."

There was no reply to that. Neither of us believed it for a minute but it was pure balm for the ego.

The time did not pass quickly, partly because we expected to hear a helicopter screaming overhead or the bark of guns from the brush at any moment. It was incredible we'd gotten this far.

Finally, however, the thing came. It came in a crazy, impossible fashion, coming in incredibly fast just above ground, keeping distance from whatever terrain, and then stopping on a dime as if for all the world the laws of inertia had been repealed. There was a *crack* sound, once.

It wasn't large—in fact, it wasn't much bigger than a

small truck—and it wasn't saucer-shaped. It looked, rather, like a stylized, very thick pair of wings, or perhaps a boomerang, with rounded corners. It hovered there, a couple of inches above the ground making no sound at all. Pauley approached it, and although that computer or whatever had never seen him before in that body it seemed to recognize something. One of the "wings" rotated with a slight humming sound, revealing an opening about four feet square.

"Let's go," he shouted. "In the hatch as quickly as possible and move down!"

I hesitated a moment, but then heard the sound of helicopter blades not too far off and the sound of engines in back of us. Both Dory and I ran for the opening which Dan had already entered. He reached down, pulled her in, then strained to help me. There was a strong vibration all around us, and I lost my balance as the hatch rotated closed, falling on the smooth, seamless floor.

And then, quite suddenly, Dory gave a yelp and fell, too, and before I could do or say anything a giant fist seemed to slam us back down hard. I could already feel the bruises.

We seemed held there, unable to move, breathing with difficulty, for a fairly long time, and then, just as suddenly as it appeared, the pressure lifted. I picked myself up, groaning a little, and rubbed my rear end. "Ow! I wonder if I'll be able to sit down tomorrow," I said.

"Don't expect any sympathy from me," Dory responded weakly. "You got a *lot* more padding than I do, and you were already down!"

I got to my feet and helped her up as well. The whole ship vibrated slightly, but otherwise there was no noise, no sensation of anything at all. We seemed solidly anchored to the deck, too.

"Damn! At least I thought we'd get to find out what it's like to do it in no gravity!" I pouted.

The ceiling was just a couple of inches above my head—my hair rubbed against it when I stood up, and the chamber we were in was quite small, no larger than, say, the back of a pickup truck. There seemed no doors or windows, and I looked around. "Now what? Where's Dan?"

She shook her head. "He headed forward as soon as he dragged you in." She looked at the solid wall. "How, though, I don't know."

The wall shimmered, and Pauley stepped through, having to crouch down to get in. "Sorry for the fast lift," he told us, "but I had to give the go-sign. They were already shooting at us. Come on forward and we'll relax a little." He turned and more or less duck-walked through the wall.

I shrugged. "If he can do it I guess *we* can, too." I went up to the wall, hesitantly, and pushed against it. I felt a tingling, and the place I touched seemed to shimmer and become intangible. I stepped through, getting the overall sensation of walking through a vibrating shower. It felt pretty good, really.

The other side was not much larger than the entry chamber, but had a soft, furlike padding all over it that you kind of sunk into a little. It was all over, a nice baby blue, on the walls, floor, ceiling. All over. There was nothing else in the room. Pauley was sitting against the wall, watching me with faint amusement.

Dory entered and looked around the chamber with the same surprise I did. "I expected a big, fancy control room or cockpit," she noted. "But, then, I guess a padded cell *does* fit better."

Pauley laughed. "Take a seat. Anywhere you're comfortable. This thing wasn't built for anything except fast landings and fast getaways, I'm afraid. We're in the half set up for humans—the other side is for Urulu."

"Where do you pilot the ship from?" I wanted to know.

"We don't. It does it itself. I just tell it what I want and it does the rest."

"Where are we?"

He shrugged. "I have no idea. It took the fast way out—sorry for bumping you around, but I didn't know if that helicopter had some nasty weapons, or if they were training missiles on us at that very moment."

I shivered. "You're forgiven. But—you mean this is it? No great pictures of Earth from space? No fancy stuff? We just sit here for who knows how long in this blue room?" I seemed to remember it'd taken three days just to get to the moon.

"I'm afraid this *is* it," he answered. "I mean, we have ships with those kind of things but this isn't designed for it. Sorry—not very exotic, I know. But we've already left the Earth's magnetic field, and, in a few minutes, the ship'll have all the data it needs for a jump—allowance for gravitational forces, solar wind, stuff like that."

"Jump?" Dory said uneasily.

He nodded. "Don't worry. It's a little too complicated to explain, and since I don't understand it myself there's no use in me explaining it. When the ship's ready, it'll give us a warning, then you just lie down flat on the rug, here, and relax."

"Faster than light drive," I noted. "So Einstein was wrong."

"As far as I know nothing can exceed the speed of light except for some little subatomic particles that do nobody any good," he replied. "No, the way it was explained to me once was that the ship kind of punches a hole in space/time, goes through it, closes the hole behind it, travels along until it gets to where it wants to go, punches another hole, re-emerges, and that's it."

I frowned, "Dan—where does it punch a hole *to?*"

He shrugged. "Damned if I know. All I know is that it isn't in *our* universe, that's for sure. I'm not even sure anybody knows—it just *is*, that's all, and you can use it. The ship flies at about two-thirds of light speed there, then emerges."

"Two-thirds of light speed," I echoed. "That's damned

fast—but unless we're staying in the solar system we're going to be *years* getting to where we're going!"

He nodded. "Probably fifty or sixty at least. But, don't worry, you won't feel a thing. We'll be in a nice, safe, state of suspension. Physically we won't age a bit."

"But we'll get back a hundred years too late to help Earth!" Dory protested.

"Nope. That's the crazy thing about this no-space business. We'll re-enter this universe about two or three minutes after we left it. I admit it wouldn't have been practical without the state of suspension, but it's convenient, and seemingly fast. Just wait and relax. You'll see. The effect is almost as if it's instantaneous."

Dory shook her head and looked at me for help but I couldn't say a thing. It made no more sense to me than to her.

There was a sharp, irritating buzzing sound. Dan looked up, although there was nothing to look at. "O.K.—here we go. Just lie down flat, face up and comfortable, on the floor here, and relax." He did it himself, and we did likewise. I didn't know how Dory felt, but I felt queasy as all hell, and I found her hand, took it, and squeezed it. She squeezed back.

There were two short buzzes, a slight pause, and then the world went green. No, I don't mean the rug changed color—everything was a sparkling, translucent green, including the air inside, and it all seemed to shimmer slightly. A tingling went through every part of my body much like the feeling I'd had passing through the wall or whatever it was—very pleasurable, like an all-over vibrator.

And then, suddenly, the green clicked off, and all returned to normal again. There was a long buzzing sound.

Pauley stirred, sighed, and got up to a sitting position, stretching. "Well," he said, sounding a little hoarse, "that's it. We're here."

*   *   *

I turned slightly. My mouth felt really dry and my eyes hurt a little like they had mild eyestrain, but otherwise I felt just fine.

"That *it?*" I managed, sounding a little hoarse myself. "That was barely a couple of minutes—not fifty years."

He smiled. "It was really a long, long time. It just doesn't seem that way. We need some fluids, though, and fast. The process is very dehydrating to human type bodies." He reached over against the wall and a small hinged panel revealed itself. Reaching down, he brought up a large cube with a strap attached to the top, put it in front of him, and touched a small area on the side. The top slid back, and he took out three tall canisters, about a liter each, and three small wrapped blocks. Dory and I each took a canister and followed Dan's example, turning the top until a slot appeared.

"Go ahead—drink it," he urged, and took a swig of his.

I put it hesitantly to my lips, then drank, overcome with sudden thirst. I drank quite a bit, then put it down for a moment. "It tastes like orange juice!"

He nodded. "That's because it's basically orange juice, with additives that'll help get your body quickly back in balance. The stuff's matched for each race likely to use this thing. The cakes look and taste like gingerbread, by the way, but will give you a lot more than plain old gingerbread ever did. My predecessor, who set up this ship for Earth, liked the tastes."

I tried the cake, and it *was* good. My stomach felt as if it had a lump in it, but the juice and cake seemed to go down quickly and dissolve the lump in a matter of minutes. The thought of fifty-year-old, half-digested food had a sort of repulsion about it, but I'm not quite sure I bought Pauley's explanations and time-frame anyway. I wondered if they would give anything real that might clue in some future Earth scientist in the way IMC had been born.

The buzzer gave several short bursts. Pauley nodded

to himself, then said, "We're within range of a perimeter ship now," he told us, "and the ship's made contact."

I was disappointed. "I was hoping we'd see a Urulu world," I told him.

He chuckled. "You couldn't go there anyway. The closest to it would be something like Jupiter in your own solar system. A big gas giant with beautiful multicolored bands of gases and a lot of heat from the pressure caused by the weight of the incredibly dense atmosphere."

"Your people could live on *Jupiter?*" Dory gasped.

He shook his head. "Probably not. It's not the right mixture. But most of our worlds are similar *looking*, anyway. My own home has a beautiful multiple ring system, like Saturn."

"And you live on a dark ball underneath all those gases?" I pressed, trying to understand.

"No, no. There *is* a planetary solid there, very dense, but we don't live *on* it. We live in the middle of the atmosphere itself, kind of like fish in water. It's quite hard to describe, but on many gas giants the protein molecules that form life are found in wide bands of gases heated by radiation from the pressure below and maintained there. We don't ever touch the solid below— the pressure alone, not to mention the heat, would kill us."

"And yet you somehow found the means to get there, even mine there, or you'd never have ships like this, space travel, or any mechanical things," I pointed out.

"That's true," he agreed, "but it's a long, complex story. Maybe, one day, when your people and mine can sit down as friends, we will be able to study the history and development of your people while you study ours. But now is not the time."

We both nodded, understanding what he meant. The sense of high adventure, of new worlds and new experiences, faded swiftly as the reason why we were here really came back to us hard.

When your people and mine can sit down as friends. . . .

That might well depend on what we said and did in the next few hours or days.

There was a thump, and a shudder went through the ship. *Jgur abrix!"* an eerie, nonhuman voice that I can not describe came to us.

Pauley sighed. "O.K. We've docked. This ship is giving the physical requirements for us. When the mother ship has a chamber prepared for us that won't kill us, we'll go through. It's pretty fast—we have to be set up to handle a variety of races and requirements, obviously."

Obviously, I realized. Body switchers who sped between the stars at near-instant speeds would need a lot of technical knowledge and skill about an incredibly varied number of lifeforms.

A clanging sound came from the wall behind us through which we'd entered. Pauley sucked in his breath for a moment, showing his own nervousness, then stood up as well as he could and headed for the wall. "Stay here," he told us, "until I see what's what." The wall shimmered obligingly and he vanished behind it. I turned to Dory. "Scared?"

"A little," she responded nervously. "You?"

"Frightened to death," I said honestly. "But what's done is done. Here we are—wherever it is."

She squeezed my hand tightly and kissed me lightly.

Pauley was gone for some time, but, finally, he returned and sat down on the blue carpeting, looking a little grim. "Look," he began hesitantly, "I warned you that humans weren't exactly common and that we were very different."

We nodded.

"Well, they've got a chamber for us, but it's little more than a big bubble inside Urulu atmosphere. I got them to darken the floor so we have some solid grounding, but it's going to be like being in a giant fishbowl. Just take it easy and remember that you're perfectly safe there, and there's a good deal of machinery maintaining proper air, gravity, and pressure, and a damned thick wall between you and the rest of what you see."

My nerves were getting the better of me. I wanted this over with, and got up.

"I want you both to take your clothes off," Pauley said, starting to undress himself. "I'm afraid you're going to have to play by the rules, and that means you bring nothing in you weren't born with."

"Well, you said it would be a fishbowl," I sighed, and complied.

"In more ways than one," Pauley responded. "You will literally be the object of a lot of curiosity, both professional and just plain gawking."

We were totally stripped now and I looked at him. "Hmm . . . Well hung, Dan."

He grinned, turned, then looked back at us. "You're going to feel a real tingly sensation as you pass out of the hatch," he warned. "Decontamination. A dry shower, sort of. Don't worry—it won't hurt you or your unborn children." With that he stepped through.

I looked at Dory. "Ready?"

She nodded. "Let's get this *over* with!"

I stepped through first, then she. I reached the open hatch and paused, bending down and looking out. I let out a gasp and felt Dory just behind me, also peering out.

Pauley's description of his home as something like Jupiter was fairly close. The world swirled around us, a sea of thick gases that were mostly yellows, reds, oranges, and purples. It was as if somebody had put a stick in Jupiter and stirred it up.

I stepped out and helped Dory down. Immediately we felt the "shower" and it was no different or worse than the other odd feelings we had had. Turning, looking forward, though, we walked out onto what appeared to be a long, flat piece of dull aluminum, circular and about ninety feet across. The air smelled fresh and sweet, the temperature was warm and comfortable, but there was no visible boundary between the "bubble" and the atmosphere of the rest of the ship.

The floor did not feel cold and metallic to my bare feet, but like soft rubber, with some give to it, and it was at air temperature.

The only features of the bubble were a shiny round protrusion in the center and four seatlike pads around it. Pauley was already at the center and gestured for us to come to him.

The eeriest thing was the silence. It was so quiet we could hear ourselves breathing and the sounds of our bare feet against the odd flooring material. I was glad that Dan had gotten them to color the floor—I felt exposed and off-balance as it was, with nothing save the floor and the protrusion in the middle to get bearings from.

Suddenly there was a loud sound behind us. We stopped and turned as one, watching as the whole rear wall shimmered and a blackish shape receded and disappeared.

"Hey!" Dory called out.

I looked at her. "The ship's gone. We're trapped in here!"

We held hands and approached Pauley. "Don't worry," he said reassuringly. "You're safe."

"I'm beginning to wonder how I got talked into this," I told him with more seriousness than he took it. I looked at the big center protrusion. "What's that?"

"We'll get food and water from the middle—the hub flips back. The water will be distilled and the food won't be very appetizing, but it'll do."

"I don't exactly feel very hungry," I mumbled, looking around. I felt adrift on a platform, lost in some nightmarish sea of colorful clouds. I had the sensation of moving because of that swirl, and it made me slightly dizzy.

"Dan—I hate to say this," I said hesitantly, "but I have to pee."

He laughed and pointed to one of the pads. "Just reach down and flip it up." He saw my hesitancy, and reached down and pushed against the top. It swung back noiselessly and revealed a rubbery-looking tube. "Just sit on it—it'll support you," he told me. "Then go."

Dory looked upset, but I was in no position to argue. It worked fine. Dory, though, seemed irritated.

"Damn it," she grumbled, "I think this is a little *too* public! I'm not sure I *like* shitting in a fishbowl!"

"Well, you're going to have to," Pauley replied. "At least until this is over."

"Dan? Where's the toilet paper?" I asked.

"There is none," he told me. "See that little indentation there by your right elbow? Just keep seated and push it."

I did as instructed, and got the damndest erotic sensation I'd *ever* had—but whatever it did, it worked. I was dry and sanitized.

I got up and lowered the lid. "Now what?" I asked him.

"We wait. I—whoops! Company!"

We turned to see what he was looking at, and got our first view of what I guess was an Urulu.

In some ways it *did* remind you of a jellyfish—a large umbra, but multicolored, below which was suspended a huge brain case of some transparent material, then a chamber I guessed had something to do with digestion, and, oddly, an irislike opening that changed. From the region where the umbra met the brain-case dangled hundreds of incredibly thin tentacles that seemed to be composed of countless tiny translucent blue beads. The whole creature swam effortlessly in the sea of gases, and was partially obscured by them, but it was *big*—perhaps ten feet across at the umbra, with the brain-case and other organs beneath three or four feet long, and the tentacles reaching down at least fifteen, maybe twenty feet. The umbra undulated constantly and the creature looked incredibly graceful, almost beautiful.

"Here comes the messenger-boy," Pauley said. "I'll be talking to him for some time, so excuse me. Just amuse yourselves."

"Never have I felt less like amusing myself," I grumbled.

Pauley went over to the edge of the bubble. The Urulu approached the same spot, and suddenly a tentacle shot out and touched the side of our shield against its world. A small, brownish disk shape appeared where it touched, and Pauley reached out and put his hand on the disk. Almost at once he stiffened and seemed to go into a trance. I realized that the two were talking in some way, perhaps related to the identity matrix transfer itself using that area as a conductor to replace physical contact.

Dan said he might be a long time, and his conversation or whatever it was dragged on and on. We sat on the spongy floor and waited, having nothing else to do and no place else to go.

As it went on, we began to see other shapes, other Urulu floating by, a few at a time. Although no eyes were evident—the iris beneath was almost certainly a mouth—there seemed no doubt after a while that we were the object of curious attention.

"You know," Dory remarked, "they really have a kind of graceful beauty about them, don't they? I wonder what it's like to float in all directions and glide through that? Kinda like a bird."

I nodded, not mentioning that I was beginning to feel like a zoo animal. Still, there was a great fascination in the huge creatures, and I began trying to deduce things from them.

It seemed impossible that such creatures could have built great machines that would fly to the stars. How would they even *see* stars in this kind of atmosphere? I thought they were probably much older than mankind, even on a relative scale. Progress, which for humans had come in comparative quick jumps, had to have come very, very slowly to such people. But—how could such as they have even developed the means to get to, let alone mine, a hot planetary center under huge pressure? Was it possible that Pauley had been giving us another untruth, or at least half-truth, about their history when he said that they had developed the body-switching technique as a defense against predators? In their element, they looked more than capable.

But what if life had developed in a layered system within a gas giant? Or what if they bred forms of life, weaved them from the floating nucleotides of their gaseous environment, that could take those pressures? Took what might have been a sophisticated communications process and discovered from it the secret of the identity matrix?

I would imagine them moving, then, from layer to layer, their minds travelling through those new creatures they made at each step tailored for that particular environment, until, in one direction, they reached the planet and in the other saw the stars. Could their sophisticated powers, then, have developed not as a result of predators but rather as the result of a frontier psychology? Would we ever really know these strange people?

They, then, would see bodies mostly as tools, form following function, a concept that would eliminate a lot of the root causes of hatred, prejudice, divisions which marked our own terrestrial people. In our society form followed function only in our tools; in a sociological sense, function followed form, as was so graphically illustrated by my own self. The fact that Victor looked like a wimp made him something of a wimp, but also produced, through social pain and introversion, a social scientist, author, teacher, whose work had to be everything in his life because his form, socially, turned him inward. I, on the other hand, was a buxom beauty who turned people on when I walked into a room. And what did *I* do for a living?

If I were at all right in my theories of the Urulu, it

explained why our form of life and theirs had taken such different paths, and why the Urulu themselves might hardly believe we could have a meeting of the minds.

I shared these ideas with Dory, but she just shrugged and shook her head. Life, I knew, was simpler for Dory than for me. Things were practical—what was, *was*—or they were beautiful, ugly, that sort of thing. She was the hardhead and I was the dreamer, which is why, I think, we complemented each other so well. Without her practicality, her good common sense, her ability to face life on its own terms as a series of practical problems to be solved, I'd not be able to survive. But without people like me to wonder and speculate on the unknowable, there would be not only no science, but no poetry, either.

"I wonder how they fuck?" she mused, showing the difference between us.

I managed a chuckle. "They probably lay eggs. Or they might not even have sex as we know it." I put my arm around her. "We just have to hope that they have love."

Pauley finally disengaged and seemed none the worst for wear. He came back over to us and sank down wearily. His Urulu contact floated off and was soon lost in the billowing gases.

"Well?" I asked him.

He shrugged. "All I did was report. Gave a readout, as it were, of all my experiences, feelings, and conclusions. Now it'll be taken higher up, then again higher, and so forth, until it finally reaches the people who make the decisions."

"There seems to be one universal law," I noted, "if even the Urulu have a complicated bureaucracy."

We rested and we waited for quite some time. Food came, and it was as tasteless and as filling as Dan had warned, and more time passed, and hordes of Urulu kept swimming by, giving us the once-over. Except for feeling like a specimen, I didn't really care about that, but I was a little worried about Dory. She seemed to shrug it off, though, after a while, perhaps concluding that these weren't really people—not her kind, anyway. And we could do little about it, anyway. Still, we felt very exposed, and I wished for some privacy.

We finally slept, and food came again, and I began to worry about things. Why was it taking so long?

"You have to remember they have to digest an enormous amount of data, sort it, analyze it, you name it," Dan consoled. "It all takes time. It's possible they might pass the buck to higher-ups, which means physically leaving and going, since radio waves would take forever. We just have to be patient."

Of his people and my speculations Dan would neither confirm nor deny anything. I understood. Deep down he was still the military man in a war, and this was a military ship.

Finally a Urulu did approach the communications point again; maybe the same one, maybe not. Dan went over and went through the touching ritual again, but did not stiffen. They were talking, somehow, not anything more.

He let go after a moment, turned, and walked back to us. "Misty, Dory—they want confirmation of my feelings, which is a really good sign. They want to examine the both of you."

Dory frowned. "Examine us how?"

He smiled reassuringly. "Look, it's nothing, really. Wait until the Grandfather gets here, then just do what I've been doing."

"Grandfather?" we both echoed.

He nodded. "That's the closest I can come in English. Call him, well, a venerated old man, a commanding general, a political leader—a lot of things—and you get some idea."

"What, exactly, is this examination like? Will we be asked questions?" I wanted to know.

He shook his head negatively. "Nothing like that. What

he's going to do is read out your matrices. He'll know the both of you better than you know yourselves."

"I don't want anybody messing with my head again!" Dory exclaimed.

"No, no. It's like taking the recording. There's no sensation, particularly, and he's not going to do anything *to* your matrix, just copy it." He paused a moment. "It's the only way."

I sighed. "All right. When?"

He looked up at the swirling gases all around us. "I'd say almost any moment. See?"

We looked, and for a moment I didn't realize what he meant. Then it registered—the hordes of curious Urulus, the gawkers, had gone. There was nothing at all to be seen except the swirling colors. The boss was coming— they were scurrying back to look like they were busy.

And then the boss came, majestically through the mist. He looked like all the others, but seemed much, much larger; so huge he almost dwarfed our little bubble. All of us could have stood in his brain-case with room left over. I realized that Urulu just kept growing as they got older. I suppose gas giants give you a lot more room.

A huge, cablelike tentacle snaked out and touched the communications plate. Pauley went over and touched it, again casually, talking rather than anything else. Finally he let go and turned back to us. "O.K.—who first? Don't worry—he doesn't bite."

Actually, it wasn't the huge creature or the idea of having my mind read out that bothered me the most. It was the knowledge that what this being learned, or thought he learned, from the likes of Dory and me might well determine the future of Earth—*would* determine it, for better or worse.

For, in the end, these were not godlike beings, but *people*—a far different sort, but people all the same.

I stepped up to the plate. "Here goes," I muttered, took a couple of deep breaths, and put my right palm flat on the plate.

Considering my IMC experience I had expected no real sensation whatsoever, but there *was* this time.

Half of me stood there, but the other half seemed floating free in space, hovering in air of spectacular beauty and fluidity. My vision was fully 360 degrees and, even as I was aware of myself, standing there in the bubble, I also saw myself, and Dan and Dory, as if from a different place. I felt reassured, warm, comfortable, yet I could sense in the great being a tremendous feeling of concern, of responsibility, which was there, tangible to me, yet just out of reach, a frame in which I was the picture.

Oddly, this feeling, this confidence, reminded me somehow of Stuart, and I felt more comfortable, more at ease.

And then, suddenly, it was over, and I was just touching plastic. I let go with some regret, and Dory hesitantly approached.

"It's all right," I told her. "It's—a real experience."

She touched the plate and stiffened, and I knew the process had, once again, begun. It seemed to take a terribly long time, but Dan assured me that, no matter how short it had seemed to me, it was no longer than mine.

"How was it?" Dan asked me.

"It was—interesting," I replied. "It seemed like I got a little into his head, too. Dan—do you miss it? Floating free like a bird or a fish, seeing a wider and different spectrum, communing with the others of your kind?"

He nodded seriously. "Sometimes I do, very much—like now. Remember, I was supposed to come back years ago."

"Will you stay, then?"

He shook his head sadly from side to side. "No, I doubt it. Not if it goes the way we hope. They'll need somebody who understands humankind, at least as well as anybody can, and I'm the only likely candidate left alive and free. I'll have to train others and ease them in. Still, I like the idea a lot better than before. It's a nicer, cleaner kind of job—to build bridges, rather than blow them up. Harder, though. *Much* harder"

Finally Dory, too, was let go, and returned to us with a dazed expression in her eyes. "Wow!" she breathed. "That's really *something!*"

Dan went over and "talked" to the Grandfather again. Then he let go and the huge creature rose majestically and vanished in the billowing clouds, causing a riot of colorful patterns as he went.

"What now?" I asked Dan.

"Now we wait some more," he sighed. "While the Grandfather and *his* bosses and the computers analyze the data." He crossed his fingers. "And then they'll tell us if I played it right."

I realized then what tension he, too, was under, and I recalled his tale of being responsible for another world, far away, being destroyed. He had told that one with too much sincerity and anguish for me not to believe him. I felt a little sorry for him, really, since I knew that this meant almost as much to him as it did to us.

And so we waited, and waited, and waited. . . .

A convulsive shudder went through the ship, starting the interior gases swirling even more and knocking us to the floor of our bubble. I was afraid for a moment it would crack, or, at least, break free and go hurling off into the void, but it soon settled down to a steady vibration.

Dan looked apprehensive but hopeful. "We're moving," he told us.

How long had we been there, I wondered. A day? A week? It was hard to tell from the food cycles and the sleep cycle had changed for us anyway, in response to boredom and the almost hypnotic effect of those clouds.

A Urulu approached the plate, and Dan went to it. He returned in a few moments, looking cheerful. "We've done it! Misty! Dory! They bought it!"

He talked feverishly, excitedly. A small task force was

being assembled, he told us, to proceed to Earth directly. The first priority, he told us, would be to hit IMC, to wipe it off the face of the Earth.

"It won't mean that they'll be destroyed," he cautioned. "It'll just set them back a few years until they can build a better computer. But it'll be a demonstration of power. Then we're going to contact those leaders of yours, not just in the U.S. but key leaders worldwide. They're going to get an ultimatum of sorts."

I was nervous. Invasion from outer space might guarantee cooperation but hardly a friendly attitude, and I pointed this out.

"No, it won't be that kind of grandstanding," he assured us. "We are going to demonstrate our power for them, once in each key country. Then, *quietly*, we will contact them. The message will be simple, yet startlingly complex. We're going to leave them alone, but we will offer complete protection against The Association—for a period. The key to the identity matrix is known now to your people—at least some. When the facts are clear, the others will start to work on it, or steal its secrets—whatever. Then we're going to sit back and watch what you do with it."

I was aghast. "But—Dan! They'll misuse it!"

"That's the one thing we plan to point out to them. If they misuse it, if they go the way of The Association, we will abandon them to the enemy, for there won't be a dime's worth of difference between them anyway. But as they learned to fear the atomic bomb so much they have never used it against one another after the first time, so they might do the same here with the identity matrix. If they use it to learn, to grow, to change their society and their attitudes, then they make history. They become the first race of their type to transcend their physical limits, their petty hatred and prejudices. If that happens, humanity will gain not only a host of friends, but the stars—and inner rewards you can't even dream of right now."

I shook my head. "It's no good. We'll blow it. We always blow it. Besides, totalitarianism seems to be the natural trend of mankind."

He smiled humorlessly. *"They* think so, too. But they're willing to give you the chance."

I looked at him. "What about you, Dan? What will you do, now?"

"I'll be there, with you," he told us. "Like I said, training others, putting evaluators in place, so we'll *know*. God bless Stuart Eisenstadt! How I'd love to find him and give him the news."

That brought me up short. "You might kill him. He's probably in IMC."

He nodded. "I thought of that. But so are some of our people, remember. Don't worry—the odds are we won't kill anybody. It's the *computer* we're after."

"And we're heading home *now?"* Dory asked, sounding anxious.

"Soon, anyway. They'll warn us when they make the jump. Then be prepared—the three of us have some work to do."

"Huh?"

"Well, *my* people can't go into IMC. They can't even breathe there."

Chapter Sixteen

When we arrived off Earth they brought a small ship for our use. The interior smelled like it had been put together expressly for us, which it might have been. If Pauley was really serious about the amount of physical time needed to traverse space, they'd have loads of time to refit whatever was necessary if they just didn't go into suspension in one part of the ship until they finished what they were doing.

It was larger than the one that had brought us—Dan could stand in it—and had one of those combination food and water dispensers and johns as well, not to mention three very comfortable form-fitting chairs. It also had a small screen that showed us where we were heading, but little else. The carpeting was yellow instead of blue.

Dan was getting information from a small hand plate near his chair. I tried it once, but the images and language were far too confusing and just made me dizzy.

"They found The Association's base," he told us. "It was pretty far out on a chunk of rock that's one of

Neptune's moons. No ships got off successfully, so they think they cleaned out the nest. It wasn't a big operation, anyway. They didn't need much."

"They sure did a lot of harm for a little bunch," Dory commented, and I nodded.

"It's not numbers but technique and knowledge, experience, that counts," he noted. "The cleanup below will be a lot tougher. Thanks to Parch the leaders have already gone underground down there and will take a lot of digging out. I'm not worried, though—they have no place to go now."

We looked at the screen, filled now with the great blue-white ball of our beautiful world. It looked just like the pictures from the orbital stations.

"Dan—how are we going to work this?" Dory asked. "What's the procedure?"

"O.K. First the big ship will move into position in orbit and assume a stationary orbit over IMC. They will train a beam on an area of about twenty square miles around IMC, essentially putting every living thing in the area into a suspension similar to the one we use for space travel. It might cause some deaths or injuries—people driving, like that—but it's far less damaging than any other thing we could come up with and its very ease should scare the hell out of the government. In the 'showers' we've been getting we've been coated with a compound that permeates the skin and will render us impervious to this kind of suspension field. The task force will cover us and the big ship, vaporizing any missiles, planes, or other nasties that might be thrown at us."

"All right," I said, "but what do *we* do?"

"See those plates next to your chairs there? Put your hands on them when I tell you."

I looked nervously at mine. It'd given me only gibberish and headaches when I'd tried it.

"They have your matrices, remember. They're going to link up through you, attuned to you. It won't last more than a few hours at best, but we shouldn't need very long."

"But the electronic security—we don't know the *codes!*" Dory protested.

"You won't feel it, but you're going to be linked to the most powerful portable computer I know of," he replied. "Just let *it* do the thinking. Once inside, I want you, Dory, to head for the programming department. You worked there and know it best."

She nodded.

"You, Misty, get down to that chamber with the chairs. Think you can find it?"

I nodded. "If the elevators work and the doors will open."

"Good. I'll free the Urulu, and we'll all meet out in front of the access building."

I frowned. "But—Dan. What do we do when we get to these places?"

"You'll know what to do when you get there. Just let us guide you. Clear out as soon as you're finished, get upstairs and outside."

"Seems like a lot of extra-elaborate trouble to go through," I noted, "when you could just short out the computer from the air."

He nodded. "But that's not the point of the exercise. There are loads of easy and quick ways to blow IMC, but *this* involves technology and demonstrations totally beyond the powers of your people. It's designed for maximum effect, to illustrate their impotence. It'll scare the hell out of 'em so badly they'll have to listen to us."

"All right," I sighed. "When do we get it over with?"

"We're approaching the terminator now," he responded. "It'll be late night at IMC, which is best for us."

Dory looked around. "Uh—Dan? Where's our clothes?"

He looked sheepish. "Damn. My people don't use 'em, and I guess they were tossed out when the emergency vehicle was cleaned. I just plain forgot."

"You mean we have to do all this in the *buff?*"

"They'll all be frozen anyway," he replied. "You'll be safer than anywhere else on the planet including your own bathroom."

"But our *keys*, driver's license, credit cards . . . ?"

He shrugged. "They can be replaced. Ready? Here we go! Put your hands on the plates *now!*"

We landed and went to the rear where the hatch opened, letting in a sudden mass of dry, incredibly hot air. We were in the middle of the parking lot and had to run barefoot across still really hot asphalt to the main building.

Everything was lit with an eery, purplish glow, which seemed to sparkle a bit with some sort of pent-up energy.

Everybody inside was frozen stiff, it looked like, suspended like still pictures in most cases, although some people had fallen over if not balanced. Even a police dog was frozen, caught in the act of a big yawn.

We walked down the hallway in eerie silence, although the lights remained on and we could hear the occasional clatter of automatic teletypes and the like still functioning even with their operators stiff.

We reached the freight elevator, with two burly Marine guards standing there, and Dan removed one key and I the other from the two men, then put them in the slot and turned. The elevator door slid open. Inside, he reached into the little compartment for the interior key, put it in, and started very slowly twisting and turning it, almost like a safecracker. Suddenly, the elevator started to move.

"It was an easy set of circuits to analyze," Dan commented, and I suddenly realized that it wasn't *he* who analyzed it, but the computer we were all theoretically connected to. I felt nothing except a slight, odd feeling of buoyancy, of unreality about it all. There had been no sensation when we'd touched the plates.

Our destinations were on different levels. Dory got off on 4, I on 12, and Dan continued down to the IMC dungeons. I was alone, heading towards Stuart's old office and that terrible theater of the mind.

Passing people frozen there, and occasionally stepping over them, was something of a novelty and a turn-on. I had a great urge to do something to them, maybe undress them or put them in obscene poses, but I barely repressed it. This was business.

I looked in at Stuart's office—it still had his name on the door, which made me feel a little better—and saw a number of technicians around, but not Stuart. I headed for the control room.

It was an odd feeling, walking into that place once again. Here Misty Carpenter had been born, Victor Gonser killed, sort of, in a cold, mechanical and technical process. It still gave me the creeps, even though I liked myself and who I was these days.

There were only a few people around, looking in the process of straightening up the place, and I sat down at the master control console, my back to the chairs. It was in this seat that a dispassionate engineer had called the shots for my, and who knows how many others', reprogramming. It felt cold on my naked skin, but, then, the whole air-conditioned place did. I had goose bumps.

Now, though, I wasn't sure what I was supposed to do. I looked at the massive screen and all the controls and keyboards but didn't know what to do next. I just put my hands out, typewriter style, and much to my surprise they started working. I had no knowledge or control of what I was doing; I was just a passenger, now, watching my hands control, adjust, throw switches, type in messages, read out outputs, and punch more messages. Academically, I *did* realize what was going on—the bosses up in orbit and their master computers were learning about this one, probing and testing and analyzing, comparing the information with what they already knew and were learning from Dory's end—and, perhaps, from Dory's matrix. She'd worked these things and had a lot of training on them.

Suddenly I stopped, but the CRT screen didn't. It filled with line after line of numbers, symbols, and the like, faster now than my eyes could follow, but it would pause occasionally and a single phrase would appear, but for a moment.

"Garbage dumped."

Then it would resume, again and again.

I felt now that I could leave it to its own devices, and got up without any hint of resistance from above. I was finished.

I headed back down the hall, stopping in on Stuart's inner office and seeing his nameplate, pipe, and even a spare lab smock. I didn't know whether, or if, Parch had done anything to his mind, but I felt certain Stuart was all right.

I headed back to the elevator, which now opened for me as I approached it. The Urulu, then, were now in complete control of the computer.

"Hey! Wait!" I called out, although I didn't really know to who. "If there's time—stop at Level 4."

The elevator seemed to jerk slightly, then continued, and opened at Level 4. I looked around. "Thanks."

I walked down the still halls, heading for one particular place. I found it easily—I knew the way well enough. Harry Parch's office. How *very* much I hoped to find him in.

But he wasn't. The office hadn't changed much, but there were only a couple of secretaries there, frozen in the act of typing. In the inner office I looked around for any sign of who or what he really was, but there was only the make-up table, the wigs, false moustaches, and wardrobe closet.

I was tremendously disappointed, but, I told myself, it didn't really matter. Parch, Kelleam, and the others involved in all this—it was more than personal. It was worse, in a way. If they hadn't found Harry Parch to do their dirty work, they'd have found somebody else. The country, the world, had no shortage of them, and the

Phil Kelleams and the rest, the bureaucrats and technicians who followed the system blindly, each a small part of the whole they never really allowed themselves to think about. It was the Eisenstadts and Jeff Overmeyers and those assistants of Stuart's who were the rare ones, I knew. The horribly outmatched people of vision and all that seemed good in the world on whom the only hope of Earth's future rested.

I turned and walked back to the elevator, meeting Dory there. She turned and smiled. "All done. I figured you couldn't resist comin' up to *his* office."

I shrugged and smiled sheepishly. The elevator door opened, and then closed and took us back to the surface.

Pauley waited for us just inside the door, between the desk staff, security men, and the still yawning police dog. He had seven other people with him, four women and three men, all of whom looked pale and drawn but happy.

"We did it!" he called out happily.

I looked around at the strange faces, suddenly conscious of my exposure. They all wore loose-fitting clothes. "Now what happens, Dan?" I asked, not waiting for unnecessary introductions.

He looked at the others. "I've told them what's going on," he said, "and they have all pretty well agreed to stay on and help. We're going to send them up for debriefing and a little reorientation, then they're all coming back to work for us."

Dory nodded. "What about *us*, though?"

He leaned over the counter and pulled up some car keys. "Why don't we all go home to your place? The three of us, that is." He looked at the big clock. It said 23:40.

"You mean—drive into Vegas? Like *this*?"

He shrugged. "We'll get in about 3:30 in the morning, hunker down and take some back streets. Maybe we'll shock a few neighbors of yours but I think you can stand that."

"What about Parch?" I asked, suddenly worried. "He's sure to come after us."

"If he does he's in trouble," Dan replied. "Parch's bosses are at this moment getting the word from on high. They'll leave you alone, Misty. They're going to be scared stiff of you. You have powerful friends."

I nodded, hoping he was right. "I *still* would like some clothes," I grumbled.

"Don't get modest now," he laughed and pointed. Dory and I both looked around and gasped. Until this moment I hadn't realized, hadn't remembered, the security cameras, which were automated and, therefore, still running.

"You mean—we've been *televised* the whole time? Like *this?*" Dory blurted out.

He laughed. "Just think of yourself as an honorary Urulu," he replied, and the others laughed, too.

Dan looked at the others a moment, particularly at one young woman who was particularly well-built and attractive. "You know, I've been getting an idea about the domestic angle of my evaluations," he said.

Driving home was a little nerve wracking, but we made it, in a nice Air Force station wagon. I kept worrying that we were going to be hauled over by a cop or something, but the only problem we had was at one traffic light in Vegas, when a couple in the car next to ours got more than their money's worth.

Dan picked the lock on our door with the government credit card in the glove compartment used by the normal driver for fuel purchases, and we entered, both of us making mental notes to install dead-bolt locks from now on.

Things looked pretty well undisturbed, although Dan assured us that there were signs of a thorough search. My little electric calendar said it was July 20, so we'd been gone less than three weeks. I chuckled. If Dan were right, I was due back at work the day after tomorrow.

I felt tired, but very good inside, and Dory seemed the same. "You know," she told me, "I've been thinking. This may yet be the kind of world I'd want my kids to grow up in. Maybe it's worth bein' an optimist, just this once."

I stared at her. "You do what you want to do, honey."

Five years. Five years ago and a world away, it seems. Mankind still hasn't changed much, but it hasn't changed much for the worse, either. Things go on almost as if nothing has happened, and I wonder, after that massive cover-up the government pulled, whether we'll ever know what effect our actions had on them, on Parch, on the scientific community that creates our wonders and the political community that directs and controls them.

Parch, if he's still around, has not bothered us one bit. I hope he got some jollies out of seeing Dory and I jiggling around IMC on those tapes! We haven't heard from anybody connected with IMC, in fact, although Kelleam just won his second term last year and Stuart is in the papers, I think. At least, I suspected when I saw the trim, youngish, somewhat sexy new National Science Advisor to the President on a talk show that he was all right. The fellow, who was Dr. Blumberg, we were told, had a most interesting set of mannerisms and a crazy accent that was mostly Americanized but had real problems with "w"s and occasionally "v"s.

When nothing happened to us, Dory relaxed quite a bit and really started talking seriously about children, a family. Of course we couldn't have each other's children, but that was easily remedied. She's had two beautiful, dark Indian babies now, with different fathers but they both look very much like her, and she's settled into what appears to be very happy domesticity. I love them so much I kept dreaming of having my own, but pregnant strippers don't make it and we were not yet secure. We are, now—Joe's little club has turned into something of a colossus, with heavy interest in casinos here and in Reno, Tahoe, and Elko, and a mini-chain of high-class strip joints now in twenty cities. My Dory-negotiated five percent interest in the original company is now worth a couple million, making us more than comfortable.

We have a pretty home now, in the mountains outside of Vegas, with a pool and other comforts and enough privacy that we could walk nude without being observed by anything but jackrabbits, yet only forty minutes from the Strip.

As for me, I'm heading towards thirty and finally decided it was now or never. I'm in my ninth month and feel like a bloated cow with a giant watermelon stuck in her stomach, and my tits have started swelling with my tummy to incredible proportions, but I can hardly wait. I could know the sex and all that, but I want it to be a surprise, like Christmas. The way it feels it *must* be a boy, and if so, I'll name him Victor Stuart Daniel Carpenter, I think. Or, maybe, I'll just have three boys. . . . I don't know. The world is fantastic right now, and I don't want anything to spoil it.

The pregnancy gave me the time, finally, to write this book. I wanted to write it, although I have no idea if it'll ever see print, at least in my lifetime. I'm forty-six, you know, going on twenty-nine. . . .

I'd like it to get published somewhere, although they'll probably just label it science fiction or something. Who would believe? Only the people who know, and Kelleam's still damned popular.

As for Dan and the Earth-based Urulu, we see them often, not only as guests at the ranch but in other capacities as well. He seems to have worked out an interesting idea for getting his people around the western world, anyway, meeting the common people in city after city, noting news reports, gossip, you name it for their reports. I wonder what people would say if they knew? The government knows, of course, but they can't do much about it. At least they can't say that the Urulu aren't earning their keep.

Tonight, in fact, I'm going down to Misty's Place if I can lug this *really* out-of-balance body there and take a night out without getting *too* tired, and watch the Las Vegas debut of Danielle Dynamite, the Red-headed Rocket from Rhode Island, finally here after her first big national tour.

I wonder if Harry Parch will also be in the audience?

CODED—TOP SECRET—PRIORITY A
DISPOSITION—MASTER PENTAGON FILE HYDRA ONLY
FROM—DIRECTOR, HYDRA
SUBJECT—OPERATION "TRIPLE PLAY"
COVERAGE—GENERAL SUMMARY AND EVALUATION OF
    OPERATION

It should be clear from the attached memoir that, despite impossible odds and tremendous risks, "Triple Play" succeeded beyond our wildest dreams. A combination of brains, luck, and tremendous dedication and sacrifice were necessary for it to succeed, and for those of some future time who might wonder at why such incredible risks were taken, let me assure you that the finest minds of this country supported by the most sophisticated computer analysis found that, while the operation had, frankly, less than a fifteen percent chance of being totally successful, there was simply no other alternative. The fact that it worked is certainly the ultimate justification, but those who might question what we did and how we did it should also consider the fact that no suggested alternative gave odds which could even be recognized as such.

Consider: quite by accident, or, if you will, sloppiness, this government was faced with two incontrovertible facts. First, that we had, in fact, been penetrated by alien beings from off this planet whose abilities and technology were far in advance of our own and whose behavior indicated that they were hostile to humankind. Second, that these beings could trade minds with us or with each other as they chose. Further, they knew enough about us to easily pass our most stringent muster, yet we knew nothing about them.

Naturally, this information was not given to the public, as the panic and paranoia it would cause would only aid the enemy. In fact, only a special team composed of the heads of the CIA, FBI, DIA and other security organizations and the Joint Chiefs were ever informed, and were directed by the President to create a crisis management team, code-named Hydra, to combat the menace. It is almost certain that, at no time, did the number of unsecured top personnel—that is, those with liberty and not living in a secured environment—exceed a dozen.

The first task, of course, was to create a security force capable of at least recognizing the enemy and perhaps placing a bit of pressure on them. This was organized under Chief Inspector Harold G. Parch, who had supervised the original team that had exposed the first aliens. Parch is a strange man, as accurately pictured in the Gonser narrative, but he is both fiercely loyal and intensely patriotic. He is also, quite certainly, dangerously psychopathic, but in a manner useful to us. I would in no case wish Parch to date my daughter, but he is the first one I would trust with the family jewels, and he was perfect for his overall security role. We owe Parch not merely for the success of Triple Play, but also for our own necks, since, in the course of the operation, all of us violated our most sacred oaths and principles in what we believed and believe to be a desperate cause.

In addition to security—which included not only tracking the enemy but also securing their existence from the outside world—there had to be a concurrent operation to find a defense against this body-switching ability. As a result, IMC was formed, with the finest minds and finest machines available at all times. As the Gonser manuscript makes clear, while we never did find out how they so easily did it, we did find a way to do it mechanically. Show the finest minds in a field that someone else can do something they can't and give them almost unlimited funds and resources and they will almost certainly do it.

Of course, just when we found a proper defense we discovered that we had not one, but two hostile alien powers, both with this switching ability, on our hands. We were, then, on the horns of a dilemma, since we found ourselves the innocent civilians in the midst of a war between superpowers we could barely understand. Obviously the only thing we could do was pick a side and try and arrange it so that it would take us under its protection. A very subtle task, not only because we had to at all costs prevent a military confrontation with either side that we would inevitably lose while, at the same time, we had to evaluate and choose the lesser of two evils among the alien powers. Since we had a number of captured Urulus but none of the opposition, we had to start with the Urulu side. Gonser/Carpenter's early work with "Dan Pauley" and her complete evaluation of them helped enormously, and the relationship developed between the two formed the cornerstone, as it were, of Triple Play.

Our problem, of course, was that time was against us, and there was strong evidence that the Association, at least, was actively engaged in influencing our affairs while the Urulu were not. It became fairly easy to tell them apart, since the Urulu switched minds totally without fail, while the Association seemed more concerned with the by-product of the process, the selective editing of the memory and personality. Faced with clear evidence of active opposition by one side, we felt we had no choice but to opt for the Urulu as our "friends."

The trouble, of course, was that the Urulu were, at best, indifferent to us and had no desire to be our friends, nor did they consider our planet and race worthy of concern no matter what was happening. In the meantime, intelligence clearly showed the Association patterns in the cult's growth and, almost by accident, stumbled on the evidence that the Association had actually penetrated the White House.

At that point Hydra's hand was forced, since the President knew of IMC and Hydra and, therefore, our liquidation or takeover despite our best efforts was only a matter of time, perhaps very little time. To buy that time, it was necessary to take drastic measures.

Triple Play, of course, was already in motion at that point. Having decided that Gonser/Carpenter and Tomlinson were the best lead to the Urulu leadership, an intensive study of what the very alien Urulu valued in other people and other civilizations based on our prior work was condensed to specific personality points, and from those we created the human personality with values and outlooks we believed would hit the Urulu where it counted. The original personality recordings of Gonser and Tomlinson, then, were edited, altered, and rewritten so that, when added once again to their created new personalities they would become the kind of people the Urulu, it was hoped, would identify with and want to help. And since they would be, hopefully, the samples, the Urulu might well take them as representative of the human race itself.

We then "discovered" them in their new security-created lives, added our modified recordings of their past selves, and arranged to have this "Pauley" broken out of IMC.

And it was here that the ultimate gamble had to be taken. We could not afford to have "Pauley" immediately spirit the women to his superiors for evaluation, since to a race that swapped minds as easily as we snap fingers the psychosurgery we had so recently performed would have been painfully obvious. Therefore, the women had to be allowed to live as their new selves for a while, to settle in and *become* those newly designed psyches we counted so much on. This, however, meant potentially losing "Pauley," and we thought we had completely blown it when so much time elapsed. Fortunately, the Association ships and those of the Urulu are quite different, and we detected no Urulu ships arriving after the escape period, nor any departing. We knew, also, that the Association had hit the isolated Urulu bases hard, thanks in part to the fact that we leaked what we knew of those bases via the President to help them out. This served several purposes. For one, it kept Pauley a fugitive and made his escape from Earth extremely difficult. Second, it convinced him of the scope of the Association's subtle attack. Third, it confirmed once and for all that the President—and, alas, as we discovered in the same way, the Vice President—were already controlled by the Association. And, finally, by leaking that information we gave the Association a reason for letting Hydra and IMC continue, at least for a while. We represented no direct threat and were a source of information on their enemy.

Finally, however, we simply were forced to act. Evidence showed that the Association was poised for a much deeper penetration of government and that Hydra and IMC were in imminent danger not of being dismantled but of being taken over by the enemy. Since Speaker Kelleam, thanks to his visit and "demonstration" of IMC, was very much *our* man, our survival became obvious. The assassinations we arranged and the terrorist attacks we perpetrated caught the Association off guard. It was pretty easy not only to break the news to the public but also smash their political apparatus. Of course, we knew this would be a temporary solution, but we were banking on them not having a significant military force deployed for us. This was one time when it really paid to be a primitive jerkwater island off in the fringes of a war.

The actions had the effect of reviving Triple Play, on which we had almost given up. Seeing what was happening, Pauley took our bait and contacted the two women. We had, thank God, judged him correctly. Knowing that, eventually, the Association would return in force, and having lived with and made friends with some of our people, he opted, as our profile predicted, to try and convince the Urulu to intervene on our side.

The foregoing manuscript shows that he, and therefore we, were successful. The personalities we created went unsuspected and contained the elements necessary for a command decision in our favor to be made.

You can certainly argue that the personality and lifestyle of "Misty Carpenter" is not one one would like or accept. *I* certainly am not comfortable with such a casual and, well, immoral lifestyle, but I'm old and very old-fashioned. But we have a younger, more pliant, more tolerant generation, and as one of those who created Misty Carpenter as she is today I can hardly kick. Thank God we always have that younger, adaptable generation! And, of course, she would be terribly shocked at my own actions in this matter if she knew them. If this is the newer generation, I might not accept—but I will not resist. Social evolution, no matter what the cause, has generated more suffering from the resistance to change than to the acceptance of it.

But it's still not *our* world, it's ours only by sufferance of the Urulu who are, I might point out, alien, not friendly on the whole, and not really any more our friends than the Association, for as long as we primitives remain at their mercy and sufferance we control not our own destiny.

It used to be simple in the old days. Two armies would march out, fight it out, and the best force would win. Or we'd plant our spies, they'd plant their spies, and we'd battle for advantage in the shadows. But a war where one superior adversary has to be tricked into taking out another superior adversary—well, nobody in history ever had to fight this sort of war before, and I think we can be damned proud of ourselves despite the ugliness we had to perpetrate. History, we all feel, will be kind to us—if, as Carpenter darkly suggests, we do not "blow it." Like her, I suspect we will—the Russians and Chinese in particular are climbing the paranoid walls even now. But we have the only defense. The rest of the world can either take the cure from us or go nuts. And, when they *do* take the cure, and get not only protection but also a little change in attitude as a bonus, then, maybe, we can allow the Carpenter book to be published. Probably not, though. We don't want anyone planting the idea of judicious editing of the mind right about now.

But we've come this far, and the great enemies in the totalitarian societies are, of course, the most fearful and paranoid of all. They've all got their own IMCs now, of course, but they're ten years or more behind in the hardware necessary to do it right and many years also behind in experimentation we've already done. When the rulers even now are afraid to shake hands with their closest aids or go to bed with their wives or mistresses, they will eventually *have* to come to us. And when *they* do, we'll have little trouble with their general populations.

What we need, and have hopefully bought, is time. Time to bring the rest of the world around. Time to educate the population. There's talk of introducing the IM process into medicine next year, for treatment of brain disorders, and after that it'll be mated with teaching machines, then . . . In our time, we hope, people will take the IM treatment so much for granted, like they now accept plastic surgery and home computers, that they'll be ready to accept the idea of routine body-switching. That, of course, will transform society beyond our imagination. And, by that point, our Urulu watch-dogs will themselves consider the process so normal and so positively used that there will be no further trouble with them. At the very least the IM will double our IQs, a tremendous leap—children might learn to read again and like it, and without the severe international tension and nihilism rampant through our century they might get the chance to use it.

The hardest part, of course, is that we remain, of necessity, behind the scenes, unknown and unrecognized. I doubt if the Hydra report can ever be known until that social revolution takes place—if it does. Still, it *will* all come out one day. Hydra and IMC are generaly safe, though. We can be just about anybody—and sometimes are. Fewer still know the real identity of Harry Parch, and what he really looks like. Still, I doubt if any of us can ever pass a burlesque house or strip joint again and feel totally secure.

As for me, I am prominent now, but with a little IM work perhaps my telltale speech patterns will vanish into, say, Brooklynese, and I hope soon to abandon the public life and restart my research work at the new IMC in Colorado, already hard at work—as it has been since before the Urulu kindly saved us the trouble of demolishing the old Nevada IMC, obsolete as it was.

But when the Urulu find out one day at last that a couple of very primitive old apes made suckers out of their godlike selves, I will be very, very hard to find. But that will be a while. Perhaps, by then I'll know how *they* switch and we can leave our dependence on machines forever behind.

Respectfully submitted,
Stuart J. Eisenstadt

Dear Dr. "Blumberg":

Caught you on TV the other night. A nice performance, but you still can't tell a "v" from a "w." Still, with you up there with the high and mighty ones, I feel like the human race is really going to become something great. My best to you,

Dan Pauley

Dear Dan:

War is hell, son.

Eisenstadt

"Drake has distinguished himself as the master of the mercenary sf novel."—Rave Reviews

DAVID DRAKE

IS

ROLLING HOT

Hammers Slammers
Rolling Hot
The latest novel of Col. Alois Hammer's Slammers —Hammers Slammers vs. a 22nd Century Viet Cong.

Hammers Slammers
The new *expanded* edition of the book that began the legend of Colonel Hammer.

At Any Price
The 23rd armored division faces its deadliest enemies ever: aliens who *teleport into combat*.

Counting the Cost
The cold ferocity of the Slammers vs. red-hot religious fanaticism.

Ranks of Bronze
Alien traders were looking to buy primitive soldier-slaves—they needed troops who could win battles without high-tech weaponry. But when they bought Roman legionaries, they bought *trouble* . . .

Vettius and His Friends
A Roman Centurion and his merchant friend fight and connive to stave off the fall of Rome.

Lacey and His Friends
Jed Lacey is a 21st-century cop who plays by the rules. His rules.

Men Hunting Things
Things Hunting Men
Volumes One and Two of the *Starhunters* series. Exactly what the titles indicate, selected and with in-depth introductions by the creator of Hammer's Slammers.

To receive books by one of BAEN BOOKS most popular authors send in the order form below.

Rolling Hot, 69837-0 ✪ $3.95 . . . . ☐

Hammer's Slammers, 65632-5 ✪ $3.50 . . . . ☐

At Any Price, 55978-8 ✪ $3.50 . . . . ☐

Counting the Cost, 65355-5 ✪ $3.50 . . . . ☐

Ranks of Bronze, 65568-X ✪ $3.50 . . . . ☐

Vettius and His Friends, 69802-8 ✪ $3.95 . . . . . . ☐

Lacey and His Friends, 65593-0 ✪ $3.50 . . . . ☐

Men Hunting Things, 65399-7 ✪ $2.95 . . . . ☐

Things Hunting Men, 65412-8 ✪ $3.50 . . . . ☐

Please send me the books checked above. I have enclosed a check or money order for the combined cover price made out to: BAEN BOOKS, 260 Fifth Avenue, New York N.Y. 10001.

BIG, BAD AND AFTER YOUR BLOOD

MARTIN CAIDIN

Not all aliens are as cute and cuddly as E.T. . . .
At last the hopes and dreams of earth-people yearning for contact with the stars are fulfilled—by six of the most ruthless and depraved convicts that a galactic system advanced only in its methods of cruelty and oppression can produce. When they and their technology team up with a band of human desperadoes it's going to be hell on earth!

———————————

And don't miss *BEAMRIDERS*, high-tech science fiction adventure as only Martin Caidin can write it!

Available at your local bookstore, or send this coupon and the cover price(s) to: Baen Books, Dept. BA, New York, NY 10001.

Prison Ship, 69814-1, $4.50 . . . . ☐
Beamriders, 69823-0, $3.95 . . . . ☐

THE MANY WORLDS OF
MELISSA SCOTT

*Winner of the John W. Campbell Award
for Best New Writer, 1986*

THE KINDLY ONES: "An ambitious novel of the world Orestes. This large, inhabited moon is governed by five Kinships whose society operates on a code of honor so strict that transgressors are declared legally 'dead' and are prevented from having any contact with the 'living.' . . . Scott is a writer to watch."—*Publishers Weekly*. A Main Selection of the Science Fiction Book Club.

65351-2 • 384 pp. • $2.95

The "Silence Leigh" Trilogy

FIVE-TWELFTHS OF HEAVEN (Book I): "Melissa Scott postulates a universe where technology interferes with magic. . . . The whole plot is one of space ships, space wars, and alien planets—not a unicorn or a dragon to be seen anywhere. Scott's space drive and description of space piloting alone would mark her as an expert in the melding of the [SF and fantasy] genres; this is the stuff of which 'sense of wonder' is made."—*Locus*

55952-4 • 352 pp. • $2.95

SILENCE IN SOLITUDE (Book II): "[Scott is] a voice you should seek out and read at every opportunity." —*OtherRealms*.   65699-7 • 324 pp. • $2.95

THE EMPRESS OF EARTH (Book III):

65364-4 • 352 pp. • $3.50

A CHOICE OF DESTINIES: "Melissa Scott [is] one of science fiction's most talented newcomers. . . . The greatest delight of all is finding out how she managed to write a historical novel that could legitimately have spaceships on the cover . . . a marvelous gift for any fan."—*Baltimore Sun*   65563-9 • 320 pp. • $2.95

THE GAME BEYOND: "An exciting interstellar empire novel with a great deal of political intrigue and colorful interplanetary travel."—*Locus*
                                     55918-4 • 352 pp. • $2.95

To order any of these Melissa Scott titles, please check the box/es below and send combined cover price/s to:

**Baen Books
Dept. BA
260 Fifth Ave.
NY, NY 10001**

Name _____

Address _____

City _____ State _____ Zip __

THE KINDLY ONES ☐   FIVE-TWELFTHS OF HEAVEN ☐
A CHOICE OF DESTINIES ☐   SILENCE IN SOLITUDE ☐
THE GAME BEYOND ☐   THE EMPRESS OF EARTH ☐